Penguin Books

GABRIEL'S LAMENT

Gabriel's Lament has received great acclaim from the critics:

'Almost Dickensian in scope and richness of detail ... he is brilliant at bringing vividly to life the eccentrics and misfits, the odd and the peculiar, all of them remarkable and resilient and memorable ... a serious, sensitive and painful book.'

Susan Hill

'A powerful study of bereavement as obsession and of the consolations of comic art.'

Hermoine Lee in the *Observer*

'Bailey's most substantial novel yet ... It is essentially a tragicomedy about a man (Gabriel Harvey) in search of his lost mother. The chief character seems to be Gabriel's fantastic, foul-mouthed, randy, mendacious, selfish and irrepressible father Oswald Harvey – as magnificent a vital rogue as we have had since the novels of Joyce Cary.'

Martin Seymour-Smith in the *Financial Times*

'Paul Bailey's most complex novel so far, seems to me a sad story, though it can be read as a funny one. Its point is that the hells of grief and shame and lost love are preferable to the grotesque pretences that people construct to deny them ... it is a book worth reading twice.'

Victoria Glendinning in *The Times*

'There is a poetic reality to this novel, a sense of the strangeness of personality and of the weight of a great city which recalls Dickens, even while the novel is also an expression of a late twentieth century sensibility.'

Allan Massie in *The Scotsman*

GABRIEL'S LAMENT

PAUL BAILEY

PENGUIN BOOKS

PENGUIN BOOKS

Published by the Penguin Group
Penguin Books Ltd, 27 Wrights Lane, London W8 5TZ, England
Penguin Books USA Inc., 375 Hudson Street, New York, New York 10014, USA
Penguin Books Australia Ltd, Ringwood, Victoria, Australia
Penguin Books Canada Ltd, 10 Alcorn Avenue, Toronto, Ontario, Canada M4V 3B2
Penguin Books (NZ) Ltd, 182–190 Wairau Road, Auckland 10, New Zealand

Penguin Books Ltd, Registered Offices: Harmondsworth, Middlesex, England

First published by Jonathan Cape 1986
Published in Penguin Books 1987
5 7 9 10 8 6

Grateful acknowledgement is made for permission to reprint an excerpt
from 'Margaritaville', words and music by Jimmy Buffett,
copyright © 1977 Coral Reefer Music & Outer Banks Music B.M.I.

Printed in England by Clays Ltd, St Ives plc

David's, always

Joys are like oil; if thrown upon the tide
Of flowing life, they mix not, nor subside:
Griefs are like waters on the rivers thrown,
They mix entirely, and become its own.

George Crabbe: 'Infancy – A Fragment'

Part One

I

I came to grief late in life – when I was forty, in Minnesota. The distress I almost failed to bear during the long nights of that hot summer was my legacy, I suppose. There are times, even now, I consider it my rightful inheritance.

'I'm leaving you something,' my father announced, from what I hoped would be his death-bed.

I reminded him, yet again, that I neither wanted nor needed his money.

'That's gone where my legs went. I'd be surprised if there's much more than a brass farthing and an old collar stud in the kitty. No, my son, I wouldn't insult you with filthy lucre. Others, yes, but not you.'

I thanked him for having my interests at heart.

'I know you'll thank me – in my absence, of course – for my parting gift. Oh, I'm sure you will. You're the only person in the entire world, Gabriel, who would appreciate it.'

I did not ask him why. I had stopped asking him questions ages past.

His hands were suddenly restless, pummelling the eiderdown. 'Signs of life, signs of life,' he hissed. 'Yes, there is definite activity below. I feel a turd worming its way out. Be a good lad and ring for my wet-nurse.'

I was happy to press the button.

I live by the Thames these days, at Chiswick. My house was built in the 1770s, fifty years after the completion of Blenheim. The 'Blenheim' in which Oswald Harvey once loved to strut arose nearly a century later, on the outskirts of the ever-sprawling capital.

I can see the river at all hours, in all its moods. Even on the darkest night, it is a glistening presence. On just such a night, a week ago, the water looked thick and still as I walked slowly home from the Steam Packet. I was almost at my door when I noticed what appeared to be a body floating on the calm surface. Had the richest of my wealthy neighbours, I wondered, succumbed to despair as the result of a setback on the Stock Exchange? Was the merchant banker a sudden pauper?

Fanciful questions, morbid imaginings – the corpse was a log. I smiled at the turn my mind had taken, and then I remembered a story told me by my ancient father before he became the master of 'Blenheim'. Perhaps it wasn't a story, for the word suggests fabrication: he might have been telling me the truth.

My mother was not with us that evening. She was probably working at her 'secret place', otherwise known as 'There'. Her husband and son had been left to fend for themselves.

We had finished eating the rice pudding she had prepared and he had allowed to burn.

'Don't let her know that we had to poke about among the charred remains, there's a good lad. I'll wash away the incriminating evidence,' he added, bearing the blackened dish to the sink. He held it absurdly high in front of him, as if it were a chalice. 'The precious bowl. It's only earthenware, but it means a lot to her. I shall have to be careful with it.'

He was. He scrubbed it with care; with equal care, he set it down to dry. As he took his hands away, it cracked in two – of its own volition, it seemed.

'Cantankerous bloody thing. "Crack," it said, and went. You saw how I treated it. You'll be my witness, won't you, lad, at the post-mortem?'

I was a bright ten-year-old. I understood. I nodded.

'Not that she won't believe her Ossie. She usually does. But if I need to call on the defence, you'll step forward sharpish, I don't doubt, eh lad?'

I said I would, if he let me have a game of dominoes.

'Dominoes? Yes, I think that's a reasonable bribe.'

We played several games, by gaslight, at the kitchen table. During one of them, he annoyed me by not making his move. He chose to talk instead.

'Your mother's a hard little worker. I'm of an age, Gabriel, and I expect I'll soon be a shadow of myself. I can't do all the providing, as I should. She's the toiler now, and will be for a good while yet. I'll be collecting my pension in a year or so, lad, and then we'll have to depend on her, the two of us, until you're old enough to be the breadwinner.'

No one had told me he already had another son, by another of his wives. It was my Swedenborgian aunt who informed me of Thomas Harvey's existence – over tea with tansy cake, that unique Easter I met her.

'I earned my first wages, my first ever half-crown', my father confided, 'in the winter of 1894, when I was just turned twelve. I was a street Arab, a rough diamond, a tyke. Can you believe it? I had to be, to survive. I was seldom out of scraps. I fought like the bloody heathen.'

'It's your go, Dad.'

'Like a savage, among savages. The police wouldn't walk alone where I walked after dark. They were so bloody scared, they trod the beat in threes. And in broad daylight, too. Anyhow, it was December, the time I'm talking of. I was on my way home – ears on the alert, eyes peeled for trouble – when I heard a splash, and then a man's voice, crying out for help. Screams and shouts were nothing special along the Highway and Narrow Street – round the clock, the saying went, there was always someone being done for. I'd got used, young as I was, to taking no notice. But this cry was different. It was coming from the river: "I'm drowning! I'm drowning!" I ran down to the water's edge, the better to see who was in the drink. I saw his wild arms, that was all. I took off my boots as fast as I could, I plunged in, and swam to his rescue. He was a goner when I reached him. He weighed a ton, Gabriel, he was that bloated. I must have had the strength of the insane, getting him back to land like I did. It wasn't until I was on terra firma – can you believe it? – that I realized I was cold. Icy cold I was, I was freezing, I could hear my teeth clanking. I'd been swimming in the Thames, in December, in God knows what temperature. It was a miracle I hadn't perished.'

There would be other miracles for Oswald Harvey – three, at least, by my reckoning.

'If he'd had a breath of life left in him, I wouldn't have been paid. Just fancy. Had it been summer, had I been swifter, I'd have collected sweet sod all for saving him. As it was, I was handsomely rewarded for his corpse. Aren't you going to ask me why?'

'Why, Dad?'

'What a joy it is to have a curious son. A man who tries to

do away with himself and doesn't succeed has committed a crime, Gabriel. A man who succeeds has committed a crime but can't be charged for it. Johnny Tuohy, bless his poor Catholic hide, succeeded – though only by a hair's breadth. He was the one I failed to rescue. The Thames police don't like their lovely river bunged up with cowards' bodies, so that's why they handed me a spanking new half-crown coin for ridding it of Johnny Tuohy.'

'Did you know him, then?'

'I knew of him. Everyone did. He was Irish, and had a mouth cluttered with daftness. Words flew out of him as fast as the porter fell in. My move, did you say?'

'Yes, Dad.'

'Then mine it is. And mine again. And yet again, I'm afraid. It looks as if I've won.'

Before 'Blenheim', before my mother vanished, before he called me Piss-a-Bed, I surely loved my father.

He was a storyteller in our house without a name. In 'Blenheim', he lectured.

He said to me once, 'I was born near the Isle of Dogs.' Then, inspired, he complained of the noise they made at night, those dogs on their special island. How they barked, through all his childhood; how they yelped.

'I don't believe you.'

'Master Don't Believe never found out, so Mister Don't Believe never grew wise. A fact's a fact, and the Isle of Dogs is called the Isle of Dogs because people aren't allowed to live on it.'

'You're fibbing.'

'Am I?'

'Aren't you?'

'Yes. No. Perhaps. Maybe. Take your pick, Gabriel lad.'

'Shall I choose "perhaps"?'

'The choice is yours.'

'It sounds silly – an island just for dogs.'

'It does sound silly, that I can't deny. What must I do to convince you that I'm telling the truth?'

It was a question he never asked me in 'Blenheim'. The lord and master was not to be doubted; could not brook contradiction.

'You can explain how they got there.'

14

'Nothing simpler.'

I indicated that I was prepared to listen by sitting at his feet.

'Once upon a time – '

'When?'

'Oh, a long while ago. A long, long while ago. In the Dark Ages, you might say, before we had proper kings and queens on the throne. If I were ordered to put a date on it, I'd hazard a guess, I couldn't do otherwise, that the time I'm talking of would be – oh, when would it be? – well, I should imagine when old Boadicea was on the war-path, winning her battles.'

'I've heard of her at school. She's proper.'

'Not proper like Elizabeth was, or the Charleses, Jameses and Georges. She was a termagant, Gabriel lad, which means – just in case you don't know – she was wild. Her behaviour wasn't regal. She was always in a frenzy. She probably slept in her armour, she had so much fighting to do. I should think she kept a tin opener by her bed, for when she wanted to breathe easy. There's a statue down by Westminster bridge that shows her on her chariot with her face set square against the world, just spoiling for trouble. The muscles that woman must have had!'

'You've forgotten the dogs.'

'No, I haven't. I most definitely have not forgotten the dogs. I was coming to them. They were brought here by the Romans, and terrible Mediterranean tempers they had. Something had to be done about them, and Boadicea was the ideal person to do it. You try leading your charger on to the battlefield with a dog yapping round its hooves. That's what she had to put up with – yap, yap, yap, with the enemy all ready to hack her army to pieces.'

'I can't follow. I'm lost.'

'You're no son of mine if you are. Think, Gabriel. It's only a matter of simple arithmetic, simple deduction. Those dogs that came to Britain from Rome left a hot climate for a cold one and there weren't any cosy firesides they could curl up near. So how did they keep warm? They used Nature's method, that's what. They bred. They went to it with such a vengeance that it was almost Biblical, the way they multiplied. Very soon, they were everywhere, up hill and down dale, the length and breadth of the land. When they started scaring the horses, Boadicea decided enough was enough. She'd had her earlier-than-medieval mind more than bothered simply coping with invaders, without having half-crazy mongrels snapping at her heels to make her lose – well, her beauty sleep. She gathered her council together (her daughters were on it, and they were termagants, too) and the whole lot of them racked what they had for brains in those days, until a lord or some such reminded Her Majesty that there was an island on Londinium's river which would make a perfect asylum for the thousands of strays who were running amok all over the capital. That settled it for Boadicea. A decree was issued immediately, and her soldiers commanded to round up the stragglers and take them, with no delay, to their own little Eden on the Thames. Which is where', he concluded, breathless, 'they have remained to the present time.'

'Dogs eat meat, don't they, Dad?'

'That's correct. They are what you might call carnivores.'

'The ones on the island – did they, do they, kill each other, then? For food?'

He stared at me for a moment before he found his answer. 'Why, they are fed by Royal Charter, Gabriel lad. Yes, that's it, they are fed by Royal Charter! Every morning a boat stops by the island and the crew chuck lights and livers and kidneys and brains to the prowling animals on the shore. There's a terrific scrummage, I'm told, and growls that would freeze your young blood, whenever the HMS, the HMS – *Canis*, yes, *Canis* – drops anchor. If I should meet the captain again – he comes into the Prodigal's Return twice a year on average – I'll ask him if it's possible for a certain Gabriel Harvey to climb aboard one day and watch the dogs fighting for the offal the King allows them. That's a promise. No more questions, lad. Your mother will be home soon from her secret place and she'll wonder why you aren't asleep. Get yourself off to bed now, there's my good Gabriel.'

I never did climb aboard the HMS *Canis*, nor did I meet its captain, whose name, according to my father, was William Bligh. His infrequent visits to the Prodigal's Return ceased altogether, and then we moved to 'Blenheim', far from his haunts.

All through that cruel winter, I bothered the storyteller whom I scarcely believed with pointed inquiries about the dogs' state of health: Who would feed them, if the Thames froze over? Would skaters deliver their kidneys and lights? Weren't they dying of cold, like people? Wasn't it only wolves who survived when the thermometer fell so low?

'The King will look after them. Rest assured.'

I pretended to accept his assurance as I huddled by the fire with our cat, Mrs McTrap, spread across my feet.

Most of Mrs McTrap's blind offspring went the way of Johnny Tuohy – except that they remained among the river's detritus. The drunkard's would-be rescuer was their expert murderer. Two or three times a year, he stuffed her new-born litter into a sack, leaving behind a solitary kitten with a surfeit of nipples from which to feed.

If ever there were mice in our nameless house, Mrs McTrap never caught them. It was birds she favoured. Day after day each spring, she crunched on fledgling sparrows. Once she threw herself on a huge crow, which she slowly and purposefully buffeted senseless with both front paws. Blood-spattered feathers rose in a cloud as her frantic tail signalled conquest.

I screamed at my father to stop her.

'Don't be a baby all your life, Gabriel lad. It's in her nature to kill. You have to admire her cunning. Just look how she's forced that great devil of a beak into the grass. And that helpless thing underneath has the nerve to call himself a bird of prey!'

We were in St Mary's churchyard, early on a summer evening. Boys whose parents didn't care for them were swimming in the Thames below. I couldn't believe they were 'filling their lungs with filth' and 'catching every disease known to mortal man', for they looked so sleek and lithe whenever they emerged. Yet my father insisted that they were shortening their chances of survival the longer they remained in the contaminated water. He talked of plagues and pestilence, like some Old Testament prophet. 'They'll soon have boils,' he said.

'Not just pimples?'

'No, not just pimples; certainly not just pimples. You don't swim through shit – you're not to tell your mother I used that word – and expect to break out in a few little spots. Pimples are for clean folk. Those guttersnipes down there, splashing about in the sewage, are in for swellings the size of crab apples, or I'm not Oswald Harvey.'

'That word you said I'm not to say you spoke – what's it to do with the Thames?'

'Gabriel lad, it has to go somewhere after the chain is pulled, doesn't it. It isn't abracadabra'd away by a magician stuck in the pipes. It can only go where it won't be noticed – out to sea.'

In the June of 1948, I learned that shit flows seawards, and that nature must be respected for being red in tooth and claw. I learned, too, that had I been free to dive and swim, as those boys were, I should not have known the love of my mother and father.

2

In 1700 or thereabouts, a dying baronet, Sir William Lilliburn, notified his executors that he had set aside a sum of money for the foundation of a charity school to be honoured with his name. It was his last wish that twenty poor boys from the parish should be educated in the arts of reading and writing and the science of arithmetic. Their humble study of God's Word – and the possible attainment of a wisdom outdistancing knowledge – was all that a mere mortal benefactor required in thanks. Sir William foresaw generation upon generation of urchins grown into wise men – which happy vision sustained him through his final earthly ordeal.

'You are Lilliburnians now,' the Headmaster told us new arrivals at our first assembly, 'and as such you will be respected in the community. You have a tradition to maintain. You have standards to keep up. You must wear your uniform with pride.'

I am not the type to wear anything with pride. I am, was then, and for ever shall be, a slovenly dresser. My mother was anxious that I looked the complete Lilliburnian: she gave my trousers guillotine-like creases and polished my boots into a state I have to call radiant. I glittered each morning as I set off. 'People can see you're a scholar,' she said approvingly.

The boys who were free to swim saw me as a 'Lily', a member of that hated tribe, the 'Lilies'. They threw my cap in the air and trampled on my satchel. They called me Little Lily Harvey and Willy-Lily. They sneered at Sir William's motto 'Better Deathe than Deceite', which I bore on the breast pocket of my blazer, beneath his coat of arms – a mysterious affair involving two stars and a shield and the profile of an eagle. 'Death-ee!' they shrieked. 'Deceit-ee!' Circling me, arms linked, they chanted:

19

Willy-boys
Are silly boys
Because they think they're Billy-boys.
They're white and pure
But they shit manure
To feed the beds
With stuck-up heads
For bunches and bunches of Lily-boys.

That awkward rhyme, I discovered later, had been sung and shouted by generations of South London urchins who were denied Sir William's charity. By the time I made my discovery, I wanted to sing it, too.

The strangeness of my name caused me to be gently mocked by my fellow Lilliburnians. I was the sole Gabriel among 30 Williams, 23 Peters, 17 Davids, 15 Michaels, 13 Pauls, 12 Johns, 10 Dennises (4 Denises), 9 Jameses, 8 Leslies, 8 Trevors, 8 Kenneths, 7 Charleses, 7 Ronalds, 6 Leonards, 6 Georges, 5 Dereks, 5 Thomases, 5 Richards, 5 Sidneys, 3 Ralphs, 3 Hughs, 3 Fredericks and 3 Brians. They were not all scholarship winners – many had parents who paid their fees – and were therefore not bona fide Lilies, as I was. My mother made certain that I was a shining example of Sir William's benevolence.

'I'm the only Gabriel in the whole school,' I told my father.

'You don't have to whisper it from the tomb, lad. You should thank your mother and me for giving you a handle that people notice. You ought to be pleased, not down in the dumps. Back-street Gabriels aren't bumped into on every corner, remember. Shake the average family tree and what falls off?'

'Tom, Dick and Harry,' I suggested.

'Exactly. Or Jack, Jim and Stan. Or Ted, Fred and Sid. It's a rare branch that can boast a Gabriel. You could easily go through life, my lad, without ever meeting another one.'

'Why did you choose it, Dad?'

'It was her choice. She wanted it. She didn't give a reason. She liked the sound of it, I suppose. Ask her to tell you.'

I did, the very next day, while she had me in her furiously refining hands.

'Oh, but you've got stubborn hair! What is it you're anxious to know?'

'Why I'm Gabriel. Why you chose Gabriel for me.'

'Because, because. I can't rightly recall. Perhaps I pictured you sprouting wings. I think that's what it was. Yes, that was all it was. I deserve to be famous for my daft notions. I thought I'd given birth to an angel. I was wrong, wasn't I?'

'No, Mummy.'

' "No," he says, the conceited little blighter. A true angel would have agreed with me.'

She stood back, to inspect her glowing earthling, whose stubborn hair she afforded a rare kiss, which she instantly combed out.

'Keep an eye on Daddy this evening, dear, and make sure he doesn't burn your supper. I'm going to be There tonight until the gates close behind the guests.'

'We've arranged a holiday for you, Gabriel lad. Nowhere special, like the seaside. No, your mother thinks it would do you good to spend a few days with Swedie.'

'Who's that?'

'My mad sister. Your aunt.'

'She's not mad, is she, Aunt Kath?'

'Kath*leen*. Kath*leen*, boy. You'll have Sister Swedie heaping the coals of hell on your head if you address her as Kath. I'd practise saying it, if I were you, before you go.'

'She isn't mad, is she, Aunt Kathleen?'

'She's never been locked up, if that's what you're asking. No, the men in white coats haven't presented themselves on her doorstep – as yet, as yet, but give her time. She passes for normal, does Swedie, but she knows I know she's loony. She can't fool her brother.'

I was confused. In what way was she mad? If her madness wasn't obvious, how could he be so certain she was loony? People with screws loose screeched and jabbered, stuck their tongues out, rolled their eyeballs and laughed when they weren't crying. At least, that's what they always did in the pictures I'd seen with him and Mum at the Super Palace. And why did he call her Swedie when her name was Kath*leen*?

'The lady herself will answer that, mark my words, lad. She'll make sure you listen – it's one of her gifts. And as for her not being as sane and as sensible as me – well, you'll soon discover the reason she isn't.'

On the station platform, seconds before I boarded the train, my mother handed me a box containing three precious fresh eggs.

'Don't let her think they've come from my secret place, even though they haven't. Promise me, Gabriel.'

'I promise.'

'She'd disapprove if she thought they had. She's a woman with principles.'

Another mystery: she had principles, too, this one and only aunt of mine, this Kathleen who was also Swedie, who passed for normal although her brother knew different ... and whose surname, I noticed now, with surprise, as my father entrusted me with a letter to give to her – 'It saves the cost of a stamp' – was di Salvo. Di Salvo: another mystery.

'Find a compartment with a woman in it, Ossie. The older the better. There are lots of funny people travelling.'

'I've spotted a fat one, Amy. She's not particularly old, but she looks cosy and comfortable. He won't come to any harm with her. You can put your mind to rest. When did you see such rosy cheeks?'

Plump Mrs Slater assured my anxious parents that I would be safe as houses, safer, in her care. She could tell, she said, that I was well-spoken: 'He doesn't have to say a word.'

'He doesn't have to, but he will, Mrs Slater. He's his father's son.'

(I suppose I was, then. After she vanished, I became hers. I actually said to him once: 'I'm Mother's son, Father. I'm Mummy's, not yours. I belong to your wife.')

That day, however, I was keen to impress Mrs Slater with a choice tale or two, in the manner of Oswald Harvey. I had a great deal of mysterious material at my command, all of it contained in the person of my aunt. Mrs Slater listened to my ramblings with smiling attentiveness. She even tut-tutted once, when I hinted at Swedie's more eccentric behaviour, which was far too peculiar – I suggested, darkly – to be discussed in public.

'She goes really wild,' I heard myself telling her.

'In what way, my dear?'

'She reverts to the jungle.'

'How distressing.'

'They say she's ferocious.'

'She would be, wouldn't she? And who exactly are *they*, my dear?'

'The men in white coats. They have trouble catching her at times.'

'I can believe it.' She beamed as she added, 'What a cruel place the world is.'

She began, haltingly, to talk of her son, whose name was Ivor. How could she describe him for me? It was difficult. She needed to clear her thoughts. My word, how difficult it was! She had never mentioned his terrible accident – except that it wasn't an accident – outside the family before. 'Are you squeamish?' she asked suddenly.

I did not understand her question, since the word was new to me.

'You're not easily upset by – how shall I say – nasty details?'

'I shouldn't think so.'

'My husband is. Oh, Lord, is he!'

Again she beamed. And again, out of politeness, I smiled.

'He turns to jelly at the very idea of pain. Especially Ivor's.'

'Does he?'

'Yes, Gabriel, he does. He does, indeed.'

The beam, now, was almost threatening. I stared into it, transfixed.

'Ivor was a gunner in the Air Force. The Germans shot his plane down over the Channel. It was his first mission. He was pulled out of the wreckage.'

I went on staring.

'His beautiful face was burnt away. His hands, too. He was bandaged up for months.'

And still I stared.

'The doctors are taking teeny bits of skin from every part of his body – his legs one week, his arms the next; then his stomach, then his back. They're snipping at him from all directions.'

'What for?' My throat was blocked with phlegm. I coughed. 'What for?'

'You don't look stupid, my dear. Can't you guess?'

I was stupidly silent.

'They call it grafting, medical people do. They're sewing those bits together so that Ivor can have a new face. And hands, too, perhaps, in time.'

'Will he get them?'

'That's what I hope. It's a long business. With any luck, the day will come when strangers won't feel immediately sick at the sight of him. As they do now. As, I'm afraid, his father, my husband, does.'

That beam, once more; once more, my strange, polite acknowledgment.

'The nurses give Ivor regular salt baths. They have to be gentle and patient with their patient, as you can imagine. He often feels raw and tender and prickly – the merest touch hurts him, he says, like hell. I wonder, I honestly do wonder, why he doesn't scream. I would. You would. Your aunt certainly would.'

'Yes,' was my response.

'Judging by what you've told me.'

'Yes.'

'Can you see my husband?'

'See?'

'With your eyes.'

'I don't know what you mean.'

'Look around you. Where is Mr Slater?'

'There's just us in the carriage. No one else.'

'Exactly. He isn't here, is he?'

'No.'

'No, he isn't. He is not with his wife, who is visiting their son this afternoon; who visits their son each and every weekend, without fail. Who knows it is her duty to, which he doesn't. Who has the full measure of his love now, and no great distance it stretches – does it? He's tending his roses at this moment. Mr Slater wants a fine show this summer. You don't bathe roses in salted water, that's a fact. He might even win a prize with them. Won't that be nice for him?'

What was my reply? An inane nod and another smile, I seem to remember.

'I shall tell Ivor I met you today. He'll be interested to hear that I've made a new friend. Shall I pass on your greetings and good wishes?'

'Yes, please.'

'There's a dear kind soul.'

I was commanded to kiss her goodbye. I did so, and was briefly, smotheringly hugged.

I waved to Mrs Slater from the platform. Her beam filled the carriage window.

'You smell of dead animals.'

Yes, I thought, my father's right: she really is mad.

24

'I knew Oswald would never take my advice. Did he tell you that I am insane?'

'No,' I said, too quickly.

'Of course he did. You're lying to protect my feelings. I shouldn't worry about those if I were you.'

Aunt Kathleen finished sniffing me.

'Oswald seldom has. How's your young mother?'

'She's very well, thank you. She gave me some eggs to give you.'

'Eggs? There's luxury!'

'Only three.'

'Are you accustomed to more, Gabriel? Does Oswald keep hens?'

'He can't. Our cat would kill them.'

'Then your young mother is being especially kind. I shall make us an omelette with them tonight.'

She snatched my suitcase from me and indicated the direction in which we would be going: 'Can your little legs manage a mile?'

She had already set off before I could answer. No one ever walked with such determination, with so keen a sense of purpose. She neither huffed nor puffed, as human dynamos are said to do. She steamed along, but she did not sweat.

Her first words to her breathless nephew when they entered her cottage were 'Breathe in! Breathe in!' I did as I was instructed. 'Do you notice the difference?'

Her question was as baffling as any put to me by Mrs Slater. 'Yes,' I said, stupid for the – oh, twentieth time that day.

'I thought you would. You're a perceptive boy. I had an idea you would be.'

I accepted her unintelligible praise with a smile that, I hoped, suggested gratitude.

'I am a believer, Gabriel, who is firmly convinced that the Lamb of God should not be sacrificed. I see no reason why Agnus Dei should be prevented by mere men and women from growing into Ovis Dei and then dying, as we all must, at his appointed time. You won't be eating him while you're my guest. In fact, you won't be eating meat at all. My kitchen is not dependent on the slaughterhouse. Your young mother's is, obviously.'

(I had planned to tell my aunt that our butcher's name was DeAth, and that we always referred to him at home as Mr

Death. I had anticipated that she would find this amusing, as we did. I understood, now, that she wouldn't.)

'Mummy cooks a lot of stews.'

'She hasn't much of an alternative, with food still rationed. I shall cook you a stew, Gabriel, that I think you will enjoy and remember.'

'Thank you.'

'Don't thank me in advance. I can't see Oswald in you, hard as I'm looking. Is his hair as grey as mine?'

'Not quite.'

'You know who I am, Gabriel. Why not call me Auntie?'

'No, Auntie. I mean, no, his hair isn't as grey as yours. He's only grey at the temples, Auntie.'

'You'll be old before he is, I prophesy, Gabriel.' She took my hands in hers, pressing them tight, and said, 'Poor Oswald. Poor Oswald.'

'He's written you a letter, Auntie. I've brought it with me.'

'I must let go of you, then, to receive my surprise. A letter from brother Oswald! Are you absolutely certain it's from him?'

'Yes, Auntie. I think it's rather long.'

'A long letter from brother Oswald! Wonder of wonders! Give it to me this minute, Gabriel, or I'll faint right away, I swear.' She gulped, to stop herself laughing. 'Isn't it kind of him to communicate, and at length, with his mad sister?'

That evening I ate my first Emanuel Swedenborg omelette, as I chose – years afterwards – to call the simple dish my aunt prepared with the three precious eggs and some herbs from her garden, chief among which was sage. I chose, years afterwards, to think it was Jerusalem sage, though it probably wasn't. The conceit appealed to me, and might have appealed to her, had I thought of it while she lived.

'I am a vegetarian, Gabriel, not a vegan. If I were, I couldn't have whipped up this delicate concoction.'

A vegan, she explained, is one who eats nothing that does not come out of the earth. Whereas she liked eggs and milk. And butter, too ... but, thanks to the war, if one could thank such a dreadful business for anything, she had grown used to the taste of margarine.

'What about fish, Auntie?'

'Of course not, silly. Fish swim, don't they? Or do until the fisherman comes along with his line and his net. Imagine having a hook in your throat, and your blood welling up and spilling out. I should say I don't touch fish!'

'Do I really smell of animals, Auntie?'

'Dead animals, yes, Gabriel. I'm afraid you do. We vegetarians have keen noses. It isn't a stink that causes everyone offence. Just us.'

I had been taught by my mother to be polite, so I probably said I was sorry, and Aunt Kathleen, in all probability, replied that if I learned to respect the lives of God's creatures, apologies would never again be necessary.

'I want to hear about your school, Gabriel. It sounds a fascinating institution.'

I told her it was. I must also have mentioned that I was the one and only Gabriel among its 211 pupils – and in tones that weren't tomb-like. I certainly let her know that the boys in my class had given me the nickname Starch-angel.

'It's because of my shirts. Mummy makes sure that I wear a fresh white shirt every day. The collars are always stiff with starch.'

'The Starch-angel Gabriel. That's most inventive of the boys, most imaginative. I can see that your young mother takes pride in your appearance, but you must allow yourself to be unstarched while you stay with me. Anyway, you have no alternative. I haven't heard enough. Go on.'

I went on. My physics teacher, Mr Carver, I said, who taught in a room in a building that was cut off from the main school – a bomb had destroyed an entire block, which fortunately was not the oldest part, which went back to 1703, which was where we assembled every morning and where we had a short service with a hymn, a reading from the Bible, and a prayer, as well as a sermon once a week from the Headmaster ...

'We appear to have lost Mr Carver. In his isolated building.'

'Yes, Auntie. When Mr Carver talks to me he never calls me by my real name, Harvey, as he does the others. It's always "Spencer's friend" or "Spencer's pal" or "Spencer's chum".' (I spelled Spencer with a 'c' then, because there was a Lilliburnian Spencer, who was definitely not my friend.) 'I keep telling Mr Carver that Michael Spencer is not my particular friend, but he only laughs to himself and says he knows better. He has inside information, he says.'

'The teasing old show-off! How clever of him, though. But we'll be cleverer, shan't we, Gabriel?'

'Shall we?'

'We shall. You must tell Mr Smartypants Carver that you prefer to be addressed as Hobbinol. I should love to be a fly on the wall when you do.'

(Aunt Kathleen was born in the same dark, damp hole as my father, in an area of London where the police walked in threes, where screams rang out day and night to no one's surprise and to no one's alarm, where girls were expected to grow into slatterns or slaves and boys into drunkards or drudges or worse; my Aunt Kathleen, of whom nothing much was expected, knew that Edmund Spenser's closest friend at Pembroke Hall was a man of great learning, Gabriel Harvey, and that Spenser celebrated their friendship in *The Shepheardes Calender* through the characters of Colin Clout and Hobbinol. It was this knowledge she imparted to me on that far-off Palm Sunday in her independent kitchen that smelled of sweet, sharp, aromatic herbs.)

I had hardly ever seen the countryside before. I had only glimpsed it from trains and hospital windows.

I had been sick for most of my childhood. No sooner was I pronounced cured of one illness than another, more severe, replaced it. Now, striding across the Downs alongside my aunt, I was blissfully certain that I would never be unwell again.

It was a warm, cloudless afternoon. Blackbirds, thrushes, tits and jays flew over and about us. A solitary lark rose gloriously in our path. We waited for it to become an unaccountable piece of the sky, and then walked on.

It was still light when we returned to the cottage. 'Let's sit in the garden,' said tireless aunt to exhausted nephew. 'I want to effect an introduction or two, if it's possible.'

We sat on the grass.

'They should be coming down in a second. I can hear them.'

'Who, Auntie?'

'You musn't say anything about this to Oswald, Gabriel. It will finally convince him that I really am crazy.'

'What will?'

'You'll discover in a moment.'

Almost as she spoke, the leaves of her Judas-tree were in a sudden commotion.

'Tabitha!' she called. 'Toby!'

At which command, two tiny creatures scampered across the

lawn. When they were close to us, I saw that they had pink, monkey-like faces with tufts of hair, like whiskers, around their heads and ears. They had long bushy tails, and claws for fingers.

'Mr Gladstone, twice over,' I said, pointing at them.

'Yes, Gabriel. There's a distinct resemblance.'

We watched them chase each other in and out of bushes, up and down the tree.

'They put on a fine show, don't they? What a joy it is to have them. They sleep in the conservatory. Today's a special day for them, being so balmy. During the war I kept no animals at all, for obvious reasons. Did I hear you say you have a cat?'

'Yes, Auntie. Mrs McTrap.'

'Good heavens! Does she wear tartan, this married feline, or does she play the pipes?'

'No, Auntie.'

'I somehow felt she wouldn't. Explain, Gabriel.'

'She was given to Dad by a Scottish knife-grinder, Jamie Deuchars, in the Prodigal's Return one Saturday night. He said that mousing ran in her family, and that she'd save us the cost of a trap, let alone the cheese to fill it.'

'What does she look like?'

'She's got green eyes, and her fur is orange and black and white. And she has a tabby tail. And why she's fluffy, Jamie Deuchars told Dad, is because one of her parents was a Persian.'

'A far-flung family, obviously. It's getting chill. Let's go in. And besides, I'm peckish. I'm sure you are, too.'

We drank gunpowder tea and ate tansy cake. I nibbled at it, rather, for its taste was strangely bitter. My palate would have to be educated, its baker said, cutting me a second slice.

'This will prolong your life, Gabriel, if you eat it regularly. It might even make you immortal.'

She grinned as I persevered.

'Poor Tom, your brother, thought I was trying to poison him.'

'I don't have a brother, Auntie.'

'If you want to be pedantic, very well. Very well – your *half-*brother.'

'What's a half-brother?'

'Tom is, Gabriel.'

'Who's Tom, Auntie?'

'Your half-brother. We're talking through the looking-glass. Tom is the son of Oswald's first marriage, to a dedicated pest of a woman. He is, therefore, fairly closely related to you. He must be nearing forty by now.'

'You're not teasing me, are you, Auntie?'

She caught the anguish in my voice, the edge it gave to an everyday question of childhood. She sensed the sudden cold I felt. She answered, gently, 'No, my love, I'm not. Of course I'm not. I'd tease you about a cat in a kilt, but not about Tom. Of course I'm not. Tom exists. Tom's real. He's Oswald's flesh and blood as much as you are.'

Many years later, twenty-six to be precise, I met the resentful flesh-and-blood of my father's *second* marriage: my half-sister Ethel, of whose existence Aunt Kathleen must also have been aware.

'So you're the clever Gabriel. I'm the not-very-clever Ethel.'

'I'm sorry. Ought I to know you?'

'I'm only your half-sister.'

'I didn't realize I had one.'

'Well, you have, and here she stands. Pleased to meet you.'

'Yes,' I said. 'Yes, indeed.'

'Your shirts may be fresh,' said my aunt, 'but your back is a depot for London impurities.'

She scrubbed the offending repository with such vigour that I cried out in pain.

'Blackheads galore. I shall have to squeeze them free. Don't flinch. I can't get at the beastly things if you flinch.'

She squeezed and squeezed ('And another! And another, oh my!') while I sat, her victim, in the quickly cooling water she had poured into the tin bath.

'Apart from this Mr Carver, are there any other eccentric masters at Lily's? Anyone Oswald would consider mad?'

Something – tact, perhaps; a feeling that this was a 'dirty' matter – had prevented me from referring to Mr Carver's oddest habit, odder by far than his annoying jokes about my friendship with Spenser (with an 's'). How could I say that he kept his left hand almost permanently in his trouser pocket, where every so often it twitched for minutes on end? No, I couldn't mention Mr Carver's daily game of 'pocket billiards', not even to Aunt Kathleen, who (I was tempted to think) might well be amused by it. She was a woman, and women were not entertained by smut.

'He's isolated in more ways than one, it seems. Does that explain your silence?'

'The music master's a bit funny, I suppose,' I responded, feebly.

'Not an out-and-outer? If a bit's the best you can offer, let's hear about it.'

'Mr Rushworth makes us sing silly words to help us remember tunes.'

'What do you mean, spotty-backed Gabriel?'

'This is what I mean, Auntie.' I sang: ' "This is the sym-pho-ny that Schu-u-ubert left un-fin-ished." That's the opening of Schubert's Eighth Symphony, you see. Do you want to hear another?'

'The night is young.'

' "How love-ly the sea is, How love-ly the sea is." Do you recognize it?'

'That must be Mrs McTrap's favourite. It's Mendelssohn's *Fingal's Cave* overture.'

'That's right. Another?'

'You have a large repertoire, clearly. Yes, please.'

'This one's difficult. "There are ten million people in China, who have not savoured boiled beef and carrots." Guessed it?'

'Too difficult, as you say.'

'That's Mozart's Fortieth in G minor.'

'Ah, yes.'

' "We're high on our horses, high on our horses, high on our horses – jockeys are we!" '

'Enough, enough. More than enough of those persistent Val-kyries. Dry yourself thoroughly, Gabriel. I shall repeat the treatment before the soot and the grime and the fog lay claim to you again.'

On Good Friday, the best of all Good Fridays I can remember, two mysteries were solved.

We had strolled on the Downs; the marmosets had put on their show; the last of my London impurities had been extracted, and now I sat at the kitchen table with my eyes closed and my hands clasped while Aunt Kathleen thanked God for the blessings we were about to receive: cabbage leaves stuffed with curried mushrooms.

'I assume Oswald has told you what kind of Christian I am?'

'No, Auntie.'

'You amaze me. It's always been a source of great amusement to him. I am a disciple, after my fashion, of Emanuel Swedenborg, whose followers founded the New Jerusalem Church. A crank among cranks, according to Oswald.'

I was on the verge of saying 'So that's why he calls you Swedie' when she asked if I wanted to learn a little more about the incredible Emanuel.

I said yes, naturally.

'He was Swedish, of course. He lived from 1688 to 1772. He was an engineer and a mathematician and an inventor and a scientist. And he was a philosopher. He maintained that Heaven and Hell are inside each and every one of us and that, as thinking beings, we can choose between them. We have to make a choice for eternity.'

That was the little I learned. She said nothing, that day, of the many spirits, some of them angelic, floating in and around Swedenborg's thinking; of her need to believe that one particular spirit was for ever present, waiting for her in the paradise which she, in her deep humility, hoped to enter and Alessandro, her husband, had already attained.

'Oswald, in his wisdom, would have had no cause to tell you there was a Swedish church near the Highway, not very far from where we were born. Well, there was. The Ulrica Eleanora. One of the congregation, Mrs Rosen, took a shine to me. I'd dashed into the Ulrica – the Ully Elly – one wet summer afternoon, and there she was, on her haunches, scrubbing the altar steps. She looked up and smiled at the snotty-nosed skinnyshanks who was only using the house of God for shelter until the rain stopped. She asked me if I spoke Swedish – me, who couldn't properly read or write my own language. I shook my head. "You pray in English?" I nodded. "Do you pray for yourself or for others?" I didn't answer; I couldn't, for ours wasn't a praying family. My mother often wondered what the Almighty thought He was up to, but I didn't say anything about that. "It's a sign of true goodness to think of others in your prayers. Do you like Swedes, child?" And then I made her laugh, laugh so that she clutched her sides and spluttered, because the first words I said to Mrs Rosen were "I like them mashed with lots of pepper!" It was minutes before she could speak. "She likes them mashed with lots of pepper!" And then she was laughing again, louder than ever. "I think it's the *rotbagga* you enjoy to eat, not us poor Swedes. I will cook some for you if you will let me be

32

your friend." She lifted herself off the floor and wiped her big red hands on her apron and came towards me. "What's your name, child?" I told her. "I am Nora Rosen. I live over the way, in one of the palaces. You will join me for tea, *ja*?" '

My aunt joined her for tea, *ja,* but not on that rainy Saturday. Kathleen Harvey was carrying a jug which had to be filled to the brim with frothless porter at five-thirty on the dot by the landlord of the Gun. 'That was my regular weekly duty, fetching my father's stout. I was given the job because I never spilled any of the valuable stuff – you'd have thought it was his life's blood – and I was never tempted to take a sip of it, either, which certainly wasn't the case with Oswald. It was darling Daddy's cockeyed notion that the local villains might well attack a boy but would think twice about setting on a helpless little girl. His knowledge of the world and its ways was curiously restricted for a dock-lander.'

She drank Mrs Rosen's tea the next afternoon, in the basement of a grand house in Wellclose Square, owned by a very old shipmaster who remembered Trafalgar and Waterloo. Nora Rosen cleaned and cooked for him, washed and darned his fancy shirts, listened to his tales of life in Wapping during the Regency, and read him his favourite essays by Charles Lamb while he sipped his medicinal brandy. Her accent, he said, made dear Charlie's prose the more melodious.

With the tea, which was slightly scented (a surprise) and pale (another surprise, for the brew at home was always near-vermilion in colour), came the daintiest, most delicious cakes my aunt had ever tasted.

'I watched Nora bake those *krumkake*. She beat three eggs in a bowl and stirred in four ounces of sugar. Then she added four ounces of melted butter and four ounces of plain flour, beating them in all the while. Finally, she squeezed the juice of a tiny lemon into the mixture and her batter was ready.'

My inquisitive aunt watched intently as Mrs Rosen effected the transformation from simple batter to surprising delicacy. Nora showed the entranced skinnyshanks a kitchen utensil common in Scandinavia but seldom seen in England. This was a *krumkake* iron. My aunt had difficulty describing it – it was a kind of griddle; it was made of metal, of course, and it had a detachable circular base, which you rested on the range. You poured a tablespoon of the batter on to the iron – yes, that was right – and then you clasped its two parts together and fitted it into the base. When one side of the batter was golden brown, you flicked your wrist (the iron had handles, you see) to let the other side brown as well.

'There was a third stage. She removed each crisp table-spoonful with a palette knife and when it had cooled she wrapped it round a cone-shaped piece of wood. Cone after lacy cone appeared until she had filled a large bowl with them. She brought them to the table. "Take one," she said, "and copy me." I took one, and copied her. I put in a dollop of cream, as she did. She had provided raspberries and strawberries – I could take my pick; I could choose whichever I wanted. I buried the fruit in the cream with a finger, as she did – "Polite ladies, they use a spoon, but we are not polite ladies, we are friends" – and opened my mouth, as she'd opened hers, in anticipation. "Together," she said. "United, we bite." Oh, Gabriel, the heavenly luxury. The sheer wonder of those *krumkake*. The joy I felt eating – no, not eating – devouring them.'

Nora Rosen was that phenomenon in 1898, a woman who had cast aside her husband. She was pious, diligent in her duties, fastidious in her person, but she was not finally respectable. She had denied Sven Rosen his sacred right to use her as he pleased, and such a denial could not easily be forgiven, especially by those who were still being used and used ... or bruised and bruised, to judge by the looks of them. The wife of a man who occasionally rose from the conjugal bed to saunter into the City (where he picked a few carefully selected pockets) was one such – this thief's wife regularly shrieked insults after the 'blastphemin' foreign muck' as the 'blasphemer' went about her harmless business. If there was one skill Nora Rosen possessed it was that of turning the other cheek, the most useful, the most necessary, of all skills, my aunt asseverated – 'Follow her example, Gabriel. Practise, practise, until it becomes a part of your nature.'

I said I would. I was not displaying my customary politeness. I said I would, and meant it.

'I believe you.'

From the afternoon of the *krumkake* until her last peaceful evening in St Bartholomew's Hospital, Nora Rosen was my aunt's friend, teacher, mentor and guide. Kathleen learned from her that there was more to live for than the two certainties wearily anticipated by Ephraim and Mary Harvey: the monthly visit of the landlord ('If you don't pay, it's the workhouse') and death. 'That's all the likes of us can expect' – how often as a girl she had been advised by her parents to mark the truth of those words. For Nora, such stoicism, if that's what it was, such hopeless resignation, could not be tolerated, even though she sympathized with its origins – 'They are wrong to infect their children so. You and your brother have the world before you.'

The *world* before them! My aunt had only ever imagined London before her, not the world towards which its dirty river flowed. That was where soldiers and sailors went. ' "There are worlds and worlds, child. I'll help you find them." Which she did, whenever I had a free hour from home – or from the garment factory where I had to clean the fluff out of the machines and then sweep it away with a broom twice my size. On Sundays, after church, I studied with Rosie Rotbagga – as we decided to call her – in the old man's basement, poring over the old man's books until my eyes ached. If the heavens hadn't opened, if I hadn't taken shelter in the Ully Elly – think of it, Gabriel, I might never have had an education.'

We sat and thought about it as we finished our meal.

'That's enough thinking for tonight. You look puzzled.'

'It's the grand house, Auntie.'

'What do you mean?'

'Well, a grand house, down there, near the Isle of Dogs, with the police in threes? It doesn't make sense.'

'Oh, I see. No, of course it doesn't. I'll try and explain. In the eighteenth century, there was great wealth in the East End. Silk merchants lived in Spitalfields and shipmasters in Wapping. Then, gradually, the wealthy took themselves and their money to other parts of London, and the whole district fell into decay. Poor immigrants moved in. One of those grand houses, built for a single rich family's comfort, now contained dozens upon dozens of families living higgledy-piggledy. The grand house Nora Rosen worked in was an exception, Gabriel, because its owner still occupied the premises. He'd remained within his father's bricks and mortar for God knows how many years. Now he was an eccentric if ever I knew one. Once a day, he would take a stroll round the square and peer through his lorgnette at his strange new neighbours. He was a pretty strange sight himself in his frock-coat and brocade weskit, which he'd had made for him during the reign of William the Fourth. Sometimes he wore a top hat of brushed black felt and when it was bitter cold he put on his inverness – the only up-to-date item of clothing in his wardrobe. He was a relic, was Mr Tiverley, a peacock from a bygone age, strutting along those dingy streets which in his youth had seemed to be paved with gold. The same streets, Gabriel, where Jack the Ripper hacked six half-starved doxies to pieces.'

'Did you talk to him? Mr Tiverley, Auntie – not Jack the Ripper.'

'He talked to me, my love, and I listened. I was in awe of him – his high boots, his cravats, his rings, his beautiful enamelled snuff boxes. His back was stiff and straight like the proverbial ramrod. He bowed to me, actually bowed to me, Gabriel, when Rosie introduced us. Imagine it! I nearly laughed at him, I was so thunderstruck. "What a charming smile the gel has," he said. I was always the "gel". "Bring the gel to me," he'd order, "I want to look at her with my one good eye." It was his custom, after the daily jaunt, to report to his foreign retainer on the other foreigners he'd spotted with that one good eye: "Pigtailed persons came into my ken, dear Nora. Chinese, I should suppose, by the noise like distraught doves their tongues were making." Or: "There are inebriated Russian bears abroad. I have returned earlier than usual in fear and trembling." Or: "I caught sight of a bow-legged Indian, dear Nora, with the woefullest countenance, bewildered by the spectacle of gabardined Polish Jews muttering to their maker in the square. I stood entranced at his bewilderment." Oh, Gabriel, how you've made me digress. You're entirely to blame. I shall have aching jaws tomorrow after all this exercise.'

She rolled an orange towards me.

'Don't stop, Auntie. Please tell me more.'

'More, you glutton? I don't know that there is much more.'

'There must be.'

'No *must* whatever, Gabriel.'

She drank some tea – 'to wet my whistle' – and continued with her digression. Mr Tiverley died. He died, you might say, with panache. ' "Read me dear Charlie's 'A Bachelor's Complaint'," he instructed his faithful Nora shortly after noon on the day of his death. "I want to hear about the airs and graces of the married." ' It was not an unusual request. She had read the essay to him a thousand times, so often that she almost had it off by heart. What *was* unusual was the hour. He was strict in his habits, and the reading from Charles Lamb had never taken place in daylight before.

'It was a Sunday and I was in the kitchen, doing what one is not supposed to do on the Sabbath – working. "He doesn't want his chop, he wants me to read," said Nora, rushing in. "And you're to come with me, Kathleen." So up to his bedroom I went. "I can't make out the gel. Is she here or is she not?" I was pushed forward. "Ah, the young phoenix. You catch my drift, dear Nora?" "I do, sir, I do." And so did I, soon enough. The old flatterer. What a compliment to pay the daughter of a hod carrier and a woman who took in washing.'

Mr Tiverley's was the rarest compliment. He echoed his hero by observing that the begetting of children was no special cause for pride. Anyone and everyone could bring them into life. He would chuckle appreciatively whenever his dear Nora came to the line 'The poorest people commonly have them in most abundance.' He would say it with her, and did so on that Sunday. '"No cause at all. As Charlie puts it, 'If they were young phoenixes, indeed, that were born but one in a year, there might be a pretext. But when they are so common – ' Does the gel understand me now?" "Yes, sir, Mr Tiverley," I said. "Be on your way then." It was a command. I curtsied and left. Warmed by his words – for they *were* his, although they were Lamb's – I returned to my studies. I was deep in my books when Nora came back: "I've put the coins on his eyes: a penny on the bad, a guinea on the good. Now let us have our dinner, Young Phoenix. Clear the table." It was a day of commands. I cleared the table, and we had our dinner.'

Mr Tiverley timed his departure with his customary finesse. Had he lived two more years, he would have been a near-pauper. Some of his shares were already worthless. Firms he had invested in no longer existed, and no one had advised him of their going. There was just enough money in his City bank to allow the sensible Nora to live in moderate comfort somewhere – for the 'palace' had to be sold. Its purchaser was one of the many workhouse-invoking landlords who battened on the likes of Ephraim and Mary – the grandparents Gabriel Harvey was born too late to meet.

'We loaded his books on to a cart, the two of us, and pushed it all the way to Southwark. When I say "his books" I mean those out of his enormous library that Nora wanted to keep. She seemed to have chosen hundreds. I still have some of them here.'

'Why did you take them to Southwark, Auntie?'

'Can't you guess, Gabriel? My Rosie Rotbagga rented rooms there. And I made the bold decision to go with her. You can imagine the warnings my fond parents gave me as my parting present: that I would come to grief, living so far from my natural home, and with a foreigner into the bargain; that it was all right for Oswald to run off because he was a boy and it was a boy's nature to kick over his traces. That was the wisdom ringing in my ears as I took myself and my bagful of belongings the short distance – it was short and it wasn't – to Southwark. I stayed with Nora up until the very day I married Alessandro.'

'Di Salvo?'

'Of course di Salvo. My husband was Italian. I am a widow, Gabriel. I didn't pluck my name out of the air.'

'I see now, Auntie. I understand.'

'Do you? You sound as if you've had a revelation.' She yawned. 'You may be seeing, but I shan't be shortly. Bed, Gabriel, bed.'

'Yes, Auntie. Thank you.'

'You've been a patient audience. Have you forgotten my kiss?'

'No, Auntie.'

Kathleen di Salvo sighed and groaned in her sleep that night. I heard her from my room.

In her sleep that night – I knew she wasn't awake; I was certain of it – she shouted something that made no sense to me.

In Sorg, Minnesota, it made all the sense in the world.

'I was right, wasn't I, Gabriel lad? Wasn't I right about Sister Swedie?'

'What a way to greet the boy. Really, Oswald!'

'You can't believe she's my sister, can you? Tell me you can't believe it.'

'I can't believe it,' I said, believing my words.

He laughed at that. I was pleased he had misunderstood me so thoroughly. I even repeated my answer.

'Our Gabriel's got his wits about him, Amy.'

'I never, for one moment, thought he hadn't, Oswald.'

We took the trolleybus home. I was back in the impure city now, listening to the bus's spikes singing on the wires. I suddenly felt disloyal to my aunt – whom I loved, I realized – for the noise assured me I was where I belonged.

'The country's too quiet. I couldn't live in it. Not like Auntie does.'

'It's a sign of age,' my father pronounced, 'is Swedie's hankering after trees and fields and birds on the bloody wing. Wasn't it Sam Johnson who said that a man who's tired of London is tired of life? Well, Dictionary Sam knew his arse from his elbow, and he hit the target when he passed that remark. You follow his example, Gabriel lad.'

'He'll follow what he chooses. In his own good time.'

'Yes, Amy, of course he will. He's got the spunk in him to do what he wishes. I was only giving him something to turn over in his mind.'

I was witnessing the edgy aftermath of one of my parents' rare quarrels. They had been bickering before my arrival at the station − her 'Oswald' instead of the usual tender 'Ossie' had alerted me.

'It would be pleasant, I grant you, living the life of a squire, in a country seat, with servants and grooms and tenants: lord and master of all you survey. That *would* be pleasant. But as for spending your days in some poky little cottage, you have to be as daft as Swedie is to want that.'

My aunt's cottage was neither poky nor little, I chose not to tell him. The absence of unnecessary furniture, of knick-knacks and ornaments, made it seem larger than it actually was. The reviled Swedie had space about her. Bowls of pot-pourri gave each of her rooms its particular sweet smell. Let him mock her, then. Let him picture her, as he obviously wanted to picture her, in the draughty hovel of his imagination.

'We only agreed − didn't we, Amy? − to your going to stay with her because the weather had brightened up. We have your health to think of, young man.'

In our poky, little, cluttered house, not far from the railway and very near the gas works, we sat down that evening to a shin-of-beef stew.

'This is the first meat I've eaten for a week.'

'It damned well isn't, I hope, Gabriel lad.'

'It is. Auntie Kathleen's a vegetarian.'

'Oh, that bloody crank of a bloody woman. I wrote to her, Amy, you read the letter, asking her − politely; politely − to give him the kind of meals he's used to. And what do you suppose she does? She goes and cooks him her compost heap.'

'What did she give you, dear?'

To start with, she gave me an omelette, I said, made with those three precious eggs; and then she gave me a tansy cake;

and then we had cauliflower cheese; and then a vegetable hot-pot, and then cabbage leaves stuffed with curried mushrooms . . .

'Mushrooms, Gabriel? My, my – mushrooms!'

'They were dried ones, Mummy. They were small and crinkled-looking until she poured hot water on them. They opened out, just like flowers, as soon as she did that.'

'And so did your bowels, if I know my sister. You're home again now, Gabriel lad, among sensible people who eat sensibly. I warned you, Amy – didn't I? – that she would feed him swill.'

I didn't say, as I should have said, that I liked my aunt's food, that I was perfectly happy to eat it.

'Does she keep an animal for company?'

'Yes, she has two – ' And then I remembered that I had promised my aunt that I wouldn't tell my father about her marmosets. My disloyalty was going to be total. 'No, she doesn't.'

'Don't lie to me. She has two what?'

I was silent. I was more silent, I thought, than I had ever been.

'Please don't lie to your father, Gabriel. Please don't.'

'No, Mummy.'

I chose, in that treacherous moment, to speak the truth to the Emperor of Deceit, the King of Liars. I chose to make my aunt the more ridiculous in his eyes, the madder, the crankier. I chose to be honest, at my mother's soft insistence.

'Auntie Kathleen keeps two marmosets. They're monkeys, from South America. They're very small, with pink faces and whiskers like Mr Gladstone's.'

'The devil they are, the devil she does. Would you believe, Gabriel lad, that she brought a lizard home once, when she was younger than you are today. She'd been given it by a Jew-boy in Petticoat Lane, who had reptiles and such crawling out of his every pocket. The thing really took to her. I trod on it, by accident, entirely by accident; I swore to her I hadn't done for it on purpose, the moment my hob-nails finished it. My hob-nails finished it, Gabriel, and she couldn't forgive me.'

3

George Fox looks down on me as I write: that same George Fox who 'saw darkness and death in all people, where the power of the Lord God had not shaken them', but whose steadfast gaze, captured by an anonymous, admiring portraitist, has always seemed benign to me.

Your gaze, George, has consoled me in room after London room, and it still strikes at my life.

Why did I never ask my father to tell me about Thomas Harvey? I suppose I decided that if he could be secretive, I could be, too. I was waiting for him to announce that I had a half-brother, to which announcement I would respond with a gloating 'I know I have. His name is Tom.'

I had another question for him: 'What are doxies, Dad?'

'How old are you, son?'

'I was twelve last birthday.'

'It occurs to me that a boy who was twelve last birthday is a bit young to be thinking about doxies. I haven't heard them called that for years.'

'But what are they?'

'They are persons, Gabriel lad, I would advise you to have nothing to do with. Not for a long, long while, if ever. They're ladies of the night. They sell their bodies. They're prostitutes.'

'Auntie Kathleen said they were half-starved, the doxies Jack the Ripper murdered.'

'They were. She's right, though it pains me to say so. They weren't the fancy floozies you find up in Mayfair, dripping with diamonds. They were poor bloody wretches; spotty, scruffy, park-railing tarts. And how, exactly, did Sister Swedie bring doxies into the conversation? It doesn't sound like the proper topic for a God-fearing woman.'

'She said that's what his victims were. She didn't explain.'

'Well, now you're wiser, lad. I shouldn't show off your wisdom when your mother's around – it's not a fit subject for her decent ears. Store it in the dirty part of your mind, there's a sensible fellow.'

HMV B9719 – those letters, those numbers made up the code that brought her to me, out of thin air, after she vanished. I jotted them down on a thousand scraps of paper – on a train ticket, once, in the middle of a journey – and Aladdin's lamp was always as good as rubbed.

My mother's decent ears had a fondness for an aria by Handel: 'Silent Worship', from the opera *Ptolemy*. She had a record of it, HMV B9719, which she played on the wind-up gramophone in our nameless house. She liked to put it on when her beloved Ossie was at the Prodigal's Return – where, perhaps, he was silently worshipping his Amy, for all she knew, for all I know, beneath the din of the crowded bar.

> Did you not hear my lady
> Go down the garden singing?
> Blackbird and thrush were silent
> To hear the alleys ringing

sang Heddle Nash on HMV B9719, to my mother's obvious joy. Sometimes she would sing with him – under her breath, a fraction of a beat behind, wispily:

> Though I am nothing to her,
> Though she may rarely look at me,
> And though I could never woo her
> I love her till I die.

I loved the singer's name before I loved Handel's music, arranged – so the label said – by Somerville. I might meet another Gabriel one day, but I doubted that I'd ever come across a Heddle anywhere – unless, of course, it was the silver-tongued tenor himself. I elected to ignore the commonplace John that preceded the strange and wonderful Heddle. The fact that he had reduced it to a paltry 'J' was indication enough to me that Mr Nash preferred his Heddle to his John.

Amy Harvey listened to him, entranced. Once, at my request, she turned the record over, wound up the gramophone, and played the other side. 'Linden Lea' did not send her into the familiar three-minute swoon – it was a nice melody, she said, but it didn't *belong* to her the way 'Silent Worship' did.

> But surely you see my lady
> Out in the garden there,
> Riv'lling the glitt'ring sunshine
> With a glory of golden hair.

My mother's hair was modestly mousy, not gloriously golden, though it shone somewhat when she washed and brushed it. As soon as she got home from her 'secret place', she released it from its imprisoning bun, shook her head from side to side, and let it bounce down to her shoulders. 'That feels better. Now I feel natural.'

In 'Blenheim', one chilly afternoon, I placed HMV B9719 on the turntable of Oswald Harvey's electric ('No more cursèd cranking and winding!') gramophone. I blew a speck of dust off the needle before lowering it carefully on to the record. Then I stood back to listen.

Heddle's inamorata was setting the alleys ringing when my father stormed into the drawing-room.

'Off!' he shouted. 'Off, this minute, Piss-a-Bed, off!'

'I want to hear it through.'

'Are you defying me, young man? Do as I say.'

'It's nearly over.'

'I've had enough of it. Take it off.'

'There's no need. It's finished, Father.'

'That dreadful, bloody dreadful, racket.'

'Father, it has finished. The song's come to an end.'

'Bloody silly schoolgirl drivel.'

I left him with his fury.

He was grinning when I saw him next. 'That was no way to behave, was it? Quite disgraceful. Not to be countenanced.' He was rubbing my mother's treasured record against his waist-coated stomach. 'What a spectacle, and all because of this worn-out thing.'

He broke that worn-out thing, ceremoniously, across his knee. He broke it into four jagged pieces.

'Oh dear. It's only fit for the dustbin now.'

His laughter sounded too calculated to be directly inspired by the thought. He had rehearsed it, I was sure.

'I shan't buy another copy, Father. Not while Mummy's away. I'll give her HMV B9719 as her coming-home present.'

'You will, will you?'

'Yes, I will. I shan't forget.'

Was it then, while he kept his grin in place, that the idea of my legacy first came to him?

'She'd like nothing better,' he said, at last.

He must have known, even then, that I was the only person in the entire world who would appreciate the inheritance he had in mind for me.

'I promise not to break the brand-new "Silent Worship". You have my word, young man.'

Was he planning his unique revenge, even then?

In August, during my long school holidays, my father received a typewritten letter.

'It looks official,' he remarked, holding the unopened envelope at arm's length. 'It looks dangerous.'

'You won't find out what it is unless you read it, Ossie.'

'It can't be from the government. It would say it was On His Majesty's Service if it was.'

'Where was it posted?'

'The mark's very faint. I think it's London EC2.'

'That's the City. Who are you friends with in the City?'

'A few ghosts. Nobody living.'

'Your hands are in a flutter, Ossie love. Am I married to a secret criminal? Are you a burglar, or worse, on the sly?'

'I'm a past master, Amy, at whatever it is I'm doing wrong, that I *can* disclose. Now who in hell has sent me this?'

'There's a simple way to answer your question.'

'Typing equals trouble, in my experience.'

'Shall I open it for you?'

'Good God, no. I still have blood in my veins, old as I am. I'm not afraid of a piece of paper.'

'Open it, Dad.'

'Finish your breakfast, Gabriel, and mind your business.'

'The boy's as curious as his mother, Ossie. We both want to know your news – if news it is.'

'It's got to be news of some kind, hasn't it? It stands to reason.'

44

'This Patience will be leaving her monument soon, Oswald Harvey.'

'All right, Amy. All right.'

My father closed his eyes for a moment or so after slitting open with the bread knife his unexpected, unwelcome communication. Perhaps he was praying.

He read the piece of paper he'd assured his wife and son he wasn't afraid of three, four, five times over before he flopped back in his chair and said, 'Well, well. I'm sixty-six and I haven't been forgotten. I've been remembered. Well, well, well. Amy sweetheart, darling Amy, I think we have prospects.'

'Do stop being mysterious, Ossie.'

'I'll stop this minute, Amy love. I am commanded – yes, I think I can safely say that it reads like a command – to show my face at the office of Bate, Morris and Warner, Solicitors and Commissioners of Oaths, 3 Rose and Crown Court, London, EC2, on the morning of August the 17th inst. at 11 a.m., when I shall learn something to my benefit. That's tomorrow. By twelve noon tomorrow, Amy, I might be a rich man.'

'Has somebody left you some money? Is that what that rigmarole means?'

'I should think so. I should hope so. By twelve tomorrow, we shall have learned how much. A thousand, do you suppose, Amy? Or more? Or less?'

'Who is it, Ossie?'

'Who is what?'

'Who is it that's died?'

'Why, Sir Vincent, of course. It must be Sir Vincent. It has to be Sir Vincent. Amy, my darling, it can only be Sir Vincent.'

'Who's he?'

'Who *was* he, you mean, Gabriel lad. He was a gentleman, and I was his servant – and a proud one at that. I waited on him years and years ago.'

In Clerkenwell, in Hackney, in Fulham, in Matthew's Georgian wilderness in Bloomsbury, I pictured Amy Harvey standing on the sawdust-sprinkled floor of Mr DeAth's shop in the vicinity of Victoria Station.

'How's your son today, Mrs Harvey?'

'He's well, Mr Dee-Ath,' replies my mother, who always calls him Death at home.

'Only well, Mrs Harvey? Then I shall have to find you something that will make him better.'

My grateful mother hands Mr DeAth our ration book, which he studies carefully.

'You seem to be due for a small joint, Mrs Harvey. It so happens that I have top-class beef on the premises, fresh in at Smithfield this morning from Scotland. What would your fragile little boy say to a slice of that on his plate come Sunday dinner time?'

'I can guarantee he'll say thank you, Mr Dee-Ath. I've brought him up to be polite.'

'I'll trim it nice and lean for you. I think I know your fads and fancies by now.'

My mother smiles. She takes the meat from 'my Mr Death' and goes to the desk to pay for it with money earned in her 'secret place', which isn't – she has hinted – all that far away from Death's on the corner. Her change is counted out for her by whichever of the younger, or older, DeAths has been appointed to look after the till. Then she waves goodbye to her Mr Death and goes out into the street.

It is a fine spring day. She decides to walk home. Passing the air terminal, she wonders what it would be like to fly in a plane. The very thought of being higher up than birds can get to, beyond clouds invisible to the naked eye, the very thought which has come to her before on this same stretch of the road, makes her feel just that bit queasy. If she feels queasy with her feet fair and square on the ground, then in what state would her system find itself if they weren't? She tells her brain to stop being fanciful, and quickens her pace.

On this day of recurring brightness, she buys violets at a stall in Pimlico. The two bunches cost her a princely eightpence. 'They'll take their time shrinking, ducks,' the flower-seller assures her. 'They'd better,' Amy responds, laughing. 'They'd better take their time, or you'll be the worse for my tongue next Friday.'

She is still smiling as she nears the hospital where her fragile little boy was tended with such love. 'You didn't want to leave, Gabriel,' she says to the son who isn't with her. Frowning now, she pauses – as she always does – by the hospital entrance and silently thanks the nurses and doctors working inside.

The Thames looks clean today – clean enough, you might suppose, for her child to swim in. There is a sparkle on the water, and it gives her heart a lift even as it makes her eyes dazzle. She crosses the bridge and sees what she had half-hoped to see: a mass, an amazing mass, of dandelions on a bomb site. She is no snob where beauty is concerned and the humble dandelion, sprouting everywhere, is warmly, goldenly beautiful, if you ask her opinion. And then she comes across a bonus in the midst of all this yellow − an improbably small cluster of precocious rosebay willow-herb. She picks as many flowers as her hands can hold, and with these free additions to her two bunches of fourpenny violets she has a bouquet fit for a ...

'Fit for me,' she says. 'It's fit for me.'

We put on our best clothes that warm August morning. My father complained that his suit stank of mothballs: 'Mr Bate, Mr Morris and Mr Warner will know by the whiff I'm giving off that I'm not accustomed to being dolled up like this.'

'Oh, Ossie, don't be ridiculous. Five minutes in the fresh air and the smell will have gone. And, anyway, what on earth does it matter what they think?'

'It matters that I shouldn't look a fool.'

'You won't. Take your Amy's word you won't. I've never known you to worry so about other people's opinions of Oswald Harvey. Why this anxiety, all of a sudden?'

'It's important that I make a good impression. Are you really sure this stink will go?'

'Really, I am. Really and truly.'

'It's bloody powerful still.'

'Stop fretting yourself. Have faith in your wife's common sense. Those three gentlemen, if that's what they are, won't have had a smarter customer in their offices for many a long year.'

An hour or more later, on the steps of St Paul's, Amy Harvey dabbed her anxious husband's face with a sweetly scented handkerchief.

'You'll do, my old darling. You'll pass muster.'

'Why are you crying, Amy?'

'Oh, call it happiness. Yes, that's what it is. I'm just proud to be Mrs Harvey.'

'I'll be off, then,' said my father, quickly consulting his pocket watch. He seemed not to have heard my mother's reply. 'I musn't be late for my date with destiny.'

'I'll be here with Gabriel when they're through with you. Fingers crossed.'

He seemed not to notice that she kissed his cheek.

He was her *old* darling, I realized: her *old* darling.

'How old are you, Mummy?'

The two of us were inside the cathedral, pretending to be interested in a marble monument to some sailors drowned off Cape Finisterre.

'How old am I? What a funny question, Gabriel. A well brought-up young man wouldn't dream of asking a lady her age, especially when that lady also happens to be his mother. I was nineteen when I had you and you're twelve now, which means that I'm thirty-one and a good large bit. Does that satisfy your rude curiosity?'

'Yes, Mummy.'

Why had it never struck me with such force before, the fact that my mother was thirty-one and my father sixty-six? He was – what was he? what was he? – he was fifty-four when she married him. He was her senior by thirty-five years.

'Gabriel, love, there are better things to peer at than this. Don't you want to see the altar?'

'Yes, Mummy.'

'Then let's walk towards it. Slowly, Gabriel, slowly. Remember this is a place of worship.'

'They gave me a glass of sherry, Amy, and a dry biscuit. Then they sat me down in a big red leather chair like a throne and told me to prepare myself for a pleasant shock.'

'Oh, Ossie, they didn't all speak at once, did they? You're making them sound like a choir without music.'

'I couldn't tell which of them was addressing me, to be honest, because of the tizzy I was in. They took their gentlemanly time, I must admit, before they came out with the good news.'

'And so are you, Ossie. Taking your time. What is this good news?'

'It's the best good news I've ever had, Amy. It's wonderful, wonderful news. I'm rich, Amy. I'm rich.'

'Are we?' My mother stopped smiling in an instant. 'We're wealthy, are we? Since you've heard it from the three wise men, it must be true, I suppose.'

'Of course it's true,' he affirmed, failing to notice her sarcasm. 'You can bet your bottom dollar, as the Yanks say. And here's the proof, if you still don't believe me, Amy.'

He had twenty crisp five-pound notes in his wallet – 'Courtesy of Mes-Sewers Bate, Morris and Warner.' These were, he explained, the tiniest tip of a gigantic iceberg. 'I shall have to do business with a bank for the first time in my life. You are talking to a man of means.'

'Is it Sir Vincent we have to thank for this – this iceberg?'

'None other. The very same. He died, according to them, over in Bermuda, where he'd gone for his health. They read me the bit in his will concerning yours truly. Sir Vincent didn't know if I was living or a goner, but if I could be traced then I was to be one of his two beneficiaries. Which, I am happy to reveal, is exactly what I am.'

'And who's the second?'

'Beneficiary? I haven't a clue. Does it matter, Amy? Does it matter to us?'

'To *us*, Ossie? No. Not to us.'

'Let's go and celebrate, then. If it's still standing, there's a place I've heard tell of in the Strand where a man of means can treat his family to some decent food and drink. Don't frown, Amy. You can smile all day today. You can afford to, now.'

I swear my mother blushed throughout our celebration lunch. Her naturally pale face was at its reddest whenever my father summoned a waiter with a click of his bony fingers and a curt 'Service!' Staring fixedly at the tablecloth, she whispered, 'Don't, Ossie love, don't. Please don't shame us.'

'I'm not shaming anyone, Amy. I was a servant once, remember. I am addressing the fellow correctly, as he himself is well aware. It isn't a crime to demand service in an expensive restaurant.'

'You could be quieter about it.'

'My glass is empty, I want it filled, and that penguin with acne is paid to fill it.'

'You'll be drunk if you have any more.'

'And why shouldn't I be? Good God, Amy, it takes more than a couple of whiskies to get Oswald Harvey pie-eyed.'

'You've had sherry, too.'

'Amy, Amy, allow me to be a little bit mad today. I feel like I've been released from prison. I'm breathing new air. You mustn't begrudge me my freedom, sweetheart.'

'You're shouting.'

'I'm at a loss to understand you, I honestly am. You could at least tuck into the steak you asked for. It's costing enough.'

'I'll finish it.'

'I should hope so.'

A long silence later, the pimply waiter returned with my father's drink.

'Soda water, sir?'

'A splash.'

'Was the main course to everyone's taste?'

'Very nice,' said my mother. 'It was very nice indeed. Thank you very much.'

'Madam is most gracious.' The waiter smiled at my father as he spoke. 'Would a dessert be agreeable? You have a choice of our own English apple tart or iced bread-and-butter pudding.'

'We'll all have the apple tart. My wife there makes the best b-and-b anyone's ever likely to eat, iced or otherwise. Is there any cream to go with it?'

'Yes, sir. At an extra cost, sir, I'm afraid.'

'No cause for fear. Money's no object. Bring us a great big jar of the lovely stuff.'

'Sir.'

'While we're still living.'

'Sir?'

'You must have hitched a ride to Scotland to fetch this whisky, to judge by the time you took.'

'Sir.'

'I am not accustomed to being kept waiting.'

'No, sir. Of course not, sir.'

'Sir would appreciate some speedy attention from the staff, sir would.'

'Yes, sir. At once, sir.'

Our house without a name, our modest 32, was 'one of Shylock's stables' now.

'The years I've been paying rent to that greasy crook! Don't expect it for much longer, though – that's my message to you, Mr Cross-my-palms-with-silver Middleton. You've had more than enough out of me and some to spare, you back-street money-grubber.'

'He isn't such a bad man, Ossie. We could have had a worse landlord.'

'Well, the day will be dawning soon when we shan't have one at all. I shall be my own master then.'

'Aren't we happy here? Haven't we always been?'

'You came down in the world when you married me, Amy, there's no denying that. Now you can go up again.'

'Oh, you old silly, Ossie.'

How warmly, and with what teasing affection, she used the word 'old'. It was as if she actually gloried in those very things about my father that had recently chilled me in the near-darkness of St Paul's Cathedral – things that suggested decay to me, like the brown spots on the backs of his hands, like the knobby blue and purple veins on his rarely-glimpsed legs, like the 'dewdrops' that suddenly dangled from his nostrils even on the warmest afternoon, like the insistent Adam's apple in his scrawny neck. Her 'old darling', her 'old silly' was made up of all these horrible things, and still her love contained them.

'A bathroom would make a pleasant difference, for a start. A good long soak in an enamel tub, instead of a strip-wash at the kitchen sink – I can't believe you wouldn't prefer that. Happy as we've been, we could be happier.'

'Just a little fresher, perhaps. Nothing else.'

'And a garden. You'd love a garden, wouldn't you?'

'I know where to find the flowers we need, Ossie.'

'Imagine, Amy, in the morning, opening the curtains and seeing your own roses, your own irises, your own what-have-yous growing in your own rich earth. Don't tell me the idea doesn't appeal to you.'

'It sounds lovely.'

'It's no idle dream, Amy. It *will* be lovely, as lovely as ever you wanted it.'

'Who'll mow the lawn, and do the pruning and the planting?'

'Why you, Amy, and me, of course, when my back isn't up to its aching tricks. We'll manage, between us, with a little assistance from the young man who is looking at his father at this moment as though his father was Satan in trousers. What's the matter with me, Gabriel?'

'It's not you, Dad,' I lied. 'I was miles away, honestly I was.'

'In Nightmareland, by your expression. Have you returned yet?'

'I think so, Dad.'

'Then stop bloody staring, boy. Look at me with respect or don't look at me at all.'

'Yes, Dad.'

'It's on the wrong side of the river, Amy, but the neighbours seem to be a cut above the ones we've had to put up with round here. No gypsies, I'm glad to report, and no Poles or Irish as far as I can tell.'

'Which is the wrong side of the river?'

'This is. And we shall be moving even further southwards, I'm afraid. The son and heir will have to leave his new home a bit earlier in the morning than he's been accustomed to, but that won't do him any injury. Will it, young man?'

(I was 'young man' now, and would remain such, with only 'Piss-a-Bed' as a later variation. Twenty-seven years were to pass before he called me Gabriel again; twenty-nine before I was again his 'lad'.)

'Where is it we're going?'

'You'll know soon enough. It will surprise the pair of you, I can guarantee. Your first sight of it will knock you sideways. I can't pretend it's the grandest pile that money can buy, but it should answer to our needs well enough.'

'And what are they?'

'Space, Amy. That's one of them. We shan't feel cramped any more. We'll be living in rooms, not rabbit hutches. We'll have electric lights instead of these cursèd hissing lamps. We'll have hot water coming straight out of the tap. We'll have a toilet where it ought to be, inside the house and not over yonder. You'll have a kitchen, Amy, that Escoffier himself would be proud of. And you, young man, will have a proper study in which to do your homework.'

'So those are our needs. They come as news to me.'

'Behave like a grown woman, Amy. What do you expect me to do with Sir Vincent's money? Burn it? Hand it out in the streets to every beggar or tramp? Save it up for a splash funeral? Give it to the church? Wipe my arsehole with it? Mr Shylock Middleton, the owner of this bloody pigsty, doesn't freeze half to death when he takes a shit in the winter, so why the hell should we?'

'Mr Middleton isn't Jewish. If he were, he wouldn't own a pigsty. Jews don't eat pork. It's against their religion.'

My father slapped my mother's face with the brown-spotted back of his hand.

'Oh Ossie, my poor old Ossie, I didn't mean to hurt you,' she said.

London's smartest firm of furniture removers sent a huge van – almost as tall as our nameless house – to bear the Harveys' possessions farther southwards. The removal men pretended to be breathless and exhausted, their backs aching and their knees bent beneath the crushing weight of a vase, a marble clock, some saucepans, a frying pan, a casserole dish, a solitary chair, a small side-table, a suitcase filled with clothes, another filled with antimacassars and tablecloths, my toys, comics and school books, my father's Cyclopaedia and my mother's Bible.

'The beds, the other tables and chairs can stay where they are. Let Shylock do with them as he pleases. I'd have left everything here, but my wife put her foot down and insisted that we take these bits and pieces with us. You know how it is when a woman makes up her mind.'

The men, barely concealing their amusement, said they knew.

'You chaps aren't often to be seen in a run-down area like this, I'll wager. Westminster's more your territory, I presume, or Kensington. Look at all those curtains twitching. The women behind them will be talking about you for months on end.'

Early that morning, while Oswald Harvey slept, my mother had pushed notes of farewell through almost every letter-box in the street. The longest, most heartfelt of these, composed the previous evening while the man of means was entertaining his for-ever-to-be impoverished cronies at the Prodigal's Return, was reserved for the hempen widow, Alice Boundy, whom many people, my father included, ostentatiously shunned. Alice's husband, Norman, a painter and decorator who coughed more often than he spoke, had been hanged at Pentonville during the terrible winter of 1947. The timid Norman, a martyr to his lungs, had stabbed a journalist to death in a crowded Bouverie Street. Passers-by were alarmed at his behaviour after the murder. 'I mustn't wipe Exhibit A,' he'd said, placing his blood-stained carving knife cautiously on the pavement. 'I shall watch over it until the police come.'

He had not had a brainstorm; there had been no motive – no, no, no, he'd insisted, again and again, throughout his trial, to the judge's growing impatience. 'Definitely no brainstorm, certainly no motive' – this remark, re-punctuated each time with a cough or a loud intake of breath (and, occasionally, an extra 'no' or two), was all Norman Boundy cared to say for himself in court.

'One of them's a murderer's wife. That's the type of district this is.'

'We've worked for plenty of criminals, Mr Harvey,' the driver of the van proudly informed my father. 'Haven't we, Jim? Haven't we, Sean?' The men nodded. 'Remember the Park Lane poisoner? We moved his Chippendale twice. And the lord who cut up his lady wife and put her in a trunk, which he had the nerve to leave in the left luggage at Euston and never came back to collect? Her Ladyship stank the office out so bad, the attendants on duty thought the trunk was filled with rotting game birds, until they opened it and found Mona in slices instead. Well, that crazy bastard owned the loveliest, delicatest china we have ever had the privilege of handling with kid gloves. He told us he would weep if we so much as chipped a single piece. We believed him, too, because his eyes were already misting over at the awful prospect.'

'You deserve a pedigree Persian,' said my father. 'Or a Siamese.'

'I'm happy with the funny cat we've got.' My mother tightened her hold on a surprised Mrs McTrap, as the animal struggled to escape. 'Lie still, puss. We'll soon be there, I hope.'

We were in a taxi, *en route* to our new home.

'Goodbye and good riddance to the mean streets, Amy. You won't have to look at them again, except when you're driving along like this.'

'Yes, Ossie.'

'Any moment now, I shall be ordering the pair of you to close your eyes. Mecca, so to speak, looms on the horizon. At last, at last – the moment's come! Do as I bid you. Tightly, tightly – no peeping, that's an order.'

We could hear the taxi's wheels crunching on gravel. 'It sounds as if we have a drive in front of our – ' House? Home? My mother choked on whichever word. 'That's what the sound tells me.'

'It tells you correctly, Amy. We do indeed have a driveway in front of our – shall I say mansion? Yes, let's settle for mansion.'

The taxi came to an abrupt halt.

'Look, Amy, look.'

'Can I look too, Dad?'

'Don't be stupid all your days, young man. Of course you can.'
I looked.

'There's ivy on the walls,' my mother remarked, distantly.

'Only above the porch, Amy. Perhaps I should say "portico",
like the estate agent did. Only above the portico.'

'It's a palace,' I said.

'Not quite, Gabriel.' My mother turned to me and smiled.

'We'd all see better if we weren't craning our necks. I'm
getting out, if you aren't.'

He trod, resoundingly, on his own gravel.

'Come on, you slowcoaches.'

My mother passed the cat to me. 'Take her firmly by the
scruff of her neck and don't let go of her, Gabriel.'

'Forget that beast for a moment, Amy, will you.'

'I'm frightened that she'll run off and – '

'Look, Amy, please look at the mansion I've bought us, for
Christ's sake.'

She crunched her way to his side. Clutching Mrs McTrap, I
joined them. We stood and stared in silence.

It was then that I noticed that our new house, our mansion,
rather, had a name. There it was, over the door, in stained-glass
lettering: a brown B, a green L, a red E, a yellow N, a dark blue
H, a light blue E, an orange I and a purple M – the whole
inscribed on a silver sword.

'It spells "Blenheim", Mummy. Why is it called "Blenheim"?'

'Ours not to reason, young man. Can't you picture it on our
notepaper?'

'Notepaper, Ossie? What in the world would we be doing
with notepaper? We seldom write to anyone, you know that,
my silly old darling.'

'Seldom's not enough, Amy. You're forgetting my new connections. Bankers, solicitors – people who move in a different
world. They have to be contacted from time to time. They have
to be notified of changes, developments. You are hereby engaged
to correct my spelling.'

'Our son can do that for you, Ossie.'

'I shan't let him. It will be your job, and no one else's. A nice,
easy task for a lady of leisure.'

'A lady of leisure? What utter nonsense. To go with the "man
of means", I assume? Oh, Ossie, what perfect drivel.'

The taxi-driver appeared to be more impressed by the interior of 'Blenheim' than my mother was. 'It's grand,' he exclaimed, as my father opened door upon door to reveal room after high-ceilinged room. 'I envy you, squire.'

My father had taken the best possible advice in the difficult matter of the furnishings. 'I wanted to surprise my wife here.'

'You've succeeded, Ossie.' She sounded unsurprised; weary, even.

'An old maid of a man, he was, my adviser. Pernickety, pernickety. What was it he said to me? Ah, yes. "You can't possibly have magenta satin cushions on a green sofa covered in uncut moquette, Mr Harvey. They simply do not *mingle*." Those chaps speak a language all their own. Anyhow, he's come up trumps, I think. I only asked him to provide the essentials, of course. My wife here will choose the rest. I'll leave the what you might call "homely touches" in her safe hands.'

My mother and I were buttering Mrs McTrap's paws when the removal men arrived with our odds and ends from Number Thirty-Two. My father instructed them to dump the pitiful things in the hallway and to join him in the kitchen for a house-warming drink.

'I have some excellent whisky, if that would be agreeable.'

The men, looking about them in something like amazement, said yes, Mr Harvey, it would be, very.

From my bedroom window, I looked down on a magnolia tree, its leaves already turning brown. Beyond the front garden was the main road, its newly tarred surface a sticky trap for walkers that warm September, and beyond the road an immense expanse of common.

The previous morning I had surveyed – for the last, happy time – a shorter, but livelier, prospect. I had followed the slow and grimly steady progress of our immediate neighbour, Gertie Wilkins, as she bore before her a po filled to within a half-inch of its brim with the piddle of Gertie, her husband Ronald and their cross-eyed daughter Emily. 'It's a miracle that her pot never runneth over,' my father had once observed in the days when he addressed me as "Gabriel lad". 'Her grip on that jordan is wonderful to behold. She doesn't spill a single, solitary drop.'

The Wilkins's urine on September 19, 1949, was amber in colour, thanks to stray shreds of tobacco from the cigarette ends that were bobbing in it. Gertie was especially stately as she trod the precarious path from scullery to privy. She was dressed in her washed-out nightgown, as usual, but for her final performance on my behalf she had shod her customarily plimsolled feet in scarlet slippers, on the tops of which pompons bounced. ' "I'm in the mood for love," ' Gertie crooned, her mission achieved. ' "Simply because you're near me." ' Empty po in hand, she waltzed her way homewards, and then disappeared, clattering the scullery door behind her.

The magnolia flowered the following April in a glory of pinkness and whiteness.

I looked down on blossom and wondered where my mother was.

4

The first of Oswald Harvey's 'Blenheim' lectures that I recall took as its theme The Suede Shoe.

'Only upstarts wear suede,' he warned me. 'A true aristocrat sticks to leather. In the days when I was on speaking terms with any number of genuine gentlemen, I never saw a one of them in suede shoes. Not a one. It was always patent leather for the opera or an evening on the town, and it was always your good stout brogues for the country. The thing is, you can't depend on suede the way you can on leather. Are you listening to me, young man?'

'Yes, Father.'

(Those terms of affection 'Dad' and 'Daddy' no longer seemed appropriate. I had stopped using them. For ever, as it transpired.)

'I'll explain why, if you really want to know. It rains a great deal in this country, in case you hadn't noticed. A soggy suede shoe is an absolutely disgusting sight, and it makes a pretty disgusting noise into the bargain. Squelch, squelch, and again squelch. The cursèd stuff has no resistance, you see. But leather, now – it would take a downpour of monsoon proportions to deprive a pair of fine leather shoes of their sturdiness.'

'Yes, Father.'

'I'm old enough to remember when the suede shoe came into fashion. Matinée idols, chaps who aren't proper chaps – those were the types who favoured them at the start. These days, it's spivs and bookmakers and film stars whose feet you find them on. People you can't trust. Sister Swedie's ice-cream husband, I seem to recollect, had a pair of them at one time, as a change from the two-toned gigolo's monstrosities he usually sported. You would be wise to steer clear of suede, that's my firm opinion, young man. I have given the matter some thought, and that most definitely is my view.'

Most definitely it was: I could tell by the way he glared at me. The lecture was over; the son and heir dismissed.

Four years and four months after the Allied Victory in Europe, we Lilliburnians were still celebrating the genital inadequacies of the German leadership. We sang, to the tune 'Colonel Bogey', in our doodlebugged playground:

> Hitler
> Has only got one ball,
> Goering
> Has two, but rather small.
> Himmler
> Has something sim'lar.
> But poor old Goebbels
> Has no balls
> At all

In class, in those last months of 1949, I was a diligent pupil. I wrote about Balaam's ass ('God granted the humblest and most stupid of His creatures a power He denied the mighty diviner. It was the animal who saw the avenging angel, not the clever man who rode on her') and won the approval – 'It's tip-top Harvey' – of our teacher of Religious Instruction, Mr Murdock, who told me that he would suggest to my parents that I should be encouraged to enter the Church.

With Mr Rushworth's erratic assistance, I learned to read music. I memorized more of his doggerel, too: the fateful 'Knock, knock, who's there? Knock, knock, who's there?', which even today caused me bemused irritation when I turned on the radio and heard the opening bars of Beethoven's Fifth Symphony. I caught myself mouthing his silly words; stopped myself singing them.

And as for History – well, I had the uncanny knack, according to Mr Nichol, the most uncanny knack of imagining the long dead as men and women who had lived. I had not assumed, as the boys he had hectored for aeons had assumed, that death had been their permanent condition. I had brought Wat Tyler to appropriately revolting life, despite some slap-happy syntax.

Which latter was the concern of Mr Penfold, the scourge of redundant adverbs, unattached participles, split infinitives, and any sentence – such as this one – that contained more than twenty words. 'Beware hyperbole, Harvey. Leave singing to the poets.' I did as he demanded, and was rewarded with ninety-nine marks. 'A misplaced comma cost you your hundredth.'

Oswald Harvey was impressed by his son's performance. 'You've done well, young man. What a pity I didn't come into Sir Vincent's money twelve years earlier, though. If that'd been the case, you would be home now for the Christmas holidays from one of the better public schools. Eton, for preference.'

'Why not Harrow? Why not Rugby? I seem to recall your being proud once that our Gabriel had won a scholarship to Lily's.'

'Of course I was, Amy.'

'And *I* still am, Oswald. Of course I am.'

'I'll pay his fees from next term on. His days as a charity boy are over.'

The second 'Blenheim' lecture, delivered on Christmas Eve, was on the subject Men of the Cloth.

'This teacher, this Murdock, has written to me, young man. It is his considered opinion, he says, that you, Gabriel Harvey, should be encouraged to pursue a vocation in the Church of England. It is my considered opinion that you, Gabriel Harvey, should do no such daft thing. You haven't given this Murdock the impression that you want to be a Man of the Cloth, have you?'

'No, Father,' I replied, truthfully.

'That's as well. It's not a profession, if that's what it is, I'd recommend. Dog-collared for life, surrounded by the worst types of prattling women – I don't know why it is that clergymen attract them, but they do. They all seem to have too many teeth, and they all put on bloody silly hats whenever there's a vicarage fête. And they have to organize a lot of fêtes, clergymen have to, and jumble sales and bazaars and such, for one very good reason, which I would advise you to keep in mind. Have you any idea what that reason is?'

'No, Father.'

'Money. Lack of same. That's what this Murdock would have in store for you. It's only bishops and archbishops in the C of E who have two ha'pennies to rub together, not the cheery so-and-soes who look after the thousands of tinpot churches all over the country. Now, if you were a Roman Catholic, which God forbid, it would be a different matter. I'm not saying you would get to be His Holiness the Pope, because that's a job they only seem to dish out to members of the ice-cream race; nor yet a cardinal; just think, though, of the perks a priest enjoys – no wife and family to support, but that doesn't stop him doing what a proper chap has to. He grovels on his knees for a few minutes, confessing his sins, and then he stands up, shakes down his cassock, and lo! he's ready to start all over again. Sinning, I'm referring to. There are bastard boys and girls the length and breadth of the Emerald Isle who'll remain for ever ignorant of the fact that they were sired by the likes of Father Flynn and Father O'Flanagan. You believe me, young man. I've made a study of the cunning devils. They are not to be trusted.'

I was tempted to ask if they wore suede shoes, but his glare prevented me.

'No, I can't say I approve of Men of the Cloth. Your mother has more time for them than I have. She's a decent woman, and takes them at their own face value. She can't see behind those smiles, the way I can. She laps up their honeyed words, whereas I won't and never could. It's the same with Sister Swedie, only more so, in her case. She'll listen to any amount of tommy-rot about paradise and eternity from some smiling ghoul. I shall write this Murdock a polite note saying that Oswald Harvey has other plans for his young son.'

Whatever those plans were, they could not have included the writing of *Lords of Light* – the book I began at the Jerusalem; the book that has made me far, far richer than my father was.

My mother cooked us a goose that Christmas, with a variety of trimmings, in the kitchen she said Escoffier was welcome to.

'Chicken was luxury enough for us last year. The grease that came out – that's *still* coming out – of this thing!'

'I had it rubbed on my chest as a child, Amy, to ward off colds and chills, and I'm standing here to tell the story.'

'That's as may be.'

'You'll change your sulky tune when you've tasted it. Is it ready for me to carve?'

'I suppose so. I can't claim to be an expert. The skin looks crisp.'

'The King will be on the wireless in half an hour, Amy. We don't want to be munching merrily away while His Majesty is talking.'

'Take it through to the dining-room, Ossie. Gabriel and I will manage the rest somehow.'

My mother had made a gravy with the bird's giblets, and a

little pudding with its neck. There was a potato stuffing at one end of the goose, and a sausagemeat stuffing at the other. And there was bread sauce.

'What a feast, Amy. We'll have to be measured for new clothes after dinner.'

'I'm not very hungry today, Ossie, for some reason. Just cut me a piece off the breast.'

'It's Christmas, Amy love.'

'Yes, Ossie. Yes, yes. Two slices, then, if it will make you happier. But, please, no more.'

'So be it. Your wish, et cetera. The young man here can have a leg.'

'Would you like a leg, Gabriel?'

'Yes, Mummy. Thank you.'

'Don't sit and stare. Help your mother to vegetables.'

'I'll help myself, Ossie, Gabriel. I'll pick and choose.'

She picked and chose a tablespoonful of cabbage, and a dollop of mashed swedes.

'I know the real name for these,' I ventured.

'I should jolly well hope so, young man. You've been eating them since you were knee-high to a grasshopper.'

'It isn't what you think it is.'

'Isn't it, Gabriel?'

'No, Mummy. Swedish people call them *rotbagga*.'

'Where did you learn that, dear? In one of your books?'

'Auntie Kathleen told me. Last Easter.'

'Did she? I might have known. Well, you're not Swedish and your mother isn't Swedish and, come to think of it, I'm not Swedish either. We have our own words in our own country, and they've proved of use, over the years, a good bloody many of them, just you remember, you just remember, young man.'

'I only said – '

'Yes, Ossie love, he only said.'

'Let's eat, shall we? Let's forget swedes, and Swedie, too. Let's enjoy our first Christmas in our new home.'

We toasted George the Sixth, his family, and what was left of his Commonwealth. We toasted 'Blenheim' and all who lived in it – in whisky, in port wine, in fizzy lemonade.

We saw the Old Year out. My father, drunk, impersonated Sir Harry Lauder (' "A verrry model of sobrrriety" ') singing 'Roamin' in the Gloamin' '.

'Oh, Ossie, old love, you really should have gone on the stage. I love you best when you're being mad like this.'

' "Ladies and gentlemen, I prrromise you healthy, innocent enterrrtainment",' said my frenetic father. ' "Nae smut, ye ken. Nae dirrrty jokes aboot sporrrans and what ye might discoverrr if ye peep underrr ma kilt." '

'Oh, Ossie, don't. You'll have me helpless. You sound more Scottish than he does, you dear old fool.'

He sang, in its entirety, 'Stop Your Tickling, Jock', and finished his performance with a dance, which he called his last highland fling. My mother and I applauded him.

'Where and when did you learn that, Ossie?'

'In my lost youth, Amy. When I was a youngster, and fancied my chances on the halls. I was full of such pipe-dreams once.'

'You would have been wonderful. Wouldn't he have been wonderful, Gabriel?'

'Yes, Mummy.'

'No time for would-have-been.'

We heard Big Ben's chimes striking midnight on our 'Blenheim' ('No more cursed knob-twiddling!') wireless. My father embraced my mother.

We wished ourselves a happy and prosperous New Year.

My father slapped me on the back. My mother kissed me, and ruffled up my stubborn hair. 'Bed for you, my tired baby.'

It was 1950.

She was slumped across the staircase when I let myself into the house.

'Mummy?'

She made no response.

I saw then, that she was wearing an amazing dress – no, not a dress, a gown; the kind of gown film stars wore in pictures, as they descended grander, wider, longer staircases than ours.

'Mummy?' I asked again, expecting a stranger to answer.

'Gabriel?' She spoke into the carpet. 'Is that you, darling?'

'Yes, Mummy. Are you all right?'

She turned slowly towards me.

'Yes, of course I am. Why should I be anything else?'

'You've been crying.'

'Everyone cries sometimes. It's the most natural thing in the world. Be a dear and help me to my feet.'

The dress, the gown, amazed me as more of it was now revealed.

'What do you think of my strapless wedding-cake?'

I thought it was beautiful, fit for a princess, I said.

It was all of silver – tier upon tier of silver silk and silver lace. Silver flowers and silver leaves covered her breasts, and at her waist there was a large, floppy silver bow. A dark red rose, made of velvet, flared from this silver shimmer.

'And what's your opinion of my coiffure, Gabriel?'

'You've had it cut off.'

'Yes, I have. See how it sweeps up at the back. This is the latest fashion, dear. The man who styles it for me said it's the rage.'

'Do you like it, Mummy?'

'I'll get used to it. I'll try to get used to it.'

'Are you going out tonight?'

'I'm not dolled up like this, as your daddy would say, just to cook your supper, Gabriel. I've left some cold cuts for you, and there's a small rice pudding in the oven. Yes, darling, we *are* going out – to a dinner-dance in a posh hotel on the right side of the river. So now I must powder the shine off my nose and will my feet into a dancing mood.'

Her evening slippers were silver, too.

'Take my word for it, young man. A cat wouldn't stand a snowball's chance in hell against a fox on the prowl, especially a vixen with cubs to feed.'

'I haven't seen any foxes on the common.'

'I'd be most surprised if you said you had. The fox is the craftiest animal in creation, as they should have taught you in that school of yours. He doesn't go gadding about in broad daylight because he's got too many enemies. He stalks his prey at dead of night, when you, young man are – or ought to be – in bed.'

'I don't believe she's been killed.'

'I know differently. Sir Vincent, being a gentleman, rode to hounds, and I heard it from his very own lips what mayhem the fox causes. You must get it into that skull of yours that the old moggy has met her match at long, long last and has ended up in the stomach of some beast or other over yonder.'

I could not, and would not, get it into my skull that any such terrible thing had happened to Mrs McTrap. I had spent most of the previous Saturday and Sunday searching for her over yonder – I had peered under every bush; called her name under every leafless tree. I hadn't found even the slightest trace of her. Had she been attacked, I reasoned, there would be a part of her somewhere. She would have defended herself to the – yes, to the death. Her fur would have gone flying. Her killer would have spat out her fur.

Day after day I walked to school and back, scouring the gutters for her corpse – perhaps she had been run over by a car, a trolleybus or a tram; that seemed the likeliest, nastiest explanation. There was, to my relief, no sign of her. She may have succeeded in her bold ambition to return to her first and happiest home, her hunting ground, her territory – for I knew she hated 'Blenheim' and its surroundings. Her growls said as much.

'Gabriel, darling, you're letting your fancy run away with you. We buttered her paws as soon as we got here. She licked them clean – you must remember. If she'd been unhappy, she'd have escaped weeks ago.'

I was not convinced by my mother's argument, and I couldn't see any sense in that butter stuff – it had to be a myth; had to be an old wives' tale.

'That's where you're wrong. It's a trick that's been practised for centuries. I hope as much as you do, Gabriel, that she's still alive.'

I visited her favourite haunts: the gas works; the disused railway bridge, beneath which my parents had waved to the soldiers returning from Dunkirk; St Mary's churchyard, where she had slaughtered so often, so contentedly; the dairy and the fish shop in the High Street – no one had seen her.

I knocked on the doors of houses where her sons and daughters lived. I knew as I did so that I was knocking in vain.

I introduced myself to the new occupant of Number Thirty-Two: a fat Welshman in a string vest.

'Pleased to meet you, like. The wife and me are having our tea right this minute, like.'

I told him about Mrs McTrap's disappearance, and described her in what I felt confident was vivid detail.

'Funny bugger of a mixture, like. Shouldn't have no trouble recognizing her, should I, like. I'll lure her indoors with a sardine, boyo, if I see her going by here. You wouldn't want me eating cold toast, would you? I'll say goodbye, like, and send you a message, like, somehow or other, when she turns up, like.'

'I'll be on the look-out for her, don't you worry, Gabriel,' said Mr Dimmock at the Prodigal's Return. 'This place isn't the same without your father. No politician loves the sound of his own voice better than Oswald does. The whale that drew breath to swallow Jonah didn't spout – couldn't have spouted – half as much. Will you tell him we all miss him?'

I promised I would. It was a promise I chose not to keep.

'The regulars noticed a change in him, Gabriel, when he switched overnight from beer to whisky. I'm not the man for words that he is, but I'd say he's become less of a wag and more of a philosopher. The gleam's gone from those wicked blue eyes of his, as we all noticed that last evening he was with us. He was tub-thumping as per usual, but the gleam wasn't there. We got the impression that he actually meant what he was spouting, after years and years of leading us on and playing the clown.'

It is the morning of Wednesday, February 1, 1950.

My mother, in her oriental dressing-gown, is standing at the foot of my bed.

'Are you awake, little lazybones?'

'Yes, Mummy.'

'Breakfast's prepared. Up with you, Gabriel. Rise and shine. Everything's ready. Your shoes are polished, your trousers pressed, and your starch-angel's shirt's laid out. I want you downstairs in ten minutes on the dot!'

On this ordinary morning, I go to the toilet, where I do my ones and try to do my twos. In the bathroom, I wash my hands and face and wipe the sleep from my eyes with a cloth on which there is the initial G. I run a comb through my stubborn hair, stick my tongue out at my reflection in the mirror, and then dash back to get dressed.

Like a thousand ordinary boys on a thousand ordinary winter mornings, I shiver as I take off my warm pyjamas.

'Time's nearly up, Gabriel!' my mother calls from the staircase.

On with my undervest, on with my underpants, on with my shirt, and on with my trousers; on with my socks, and, finally, my shoes – the hurried ritual of every ordinary morning.

I do up my shirt and trouser buttons as I make my frantic way down to the kitchen. I dart across the tiled hallway, my shoelaces still untied.

'You only just made it!'

Steam is rising from the bowl of porridge my mother sets before me. She sprinkles salt on top of it and tells me, as she always tells me, to wait for it to cool.

'You weren't born with an asbestos throat.'

While I am waiting, I talk about the ordeals ahead of me. Wednesday means Chemistry, Physical Training, Science and Mathematics. Wednesday is when I am hopelessly stupid.

'Try your best, Gabriel. No one expects you to be clever at everything.'

The boy who doesn't clean his bowl doesn't get to eat his bread and marmalade. I therefore clean my bowl of its body-building porridge and am given the food I really want as a reward. I finish my unsurprising breakfast with a cup of strong tea.

And now I have to stand up and be inspected. 'Sloven's the word for you, my darling. Will you ever improve? The backs of your ears are a positive disgrace.'

'Sorry, Mummy.'

'Your nails need scrubbing, too.'

Ears washed, nails scrubbed, properly uniformed, I submit to my second inspection – a regular event on these ordinary mornings.

'Yes, you'll pass muster, Gabriel.'

She kisses me in her usual way. She doesn't hug me to her. She doesn't fight back tears as she hands me the beautiful leather briefcase that marks me as a scholar from 'Blenheim'. (My scruffy satchel has been cast aside with Sir William's charity.) She simply pecks my cheek and smiles her usual smile and says her usual 'Work hard, Gabriel', because this is a morning like any other.

There is nothing untoward about this first cold morning of February 1950.

At the end of the drive, I open the gate. I close it behind me and wave to my mother. She waves back, as she always does.

I do not see her go into the house. I am already running to catch the bus, as on every other ordinary morning.

'Your mother cooked us a fish pie before she left.'

'Left?'

'That's what I said, young man.'

'Has she gone out for the evening, then? She didn't say she was going out this morning.'

'No reason why she should. You're only a little boy. There's no earthly reason why she should let you know her plans.'

'I suppose not.'

'You suppose correctly.'

'Is it all right to ask you where she's gone?'

'Yes, it is. I shall answer you in my own good time, though. I wish not to be pestered.'

I was in no doubt that his wish had to be respected.

'You can pour me a whisky and soda. That would be a useful thing to do.'

'Yes, Father.'

'Just a splash. No more.'

'Okay.'

'I hope they're not teaching you to speak those Yanks' words at the that school of yours. "Okay" is for gum-chewers and loud-mouths.'

'Yes, Father.'

'Bloody Americans. They come into two world wars at the eleventh hour, and they demand to be treated like heroes. The nerve they have. The impudence. "Scram, Sam" – that's my message to them.'

I gave him his drink.

'The pie we'll be eating, the two of us, is made up, your mother told me, of haddock, shrimps, parsley and mashed potatoes. We're in for a feast, by the sound of it.'

'Yes.'

'This would seem to be the right mixture. No complaints, young man. Why don't you help yourself to some squash?'

'Lemon, please.'

'As you will. My mouth's watering, as I'm sure yours is, at the thought of that pie. Haddock and shrimps sounds a delicious combination.'

'Yes, it does.'

'With some grated cheese added at the last minute.'

'Can I do that, Father?'

'No, no. She's left – she's given me precise instructions. I'm in charge of the cheese tonight.'

'I managed to jump over the horse today.'

'What?'

'The wooden horse, Father, in the gymnasium. I managed to jump over it.'

'Did you?'

68

'Yes, I did.'

(Betrayal: this good news was for my mother, for Mummy, not for him. She should have been the first to hear it.)

'So you're an athlete now, are you?'

'Not really.'

'What do you mean – not really?'

(What I meant was: I had a pitifully skinny body, with a chest that seemed to retreat into itself; what I meant was: I was the laughing-stock of the entire school, because my bony legs gave way beneath me, the very moment they were exposed to view; what I meant was: I couldn't imagine anyone weaker, feebler than pathetic little Gabriel Harvey – that's what I meant.)

'I mean, I live more in my mind, I think.'

'That's been your way from the start. You're a bit like me, in that one respect.'

He spoke without warmth. I was a bit like him, but only remotely.

'I'd feel more at ease if you sat yourself down. I never could abide children hovering.'

(Had Thomas Harvey – my half-brother, Tom – been a child who hovered?)

'Yes, Father.'

'That's better. I have something to say to you. I want you to listen to me carefully. I do not intend to repeat it for your benefit. Is that understood?'

'Yes, Father.'

'Well, it's like this. Amy – your mother – has decided – on a whim – in typical woman's fashion – to treat herself – to a holiday – yes, to a holiday. She's been working too hard for too long, and she needs a rest.'

'But she doesn't work at her secret place any more.'

'True, true. Just think, though, what it knocks out of her, running a house this size. And there was all the effort of making Mr Shylock Middleton's two-up, two-down into something bright and clean and cheerful. That must have taken its toll. It's a break – a break from routine – she's seeking.'

'Where?'

'Where?'

'Where is she seeking it?'

'Well, to start with, on the south coast. In Brighton. To start with. She may decide to come home in a day or so, but then again, she may not. She may decide, young man, to attempt a trip abroad.'

'Abroad?'

'She's often said that, if we ever came into money, she would like to see the world. Now's her chance.'

'Chance?'

'Of course, she could hesitate. She could change her mind at the last minute. It's a big step in a person's life, and she could develop cold feet. That's what you're hoping, isn't it?'

'Am I, Father?'

'I am. I don't want her away. I want her right here, by my side.'

'You could still have her by your side if you went with her.'

'And who, may I ask, would look after you, young man? No, I've already told her if it's foreign countries she's anxious to explore, then she'll have to go exploring on her tod. I'm too old for such adventures. Give me the creature comforts of my own fireside. I've no inclination to travel.'

'Won't you be afraid, Father? If she does decide on a holiday abroad?'

'I can't say I catch your drift.'

'Afraid *for* her. She is a woman, after all. She might come to harm on her own – in France, or Italy, or Spain, or somewhere.'

'It's obvious to me that you haven't got the measure of your mother. She is far tougher than she seems to be, young man.'

My mummy tougher than she seemed to be? I was perplexed by his remark.

'You don't imagine I married a sugar-and-spice type, do you? A wallflower? Because if you do, I didn't. Amy Harvey, let me correct you, has pluck and spirit. You're mistaken if you imagine otherwise. Afraid for her? Me? I should say not.'

There were to be no more questions, he insisted. He would keep me informed of her movements, whatever they were. A holiday was a holiday, and did not last a lifetime. Absence only makes the heart grow that bit fonder.

It wasn't until we had eaten her delicious fish pie that we both remembered the grated cheese we should have added to it.

I made myself breakfast in the chilly kitchen. I boiled myself a three-minute egg and cut myself a generous chunk of bread, over which I smeared more marmalade than I was usually allowed. I brewed strong tea.

At school that Thursday, no one bothered to notice that I was no longer a starch-angel, that I was wearing Wednesday's shirt.

5

'Your mother has made her decision, young man. She phoned me early this afternoon to say that she will be going abroad tomorrow at the crack of dawn. Ours not to reason, et cetera.'

'Did she send me a message, Father?'

'A message? She sent you her love, that was all.'

Her *love*, that was *all* – so spoke the Great Dissembler. That was all my mother had sent me – her love.

'She's bound for Paris. Gay Paree, she said.'

'How is she getting there?'

'Questions, questions. Oh, by boat and train, from Dover to Calais.'

'Why don't we see her off? Kiss her and wave her goodbye? It wouldn't matter if I missed the morning classes. The Head would understand if I told him the truth.'

'You weren't listening properly, were you? She is leaving at the crack of dawn, six o'clock, *ante meridiem*.'

'We could set the alarm for five, couldn't we? Or half-past four? I'd rather see her off than go on sleeping. Couldn't we?'

'We could not. Don't you think I asked her if she wanted us to be there at Victoria? I most certainly did. And what was her reply? It's the one that Garbo woman keeps making – "I want to be alone." In the circumstances, we should respect her wish.'

'It would be a nice surprise for her.'

'She seems to think it wouldn't be. Let's turn our attention to other matters, shall we? Our bellies, for a start. A man needs sustenance, and that includes you. I'll fry us some liver, bacon and onions.'

He drank whisky as he cooked.

'Sir Vincent was partial to l, b and o. Gentlemen, I've found, often have simple tastes. What's your verdict, young man?'

'I didn't like it.'

'You didn't like it?'

'No. I'm a better cook than you are. You let things burn. I made Mummy an omelette one day, when you weren't here, and she said it was perfect.'

'You're her son, that's why she praised you. She was giving you encouragement, my Amy was. You'll eat what's put before you – like or not like – you just remember, young man.'

'A telegram came while you were out. "Arrived safely Paris Stop Love to my boys Stop Amy" – that was the gist of it.'

'Show me.'

'Not possible. I threw it on the fire.'

'You wouldn't have done that.'

'Why ever not? You heard what she had to say. "Arrived safely Paris Love to my boys Amy" – it didn't take a minute to memorize, with or without the two stops. No point in keeping it.'

'No, Father.'

'Oh, for Christ's sake buck up. I've given you good news, young man, not bad, not bad news in any way. She's safe in France and you ought to be pleased to hear it, not down in your usual bloody doldrums.'

'I'm sorry.'

'As you should be. I won't have this gloom around the house. I warn you, I just won't have it. It isn't natural in someone your age. We'll be eating corned beef with cold potatoes for supper, so I don't expect any complaints about my cooking, either. You can curse the Argentinians if the meat isn't to your liking.'

The arrival, that Monday, of Ellen Gould precipitated another 'Blenheim' lecture: Men Who Cook.

'Mrs Gould will only be with us until your mother chooses to return. That's the arrangement I've made with her.'

'I said I would cook. You know I did. I've told you I can.'

'Yes, yes, yes, and I'm very grateful.'

'You can't be if you're paying her to do it.'

'Amongst other duties. She will be keeping the house spick and span as well. She showed me excellent references. Stop scowling – in a week's time, a mere week, she could be gone.'

'I hope so.'

'I echo your hope, believe me. The sun has been over the

yard-arm for nigh on ten minutes, which means you can make yourself useful and mix me a whisky and soda.'

'Yes, Father.'

'Jump to it, then.'

I knew, once I had handed him his drink, that thoughts had come to him. He was wearing his lecturer's glare.

'I've been thinking', he began, 'about your so-called talent for cookery, young man. I have yet to see any evidence for it, but I dare say your mother's praise may have been warranted.'

'She said my – '

'Your omelette was perfect, yes. I'm sure Escoffier himself started with simple things like omelettes and scrambled eggs before he went on to create his famous dishes. Old Auguste, I seem to recall, lived to a great age – ninety-odd, if I'm not mistaken. But he was a rare example of his kind. I'm here to tell you.'

'Was he, Father?'

'He most definitely was. Men who cook don't last the course, as a general rule. What's that I said? "Men who cook don't last the course" – completely unintentional play on words, I assure you. Because they don't. They're nervy by nature and quick-tempered; even prone to violence, some of them. Sir Vincent's chef that was is a good case in point. He had a staff of three beneath him, doing all the donkey-work. They slaved for Albert, those three, they really did, what with preparing his vegetables and clearing up the colossal bloody mess he always left in his wake – they deserved medals for bravery in the front-line, that's my view. Albert was polite enough to them outside his kitchen, but inside it, no, he screamed, he stamped his feet, he raved and ranted, he called them names, and – worst of all – he threw things at them. Plates, cups and saucers, his rolling-pin, anything that was to hand. Forks he threw, and knives – yes, young man, knives. He was a menace then. Those three – Henry, Phyllis and Maud – were experts at ducking, though one knife he sent whizzing through the air grazed Phyllis's arm and she had to have it bandaged. The walls of that kitchen had marks and holes and cracks and scars from the pots, pans and assorted what-have-yous that Albert had slung at them. If you're listening, which I trust you are, I shall let you know precisely why men who cook tend not to last the course.'

'I am listening.'

'The demon drink is the reason. The better the chef, the bigger

74

the tippler. They're artists, you see, and the strain of producing beautiful meals day after day, night after night, sends them bottlewards before they know it. My word, could that Albert guzzle! I'm a pillar of the Temperance League by comparison. When Sir Vincent was entertaining the high and mighty to dinner, that's when Albert hit the hard stuff with a purpose. His and Her Grace, or Whoever, would coo with delight over the wonderful concoctions on the table, while Albert would be breathing out firewater behind the green baize door. Had you lit a match near him, I'd swear he'd have been – how do you say? – combusted. He had no appetite for food, no appetite at all. Old Auguste Escoffier must have been the odd man out, because from everything I've heard most men who cook are the Albert type – chaps who can't eat from sheer worry. The effort they put into satisfying the taste buds of others causes them to lose their own. It's a sad and terrible business.'

'Yes, Father.'

'Yes, it is. Women, now, women who cook, they're totally different. Cooking's a task to them, a chore, something that's got to be done. Your mother does it well, as you know, but even Amy Harvey is no match for an Albert. And thank God, too. A sober Amy is an Amy who'll last the course, young man. She won't go to pieces if her bloody soufflé fails to rise. She wouldn't attempt a soufflé, anyhow – which is where she's sensible.'

'What's a soufflé?'

'Find out for yourself, as I had to. You have a French dictionary, haven't you?'

'Yes, Father.'

'Look it up then. I don't need to spell it for you, do I?'

'No, Father.'

'Where was I? Ah, yes. Yes, women cooks retain their sanity. They soldier on, as your mother does, feeding kith and kin and not bothering themselves with that high-falutin, fancy stuff. Women have strange habits, as you'll discover, but they usually keep them out of the kitchen – unlike men, who turn into bloody demons as soon as they catch sight of a stove. Heed my warning, young man: cook when it's necessary, when you've no alternative, but leave it to your wife when it isn't and you haven't, if you follow my meaning. You're not likely to be given wiser advice.'

'If there's one thing I can't abide, it's lumpy porridge. This is how my husband likes it, dear – on the thin side, with a lovely smooth surface. I've already fed him this morning, before I set off to come and look after you. Sugar, dear?'

'No, thank you. I have salt on mine.'

'Do you? You'll grow up to be big and strong then, won't you?'

'Perhaps.'

'Tea, dear?'

'Yes. Please.'

'You've a lot in common with my husband, dear.'

'Me?'

'You.'

'Have I?'

'Yes, you have. He's surly over breakfast as well. He favours me with a dawn chorus of grunts.'

'I talk to my mummy. When she's here.'

'What do you talk about?'

'School.'

'Talk to me about school, Gabriel.'

'No. Thank you.'

'I shan't press you, dear. Your father loves to strut, doesn't he?'

'Loves to what?'

'Strut.'

'What's that?'

'You do surprise me. I was led to believe that your brains are the equal of Einstein's. To strut is to swagger, dear. Like a peacock.'

Soufflé, strut – my vocabulary was increasing.

'Quite the toff he is, in his tweed suit. I had to laugh to myself as he showed me over the house, dear.'

'Why?'

'He kept asking me for my opinion of his mansion. Wasn't it grand, wasn't it spacious? I didn't have the heart to tell him it's no bigger, his mansion, than my own mansion in Nightingale Lane, which looks much the same as this place, except for those two turret-things you've got at the front.'

One of those turret-things was my bedroom, the other was my study.

'He's what I call a character, your father, dear. You can't object to his swank, for he means no harm.'

'How old are you?'

76

'How old is Ellen, or even Mrs Gould, at a pinch – is that what you wish to know?'

'Yes, it is.'

'Persons who make polite inquiries sometimes receive polite replies.'

'How old are you, Mrs Gould?'

'Let me see. I have a little catching-up to do on Methuselah, years rather than months, and that's the truth. I'm twelve weeks short of fifty, dear.'

'My mummy will be thirty-two in March.'

'Did I hear you aright?'

'On March 7. She'll be home by then and you'll be gone.'

'No doubt, dear. Thirty-two!' She pointed to the ceiling. 'And the sleeping toff?'

'Sixty-six.'

'Would you credit it? I wouldn't. And when's your birthday, dear?'

'After Mummy's. On the twentieth.'

'I shall bake you a cake, dear.'

'No, you won't. Mummy will.'

'How many candles will it have?'

'Thirteen.'

It was pitch black, and I was wet. It was the middle of the night, and I was wet. I was in bed, and I was wet. I was warmly, pleasantly wet, and a fountain was flowing beneath the eiderdown.

I awoke completely when the fountain reduced itself to a trickle.

It ran dry. I turned cold.

I turned cold with fright. I lay in the sticky wetness and wondered at what I had done. I knew it was dirty, it was terrible, and that only I could have done it. I knew that I had to be ashamed.

I lay wet and cold and frightened in the darkness.

I remained there, immovable, too scared to sleep, until the light of a new day stirred me into courage: This won't happen again, I told myself, as I took off my sodden pyjamas; as I stared at the dirty, terrible stains the once-warm fountain had made.

'You're grumpier than usual this morning, dear.'

'I'm not your dear. I've made a mess upstairs. It just happened. I'm not your dear, Mrs Gould. It really did just happen.'

'What did, Gabriel?'

'Go and see.'

'In your turret?'

I nodded.

'Sherlock Gould will investigate. Start your breakfast.'

There was warmth at first, and then there was shame.

'Let's strike a bargain – shall we? – young man. You'll make a promise to me, and I, in return, will make a promise to you.'

'What for?'

'Your mishap of last night is what for.'

'I swear it just happened. I woke up, and there it was.'

'Mrs Gould has sent the offending sheets to the laundry. She has also aired your mattress. Being a woman, she took the accident, if that's what it was, in her stride.'

'It *was* an accident, Father.'

'It was something you never did as a child. Even when you were very ill you always managed to let Nurse know that you needed the potty. Other boys were piddling in their cots, but not Master Gabriel Harvey. Until now, that is.'

'I'm very sorry, Father.'

'You didn't do it, either, when you had to trek the length of the back yard to reach the privy. What you didn't do in Mr Shylock Middleton's house, young man, you have done in mine. I am not pleased with what you did.'

'No, Father.'

'Hence the promise or bargain. I want you to give me your word that there will be no repeat performance of your smelly mishap. Can I count on it?'

'Yes, Father. It won't happen again.'

'In that case, and so long as it doesn't, I give you my word that I shan't call you Piss-a-Bed.'

I slept fitfully that night. Each time I awoke, I felt the bed linen to test that it was thoroughly dry. It was. It was. It was. It was.

On the morning of February 11 at about a quarter to five, it wasn't. My word was nothing, then. I was Piss-a-Bed now.

'You don't deserve to hear the good news.'

'From Mummy?'

'Your mother, yes. She phoned from Paris this morning. She's in fine fettle, she said.'

'I couldn't help it, I swear.'

'She chatted merrily on, the way women do. Typical, really – absolutely no thought of the expense. She was full of something called the New Look, which is – apparently – what all the smart French women are wearing. I told her to go ahead and buy herself this New Look, if that's what she'd set her heart on. Why do you suppose I told her that?'

'To make her happy?'

'Of course, to make her happy. Naturally, to make her happy. Do you live with the delusion, Piss-a-Bed, that I treat her to whatever she wants in order to make her miserable?'

'No, Father.'

'Then stop your nonsense. Be useful for a change and mix my drink.'

'Yes, Father. Can I hear the good news?'

'When, and if, I'm ready.'

'Is she coming home?'

'Your mother is considering doing so. In a few days, perhaps, or a little longer – depending on her whim.'

'She will come back, won't she?'

'You're at your nonsense again. Why in hell shouldn't she? Listen to me, young man, carefully. I have money now, enough to afford certain luxuries. One of those luxuries happens to be a holiday for my wife. There is nothing unusual or out of the ordinary about a mature woman, married to a man of means, taking a holiday on her own – getting, as they say, away from it all. I have said this to you before, on several occasions, but that skull of yours would appear not to have registered a single bloody iota of same. Why do you suppose I told her to treat herself to this New Look?'

I had no answer for him.

'Well?'

'Because it's smart,' I replied desperately.

'Yes, because it's smart, because it's the smartest outfit on the market for Amy Harvey to return to England in. It's what her Ossie is giving her as her homecoming present.'

(She could have worn weeds, and I'd have run to welcome her. She could have worn rags. She could have decked herself out in the Oldest Look conceivable, a Look so Old as to be prehistoric, and I'd have rushed to greet her. What were clothes?)

'She inquired after your health. She was worried, your mother was, to learn that you've begun to be a bed-wetter. To speak truly, she was more than worried, she was shocked.'

'Was she?'

'Yes, indeed. Bewildered, too.'

'So am I, Father. I am. I don't know why it happens. Happened.'

'I'm hungry. No, I'm not. I'm bloody ravenous. Go and see what Gould is up to in the kitchen.'

My father bought me a rubber sheet.

'You'll be sleeping on this cursed invalid's contrivance until you start behaving like the Gabriel Harvey I used to respect.'

'Yes.'

'That's an expensive mattress you're ruining.'

'Yes.'

'Christ, young man, Piss-a-Bed, I'm nearer to the age of helpless bloody incontinence than you are – by a good half-century and over – and you stand there looking stupid and say yes, yes, yes. Has the spunk quite gone from you?'

'It just happens.'

'Happens! You're goading me, you are, with that constant bloody "happens". I can't believe you don't have any control over your widdle. A few years back, when all three of us huddled together in the Anderson shelter, waiting for the whizz-bangs to drop and listening as they came nearer and nearer, you didn't piss yourself then. It's my belief that this is deliberate.'

'No, it isn't. It isn't, Father.'

'Shouting won't convince me.'

'What will?'

'The stench in here is offending my nostrils. I need fresh air, and quick. You can fit that rubber thing on the bed yourself. It's a very popular piece of equipment, I hear tell, in lunatic asylums.'

I was seventeen when I threw my special sheet away. It belonged in the house I was leaving and I knew, even as I dragged it behind me down the staircase, that I should never require a replacement – it had served its 'Blenheim' purpose.

Was it loyalty, or the residue of love, that made me resist Ellen Gould's efforts to turn me into a conspirator?

'Bless him, he thinks he can fool me, Gabriel.'

'What are you talking about, Mrs Gould?'

'Your father, dear. You don't really object to my calling you dear, do you? It was just the way you were feeling that morning, wasn't it? Your father, dear – he can't fool me.'

'Can't he?'

'It's his accent.'

'Is it?'

'Yours is the right one. His comes and goes.'

'Right one?'

'His vowels let him down.'

'Do they?'

'You're pretending you haven't noticed.'

'I'm not.'

'Then you are dull today, dear. The old strutter wants me to look up to him as a gentleman – me, who looks up to no one except my Maker. I'm saying to you that his vowels aren't out of the top drawer. They're Cockney, aren't they? He'd like me to think they weren't.'

'I sound right, do I?'

'Yes, dear, you do.'

I had a gentleman's voice, it seemed. I could pass, Mrs Gould assured me, as the genuine article, should I so desire. But as for the strutting peacock above, looking down his nose at the rest of the world ...

'I'd rather you didn't refer to my father in that way, Mrs Gould. I don't think I like it.'

'Gabriel dear, I intend no disrespect. He amuses me, bless him, with his airs and graces. Let him enjoy being cock of the walk. It's his harmless pleasure.'

Then there were lecture-less days – days without his awful warnings; days free from his pronouncements.

'You're not ill, are you, Father?'

'Ill? Me? I'm in the bloody pink, you oaf. Why in hell should you suppose I'm ill?'

'You haven't been talking much.'

'And since when has a closed trap been a sign that a man is out of sorts? What nonsense are you cramming into that skull of yours? A sensible person only opens his mouth when he has something to say, young man.'

'Yes, Father.'

'Not gabbing for the sake of gabbing.'

'No.'

'As most of the so-called human race chooses to do.'

'Yes.'

'My glass is empty. Make yourself useful.'

I performed my single useful function.

'Gould has cooked us a steak and kidney pie for our dinner. It won't be up to your mother's standard, but it shouldn't poison us either. Mention of kidney reminds me that yours seem to be behaving themselves of late.'

'My kidneys?'

'The very same. I hope they will continue to remember their manners in the near future.'

He chuckled at this conceit.

'The unruly pair.'

On the morning of Tuesday, March 7, 1950, Ellen Gould served me breakfast in 'Blenheim'.

'What's in the envelope, dear?'

'Mummy's birthday card.'

'Do you know her address?'

'Here. Here's where she lives.'

'Silly me.'

'I'm leaving it by her place.'

'That's thoughtful.'

'I'm going to buy her a box of chocolates on my way home from school. If you see her, don't tell her, will you? I want them to come as a surprise.'

'Of course you do. No, I won't utter a word, dear!'

'Do I pass muster, Mrs Gould?'

'I beg your pardon?'

'Look behind my ears.'

'Spotless.'

'And my uniform? And my shoes?'

'You must have risen with the lark, dear, to have worked such wonders.'

'I did.'

'Don't get too excited. Stay calm and collected. Eat up your porridge.'

'That laundry is terrible, Mrs Gould, the way it treats my shirts. It breaks the buttons in two.'

'I'll wash the next batch for you, dear. With my own fair hands.'

'No, you won't. Mummy won't let you.'

'She's the specialist, is she?'

'Yes, she is.'

'Cold tea won't warm your insides, and that's a truth. Drink.'

'All right, all right.'

On the afternoon of that same Tuesday, I bought my mother's chocolates in a shop on Lavender Hill.

'They're for Mummy,' I told the woman behind the counter. 'She's been in Paris for her holidays.'

My heart was thumping as I let myself into 'Blenheim'. Was she upstairs, unpacking? Would she be in the kitchen Escoffier was welcome to, preparing tea for the three of us? Would she be taking a bath, perhaps, after her long and tiring journey?

She was not in the hall to greet her Gabriel.

'You'll have to suffer my company, dear,' said Mrs Gould, emerging from the sitting-room. 'Your mother hasn't returned, and your father has had to go off on business. He bolted down his lunch and dashed out of here as fast as his legs could carry him, if not faster. You'll not be seeing him again today, because his business will be keeping him in Paddington until very, very late. Cheer up, Gabriel.'

'You're not teasing me, are you, about Mummy?'

'No, no, a thousand times no. I was looking forward to meeting her, believe me.'

That Tuesday evening, I listened keenly for my mother's step in the drive. There were hours yet before March 7 was over. Her boat, her train, had been delayed.

The telephone rang – a rare event in 'Blenheim'.

'Answer it, will you, dear?' shouted Mrs Gould. I had already lifted the receiver.

'Hullo, Mummy. This is Gabriel.'

A man's laugh was the reply.

'Who are you? Who is it?'

'Is your father there, Gabriel?'

'He's out. On business. In Paddington.'

'Paddington, eh? Business, eh?' The laugh came louder. 'Have you any idea, Gabriel, what that business might be?'

'No, I haven't. Who are you?'

'I am someone, Gabriel, who would never dream of doing business in Paddington.'

And that was the end of the conversation. I did not know, then, that I had been speaking to my half-brother, Thomas. It was in the hospital where our father's left leg was amputated that he informed me that we had talked before: 'When you were still a boy and I still had some youthful blood in me.'

That Tuesday evening, Ellen Gould regaled me with stories of her twin daughters, Jane and Joan, who were indistinguishable to the world at large, but not to themselves, it went without saying, nor to their parents, except when Mr Gould took a drop too much and Joan became Jane, and vice versa, and pandemonium ensued.

Jane and Joan were young women now, proper little minxes, their minds full of nothing but clothes, make-up, and going to the flicks of a Saturday night for the purpose of sitting in the back row with good-looking young men – 'I make a point of asking them if they enjoyed the film. "Yes, Mum," they usually say. "Tell me what happened in it, one of you." "It was all about this murder" is the answer I get, or "It was ever so romantic" or "There was a lot of singing and dancing." I always smile on Sundays, dear, when we have our picture post-mortem.'

Jane and Joan, bless their dizzy heads, had recently competed in a beauty contest. Joan had won the title of Miss South-West London 1949, but Jane – her spitting image – had come absolutely nowhere, twenty-fifth to be exact. Only the Gould family knew that it was the loser who breezed up on to the platform to collect her winner's sash and a year's supply of Palmolive soap, while the real Miss South-West London fought back tears that weren't ready to flow, among the girls who had been cast aside by the judges. 'I was proud of the pair of them, Gabriel, for their last-minute switch-over.'

After the meal that Tuesday evening – 'supper' in our nameless house; 'dinner' in 'Blenheim' – I played dominoes with Ellen Gould.

'You're far too brilliant for me, dear, even with your thoughts miles away from the board – as they are, if I'm not mistaken.'

'I was sure Mummy would come home today.'

'I know you were. You had no reason to be, did you, Gabriel? You haven't been told for certain, have you?'

'No.'

'There's a sensible lad. If you'd said yes, I'd have been cross with you for deluding yourself.'

She leaned across the table and kissed me on the forehead.

'I haven't shown you my temper yet. There are enough delusions in this place, if you want my opinion, which you probably don't. It's cocoa for you, Gabriel, and a dreamless sleep to follow, I hope and trust.'

I was yanked out of bed by my father early on the morning of March 8.

'I had a hunch you would be pissing yourself. Look at you – you're wet bloody through, you stinking, snivelling, ungrateful apology.'

I watched, from the floor, as he sprinkled pepper on the latest and freshest of my stains.

He grabbed me by the scruff of the neck and pushed my face into the peppered piss.

'Breathe it in. Smell it. Sniff it. Savour it, taste it, damn you. Fill your flimsy lungs with it. Go on, go on.'

Fear of suffocating gave me the strength to fight him off. I began to sneeze as soon as I was free, and then I began to sob. I sneezed and sobbed, sobbed and sneezed, by turns – of course by turns, for it was difficult to do the two together.

(When I went to pieces in Sorg, Minnesota, I counted it the smallest of blessings that I wasn't sneezing while I was sobbing. I remembered the discomfort the combination caused me.)

'Let that be a lesson to you.'

I let it be precisely that, and I learned accordingly.

I became, by gentle degrees, the conspirator Ellen Gould had guessed I already was.

'Do you think, Gabriel, that your father's friend, August S. Coffier, will approve of the birthday cake I've made for you?'

'He's dead.'

'I'm safe then. I can stop shaking in my boots.'

'He might say it's not in the same class as Albert's.'

'Albert's? Is he August S's younger, surviving brother, by any chance?'

'No, Mrs Gould. Albert was English. He threw knives when he was drunk. He's dead, too.'

'That's a relief.'

'He ranted and raved if his soufflés didn't rise.'

'So would Gould.'

'Do *you* make soufflés?'

'Is the Pope Catholic? Is modesty a virtue? Yes, Gabriel, *I* make soufflés.'

'From what Father said, I got the impression that only men cooks bothered with them.'

'Fiddlesticks, dear. Bless him, the stuff he would have you believe!'

I returned her smile of complicity.

Six Lilies, wearing their Sunday best, came to 'Blenheim' to help me celebrate my thirteenth birthday. My father shook hands with each startled boy on arrival: 'How d'you do, young man. Do you see the name of the house? I'm plain Mr Harvey, I'm afraid, not the Duke of Marlborough. You won't have to bow to me. Just mind your manners, that's all I ask.'

Hitler's solitary ballock was not crowed over that afternoon, for my father was in constant attendance and manners were minded.

While we consumed fishpaste sandwiches, jellies, blanc-manges and custard tarts, my father sat at the head of the dining-table drinking whisky and soda from a teacup. He had prepared the mixture in the largest teapot he could find – 'I don't take milk and sugar,' he announced to my silent, staring friends, the first time he poured himself a cupful of the 'delicious brew'.

There was one particular Lily, I noticed, by whom he seemed to be intrigued: he merely glanced at the other five, but Peter Fisher he afforded a special attention.

'Is there something the matter with me, Mr Harvey?'

'What?'

'You keep looking at me.'

'Your imagination, young man. Entirely your imagination. If there *is* something the matter with you, you're better placed to know about it than I am.'

Seven Lilies listened to his chuckle.

'Decidedly better placed. Most definitely.'

Seven bewildered Lilies watched him as he rose from his chair and went to the door. 'Gould!' he bellowed.

'Yes, sir?'

'These young men are ready for the cake, I think. Kindly bring it in, would you, Gould?'

'Certainly, sir.'

'In all its splendour.'

She brought it in, set it down before me, and told me to blow out the thirteen candles in a single deep breath.

I blew.

'Come on, young man, that's not good enough. You've only conquered four.'

86

I blew again.

'Don't blow on the ones you've already put out.'

I blew yet again, and extinguished the remaining nine.

'Sing, boys,' commanded Ellen Gould. 'Loud and clear, if you please.'

They sang 'Happy Birthday to You' neither loudly nor clearly. Their performance did not please her: 'Oh, what a miserable noise. What moaning and droning. You gloomy wretches.'

'Too many full stomachs, Gould. That's the explanation for their faint-hearted singing. The man who sings best is the man who has to sing for his supper. You have fed them too well, Gould.'

'They've hardly begun, sir. A slice for you?'

'No, no. This tea is sufficient.'

The gloomy wretches looked gloomier, if that were possible, as the ceremony dragged on.

'Father, can we get down and play?'

'Play, young man?'

He was fixing me with – I recognised it and shuddered inside – his lecturer's glare. He was in a speechifying mood.

'You wish to get down and play?'

'Yes, Father.'

'I believe, on an occasion such as this, that play is not in order. I should like you all to put your thinking caps on and give your brains some exercise. You play games every day, as my ear-drums know from the din I hear you making whenever I pass by the school. Well, let today be different. Thinking caps – yes?'

'Yes, Mr Harvey,' said Peter Fisher.

'You are on what I call the threshold of life. A threshold is a very good position from which to take in the view. Standing on a threshold, you can see what lies ahead – providing your eyes are open, of course.'

'Of course, Mr Harvey,' Peter Fisher agreed.

'I stood on that threshold once myself and the view was not pleasant, I can tell you, young man – beg pardon, young men. It most definitely wasn't. I don't know if my son and heir here has told you anything about my early years, but if he hasn't, which is more than likely, I shall now proceed so to do, in a few choice words.'

He would take a little refreshment first, he said, to oil the larynx.

'Some of you, I shouldn't doubt, come from poor homes. I, Oswald Harvey, came from a very poor, a dirt poor, home. The threshold I stood on when I was your age led to nowhere – at least, that's what I assumed. Fate, and my own perseverance (I shan't be modest, for a change) decided otherwise. I could have been one of a thousand – nay, a million – paupers, living from hand to mouth as my weak-willed parents lived, waiting for the monthly visit of the Shylock landlord. I could have been, but I wasn't.'

My father, in his boastfulness, had chosen to forget that in March 1949 he was paying rent to Mr Middleton; that he was a poor man then, dependent on his wife, my mother, who was supplementing his meagre pension with the money she earned at her secret place; that 'Blenheim' and its possessions were, a mere twelve months ago, on the far side of a very distant moon.

Six Lilies endured what the seventh had once absorbed with pleasure: the decorative details (the police walking in threes; the near-rescue of Johnny Tuohy) of his deprived childhood. He spoke in his lecturer's voice, glared his lecturer's glare. It was imperative that we marked well what he was saying.

What was he saying? Something about pluck and spunk, the qualities he displayed when he leapt into the river that 'keeps rolling along, down to the mighty sea' (his larynx required re-oiling after singing this snatch) – he was giving his leap, I understand now, a certain symbolic significance. Oswald Harvey had not stepped cautiously off his threshold – no, not he. He had plunged right into the filthy, ice-cold water and had earned his first honest wages as a result.

The seventh, most embarrassed Lily, his thinking cap askew, became aware that the lecturer had begun to falter.

'Hadn't been for leap, never have found courage to knock on doors. Offering my services. Told to buzz off, common brat. Flea in my ear. Slept nights Vauxhall Gardens. Kept knocking by day, offering serve. Never gave up. One door in particular. Not told to buzz, no flea. Door belonging to Sir Vincent. His – wasn't it? Sir Vincent proper aristocrat. Not jumped-up upstart. Took boy in, boy being me, Oswald Harvey. Aged thirteen. Boy on threshold. Worked for Sir Vince twenty – tell a lie – twenty-*two* years. Sir Vincent never forgot him, boy on thresh. Remembered, he did, Sir Vincent.'

There was only a trickle left in the teapot.

'Goodbye, Mazzawattee. Any boy here who wets the bed,

will he have courage to raise his hand? Doesn't matter which.'

Six Lilies, glared at in turn, shook their heads – 'Not me, Mr Harvey'; 'No, Mr Harvey'; 'No'; 'No'; 'No'; 'No.'

And then silence – defiant, sickening silence from the seventh.

'Somebody here's a bloody little liar. In my opinion. That's my opinion.'

'Is it, Mr Harvey?' asked Peter Fisher.

'It bloody is, young man. A liar. In this very room. At my table.'

'It isn't often – in fact, I can't recall it ever happening before – that I fall asleep in the daytime. Were your pals still here when I dropped off?'

'Yes, Father.'

'You could have nudged me awake. You could at least have had the forethought to have woken me up.'

'Why?'

'Out of politeness to your guests is why. A fine sight I must have looked, Piss-a-Bed, lost to the world while they were leaving.'

'I didn't think you would want to see them off.'

'You didn't think! You seldom do, these days. They appeared to be presentable chaps, with one exception. I should have liked to have been on my feet to bid them adieu. Was Gould on the premises when they left?'

'She was washing the dishes.'

'I shall have words with her in the morning. That boy who answered me back, that lip-merchant, what is his name?'

'Peter Fisher.'

'Sounds English enough. You can tell him from me he needs to mind his manners. Where's he from?'

'London. Hammersmith.'

'No, you oaf. I mean *from*. Originally.'

'Originally?'

'Origins, young man. Origins.'

'Peter's Anglo-Indian, if that's what you want me to say.'

'Is he, by God? I knew it. I knew it in my bones that he isn't completely one of us. I suspected a touch of the tar-brush the moment I clapped eyes on him.'

'Tar-brush?'

'Coloured blood. He's part-nigger, your pal. I'd tread warily with him, if I were you.'

(I am his daughter's godfather, Oswald Harvey. Did I tell you that while you were alive? I hope I did.)

'Indians, I grant you, are a mite more civilized than Africans. They didn't have to come down from the trees. They're sly, though. They bow and scrape, but it's all show. That Sahib stuff they mutter, it's only a cover-up for what they're really thinking. You watch yourself with that half-Abdul.'

'Yes, Father.'

'This, young man, is the kitchen.'

'I know it is. Of course it is.'

'If you know it's the kitchen, why are you reading in it? You have a study at the top of the house. You are not living in a hovel any longer, remember. Go up there now, and you will find your birthday present. It's a wireless, a radio. There's method in my generous madness, because you'll be able to listen to that cursed music you're so fond of out of my earshot, thank you very much. I'm giving you the thing a day early so as to get the agony over and done with.'

'You've missed her by ten minutes. If you'd put your skates on, you could have spoken to her through the crackle.'

'Mummy?'

Your mother, yes. She phoned to wish you many happy returns.'

'She's coming home?'

'Quite the opposite. She's going on a cruise.'

'A cruise?'

'On a boat. Like in the song "A Slow Boat to China". Except that she's not China-bound. She's heading for the Mediterranean. Ice-creamland and thereabouts. I'll have to ask the bank to wire her some extra money.'

There was no card from her, no letter – just the greetings my skateless feet ensured I should not receive.

My dear little Starch-angel,

So you dwell in Blenheim now, do you? Oswald wrote to me on his fancy notepaper to tell me he has become a man of means. Does he go from room to room singing

'Malbrouk-s'en-va-t'en-guerre?' No, that was Malplaquet. The wrong battle altogether.

I have not heard from you since you moved into your Blenheim. Pick up a pen one day, Gabriel, and describe it for me, as I am far too lowly – and mad! – to ever be invited inside. Do the Churchills drop in for tea?

Enclosed is a gift for you. It's probably above your head at the moment, but you will make sense of it one day.

Inform my brother that I am still in the Land of the Living. Give my regards to your young mother.

Your loving Auntie Kathleen
PS Wicked boy for mentioning my marmosets!

The gift that was above my head – indeed, it was; indeed, it is – turned out to be, after much unwrapping, a copy of Emanuel Swedenborg's *Heaven and Hell*. On the title page she had written some of God's Instrument's own words: 'It is the life of our love which we live, and that life is of such quality as the love is.'

On Monday March 27, I was met at the school gates by Ellen Gould.

'I'm taking you home with me today, Gabriel. Jane and Joan are dying to meet you.'

In the Goulds' house that evening I ate a fish soufflé – 'I hope it's up to August S. Coffier's standards' – and suffered the twins' compliments.

'You're so pretty,' cooed Joan or Jane.

'I wish I had your skin, Gabriel,' said envious Jane or Joan, brushing my cheek.

'What about my London impurities?'

They giggled when I explained how my aunt had squeezed those 'beastly things' from me, one at a painful time.

'You're small for your age,' Joan or Jane declared.

'I've never seen a boy so pretty,' marvelled the twin who hadn't remarked on my height.

'Heavens, girls, he'll grow up with a fixation if you carry on any more. He's handsome, is Gabriel. Leave him be.'

'I wish my eyes were as blue as his.'

To change the embarrassing subject, I asked Mrs Gould where her husband was.

'In prison, dear.'

Jane and Joan crowed with laughter at my astonishment.

'He's a warder, over in Brixton. He's in charge of some really nasty brutes, is my brave Charlie.'

I was alone in 'Blenheim', naked on my bed, idling the summer afternoon away.

In the hospital near the Thames, the nurses had called me 'the boy with the troublesome twos'. How often they had strained in sympathy for me as I pushed and pushed and pushed to make a motion.

That idle afternoon, I had no cause to push, no need to strain. As I lay there, my mind on nothing but being deliriously lazy, a turd moved steadily, swiftly out of me.

I captured it in my hand.

I lifted the captive to my face. I began to daub myself. I did it quickly, using my fingers as brushes.

More swift and steady escapees appeared, and I employed both hands to collect them. I daubed my throat, my chest, my arm, my legs, and the cock that intrigued my fellow Lilies because it lacked a curtain. I lay there, happily brown, letting the paint harden on me.

I tried to frighten myself. 'You're foul,' I said. 'You're disgusting. You're unnatural.'

I failed in my attempt. I went on lying there, lazily happy. Hours later, I scrubbed my smeared body clean. I slowly, dreamily worked my mother's scented soap into a lather – the purple bar that no one had touched since she left for her holiday.

'You bloody wretch,' said my father when I handed him his first drink of the evening. 'You smell of her. You bloody wretch, I'll thrash the living daylights out of you if you smell of her again. You keep your distance from me.'

6

On Saturday, November 24, 1956, I returned to my room on the top floor of a shuddering house in Vineyard Walk, Clerkenwell, switched on the radio and learned that Guido Cantelli had been killed in a plane crash on the outskirts of Paris.

I listened to every news bulletin that long black day: perhaps there had been a terrible mistake; perhaps Cantelli had been on a different flight; perhaps the great conductor, whom I hero-worshipped, was even now about to land in safety at another airport, in another country.

'I could never fly,' my mother had said to me. 'I'd be too scared. The thought of being higher up than birds can get to, beyond clouds invisible to the naked eye – oh, the very thought makes me feel queasy. And if I'm queasy with my feet fair and square on the ground, Gabriel, what state would my system find itself in if they weren't?'

The next morning, the fatal accident wasn't mentioned: it was already relegated to history. That official silence convinced me he was dead.

I had been Cantelli's most fervent admirer – no one more fervent – since 1952, since October 5 of that year, on which Monday evening in that 'cursèd modern eyesore', the Royal Festival Hall, I heard, and watched, him conduct the Phil-harmonia Orchestra in Ravel's Pavane and the Second Suite from *Daphnis and Chloe*, in Haydn's Ninety-Third Symphony and in Beethoven's Seventh. It was the Beethoven I hummed and conducted – those bits of it, rather, that I knew by heart – as I walked from Waterloo to 'Blenheim' in a daze of happiness.

Excitement and consolation were what I craved, and music alone provided them. Cantelli's interpretations always thrilled and moved me: they belonged in a world that Oswald Harvey couldn't occupy; they made me forget, while they lasted, my mother's continued, inexplicable absence.

'You are a Romantic, Harvey,' said Mr Nazareth, when I told him the reason for my long face. 'A dyed-in-the-wool specimen, I truly swear. There are, and will be, other conductors.'

Of course there were: of course there would be; but none of them were, or would be, mine, I did not explain to Mr Nazareth.

'Yes, plenty of others. You're right, I suppose.'

'It's a simple matter of logic. A maestro is a replaceable entity, like a doctor or a politician. Orchestral life must go on.'

Mr Nazareth's worldly-wise smile curbed any temptation I might have had to deplore the cruelty of Fate, to complain that a faulty piece of machinery had caused the early death of the man I revered. 'You're right. It must.'

Every Sunday evening, I went with Mr Nazareth to the Three Crowns for a drink. And *a* drink it was – a solitary pint of what he called 'your good English beer', lingered over, sipped appreciatively, seldom guzzled. I was usually happy to join him in this one of his various frugal rituals, though on the 'night of the long face' I did not give him my complete, bemused attention. I was thinking of all those memorable concerts I had seemed certain of attending, in an unblighted future.

Mr Nazareth lived immediately below me in Mrs Sparey's lodgings. His age was a mystery he did not allow his nineteen-year-old friend to solve; he might have been an oldish thirty, or then again a youthful fifty; he chuckled as I guessed. He was born – 'On a day in the present century, Harvey' – in Goa, of Christian parents. The Portuguese invaders had given his far-distant ancestors the name Nazaré: 'The Anglicizing "th" is my addition.' He had come to 'your cold little island' to amass large sums of money: slowly and surely to start with, and consequently – he smiled as he said it – at a 'rapidly accelerating rate'.

'Why did you choose England, Mr Nazareth?' Why not America?'

'A pertinent question, Harvey. This beer, perhaps. No, I joke. To be a dark-skinned millionaire in a country like yours, where real wealth is in so few, and such white, hands – that, Harvey, is my grand scheme. I do not intend to fail. Why not America? The place is too vast; it has no history, and besides, they have more than prejudice there . . . they lynch people like myself; they castrate them, too, I have read. I can endure verbal abuse,

Harvey, indeed have had to – punishment more severe I should be foolish to encourage.'

'But that's only in the Deep South, isn't it – the lynchings?'

'So one hears. Who knows? My beliefs would spell danger for me anywhere in the United States, Harvey.'

'You don't have any beliefs, Mr Nazareth.'

'I believe in not believing, and that in itself is a belief. Religion is poppycock, Harvey, as I keep on insisting. Imagine how I would fare in the land of the Baptists, the Seventh Day Adventists, Mormons, Lutherans and Jehovah's Witnesses – not well, not well. An atheist calling himself Nazareth: explosive, Harvey, undoubtedly explosive. Most millionaires in America are God-fearing, or pretend to be. They use piety as a justification for their greed. I have no intention of piously justifying my heartfelt desire to become, as you say here, *stinking* rich. I am going to stink for my own glory, not some god's, and I shall revel in the odour. When I die, it will perhaps be said of me "Nazareth prospered". Those two words will be sufficient recognition of my extraordinary achievement.'

'What if you die next week or next year? Before you've had a chance to prosper?'

'I am taking every precaution to ensure that I don't. I avoid all excitement and I cross roads carefully. My body is not my master – rather the reverse. No, no, you doubting Thomas of a Harvey, you will not cast a shadow over my bright horizon, therefore please desist in the attempt. I cannot be deflected.'

People, landlords mostly, had not succeeded in disheartening Mr Nazareth; so why should I, who had no such purpose in mind? He had knocked on dozens of London doors, had been told at dozens of London boarding-houses and dingy hotels that no rooms were vacant – often at 'establishments' where cards and signs advertising vacancies were prominently displayed.

'It is a strange thing, Harvey, but I began almost to admire – yes, yes, admire – those men and women who turned me away because of my colour. The feeble excuses the others offered me! The embarrassment they suffered! The blushes that came to their cheeks! How they slithered, metaphorically speaking, and squirmed! My declared enemies stood secure on their steps, though. They did not slither or squirm. They advised me, some of them, to return to a country I have never visited: Africa, Harvey. Very droll. One gentleman in particular I found hugely – yes, hugely – diverting. "This no jungle," he observed, before

I had even opened my mouth. "Understand, darkie? No jungle here. Jungle in Notting Hill. This street civilized. White man province. Black boy not welcome." An amusing Englishman, Harvey. I thanked him with exaggerated courtesy for his invaluable information and asked him if he knew where I could perhaps hire an elephant: I had a fold-up howdah, I said, in my briefcase, which I carried with me especially for jungle travel. The look of bewilderment that crossed his hideously purple features was deeply satisfying to me, I truly swear. I bowed to him, Harvey, and touched my forelock – yes! and wished him the best of health. My polite departure, bowing all the while, had a startling effect on him: he jumped up and down like an angry child, spluttering and shrieking. He was still doing so when I turned at the corner of his civilized street and waved goodbye. Oh yes, Harvey, a hugely diverting episode.'

While I was living at Mrs Sparey's, I bought my first piece of furniture: a school desk, of the kind I had used as a diligent, and then a listless, Lily. Its top is scored and scarred with mysterious initials, FK, PA, RW, JB – and the message WRIGHTS ALWAYS WRONG (TRUE) is engraved on its seat. Within its confines – the traces of unknown boys or girls before me, the truth about Wright's wrongness below – I wrote and wrote my *Lords of Light*. I shackled myself for the task. I was certain that I had to; it was imperative; I should have been indolent otherwise.

I had failed as a Lily, seated at just such an imprisoning desk. I had dreamed and dozed there, my mind not bothered with the Gordon Riots, the hypothesis of Avogadro, the Revelation of St John the Divine. My mind wasn't bothered with anything scholarly, with anything that might test or expand it. My academic regress was recorded – at first amazedly, then sadly, then angrily – in a succession of dismal reports. 'What are you playing at, Piss-a-Bed?' my father demanded, not waiting for, or even expecting, an answer. 'I seem to recall that you had brains a while ago. So do these teachers. They say they find it hard to understand what you are about. You are no longer the bright boy you were. You've become a dunce, that's their opinion. A dunce, you cursèd oaf – a bloody stupid, good-for-nothing dunce!'

'Yes, Father.'

'A fine start you're making for yourself, I don't think. Mooning around to music, that's all you're fit for. And emptying your bladder where you shouldn't. What a specimen of young manhood I've produced.'

'I'm Mother's son, Father,' I heard myself telling him, with a firmness that surprised me. 'I'm Mummy's, not yours. I belong to your wife.'

'You do, do you? What's between my legs can take some of the credit for Gabriel Harvey, just you remember. It's as bloody basic as that. If your mother had sent it packing, which she didn't; if she'd begged me to stop, which she didn't; if she hadn't behaved like a red-blooded woman, you would be nowhere now, which you aren't. The airy-fairiness you store in that skull of yours astonishes me at times, Piss-a-Bed, it really does.'

'I'm hers, and always will be. I can choose what I want to believe. You can't alter that.'

'Listen to your nonsense. Wherever Amy Harvey is, you don't seem to matter much to her, do you, young man? If she's thinking of you in sunny climes, she doesn't leap out of her deck chair – does she? – to put her thoughts on a postcard. No, her precious Gabriel isn't precious enough to deserve a "Wish you were here" or a "Hoping this finds you as it leaves me" – that's how it looks to her husband, who's stuck at home with her precious little love.'

('Sunny climes' – that was the dissembler's phrase, the liar's cliché. He knew where she was, yet he could still speak of sunny climes. Possessed of his terrible knowledge, he could still invoke a deck chair, a postcard from some far-off country, the vapid messages of a contented holiday-goer. Knowing what he did, he could still conjure up a picture of my mother on some crowded beach, happily browning her body at his expense. He could still talk so, and without shame – as I discovered in Sorg, Minnesota, the year after he died.)

'Going back to school, are you?' asked the junk dealer who sold me the desk.

'Probably,' I answered.

'You're the right size and shape for it.'

Mr Nazareth helped me carry it to our lodgings. I promised him an extra pint of 'good English beer' for his trouble.

'One a week is sufficient for my needs, Harvey. You will not lure me into excess.'

In room after London room, I stared at the wooden reminder of my failure. When would I be able to sit at it and prove myself? That, surely, was the reason for its purchase – the proving of

Gabriel Harvey, the testing of his will to succeed. At what? In heaven's name, at what? I did not know.

Long before I sat down to write my study of itinerant preachers, I added to the inscriptions on my stocks-to-be: I carved HMV B9719 at an angle between FK and RW, with a penknife that set Heddle's alleys briefly ringing, to my absent mother's brief delight.

'I heard from your mother today, Piss-a-Bed.'

'She phoned, I assume?'

'You assume correctly.'

'While I was out.'

'While you were out, of course.'

'Of course.'

'Prepare yourself for a shock.'

'Mummy can't be dead if she spoke to you. What other shock could there be?'

'She's met another man,' he said, with a totally convincing catch in his voice. 'A foreigner, by the sound of him. He's younger than her old Ossie, nearer her own age. She wants a divorce.'

'A divorce? From you?'

'Who else is she married to, you oaf? Yes, it is me she's ditching.' He went on, in husky tones suggestive of injured nobility, 'I told her I had no alternative but to agree to her request. Her happiness has ever been my main concern. She said she'd known all along that I would understand, I was that kind of husband – generous, thoughtful, considerate of his Amy's wishes. There wasn't a whim of hers he didn't pander to. So there you are, young man. That's it. She's made her choice and it isn't yours truly any more. If she decides to honour England with her presence again, she won't be wending her way home to "Blenheim", you can rely on that. I shall have to reconcile myself to facing the future – what little of it's left to me – without her.'

'Where was she phoning from?'

'Where? Who's to say? The crackle on the line was so bad, I couldn't hear what the operator at her end was gabbling on about. The last lot of money I had the bank send was to Malta, a few weeks ago, so I shouldn't imagine she's strolled very far. Yes, it was probably that part of the world, in the Malta region.'

'Did she mention me?'

'As a matter of fact, she didn't. She was too full of her romance to inquire after her beloved Gabriel. Don't look surprised. When a woman's in love –'

'In love?'

'As she must be, or thinks she is, she forgets everything else – even, I'm afraid, her nearest and dearest.'

In love? My mother in love? 'She can't be in love.' I was almost shouting.

'She can. She asked for a clean break. It's yours, I said, seeing as how this lover-boy you've found seems prepared to do his best for you.'

'He's not a boy. If he's Mummy's age, he's thirty-six.'

'You keep count, do you?'

'Yes, I do.'

'You haven't seriously been expecting her back, have you? After four, coming on five, years? Not seriously, Piss-a-Bed?'

'Yes, Father. I have. Seriously.'

'Hope springs eternal, does it, eh? I must tell you something. Man to man. You and I, Oswald and Gabriel Harvey, belong to her past, which she has put behind her. Get it fixed into your skull that she won't be returning – not to us, never to us, most definitely not to us.'

(He was telling the truth at last, a fraction of it, anyway. The 'lover-boy', the demand for a divorce, the abandoned husband's thoughtful and considerate behaviour – all that was his perverse invention.)

He was launched into a 'Blenheim' lecture – The Fool Looks Backward, The Wise Chap Plans Ahead – when I decided to escape. I had run away, childishly, before; now I would surprise myself and him by leaving for ever. A disgraced and disgraceful Lily, I was fit only for manual work: lacking the necessary written proof of my intelligence, I had no prospects of the sort that would meet with the glaring lecturer's immediate approval – that proud man of property who had once been a roadsweeper. I heard him accuse me of daydreaming, of wasting my chances, of being bloody bone idle for reasons he hadn't the time or patience to get to the bottom of. They were familiar accusations.

'The chap who plans ahead is a different kettle of fish altogether. He may have been a backwards-looking fool as a youngster, but there comes a day in his life when he gets up with the lark and tells the world he intends to make it his oyster. The sooner that day dawns for a certain ne'er-do-well, the happier he and his sorely tried old parent will be. That ne'er-do-well is you, Piss-a-Bed. Are you catching my drift? You could still buckle down to it and turn yourself into a man of substance. With my money to support you, you've a sure foundation to build on. I shall go on dipping my hands into my pockets for a little while longer if you promise me you'll sit and pass those cursèd bloody exams you failed. It could be arranged for you to do so. Strings can be pulled.'

'Keep your money, Father.'

'What do you propose to live on? Tea leaves? Keep it, indeed!'

'Yes, Father. Keep it.'

I had twelve pounds in the Baptist Missionary Society collecting box ('The Baptist Mission was founded in 1792. Its objects are the preaching of the Gospel of Christ, the translation of the inspired volume into the various languages of the Heathen, and the promotion of Education amongst the youth of both sexes') which I had discovered in the cellar at 'Blenheim'. I had used it as my piggy-bank for years, emptying it whenever I treated myself to a Cantelli concert or a Sunday afternoon at the Zoo or a gramophone record I would have to play while my father was hobnobbing with his new cronies in the Windmill or the County Arms. 'All donations can be addressed to the Secretaries, Baptist Mission House, Castle Street, Holborn, EC.'

With twelve pounds in threepenny bits and sixpences, I was rich enough to leave. I should have to find a job that Oswald Harvey considered beneath me, and there were plenty of those. I had to find a room as well, and that would mean trudging the streets. I had to go to an area of London where he couldn't find me in a hurry – on what he still called the 'right side of the river', beyond the City, perhaps. Well, I would trudge and trudge until I was safely hidden from him. I might even take refuge among those ferocious Mediterranean beasts on the Isle of Dogs: Bite him, Romulus; Sink your teeth into his trousers, Remus. That would be really crafty of me.

'It's nothing to smile about, your pig-headed refusal to grow up.'

I rose with the missing lark the following morning. A pigeon continued to sleep soundly in the guttering beneath my turret window as I carefully picked out the clothes I would be wearing in another part of London in my first weeks of freedom. My mother's Bible went into the suitcase, and *Moby-Dick* and

Keats's poems, and the wireless my father had given me on my thirteenth birthday: I'd be able to listen to that cursed music I was fond of several miles out of his earshot now. I bathed and dressed. Within an hour, I was ready to set off.

I dragged my special sheet behind me down the staircase, knowing as I did so that I should never require a replacement – I was leaving 'Blenheim', and it had served its purpose. No more shame; no more humiliation; no more taunts of Piss-a-Bed. I dumped the wretched thing next to the dustbins by the tradesmen's entrance.

I made myself tea in the kitchen no longer ruled over by my kind fellow-conspirator Ellen Gould. Her brave Charlie had been appointed a chief warder ('With special responsibilities') in a maximum security prison 'a stone's throw from Scotland', and she and one of the twins had joined him in that rugged town – 'The people here speak a different language, I swear, Gabriel. Joan and me are deaf from the effort of trying to understand them. Tell your old pater I haven't spotted a single toff since we arrived.'

I ate three boiled eggs and four slices of toast with marmalade. I was properly stoked up for what could be a long and tiring journey, for I was determined to walk all the way to my meagre new abode, wherever it turned out to be. The moment for departure had come: it was seven-thirty, and Mrs Quinlan, Ellen's steely successor, was due at eight. It was a Thursday, which meant that Mr Cole, the gardener, was also expected. The son who did not wish to be an heir opened the front door of his father's house and was suddenly sick with fright: 'I can't,' he said loudly; and then, even louder, he corrected himself: 'I can.' He paused on the step – the door of 'Blenheim' temptingly ajar behind him – and stared up at the silver sword with the multi-coloured letters on which he had remarked to his mother five years earlier: 'What does it mean, Mummy?' He put his hand on the doorknob and pulled it towards him. He heard the final, decisive click. He halted. Security – of a terrible sort, but security none the less – was in there, and he was on the brink of rejecting it. He halted.

It was the Gabriel Harvey who had twice run away from that terrible security who halted on the very doorstep of 'Blenheim'. The police had brought him home after his second break-out: 'We found your little lad half-asleep and half-frozen to death under the arches by Charing Cross station. We didn't approve of the company he was keeping, sir – tramps, drunkards, West End riff-raff, the lowest of the low. We'd advise you to watch him closely in future, sir. He has a wild streak inside of him, your well-spoken boy.'

The same halting Gabriel had slunk back to 'Blenheim' on his aunt's stern insistence: 'My brother is not devoid of feeling, Starch-angel, in spite of his fixed belief in my madness. It is possible – difficult, but possible – to hurt him, I do assure you. Gabriel, you are to catch the eight o'clock train tomorrow and return to him, with or without the proverbial tail between your legs – that, my love, is an order. You can't stay here with me; you know you can't. I'm settled in my widow's habits. I have faith in you. Let that be enough.'

'Please, Auntie'.

'You'll thank me, Starch-angel, I promise you. Oh, you're too citified to live in my peace and quiet. I'm happy alone. I'm one of the chosen.'

'Please. Please.'

'Bear with him, Gabriel. Try to bear with him. I couldn't, I confess. You will be a true man if you do.'

I walked the length of the drive, slowly. I climbed the gate and jumped down to the pavement – a rare gymnastic feat for a sickly youth carrying a heavy case. I spared myself a last glimpse of 'Blenheim'. I stepped forward, briskly, into the real world.

Mrs Sparey was my short-sighted rescuer. 'Stand under the electric light, would you, and turn round slowly.' When she had finished inspecting me, through glasses held together by sticking plaster, she nodded vigorously and said, 'I've only the attic. It's two pounds a week. A bath will cost you a shilling each time. You mustn't be afraid when the house shakes – just blame the traffic in Farringdon Road and pray to your Maker, if you're lucky enough to have one. What did you say your name was?'

I hadn't said. I now told her.

'Gabriel? That has a pleasing sound. The bringer of good news, I hope. Can I anticipate angelic behaviour?'

'I'll do my best.'

'You look famished, from what I can see of you. Cheese and chutney be agreeable?'

'Yes. Thank you. I wasn't expecting food.'

I certainly wasn't expecting the attic. Dozens of doors had

been slammed in my face that day: 'I don't let rooms to runaway children'; 'Try an orphanage'; 'This is a respectable lodgings, not a nursery.' I had pressed Mrs Sparey's bell with every expectation of being told what I had been told so often – that since I was too young to earn a living wage it therefore stood to reason that I would be unable to pay my weekly rent. It was already late in the evening, and I was beginning to wilt. My head ached, my feet hurt, my clothes were sticking to me. I pressed Mrs Sparey's bell a second time, wondering if I could summon up the energy to protest at her inevitable refusal. 'Be patient, whoever you are. You caught me doing something you can't do for me. You've come about the room, I suppose?' 'Yes,' I replied to my unseen questioner. 'Don't dawdle, then,' she said to me the moment she was visible. 'It's not my custom to interview tenants in the street. Please enter.'

I entered, and immediately stumbled. I was advised to watch my step. 'The carpet was new once. Go right to the end of the passage, and proceed with caution.' I walked warily in the near-darkness. 'The bulb went kaput an hour ago. All my waifs and strays are out on the tiles tonight, including Countess Bolina and Mr Nazareth, who are both stay-at-homes as a rule, so I've no one to change it for me. I get chronic vertigo just standing on a chair, you see. Two feet from the floor, and I could be at the top of the Eiffel Tower – it's quite absurd, and quite unavoidable. The silly trials our bodies are forced to endure.'

'I really wasn't expecting food,' I said to the small, grey-haired, almost grey-bearded woman who had just scrutinized me from every angle. 'I don't wish to cause any bother.'

'You can dispense with that kind of politeness straight away. It's so bloody English. I offered you grub, you accepted – that's enough. Park your behind at the table while I raid the larder. Tea?'

'Yes, please.'

'Good boy. That's all you need to say. And you *are* still a boy, aren't you?'

'I'm seventeen. I –'

'You haven't asked my name. It's Sparey. Diana Sparey, wife of Walter Sparey, who was shot dead in Spain in 1937, fighting for the Loyalist cause. He's the one with the nose in the photo on the mantelpiece. Your age doesn't worry me, Gabriel. If you want your independence earlier than most, that's your affair. I was only a slip of a thing when I flew from the nest myself. I've never regretted taking off when I did – not for a minute. If I hadn't come to London, I wouldn't have met Walter, which doesn't bear thinking of. It isn't my policy to bombard you with questions, by the way. Prying isn't in my nature. You needn't say another word.'

'I don't get on with my father,' I confided. 'I don't get on with him at all.'

'I had the same problem twice over. I can't make up my mind which of my parents annoyed me more – him with his everlasting talk of cricket or her with her silly little yapping dogs. Mine was what is called a "good" family, damn it. It still is, probably. I cut my ties in the ancient past and it's far too late to knot them back together again. Not – without a "k" – that I want to.'

'I don't know where my mother is. He said she was on Malta last, but I've stopped believing him. I wouldn't be sitting here, Mrs Sparey, honestly I wouldn't, if she were in "Blenheim".'

'Are my ears deceiving me?'

'It's the name of my father's house.'

'Is it, by George?'

'In Clapham. It looks over the common.'

'You are talking music now, Gabriel,' she said, and laughed.

'I don't think I understand, Mrs Sparey.'

'It is a great relief to me to hear that you've done a flit from the Clapham Common "Blenheim", rather than – well, the other one. A second aristocrat under my roof and I might be driven to murder. The Countess is a pathetic old duck, a dear soul at heart, but I must confess that there are times when I come close to wishing the Bolsheviks had got her in their line of fire. She's been here longer than you've been alive, Gabriel, and she still treats me like a servant – when she's even acknowledging my existence, that is. I made this chutney myself, with my own window-box tomatoes.'

I could have guessed that Mrs Sparey's chutney was home-made, by the number of human hairs in it.

'I have two gigantic boil-ups every year. I buy a ton of Seville oranges in Exmouth market for my coarse-cut marmalade. I'll give you a pot if you stay. I hate the daily routine of cooking – I fry or roast with my mind elsewhere – but my preserves seem to find favour. I throw myself into them.'

Head first, I thought.

'Eat as much as you want. It's not often I play hostess.'

'Yes, I will. I'm very grateful, Mrs Sparey.'

She could not gauge the extent of my gratitude. No one could.
I sat at a rickety table covered in oil-cloth, in a stuffy little room
adjoining a kitchen that would have broken the spirit of August
S. Coffier, and felt almost hysterically peaceful – if such a state
of happiness can be imagined. I had found myself a home, a
hiding place. I had yet to see the attic, but I knew I should be
my own master there.

'If you have a delicate constitution, you won't approve of
this,' my scruffy saviour declared as she handed me a chipped
Welcome to Margate mug filled with dark red tea. 'I like a brew
with a kick in it.'

'So does my mother. So do I. Everything's delicious.'

'You're determined to be the perfect lodger, aren't you? I'm
not accustomed to such politeness, I'm really not. It might go
to my head.'

'Shall I change the bulb for you, Mrs Sparey?'

'Yes, please. The Countess will fall on her face if you don't.
She can be very insulting, in several languages.'

I was thanked profusely for averting the wrath that would
otherwise have come; I was envied for my steadiness while
divorced from terra firma; I was told I had got off to an angelic
start; I was offered more tea, more cheese, more chutney.

'Could I, perhaps, see my room?'

'Why perhaps? It's yours now, Gabriel. I'll give you some
fresh sheets and pillow-cases to take up with you. You don't
object to scaling the heights by yourself?'

'Of course not, Mrs Sparey.'

'Follow your nose to the top floor then. You can't miss it.
You may well wish you had – missed it, I mean – when you
look inside. You'll probably be beetling back to "Blenheim"
tomorrow.'

'No, I shan't.' I realized I was shouting. 'No, I won't,' I said,
with quieter conviction.

'Mr Nazareth swept it only last week,' she called up the stairs
after me. 'You should find the floor clean, I hope, at the very
least.'

The sheets Mrs Sparey gave me had not been invisibly mended.
It was difficult to ignore or avoid the lumpy seams that held
them together. Those meandering repairs – 'Sparey's snakes', as
they were known in the local laundry – outwitted my twisting
and turning body the entire time I lived in Vineyard Walk. I

would emerge from sleep the reddened victim of their stealthy pressure.

That first night, though, I was not to be daunted by such petty irritants as hairs in my food and lumps in my bed. I was too excited and exhausted to be upset by the apparent dinginess of my hideaway; I stood on cracked linoleum beneath a sloping ceiling and spoke my incantation and all was well. 'HMV B9719,' I said aloud, and there she was with me, warm at my side, taking in deep breaths of the same musty air.

Fresh white paint was the answer, I decided. I should need gallons of the stuff. I already had Mrs Sparey's permission to remove the faded wallpaper: 'It's had its day, I suppose. It was new once. Walter chose it. He always referred to your room as his eyrie, because he liked to joke about his aquiline features – alias his bloody great beak. He wrote his best pamphlets up there. If you're planning a revolution, Gabriel, you couldn't have picked a finer place to do it in.'

For the boy from 'Blenheim', revolution meant severed heads rolling into baskets, to the sound of furiously clacking knitting-needles, and far, far better things being done at the best of times, the worst of times; it meant that 'demmed, elusive Pimpernel', the frivolous fop Sir Percy Blakeney, whom 'they' sought here, whom 'they' sought there, but never managed to capture, ha ha; it did not mean Friedrich Engels studying the poor in Manchester, and Karl Marx swotting in the British Museum, and the First International, and Lenin rising to power and Stalin ousting Trotsky – not then. In September 1954, I was staging the tiniest of revolutions myself. The vast intricate world beyond me could look to its own concerns.

'He liked to play chess with Countess Bolina after a tiring session up in the eyrie. He used to tease her between moves about his modest proposals for the Hanoverian occupants of Buckingham Palace – how he'd have them shifting the London sewage, or digging for coal in Wales. The filthiest jobs were to be reserved for royalty in Walter's scheme of things to come. At his command, dukes and duchesses, princes and princesses, kings and queens – even ladies-in-waiting – would descend to the bowels of the earth in all their finery. That was what appealed to him most – the thought of those blue-blooded creatures, dressed for state occasions, crawling along underground tunnels and shovelling their subjects' shit in the sewers.

"Watch your ermine, Your Majesty, it's a bit dusty down here"; "Isn't that your crown floating in the-er-water?" – those were the kind of remarks he imagined the future Commander Sparey making. He drove the Countess into such a temper once that she swept all the pieces off the board.'

Walter Sparey's revolutionary ideas did not encompass interior decoration. There was nothing original or daring or subversive about the bunches of red roses tied with green ribbons that covered the walls of the nest in which he hatched his plans for a liberated England. I had seen those flowers before, in the Wilkins's front room. 'It's like a tart's parlour, Gabriel lad. Don't tell your mother I said so, but that's what it reminds me of. Not that I've ever been in one. Just hearsay.'

What tearing, ripping, clawing and scraping it took to clear my retreat of Walter Sparey's chosen paper – a whole weekend of manic effort. It was only when I had finished, when I descended from a chair and surveyed my handiwork, when I was welcoming the prospect of fresh white paint and wondering if my vertigo-afflicted landlady actually possessed a stepladder, that it occurred to me I should have to find a job, and quickly. I had paid a month's rent in advance; I had spent nearly thirty shillings on food; I now had a mere one pound eleven left in my Baptist Missionary Society savings. The might-have-been heir of 'Blenheim' was desperately in need of money.

Words, words, words – millions upon millions of them, and not one for me.

'You'll be able to sort these with your eyes shut, once you've got the knack.'

'That doesn't make sense. How could I see the addresses?'

'My feeble joke, youngster. What I meant was that you won't have to study each and every single solitary letter like it was Holy Writ, once you've got the knack. "With your eyes shut" was just a manner of speaking.'

'I understand.'

'South-west, North-west, South-east, North-east: watch me and you'll soon be doing it in your sleep. In a manner of speaking.'

'Thank you, Mr –'

'The name's Mude. If it didn't have an "e", my name would be Mud. Another of my feeble jokes, youngster. Harold Mude is who I am.'

'Harvey. Gabriel Harvey.'

'Gabriel? There's a spade who cleans the gents' bogs at King's Cross station, a real philosopher he is, tribal marks down both his pitch black cheeks – well, he's Ezekiel. Next time I wash my hands and powder my face – in a manner of speaking – in his vicinity, I'll let him know I've met a man after his own heart. You and he could strike up a really interesting conversation, youngster, what with your wherewithal about the ram with two horns and the rough goat, and his being so nifty with those dry bones, putting flesh on them like he did – yes, I'll inform Ezekiel I've made your celestial acquaintance, you can be sure. That letter you've got in your hand goes in Surrey – three boxes to your right. If my sense of humour doesn't drive you barmy first, you'll cope, I'm certain.'

'I hope so, Mr Mude.'

'I'm Mudey to my mates. Did you ever see that picture *The Outlaw*?'

'No, I didn't. I wasn't allowed to. I think my father saw it.'

'I bet he did, the rascal. I bet every father in the land sneaked out of the house to get an eyeful of that Miss Jane Russell putting her best breast forward. Even *I* went missing from the wife the week *The Outlaw* was showing at the Odeon, I have to be honest with you. There was this phrase on the poster advertising the film – it said "Mean, Moody and Magnificent". If you ever hear shouts of "Mean!" and "Magnificent!", you'll realize it's me – Mudey – who's wanted. I do believe you're smiling.'

'Yes, I am.'

'It's healthy exercise for the face muscles. Keeps them in trim. Guarantees that your lips won't curl up at the edges in a sneer. I do believe you're laughing. Mock not, youngster, mock not. You're doing your lungs a good turn now.'

'Making Mount Pleasant pleasanter' – that was Mudey's avowed purpose. 'When you consider the miserable wretches who were cooped up in this neighbourhood a century back, it becomes your bounden duty to act cheerful. That's my way of looking at it, youngster.'

Which miserable wretches were they, I asked?

My plump fellow-sorter answered me in what his high, bright voice could manage of sombreness. The *which*, the *they*, were those poor dregs of humanity who were thrown into the Cold

Bath Fields Prison – an institution so terrible, its very name made folk quake in their innocent boots. It had stood, give or take a yard or two, where we were standing now. 'I sometimes think of those luckless perishers when I'm on night-shift. I know I shall be going home to a bed the wife's kept warm for me, followed by a blow-out of a breakfast in the early afternoon – and I wonder at those rows and rows of criminals who were made to suffer for their sins, great and small. And when I've stopped shivering – in a manner of speaking – I smile at my good fortune.'

(On an afternoon of intense heat, in Sorg, Minnesota, I had a hasty vision of the resolutely happy Mudey acknowledging the greetings of his workmates – 'How's the world treating you today, Mean?'; 'You'll be grinning at your own funeral, you will, Magnificent' – in the sorting office where he befriended me in the autumn of 1954. I had been lying in Dr Olson's hammock, slung between two trees in Dr Olson's yard, flicking through the pages of the Nonesuch *Coleridge*, when I found myself reading 'The Devil's Thoughts', the satirical poem Coleridge composed with Robert Southey:

> As he went through Cold-Bath Fields he saw
> A solitary cell;
> And the Devil was pleased, for it gave him a hint
> For improving his prisons in Hell ...

The Coleridge/Southey Devil was an early visitor to the prison, going through as he did in 1799, when it was only five years old – its terrors were thus already established in infancy. I remembered the history lesson Mudey had given me on that long-ago October morning, as he deftly aimed each letter into its appropriate box: 'There's no evidence to suggest that this little stretch of London was ever pleasant. As for the mount, I think it was no more than a hump on the far bank of the Fleet River. People throw their rubbish there, and by rubbish I mean the putrid stuff that grows into a laystall. "What's a laystall?" you'd be asking if I drew breath. It's a tip, youngster, of a kind that's vanished along with the word. Stillborn babes were chucked on it in the dark. The next time you walk down Laystall Street, just stop and think how it got its name. The man who dreamed up "Mount Pleasant" must have been a wag-and-a-half. I should like to have met him, youngster, and shaken him by the hand. He knew the meaning of, the value of, humour, if anyone did.')

'Mudey, this is from Malta!'

'What are you interrupting me to say?'

'This postcard has come from Malta.'

'And what's so surprising about that? You'll see hundreds of those while you're here. Had it come from Surinam, now, or the North or South Pole, it would have been worth remarking on, but not when it's from a common-or-garden place like Malta.'

I did not tell Mudey that my wandering mother had been, and possibly still was, on the island; that a hope was rising in me that while I was here, at the source, I might dip into a sack and bring out a card or letter written by Amy Harvey and addressed to – to whom? Her son, perhaps.

'It's a view of Valletta.'

'I'm sure it is.'

Perhaps she kept in touch with someone in her 'secret place'; perhaps there was a relative somewhere with whom she still corresponded: I'd know her handwriting instantly. I would have to keep my eyes peeled for her Greek 'e's, her always slightly isolated 'w's.

Without intending to, I memorized the message from Dilys in Valletta: *Dearest Chesty – Weather but Glorious – Too too solid Flesh positively melting fast – Raising my Pimms to you avec Love et Kisses* ...

Dilys's 'Chesty' was a Mr Valentine Gray, I insanely recall, who lived in Nectar Cottage, in Herstmonceux, in Sussex.

My father's perpetual 'young man' indicated that I had offended him in some deeply devious way. I might have pleased him had I contrived to bypass adolescence, or so I supposed then. 'What's in that skull of yours is beyond my comprehension, it really is, young man,' the expert on suede shoes, drunken cooks and sundry arcane subjects had recently observed. 'I may yet live to see you grow up.'

Mudey's 'youngster', by contrast, recognized, even celebrated, my greenness. There was no hint of reproach in it. He used it casually, the right word among others. I was willing to play pupil to his teacher – for such, from the very beginning, was the nature of our relationship. I was a listener again, the more docile for not being glared at. I suddenly wanted to be possessed of knowledge – Cold Bath Fields knowledge, laystall knowledge; the kind that often invites indifference, scorn, derision. I wanted to have it at my fingertips.

(I did not have it there until I sat down at my accusing desk a decade later – sat myself down to write, that is; not to doodle, not to scribble.)

'The wife's a stickler for tradition, youngster. She was brought up as a kiddy to eat fish on Fridays – even if it was only a pennyworth of sprats – so fish on Fridays it still is. We're not Catholics, I can't say exactly what we are, but she's got it fixed in her mind that some terrible fate is lying in store for us if we make a change. That's why it's steamed cod tonight, so help me.'

I did not learn Mrs Mude's Christian name for several months. The revelation that she was Ivy as well as 'the wife' came in unusual circumstances. The lady herself wasn't present because 'she lives with the radio of an evening' and 'crowds bring her out in a rash', and Mudey and I were at Collins's Music Hall on Islington Green. We were there for two reasons: the first was that I had 'successfully failed' to be enlisted for National Service, and that was 'no small cause for painting the town'; the second was that Mudey had an old chum who was 'nearly topping the bill' – 'He rarely does London these days. Confines himself to Glasgow and Liverpool, where he maintains he's better appreciated. His act's worth catching, youngster. You won't see another like it.'

Stanley ('The Mortal') Vale began his unique performance by forcing himself out of a coffin. The lid once open, he stared for a long minute at the world he had been about to leave: 'Goodness me, that was a close shave!' he whispered eventually. He stood up slowly, taking in deep breaths, and then stepped daintily on to the stage: 'Accidents *will* happen, won't they? I wonder if they did a post-mortem? Shall I look for the scar? Yes, please, I didn't hear them answer. They always sew you up again, don't they? Makes a nice impression.' 'The Mortal' turned his back on the audience, opened his black coat and unbuttoned his white shirt and gasped, 'It's here. Straight down the middle, as golfers say. They've done some beautiful sewing – beats my white-haired mother's cross-stitching any time. I wonder if they put everything back? I wouldn't like to think that I'm walking around with a bit missing. Hospital cats get hungry ... Talk among yourselves, if you please, while I adjust my clothing.

Gorgeous handiwork as it is, it's not a sight for sensitive souls. Yes, you do hear stories,' he reiterated, facing us once more. 'You hear alarming stories.'

'The Mortal' told some of them, in a voice that was not alarmed. They had a common setting – an infernal operating theatre in which the wrong limbs were removed and the wrong parts replaced. Surgical instruments were dropped by distracted nurses into the helpless bodies on the table, only to be sewn inside when the surgeon was done: ' "It's just a stomach ache, Mr Golightly. Nothing more complicated. What a hiatus over a little hernia!" '

Mr Golightly went. 'Heavily, ladies and gentlemen, thanks to the scalpel stuck in his – begging your pardon – guts.' Mrs Golightly went, too: with a thud, in the coroner's court, after hearing the reason for Mr G.'s surprising exit. Pale hands were rubbed at the undertaker's when the young Golightlys – pinching each other to check that they hadn't gone as well – asked for a slap-up send-off for their scalpelled Pa and struck-down Ma and were promised the best the parlour could provide by the ever-so-solemn Mr Graves: ' "Rely on us" – rub, rub, not too fast, rub, rub – "in your hour of *double*" – rub, rub – "need." Rub-a-dub-*double*, thinks Mr Graves, his palms itching as they always do when business is brisk. He says to himself – rub, rub – "This is the life, this is." '

'Picture those poor Golightlys, shaken with grief, eyes be-dimmed –' ('Kindly show some respect,' ' The Mortal' admonished a woman in the circle, whose laughter rose in a shrill crescendo above everyone else's. 'Your cackle, Madam, is most unseemly') – 'with eyes *bedimmed*, as I was saying before I was so *disrespectfully* interrupted, Brother and Sister Golightly took their leave of Mr Graves – rub, rub – and joined the passing throng outside. They needed to cross the road – didn't they? – to catch the bus that would transport them to their once-happy abode, where Ma would not be waiting with a delicious tea and Pa would not be sitting with his nose stuck in the evening paper. That's what they had to do. But they didn't look right, left and right again, did they? They couldn't see – with their *bedimmed* eyes – a huge great articulated lorry heading straight in their direction. If anybody here doesn't know what an articulated lorry is, allow me to correct their abysmal ignorance. It's a vehicle – ladies, gentlemen, and cackler – what is driven by a well-spoken driver. You are required to have a cut-glass accent if you wish to manoeuvre an *ar-tic-u-la-ted* lorry. Lesson over. Anyhow, can you guess what happened? Did the lorry avoid Master and Miss Golightly? It pains me to say it didn't. Mr Graves couldn't believe his luck – rub, rub; rub, rub. His eyes – which were professionally bedimmed, which means they weren't really – blinked pounds, shillings and pence as he surveyed the wondrous cross he would be ordering for no less than *four* Golightlys – rub for Pa, rub for Ma, rub for son, rub for daughter. But Fate had different plans up her back sleeve for that smug Mr Graves, standing there a-rubbing and a-rubbing – I'll say She did. She didn't tell him he was looking at the last of the Golightlys and that their only surviving relation was so distant as to be invisible – and stony-broke into the bargain, somewhere high in the mountains of Mourne. Mr Graves had a quartet of unclaimed Golightlys on his premises and no one to pay for their slap-up send-off: rosewood coffins, as requested by Master Golightly; marble monument, ditto; the Works, in fact. The shock, when it came, was too much for Mr Graves. His ticker stopped at a quarter-past three on a wet Whit Monday and Mrs Graves had to be given smelling-salts to bring her round. Thus ends my *cautionary* tale. Walk a straight line when you leave this house of sin and disrepute, ladies, gentlemen, and the person having hysterics in the upper vault, and *do* be *cautious* when you step off the kerb. Remember – too much liquid refreshment bedims the peepers, and you could find yourselves in the path of a well-spoken driver. Exhibit *caution*: that's my advice, isn't it, Paderewski?'

'The Mortal' peered into the orchestra pit. 'Paderewski accompanies me on the joanna, I must warn you. When he's here, I mean. Ah, there he is, emerging from the Stygian gloom. I have to catch his unbedimmed, because he's deaf as the last post. I've got him now. He's flashing his tombstone teeth at me. Music, Maestro, p-lease!'

As Paderewski played the Dead March from *Saul*, 'The Mortal' announced that he was going to wind up the proceedings with a little ditty of his own decomposing entitled 'I'm Pushing Up the Daisies'. He jumped on to the coffin, cleared his throat, and began:

> I'm pushing up the daisies –
> Ain't they lovely how they sprout?
> Every time you pick one

I give a silent shout –
Ooh! Ouch! Care-ful!
That's ME you're pulling about!

He then executed (his word) a tap-dance of sorts. 'I'm available for wakes at a very moderate price.'

We're pushing up the daisies,

we sang, at his invitation,

Ain't they lovely how they sprout?
Every time you pick some
We give a silent shout –
Oooh! Ouch! Care-ful!
That's US you're pulling about!

(I was often to recall that Saturday evening at Collins's while I was working on *Lords of Light*. I liked to remember Stanley ('The Mortal') Vale inviting his admirers to join him in a jubilant chorus or two: 'All together, daisy-pushers – and don't forget you are "we" not "I". I want you to hear you "we"-ing, loud and strong.' I would leave my preachers to their hectoring and imagine myself back in that vanished auditorium, among those happy hundreds happily invoking a daisied future. No hell-fire, no harps, no leering Satan or welcoming Saint Peter – just daisies sprouting; the common day's eye that opens in the first fierce light of spring and winks itself slowly shut with the late autumn mists. A perennial flower, the *Bellis perennis*, the weed of rich men's lawns and poor men's plots – 'Oooh! Ouch! Care-ful!' I say to myself several times a year on Putney Heath, in Richmond Park, whenever I stamp on it by accident.

Looking up from my manuscript, abandoning Pastor Spurgeon in his Metropolitan Tabernacle, I would wonder at the comfort the music halls provided. On nights when my mother was at her 'secret place', my father had stopped occasionally in the middle of a game of dominoes and talked of George Robey and Marie Lloyd as if they were his dear friends, his soul mates. He declared, once, that they and their kind had been his comforters. I had been impatient for him to make his disastrous move, and had listened to him with most of my mind occupied with winning tactics.

Comforters, dispensing balm – in jokes and ballads, in sketches and songs, in novelty acts as grotesque as they were macabre. Comforters with lived-in faces, singing of brutal or feckless husbands, charm-encrusted bigamists, gin-guzzling doctors, shifty clerics, hard-hearted rent collectors – a vast assortment of everyday scoundrels. Comforters, lightening the pain of the here-and-now with mockery – for they were veterans when it came to distress. Their comforting art had been nurtured on an abundance of indignities. Plaster cherubs, some plumper than others, beamed down on Cockney vestal virgins knocked off their plinths by dashing young cads who knocked them up as a consequence before deserting them for ever; on ferocious mothers-in-law, rolling-pins at the ready, waiting for the objects of their misguided daughters' affections to stagger home drunk from the pub on pay day; on *lions comiques*, those upstarts from the back streets who transformed themselves into Champagne Charlies and breakers of foreign banks – on such familiar scenes, on such vital people, those wise little angels of the second order beamed down for a century of comfort, in a thousand Alhambras and Empires throughout the British Isles.)

'I thought you might have forgotten me, Mortal.'

'Forgotten you, Harold? Of course I haven't. A modest bastard like you? You're the rarest bloody bird among all the rare birds I've met in my travels. Come in, old pal, and have a drink.'

Mudey pushed me in front of him as we entered Stanley Vale's dressing-room.

'I see you and Ivy have been busy in the intervening years.'

'What do you mean, Mortal?'

'This blushing lad is the fruit, as they say, of your loins, isn't he? In other words, your son, Harold. You've been typically quiet about him.'

'He works at the sorting office with me, does Gabriel. He's Mr and Mrs Harvey's, not mine.'

'Pleased to meet you, Gabriel. Who do you remind me of? Don't give me a clue. Let me guess. You're the very image of him, whoever he is. His name will come back to me in a minute.'

Stanley Vale's face, without its deathly white make-up, was the colour of beetroot.

'I can only offer you milk stout. I thrive on the stuff. There's a crate of it in the corner, Harold. Be a gent and do the honours.'

'I brought the youngster to see you, Mortal, because I thought it would be an education for him, your sense of humour.'

'An education my backside! I've never known a man to take being funny so seriously. Education! You haven't changed, Harold. Is this your first visit to a music hall, then, Gabriel?'

'No, it's my second,' I said. 'I went with my mummy and – I went with my parents, when I was small.'

'Smaller,' he corrected me. 'You're small now.'

'Yes, I am. When I was much younger, when I was nine, I went with them to the Grand at Clapham Junction. The artists were very, very old; even older than my father. He kept saying, "She was a beauty thirty years ago" and "He's past his peak". I was confused, Mr Vale. I don't think I enjoyed myself.' I added, in a rush: 'As I did this evening.'

'That's gracious of you. I *was* on good form, though I speaks as shouldn't. That female hyena helped – I wouldn't have got half the laughs if she hadn't given her throat an airing. She set her neighbours off, and I was away on a cloud. I ought to hire her to follow me around. Where's my drink, Harold? I'm parched.'

'Here you are, Mortal. I've poured it as you like it, with just a whisker of foam on the top.'

'Thank you kindly, Harold. Is Gabriel of an age to partake?'

'I'm eighteen, Mr Vale.'

'He deserves a glass tonight. He failed his army medical yesterday. I'm pleased to say he failed it with honours, Mortal. They told him outright, the doctors did, that they didn't want him. "You're totally unfit for service in Her Majesty's forces," they said. That's worth celebrating – wouldn't you agree, Mortal?'

'My sainted aunt, Harold, you really are the most peculiar bugger in the entire universe. Listen to me, Gabriel. That man there was decorated for bravery during the war. Yes, he was. That same man who's happy that you haven't been called up has had a cross pinned on his chest for bravery in battle – in Africa, in the desert, wasn't it, Harold?'

'Never mind where it was. Enough of that, Mortal. The youngster's got shot, in a manner of speaking, of the whole mucky business, and I for one am totally delighted.'

'Don't snap my head off. You're a hero in my book, and so you ought to be in Gabriel's, too. Chin chin, chaps. What did you connoisseurs make of Kevin O'Strangled?'

'Who?' asked Mudey.

'The Irish tenor, so-called, who topped the bill. That's my name for the Brylcreemed bogtrotter with the famous lilting larynx. I'd spare my worst enemy the ordeal of having to hear him throb his way through "Sanctuary of the Heart". And when he does his nightingale impersonation, I want to heave my dinner up –' He stopped, looked at me intently for a moment, then clicked his fingers and said, 'That's it! Now I know who it is you remind me of – the nightingale man himself. It's John Keats you resemble.'

'Oh? Do I? Me?'

'You honestly do. The Severn drawing of 1816, with the wonderful left-eyed stare. Keats was a short-arse, same as you. His friends threw tufts of daisies on his grave in Rome. I had him somewhere in my mind when I bashed out my silly ditty thirty-odd years ago. That would be before the song-strangler in the star's dressing-room was conceived – if that *is* how he came into the world.'

'You admire Keats, do you, Mr Vale?'

'I detect surprise in your question. Reverence is what I feel for the little lad. Nothing less.'

While the comedian took off his 'Mortal remains' and changed into his 'living vestments', I asked him if he wrote his own material.

'I do and I don't. I collect it from life, Master Keats. Take tonight's cautionary tale: it actually happened. Imagine the sheer bloody joy that swept over me when I found it there, in print, in a Sunday newspaper. I couldn't have fared better if I'd been doorman at the House of Atreus. The scalpel in the stomach, the widow croaking in the coroner's court, the kiddies mown down by a lorry – true, true, and again true. Facts, I'm afraid; not my fancy roaming. My pathetic imagination could only dredge up the names Golightly and Graves.'

In Glasgow, he said, he provided his canny customers with more elaborate details, of the medical variety. They lapped them up, up north. 'Mention rigor mortis and they start slapping their sides. Ghoulish, they are. That was my tactful version you just witnessed. Christ, this eau-de-Cologne stings! It must contain acid. All in a good cause, though, if it makes my armpits charmpits.'

'Casanova time, is it, Mortal?'

'When isn't it, Harold? My craving for the female form divine shows no sign of abating, I'm happy to report. The barmaid in the pub across the green has taken a fancy to yours truly, a fancy – need I say? – that's healthily reciprocated. Why don't we leave this pox doctor's cubby hole and have a pint or two in there?'

'They won't let me in,' I said. 'I look too young.'

'Oh yes, they will, never you fear. I'll vouch for your maturity, Gabriel Keats. If needs must, I'll spin them a yarn about you being one of my long-lost sons.'

'You bloody rogue, Mortal.'

'That's me. Have you got a father, Gabriel?'

'What kind of question's that? He'd be a right freak if he hadn't.'

'I meant living, Harold. I got the impression from what the boy was saying that his dad was a late starter in the siring trade.'

'Yes, I have, Mr Vale.'

'And a mother, I expect? Living?'

'Yes, Mr Vale. Mummy's alive.'

'The Countess ordered me to give you this,' said Mrs Sparey, handing me a grubby envelope. The Countess's name and address had been crossed out and the words 'The New Resident' scrawled alongside them. Inside was a scrap of notepaper on which was written: 2 *eggs,* BROWN *ones, I cannot endure the white they are inferior and taste* STRANGE. *Also a small cabbage with a firm heart. Look at it carefully Diana before parting with my money there was a* SLIMY SLUG *in the last one you purchased for me. No bread today. Pound note enclosed.*

'It's a message for you, Mrs Sparey. About eggs and a cabbage.'

'Your command will be on the reverse, I should think.'

It was. It read: *The Countess* BOLINA *requests the pleasure of The New Resident's Company for Tea in her portion of the house at 4 of the clock* PRECISELY *on Sunday next.* RSVP.

The following Sunday, at the appointed hour, I knocked on the door of Countess Bolina's room.

'If that is the new resident, enter. If it is not, vanish.'

A rabbit confronted me: a human, female rabbit, with a rabbit's protruding glassy eyes overhanging her heavily powdered cheeks; a nodding rabbit, with hair that was fiercely red above the brow but a pale orange beyond; a jewel-laden rabbit (pearl necklace, jade bracelets, rings on every finger) in an apple-green silk dress, which had its waistline sashed and bowed with striped velvet ribbon at the hip; a talking rabbit, who said, 'It is by Jean Patou, from his 1923 collection. It was designed to last, and it has. The fragile look is deceptive'; a rabbit who showed her rabbit's yellow teeth at the new resident, who stood amazed by the sight of her.

'Good afternoon. Your name is?'

'I am Gabriel Harvey. I've moved in upstairs. Good afternoon.'

'Be seated.'

She indicated a very low chair, of the kind known to the Victorians as a 'nursing'. There was one in a corner of the drawing-room at 'Blenheim' – 'That old maid recommended the useless thing. I took him at his word. Nobody's arse is ever likely to get parked on it, unless I befriend a midget or a dwarf. That means smaller than you are, Piss-a-Bed.'

I did as I was instructed, and found that my knees were almost level with my face.

'I shall not embarrass you by speaking French.'

I didn't reply that I would have little difficulty understanding her, that neither of us would be at all embarrassed, since I still had a reasonable command of the language, despite my three years' laziness as a Lily.

'The English are appalling linguists, Mr – Mr – '

'Harvey.'

'Harvey. It may surprise you to hear that I was speaking French before I was acquainted adequately with my mother tongue – which is Russian, as Diana has no doubt already informed you.'

'Yes, she has, your – um – '

' "Countess" is sufficient, and appropriate.'

'Thank you, Countess.'

'I was not always so *confined*, Mr Harvey. You cannot begin to envisage the life I once led.'

'No, Countess.'

'No, indeed, Mr Harvey. You cannot. It is impossible for you, quite impossible. You see me here surrounded by the few possessions I have been fortunate to save – or, to be accurate, retrieve. Diana insults me by calling them clutter. Clutter! Such an ugly English word! Is Sèvres clutter? Is Dresden? I have a few pieces of both. You see a worn-out survivor, not the true Countess Bolina, Mr Harvey.'

What was I required to say? 'I do?' 'Do I?' I was silent.

The worn-out rabbit-Countess had retained enough energy to talk, however. I tried hard to follow the monologue she kept interrupting with sudden, private chuckles. She was offering me her autobiography in miniature, I soon realized. 'I was born in St Petersburg, twenty-three years before it was changed to Petrograd,' she began, coyly. Her brisk narrative swiftly accounted for the annual ceremony of breaking the ice that covered the Neva; her beloved brothers Dmitri and Nikolai, whose heads were shaved every summer to protect them from vermin; the family's *dacha* near Krasnoe Selo; the imperial funeral of the Tsar's uncle, Alexey Alexandrovich; the Bronze Horseman, the Nevsky Prospect, the Hotel d'Angleterre; her father, a senior civil servant; her mother, an addict of George Sand's novels; the Vorontsov Palace, where Dmitri and Nikolai joined the Corps of Pages and learned to dance as well; her first encounter in a ballroom with the desperately handsome Bolin; her marriage to him in – oh, never mind the year!; the wretched Kerensky; murmurs of another, bigger revolution; escape to Paris with her astute husband, who was quicker than most to read the writing on the wall – 'Our escape led to permanent exile, Mr Harvey.' On she went, in a rush, about her twin passions – the ballet and *haute couture* ('Fashion, Mr Harvey'); Nijinsky's leap through the window in *Spectre de la rose* ('*Spirit of the Rose*'); Karsavina's Torch Dance in *Une Nuit d'Égypte* ('*A Night in Egypt*'); dear, sad-at-heart Sergei Diaghilev; Stravinsky – ah, what a shock to the musical system!; 'Coco' Chanel – '*Quelle simplicité!*' (This observation was not translated); darling, darling Patou – 'Poor Mr Harvey, you have only my feeble memory to guide you through the maze. I crave your forgiveness.' Her arrival in London was remembered next, in the same breath: 'The Count and I were cast down by its drabness.' There were certain compensations – opera at Covent Garden, dinner at the Savoy, trips to Ascot and the tennis at Wimbledon, the giddying social whirl. Bolin had secured a most attractive appointment in a finance company and the future looked rosy for them in exile. 'Rosy, I don't think!' shouted the Countess, causing me to start forward. 'Bolin was poisoned, in this dirty city, and my grand life was over – whoosh! – in an instant. That is why you see me here, Mr Harvey, in my

Clerkenwell confinement. Let us have tea now. The samovar is ready.'

After my friend Peter Fisher left England for Cyprus, where he was to be stationed with the army, I knew no one of my own age, with my own interests. I kept the company of talkers, older people who had much to tell me: Harold Mude, whose wife preferred to listen to the words coming out of her radio; Diana Sparey, mocking the Countess ('A bad oyster polished off her husband, not a Soviet agent'); the Countess, complaining of Diana ('She has no right to be so perverse'); and an initially distrustful Mr Nazareth, who revealed his ambition to me when he had decided that I was hopelessly impractical and unlikely to hinder his advancement. 'The realist meets the dreamer, Harvey. We shall get along fine. Shake my hand, if you please.'

Between their confidences, away for a while from their chatter, I stood in the 'cursed modern eyesore' and gave my ears the holiday they needed.

7

'Mr Harvey! Mr Harvey! There is a frightfully common man in your room. He banged and banged on the front door until I was driven to open it. He insisted, but insisted, on going up. I told him he was intruding on private property. He is most vulgarly attired, in a loud check suit. He has the manner of a commercial traveller.'

'Thank you for warning me, Countess.'

'He is older, I think, than he appears. He is past his prime. I cannot imagine how you met him.'

'I can't, either. Until I see who he is.'

'He boasted that he knows you better than anyone else. He said he wanted to give you a pleasant surprise. And then he leered, Mr Harvey. Leered.'

It was inevitable, I thought, the moment I saw him: I am really surprised that it has taken so long.

'The starving artist in his garret, eh, young man?'

'I'm not an artist, Father. And I'm not starving.'

'You're not strong enough to join the army, are you? If this great country of ours was under attack, you'd be up a gum tree, wouldn't you?'

(You did not fight in Flanders, Oswald Harvey. You did not answer Kitchener's call to arms. You were never shell-shocked or gassed. You contrived not to serve in the trenches, according to your other son, Tom. How I laughed at that ancient news, passed on to me by your disdainful first-born: 'Our beloved Daddykins at the front? The only conflict he's ever experienced is with his wives.')

'Wouldn't you?'

'It's a hypothetical question.'

'I've known of your whereabouts for months, young man. I thought I'd let you stew in your own juice for a bit. I was damned if I was going to help you. My presence here is purely accidental, you might say. I've been in the City all afternoon, consulting my cursèd solicitors on the little matter of my last will and testament and the idea struck me of paying my boy a friendly visit. And here I am.'

'Here you are,' I said.

'Unable to sit down, it seems. Is that bloody desk contraption the nearest thing to a chair you've got?'

'Yes, it is. Try the bed.'

'And have the stench of your piss up my nostrils? No, thank you.'

'There isn't a stench any more. Your nose won't be offended.'

'You mean you've stopped?'

'Yes, I have. Completely.'

'I think I'll stand, just the same.'

'As you wish.'

'What's the name of the place in France, that shrine, where all the Catholic cripples go?'

'Lourdes.'

'Did you pop over there, then, for your miracle cure?'

'Of course not.'

'Will-power?'

'Probably.'

'Nice to know you've gained some. How's your job?'

'I sort a lot of letters.'

'You've only yourself to blame for that.'

'I quite enjoy sorting a lot of letters.'

'Like hell you do.'

'What do you want with me, Father?'

'I want you to come to your cursèd senses, that's what I want with you, young man. Look at this dump. Is that apology for a sink all you have to wash in?'

'There's a bathroom downstairs, for your information. I share it with the other residents.'

'Residents? "Inmates" would be nearer the mark, to judge by that daft old foreign biddy who let me in.'

'She's a genuine aristocrat,' I told him. 'She's a countess.'

He was silent for a moment.

'I remember Sir Vincent telling me once', he began, slowly, 'that one of the differences between us English and other nations is that we don't have a surplus of titles. We don't have counts and countesses galore, as they have all over Europe. We've made sure, in this little island, that our gentry is real gentry, a gentry to look up to and respect, not a collection of odds and sods.'

'Is that so?'

'It is, believe you me, young man.'

I lay down on the bed on which my father scorned to sit. I would hear out his lecture in comfort.

'Come to think of it, we don't have countesses in England at all. We have duchesses instead. They're very high up, they are – just a rung short of royalty. They don't end their days in Clerkenwell doss-houses, screaming their heads off at respectable callers, like that mad bitch I had the honour – ha, ha – of meeting an hour ago.'

(Did my father, the master of 'Blenheim', consider himself sane? I remembered how, on the morning after my thirteenth birthday party, Peter Fisher had said to me in the playground at Lily's: 'Your dad, Gabriel – he's not all there. He's gone in the head, isn't he?' And I had answered, without hesitation: 'Yes.' Our friendship, I understand now, had deepened instantly.)

'Sir Vincent, of course, was a baronet, young man.'

'Was he?'

(Why, why did I ask? Of course Sir Vincent was a baronet. I knew he was. How could I not know, having been told so often?)

'He certainly was,' continued the glaring trespasser, encouraged by the asinine question. 'And they don't come two a penny, baronets. I suppose you feel you're mixing with the mighty, do you?'

'No, Father. I never even began – '

'Because you aren't, most definitely you aren't. Half the Poles in Shepherd's Bush are counts, young man. They serve you in the shops, and collect your fares on the buses. They're everywhere in West London. I met a matchseller once said he was a count, and I believed him, titles being as tinpot as they are across the Channel. She's Polish, is she?'

'Countess Bolina is Russian. *White* Russian, she says.'

(I did not tell Oswald Harvey that I was the Countess's part-time serf, her occasional errand boy. I had been granted the privilege of purchasing her 'few little luxuries' for her: packets of tea from the Algerian Coffee Stores in Soho; tiny pots of Danish lumpfish roe – 'Let us make pretend they are the sturgeon's' – from a German delicatessen in Kingsway; and a monthly bar of dark chocolate from Charbonnel et Walker in

Bond Street, of which I was given – 'A present for going' – a single square, neatly broken off, which I ate very slowly, pondering its immense cost.)

'Anyhow, young man, I didn't walk all the way here from Rose and Crown Court just for a natter about Poles and Russians, white or otherwise. I've been on last-will-and-t business today. I'm an old man, in case you hadn't noticed, and it stands to reason that I haven't long to live.'

(Only another twenty-four years, Father. Only another twenty-four years.)

'You'd welcome some spending money, wouldn't you? You can't be earning much, sorting letters. Fifteen brand-new oncers would burn a pleasant hole in your pocket, eh?'

'No, thank you. Put your wallet back.'

'They'll cut your hands, they're so crisp and sharp.'

'No, Father. Thank you.'

'You can't say I didn't offer.'

'That's true. I can't.'

'I tell you what. Why don't I treat you to a three-course meal? Change into your suit, if you still have it, because Oswald Harvey doesn't take his custom to the kind of restaurants where proper clothes aren't worn. Best bib and tucker, if you please, young man.'

'I have a prior engagement,' I announced, delightedly.

'You've what?'

'A prior engagement, Father.'

'A prior my arsehole! Cancel it.'

'I don't want to.'

'Stop being a stubborn ass. Throw in the towel, can't you. Anyone would think I'm your enemy, instead of – well, who I am. We could go on to a night-club afterwards.'

'No, thanks.'

'You're seeing a girl, you sly young sod, aren't you? I'm glad to hear it. About bloody time, if you want my opinion. I'd already started rogering when I was only knee-high to a grasshopper, I'll have you know.' He guffawed suddenly. 'When you're not sorting them, you're wearing them, eh?'

'Wearing? Wearing what?'

'French letters, you villain. At least, I *hope* you're wearing them. You'll pay the price in bastards if you aren't. Accept that fifteen quid and put it to a good cause, there's a sensible fellow – go out and buy yourself a lorry-load of rubber protection. Trap your wild oats before they can lead you into trouble, that's my advice.'

'I don't have a girlfriend. I don't need or want your money.'

'Oh, come on, be open, be honest with me. You're at the age when a chap who's really a chap thinks of nothing else. Listen, if she's presentable, this girl of yours, if she's not the tarty type, if she's well spoken and polite and not just a knicker-dropper, why don't you invite her to join us? I'll be on my best behaviour, never fear. I'll charm her, I promise. I won't embarrass you.'

'Father, stop – '

'Have I been too near the knuckle for you? It's love, is it? You're saving yourselves, the pair of you, are you? Well, that's very good, that's very noble. I wish I'd had some of your self-control when I was – '

'Didn't you hear me? Stop, will you. I don't have a girlfriend, I'm not saving myself. I'm not in love – '

'Yes, you are. You wouldn't be shouting at me if you weren't. I've hit on the truth. "A prior engagement" – I get your meaning now. You've gone and got yourself engaged, I'll be bound.'

'Then you're bound wrongly – '

'I'd wait a bit, if I were you. I'd play the field. I'd have a few more bites of the forbidden fruit, I would, before I tied myself down – '

'Father, I am going out to eat this evening with a fellow-lodger. Or an inmate, if you prefer. I'll introduce you to him. Then you might believe me.'

Mr Nazareth said he was 'most curious' to meet 'the abandoned parent'. He would present himself in what Mrs Sparey called 'a jiffy'.

My father was still standing when I returned to my room.

'He'll be up in a – in a jiffy.'

'Will he? Who's the funny chap in the hat?' he asked, pointing at the picture above my desk.

'George Fox. The founder of the Quakers.'

'Thought his mug looked unfamiliar. He's on the porridge packets, isn't he?'

'Someone like him.'

'Joined the faith, have you?'

'No.'

'That's a relief.'

Mr Nazareth had his own interpretation of the meaning of the word 'jiffy'. Long, silent minutes passed.

'You haven't asked me if I've heard from your mother.'

'I'm aware I haven't.'

'Which is strange. I'd have thought it would have been "Mummy this" and "Mummy that" the instant you clapped eyes on me. That's always been your way.'

'Not any more.'

'No?'

'No.'

'As it happens, young man, I haven't had a peep out of her since you went and did your bunk. Ours not to reason, I suppose.'

'I can't understand why you even bothered to mention it.'

'Keeping you up to date, that's all.'

I thanked him for having my interests at heart.

'I am not intruding, Harvey, I trust,' said an invisible Mr Nazareth from the landing.

'Do come in,' I called.

My father stood stupefied as Mr Nazareth walked jauntily into my room.

'I am delighted to make your acquaintance, Mr Harvey. Put it there,' he said, offering his right hand.

My father, in his stupefaction, did Mr Nazareth's friendly bidding.

'Good grief.'

'My name is Nazareth. I am nevertheless an atheist. My ancestors were hoodwinked – I think the word is – by mumbo-jumbo.'

'Mm? Were they, now? Were they really?' my father managed.

'Your son, Harvey here, assures me that you are a Darwinian.'

'A what? Darwinny-what?'

'Evolution, Mr Harvey.'

'Charlie Darwin, you mean? The scourge of Sunday schools? Yes, well, I know all about him.'

'His books are regularly banned and burned in America, one hears.'

'Well, yes, that's Yanks for you.'

'They are frightened, no doubt, of the truth.'

'Yes, well. There you are. Quite so.'

'I am truly pleased to meet you,' said Mr Nazareth, releasing my startled father from his grip. 'Harvey here has described your beliefs and habits to me in such detail that I feel I almost know you already.'

'Has he, now? Do you, now?'

'Oh, yes. Yes, indeed, Mr Harvey.'

(Niggers and part-niggers; Africans descending from trees, and Indians bowing and scraping – I had passed on Oswald Harvey's opinions to a bemused Mr Nazareth in the Three Crowns one Sunday. 'In the unlikely event of my ever meeting your pure progenitor, I should bestow upon him the courtesy he merits. You have had no occasion as yet, my friend, to see me at my most effusive.' I had occcasion now.)

'Well, yes, I ought to be flattered, I suppose. Better to be slandered than ignored.'

'Slandered, Mr Harvey? You misjudge your son.'

'Do I?'

'You do.'

'Well, if you say so. I'll have to believe you, since I haven't got much choice.'

Mr Nazareth smiled at my father and nodded.

'I am hoping you will join us for our monthly meal this evening, Mr Harvey. Do please honour us with your presence. You would have to go Dutch, of course. Such a quaint English expression – "go Dutch"! We cannot, alas, with our restricted funds, settle your portion of the bill.'

'Settle my portion? Nobody settles Oswald Harvey's portion, thank you kindly. Nobody. Never.'

'I did not wish to offend. The Taj Mahal is the restaurant of our choice. I have looked forward with eagerness to my prawn curry all this week. I am salivating at this moment. I shall have to exercise restraint when the waiter sets it down before me.'

'Curry? Did you say curry?'

'I certainly did, Mr Harvey. The Taj Mahal is an Indian restaurant – '

'The devil it is. It could hardly be anything else, could it. And you, young man, will you be eating curry?'

'Yes, Father. I usually have a Madras.'

'That settles it. That settles my portion, that does. I shall be dining alone tonight. Most definitely.'

'You are declining our invitation?'

'Invitation? Threat, more like. Yes, I am declining, you bet I am. I have eaten a curry but once in my life, and my bowel still bears the scars. I was shitting through the eye of a needle for days afterwards,' said my father, glaring at Mr Nazareth. 'For three days afterwards. My arse was on fire.'

'How regrettable.'

'On bloody fire. You chaps from down there must have cast-iron passages, that's all I can say. How else could you eat that stuff year in, year out?'

The question elicited a worldly-wise smile from Mr Nazareth.

'I don't want a burning bum tomorrow morning, young man, even if you do,' my father declared, limping to the door. 'I shan't have a volcano in my trousers, like a certain person I could name.'

'Is there something wrong with your foot?'

'No, there bloody isn't,' he snapped. 'By the way, I forgot to tell you, what with all this idle chatter about Taj Mahals and settling portions – your beloved aunt, old Swedie, is in hospital.'

'In hospital? Why?'

'Why is anyone in hospital, you oaf? Because she's ill, that's why. Under observation.'

'Have you seen her?'

'I try not to enter those places. They don't agree with me, so I give them a wide berth. She's in the Prince Regent Infirmary at Brighton, should you decide to play the dutiful nephew.'

I listened, enraged, as he clumped slowly down the stairs.

'Good night, gentlemen!'

'Good night, Mr Harvey. It was a pleasure meeting you.'

The front door was eventually slammed.

'A touch of gout, I expect. In your father's foot, Harvey. In his big toe, to be precise.'

'Let's get to the Taj Mahal. It's eight already, and I'm starving. I feel like ordering the hottest curry on the menu.'

'I can't seem to make them understand, Starch-angel. The Sister is convinced I am Italian, and therefore difficult. She and her nurses neither believe nor accept that I have an aversion to meat. Last night they brought me chicken soup and were indignant when I refused it. It's all very wearying.'

'I shall complain, Auntie.'

'Try sweet reason instead. I have complained till I'm hoarse. They must find me an impossible old harridan. Yes, Starch-angel, please beguile them with honeyed words – you might even persuade them that I'm not a member of the Church of England, as they will insist I am. Say the name Swedenborg to them in your most dulcet tones so that it registers in at least one brain, and I shall be the happiest of women.'

I promised to do as she wished.

'How did you know I was ill? And incarcerated?'

'Father told me.'

'You two are reconciled?'

'He paid me a surprise visit.'

(I did not tell my aunt that he had conveyed the news of her illness to me as though it were of no more importance than a change in the weather. There had been no hint of sadness in his voice, no sense of urgency.)

'That's a surprise he won't be paying his sister. He's been scared of hospitals since he was a youth. I should have to have him kidnapped, and bound hand and foot, to get him in here. And then he would fight his way out. Poor Oswald.'

'You're not angry with him, Auntie?'

'I've given up being angry with him. It's his nature, you hard-hearted Starch-angel. Your father can't endure the thought of not existing, and hospitals remind him that he has the same destiny as the rest of us. Surely you must have seen how quickly he walks past funeral parlours, with his head down in his chest. Few people have ever found the pavement so interesting.'

(I should have mentioned Johnny Tuohy then, and how my father had tried to save him. That dive into the icy Thames was not the act of a coward. His bravery had been immediate and self-regardless – or so he would have had me believe. Perhaps I feared Aunt Kathleen's possible revelation that Johnny's near-rescue had never happened, that her brother's leap was wholly imaginary. At that moment I wanted not to talk about him: I had travelled to Brighton to discover how *she* was, to express my sympathy, to offer her – I hoped – some comfort.)

'I'm glad they've put me on this side of the ward, Gabriel. I feel just that little bit closer to the sea. There was a storm yesterday, and the waves were making the most wonderful commotion. That silly creature in the next bed – may God pardon me for speaking with such contempt, but she really is unpardonably silly – actually asked the nurse on duty to please, please do something to stop the noise.'

'What did the nurse reply?'

'Lean over and I'll whisper it. Oh, but it made me chuckle! She said "Britannia rules the waves, Mrs Denton. I'd advise you to seek her assistance, because I doubt very much that they'll listen to me." Isn't that droll, Starch-angel? Isn't that choice?'

'Yes, it is.'

'There's more. Mrs Denton, silly Mrs Denton, was not amused by the answer. "Do you take me for a fool?" she shouted. "My late husband was a magistrate, I'll have you know. He sat on the bench!" The nurse remained wisely silent. "Monty would not have brooked your insolence!" And that, Starch-angel, is the only entertainment I have had in this building. I had to press my face into a pillow, to stifle my laughter.'

I was invited to help her stay skittish: 'Give me all your London gossip, dear. It won't matter a jot that it's concerned with total strangers. I'm sure you will bring them to life for me, as you did those funny schoolmasters years ago.'

I like to think I kept my aunt happy for an hour or more on that last of her coherent days. I began my performance – 'You're a natural mimic, my love. You've a gift for hitting people off' – with a description of the juddering house in Vineyard Walk, pointing out the many aspects of its varied dinginess in the manner of an eager and enthusiastic guide. I introduced her to its tenants, one by one. Of Mr Pringle, who occupied the basement and whom only the landlady, it seemed, had ever met, I could say nothing compelling. He was shy to the point of mania, and fled London every summer for the Yorkshire moors, where he cast off the cheeriness that engulfed him each hour of his working life – for Mr Pringle was a poet by trade, employed to compose a thousand different Yuletide greetings by a firm that produced Christmas cards. *We stand beneath the mistletoe/To see how far a kiss'll go* were the lines that had secured him his job in the desperate weeks following his demobilization from the navy – lines, Mrs Sparey said, the poor, haunted man still regretted having penned. Mr Nazareth had sighted him once, scurrying down the area steps, and was inordinately proud of the fact: 'I tend to opine that he sports a moustache, Harvey.'

Nazareth? Had she heard aright? '*Mister* Nazareth, Starch-angel?'

'Yes, Auntie. He's an Indian, from Goa.'

'That would make him a Catholic, then.'

'Not Mr Nazareth. He's forsworn the faith. He believes in not believing. He thinks religion's poppycock. Mumbo-jumbo.'

'A philosopher in Oswald's mould. The two great minds ought to meet.'

'They – '

'Madness, madness. My brother would disagree with your

131

Nazareth on principle. I must be wandering already. Please carry on as if I hadn't interrupted.'

In Hatton Garden, late one Sunday afternoon, I had seen on Mr Nazareth's face the rapt expression of a zealot, I said. 'Wealth, Harvey,' he had whispered. 'Wealth, wealth, wealth – oh, there's so much of it here!' I could picture it only in his bright eyes, however, since the diamond merchants' shops were shuttered up and barred, the treasures they contained invisible: 'I ache to be rich. Ache, Harvey.'

From the millionaire-to-be I turned to the disinherited Bolina, receiving me in her Jean Patou dress that was designed to last. I munched her words, rabbit-like – 'Is Sèvres clutter? Is Dresden?' – for my aunt's amusement. I described her feud with Diana Sparey, the revolutionary's widow, and tried to explain the deep affection that flourished beneath the insults the two women automatically afforded one another: 'You are not going demonstrating in this weather, Diana, for God's sake! You are far too old for such folly. Your leaflets and your banners will change nothing, and you might catch pneumonia'; 'So might you, if you once got up off your aristocratic behind and showed some concern for the human race. Things were changed in your country, you bloody fool, in case you've conveniently forgotten, and no thanks to Countess "Let them eat cake" Bolina!'; 'You really must invest in a new pair of spectacles, Diana, my dear – that sticking-plaster is so unbecoming!' Yet Mrs Sparey still shopped for her, still satisfied most of her demands, still called the unmistakable rabbit a 'pathetic old duck', while the Countess occasionally referred to the 'Clerkenwell cross I am fated to bear' in the happily bad-tempered tones of a person who knows of worse crosses, uglier fates. I detected love, I thought.

'It's indignity time, I'm afraid, Starch-angel. I need to pass water and I can't do it without assistance. Give me a goodbye kiss and ring for the nurse. In that order.'

I kissed my aunt's forehead. Then I rang a little handbell, and a nurse came.

'What is it now, Mrs Salvo?'

'The potty.'

My farewell kiss, Aunt Kathleen. And your farewell words in my hearing:

'The potty. Quickly.'

Dearest Starch-angel,

It was kind of you to visit me today. How inadequate that sounds. It was more than kind, my love – it was wonderfully thoughtful.

And what sweet reason you must have showered on that fearsome Sister Elstone, for tonight they brought me my own special salad – lettuce that was almost crisp, a ripe tomato, a few thin slices of cucumber, a pair of plump radishes and some sticks of celery. I munched away like that rabbity countess you mimic so amusingly. I swallowed everything on the tray, despite my lack of appetite, to prove to them that I am serious about not being a meat eater. I am now moderately hopeful that I have supplied them with ample evidence. If my pointed use of the word 'delicious' has not convinced the Sister and her staff, then nothing will. A perpetual optimist, your Aunt Kathleen.

Two more surprises followed swiftly upon the surprising dinner. The grim Elstone suddenly appeared with a bottle of sherry, from which she poured me a generous measure. No sooner had I taken a sip than Doctor Willis suddenly manifested himself at my bedside also and announced that he would operate – on me, that is – tomorrow. And that is why I am writing to you this evening, Starch-angel, rather than later – because I know what the evasive doctor knows, but hasn't told me. I am shortly to die.

My mortal self will have been returned to its elements by the time you receive this letter. The body is just an envelope, and the spirit goes on to the spiritual world – and that is where I feel I belong. Consider it your good fortune that the first bereavement in your life should be a tired aunt who is not – was not – distressed at the prospect of death. Which is not say to that she doesn't want you to mourn her! Please do so, she begs, but in the knowledge that she will be with Alessandro and Nora Rosen – whose eternal company she hopes and prays she merits.

Later, after a soothing hot milk drink:
I am worried, Starch-angel, by the turn your life is taking. I fear I have to offer you what is known as 'friendly advice', which is often a euphemism for 'arrogant inter-ference'. Here it comes, nevertheless. Try and heed at least a fraction of it, if you can.

I hate to think of you living on the outside of things, as you seem to be at the moment. The periphery, my love, is no place for a young man with your gifts: no place at all. You must make a move towards the centre. You will find it warmer there.

Let me explain myself. You strike me, Starch-angel, as a commentator rather than a participant. Your father is the same, even though he married three times –

'Three times!'
'Mr Harvey? Something's surprised you?'
No. No, Sister. I was only muttering. A habit I have.'

– even though he married three times. I had one husband and a perfect marriage, and wanted nothing more after Alessandro was cruelly taken from me. Poor Oswald was no sooner out of one pickle than he had got himself into a second – though how he fared with your young mother I can't say, since I hardly saw him during your childhood. He has always kept his distance, your father. He is happiest on the outside, where he can mock and scoff and voice his opinion that everyone else is crazy. As you are well aware, I have been raving mad for decades – in Oswald Harvey's distant view.

You were diverting company this afternoon, my love – for which many thanks. Do beware of becoming a collector of people (eccentric people) won't you. Look at yourself occasionally and have cause to laugh or wonder. And do please make a friend or two of your own age. And do do do give yourself to someone one fine day and shut the door on boarding-houses for ever. I have a horrible vision of Gabriel Harvey growing lonelier and lonelier in a succession of rooms ...

Your young mother has gone from you. She has left you, and now you must repair yourself. That should be your mission, your goal.

Even later, with a promise that my ramblings are nearly at an end:
You will be receiving a little money from me, dear, and twenty of my most cherished books. My neighbours, the Lindleys, have kindly agreed to scatter the remains of the burnt envelope on the Downs ...

134

I have a last wish. I want you to visit your distant father now and then, for my sake and in my memory, Starchangel. You will be a true man if you bear with him, you have my word for it. He is a poor creature, and he should be pitied.

Au revoir, my dearest. God bless you and keep you.

Your Auntie Kathleen

PS 'All religion has relation to life, and the life of religion is to do good.'

'Auntie knew she was dying.'

'Yes, she did. She let us know she knew as well. She bombarded the doctor with questions, Mr Harvey, and almost got out of him the straight answer she craved. When he told her the operation would be chancy, she smiled and said, "Just as I guessed." A strong-willed woman, Mrs Salvo.'

I did not correct Sister Elstone, who had yet to reveal her grimness to me.

'She found courage in her faith.'

'Ah, yes. It has an odd name, hasn't it?'

'She was a Swedenborgian.'

'Each to his own, Mr Harvey, each to his own. I'm a plain, common-or-garden, down-to-earth, Church-of-England Christian myself. Nothing different or peculiar. You're not, are you, a whatever-it-is?'

'No, Sister. I can't follow his thinking, to tell the truth. Swedenborg's, I mean.'

'Mrs Salvo must have followed it, I presume.'

'To the letter,' I said, in my ignorance.

'Hers was a good death, Mr Harvey. She simply drifted away. You really are her nephew, aren't you?'

'Why do you ask? Of course I am.'

'How rude of me. It's because you look too young. Far too young.'

'Her brother married my mummy when he was fifty-six,' I explained. And then I passed on the brand new information my aunt had sprung on me: 'She's his third wife.' I did not sound surprised. 'It seems there were two before Mummy,' I added, as flatly. 'Other Mrs Harveys, Sister Elstone.'

'"Blenheim". Oswald Harvey speaking.'

'Father —'

'Who the hell's there? That isn't you, Tommy Rotter, is it?'

'It's Gabriel, Father.'

'My, my, young man. To what do I owe this unexpected honour?'

'I have some news for you.'

'That's a good enough reason for picking up the telephone.'

'It's about Aunt Kathleen.'

'Then it must be news from the beyond. I was told only yesterday that she was dead.'

'Who told you?'

'Mind your manners, if you please. Who told me? Who do you think told me? The hospital told me, you oaf. They told me because I happen to be Swedie's next of kin, in case you hadn't realized.'

'I hadn't realized you'd been to visit Auntie,' I said, after a silence in which I decided against slamming down the receiver. Here was the first test of my true manhood, and I intended to pass it.

'As a matter of fact, I didn't manage to get to Brighton, though I toyed with the idea of paying her my respects. I don't know why it is, but hospitals and Oswald Harvey do not click, young man, they do not click at all. She had her religion, anyway. That was Swedie's compensation.'

'I've no more spare change, Father. I'll have to hang up.'

'Reverse the charges.'

'I'd rather not. Will you be at home – I mean, at "Blenheim" – for Christmas?'

'I've made no other plans. "Yes" is the answer.'

'Shall I come and spend it with you?'

'That's your affair. The board will be groaning at midday, as per usual. I'll see to it that the Quinlan woman cooks a sufficiency. But it's your affair, remember, young man. Yours entirely.'

Then he did the slamming.

It was as if a plague had hit the capital: London, that Christmas morning, was a city of the dead. A distraught ginger cat seemed to have the entire length of Holborn to itself – the creature's frantic mews followed me into a deserted Kingsway. A slumped drunkard snored on the steps of the Aldwych Theatre, but there was no one in the Strand – where I stopped for a moment by the restaurant in which the man of means had treated his wife and son to a celebration lunch eight Augusts past. 'Oh, Ossie love, please don't shame us.'

I marvelled at London's silence as I walked down Whitehall. The two mounted troopers of the Household Cavalry on duty at Horse Guards were impervious to the greeting I dared to shout across at them – I waited for a sneaking sign of recognition, the trace of a smile perhaps, but none came. I went on. I turned into Bridge Street and instantly bumped into a policeman who asked me if I was planning to blow up the Houses of Parliament: 'I'm in charge today, worse luck. Where are you off to, looking so guilty?' 'To see my father,' I answered. 'He lives in Clapham.' 'You'll have plenty of blisters to put into soak tonight, trekking that distance, you will, you young martyr.'

And there, by Westminster Bridge, was Boadicea, or Boudicca, with her daughters, speeding ahead in the family chariot. Seeing the spikes on its wheels, I smiled at the thought of those yapping Mediterranean dogs causing the ferocious Queen of the Iceni even so much as a second's annoyance. I had heard from my friend Mudey that she was buried beneath Platform 10 at King's Cross Station – though it was said that she also had graves in Stanmore and Epping, scenes of her humiliating defeat at the hands of Suetonius Paulinus. 'Termagants,' I whispered to the trio in bronze, and remembered, for the first of many times that day, the happiness I had known before 'Blenheim'.

South of the Thames, among the blackened factories and warehouses of Nine Elms, I quickened my pace. The silence was menacing now. I looked back frequently, convinced that a murderous gang was on my trail. I sensed eyes everywhere – behind soot-stained windows, they marked my feverish progress. I started to whistle the opening bars of the sym-phon-y that Schu-u-ubert left un-fin-ished, but stopped when a ship's siren wailed. The eerie noise was a signal to the watchers all about me, I felt: they would soon pick it up, and pounce. Absurd, absurd. I was twenty, I was walking in London, in broad daylight, and I was wretchedly afraid.

Absurd as it was, that feeling. I did not rid myself of it until I was once again in streets where the silence could be trusted. Fairy lights twinkled on Christmas trees behind clean front-room windows, and as I lumbered up Latchmere Road – Battersea's Everest – I began to hear laughter and singing. A car passed me, its driver waving, then honking, his compliments. I waved after him.

I pushed open the gate at 'Blenheim' and a dog suddenly barked. 'Shut up, Rubens, you nincompoop, for Christ's sake,' bellowed my father. 'You're supposed to sound the alert at night. That's when burglars come. To heel, to heel.'

The door was unbolted, and a huge Dobermann bounded out. I tried to back away, but he was too swift for me: had he not immediately placed his paws on my shoulders, had he not sniffed my hair, had he not licked my face, I would have registered fright. Touched by this lavish display of affection, from so brutish a source, I stroked his silky head and was honoured with a growl that was not a growl, for I could detect no anger in it. I took it to indicate friendship.

'Down, Rubens. Down this minute, sir. To heel, you cursèd animal.'

'Is he yours, Father?'

'He's been mine for three years or more. If you'd ever bothered to drop in on your old dad, you'd have known he was mine. He's of Kraut extraction, so killing's in his blood. He's company for me, is Rubens. He usually obeys his master.'

'Why "Rubens"?'

'You're curious, are you? I'll unravel the mystery when you've stepped inside. Leave him be, Rubens, or I'll take a strap to you.'

The word 'strap' sent Rubens's ears upwards, his body downwards. He barked briefly at my father, and padded into the house.

'You *are* coming in?'

'Yes, Father.'

'Well, show a leg, then. He who hesitates, et cetera.'

Under the sword I went, to my father's obvious delight.

'You were asking why and how I gave the dog his name. I bought him when he was still a puppy. I saw him guzzling on his mother's tits, and then – call it a fluke, call it a brainstorm – a picture that belonged to Sir Vincent came into my mind. It was painted by Peter Paul Rubens, a chap who cared for his tit if anyone did. She was a big buxom wench, with lovely pink nipples, and it was Sir Vincent's opinion she was mythological. Andromeda, chained to a rock, that was who she was. I saw that terror there, having the guzzle of his young life, and, yes, I thought of Rubens. Ours not to reason, but that's exactly what passed through my head. A funny connection, wouldn't you say? Typical of your old dad – a dog and a painter – isn't it?'

The question was rhetorical, self-admiring. I made no reply. I stared down at the tiled floor, across which Amy Harvey had walked on Wednesday, February 1, 1950: 'Your mother cooked us a fish pie before she left.'

'Come into the warm, young man. It's icier than a harlot's heart out there.'

And we had forgotten, the pair of us, to add the grated cheese.

'What's the matter, young man?'

'Matter? Nothing's the matter, Father.'

'You're not planning to stay in the hall, I hope. Let's go into the comfort.'

Comfort? Oh yes, the sitting-room at 'Blenheim' had always been comfortable. Didn't it boast the 'best reproduction antique furniture money can buy'?

'Just the same as it was when you did your flit – except for the new television set, of course. That cursèd thing I bought to watch the coronation on – can you guess what happened to it?'

'No, Father.'

'It exploded. In the middle of a variety show, it exploded. I reckoned my number had come up at last, I can tell you, young man, when I caught sight of that infernal smoke billowing all over the place. Rubens didn't turn a hair, being fast asleep at the time, dreaming of his next bone.'

'As he is now.'

The animal was already stretched out before the spitting and crackling log fire.

'As he is whenever he wants, the spoilt brute. Aren't you going to follow his example, then? Sit yourself down, young man. Let me fix you, as the Yanks say, a drink.'

'Thank you.'

'Which poison will it be?'

'I'm not sure. Beer, I suppose.'

'Oh, come on, take something stronger. It's Christmas.'

(I took something stronger, in large quantities, Father, when I came to grief that summer in Sorg. You would have been surprised, even – perhaps – impressed, by my capacity.)

'Scotch? Gin and tonic?'

'A beer, please. A light ale, if you have one.'

'I have one, young man. I have a whole crate of the stuff. That wrapped-up bottle you've been carrying since you arrived – would it be a present, by any chance?'

'Yes, Father. It's for you.'

'I did wonder, I must say. I was racking my addled old brain as to who or what you intended giving it. Shall I relieve you of the burden?'

'Yes. Here you are. Happy Christmas, Father.'

He quickly tore off the wrapping that concealed the gift I had not racked my imagination to find for him.

'Whisky. It's not the brand I favour, to be honest. I haven't quaffed this particular one in a month of Sundays. You really shouldn't have bothered.'

'I wanted to,' I lied.

'It *is* the thought that counts, isn't it? Thanks for thinking of me.'

I noticed that my father limped towards the Jacobean-style cocktail cabinet at which I had often made myself useful.

'Have you got gout?'

'Me? Gout? That's a port-swigger's complaint. No, I don't have the dreaded go-out. It's a simple pain, a twinge, nothing more.'

'Have you seen the doctor?'

'Stop being an oaf. Sit down, sit down. I never could abide people hovering. Of course I haven't. Whatever it is, I can cope with it, believe you me. I'm at an age when a chap gets alarmed if his joints *aren't* giving him trouble. You're certain you want a light ale?'

'Positive.'

'So be it.'

(In the Prodigal's Return, in the days when he and his family occupied one of 'Shylock's stables', Oswald Harvey had consumed pint upon pint of the beer he now scorned. Whisky, then, had been beyond his income. 'Your dad's a wag when he's had a few, Gabriel. The gleam in those wicked blue eyes!')

'The Quinlan woman is not the cook your mother was.' He hesitated. 'Still is, probably.' We had our drinks, and were both seated. 'And she's not as good as Gould. What's that I said? "Good as Gould" – completely unintentional play on words, I assure you. Your beloved Gould was no Escoffier, but she prepared her fair share of tasty meals. The Quinlan's lucky if she doesn't burn the food I buy to cinders. Fingers crossed, young man, that we don't find a burnt offering on the dining table today.'

'What are we eating?'

'Capon. The cock who loses his balls for the sake of flavour.

I've given her strict instructions that she has only to roast and baste it. No culinary hanky-panky. I've threatened her with the sack if she doesn't follow them. I'm too soft-hearted to sling her out, and she knows I am, deep down she knows, but I'm determined we're going to have a decent Christmas dinner – correction: lunch. Determined. Just because she has problems with her digestion, it doesn't mean that we must suffer, too.'

'Is she ill – Mrs Quinlan?'

'She has an ulcer. It's her one topic of conversation. She had a sharp, interesting tongue when I first took her on, but now it's ulcer, ulcer, ulcer, round the clock. Thank Christ I've got Rubens to chat to of a morning.'

The dog stirred slightly at the mention of his name.

'Listen to me, young man. Watch what you eat or you'll end up like Swedie, with a bloody great lump in your stomach. I warned the old crank that nuts and leaves and grass and whatnot were fine and dandy for rabbits and squirrels and so forth, but human beings – I told her until I was blue in the face – need sustenance, which means beef in my book. Did she heed her brother? Did she hell. She knew better, didn't she. As per always.'

'My son here keeps strange company. Tell Reggie and Marge about this Mr Bethlehem you introduced me to.'

'Mr Nazareth, Father – '

'Same part of the world,' said Reginald Van Pelt. 'Easy mistake to make.'

'My friend was born in Goa. That's Portuguese territory.'

'Typical Indian, wherever he comes from. Colossal gift of the gab. I saw through his ploy the moment he first spoke to me.'

'What ploy was that?' asked Margery Carstairs, the owner of Clapham Corsets, and 'Reggie's blushing bride-to-be'. ' "Ploy" is a funny sort of word, Oswald.'

'It suits, Marge. It fits. I associate it with cunning, and cunning's what this Nazareth or Bethlehem person has by the cartload.'

'What's his ploy, then? Get to the ploy, Oswald. You have me curious.'

'Patience, Reggie. His ploy – '

'Turnip on your shelf, mucky girl,' said Margery Carstairs, wiping her powdered bosom free of a dollop of the vegetable with a napkin on which the legend 'Blenheim' had been sewn. 'Terrible manners for a lady.'

'Ploy, Oswald. Ploy.'

'I'm coming to it.'

'Magnificent feast, Oswald.'

'He's coming to his ploy, Marge. Don't interrupt.'

'It's not his ploy, Van P. It's this Portuguese fellow's ploy. You never listen properly. And I was not interrupting. I was exhibiting common politeness to our gracious host.'

'Lovely grub, Oswald. Does that satisfy you, Marge? Now the ploy, please, Oswald. In double-quick time.'

'Everything to everyone's satisfaction?' inquired an anxious Mrs Quinlan, putting her head round the door.

'Positively scrumptious,' replied Margery Carstairs. 'I'm happy to say that for once I am making an utter pig of myself. I shall blame you, I promise, if I have to let this dress out.'

'You're very kind, Miss Carstairs. I only wish I could partake, too. I'm having a little something eggy on my tray in the kitchen, with a couple of slices of dry toast. I envy you your healthy constitutions.'

'Damned impertinence,' said my father, after Mrs Quinlan had disappeared. 'She didn't even knock. Treating the house like Liberty Hall. Accept my apologies – Reggie, Marge.'

Oswald Harvey's guests, befuddled as they were, looked almost soberly mystified. Both were silent.

'None necessary, Oswald. The ploy – yes?'

Yes, the ploy. Mr Bethlehem's – no, he would be calling him Mr Palestine next, if he wasn't careful – Mr Nazareth's ploy was all too familiar to him, accustomed as he was to a certain cast of the coloured mind. You dazzled the native – the native in this case being Oswald Harvey, not Mr Nazareth; a native Englishman, born and bred in Albion – you dazzled him with his own language. You dazzled him to such an extent that he scarcely recognized it as his own any longer. Were Reggie and Marge with him?

'Speaking for myself, Oswald, frankly, no.'

'It's simple, Marge. You – meaning Nazareth, not me – you spend years poring over the *Oxford English Dictionary* in some mosquito-ridden outpost, for the sole purpose of making Englishmen look stupid. That, in a nutshell, is the ploy. You swat up the kind of words a plain-spoken chap – and we are a plain-speaking race, I think we can agree – would never use, under any circumstances. The plain-spoken chap I'm referring to, of course.'

'This wallah with the ploy – did you say he is a friend of your son's?'

'I did, Reggie. I did, indeed.'

'Extraordinary. Tell us why you have made his acquaintance,' Margery Carstairs demanded, picking a Brussels sprout off her 'shelf'. 'Oh, you mucky slut. Yes, you just tell us why.'

'I like him. I find him interesting.'

'Go on.'

'I don't wish to, Miss Carstairs.'

'He was the same at Lily's. Out of all the boys in the school, who did he choose to be his best pal? A half-caste.'

'Extraordinary.'

Reginald Van Pelt and Margery Carstairs had swayed into my consciousness an hour earlier. He had laughed upon seeing me: 'This is yours, Oswald?' And she had boomed, 'You're very small, aren't you? Was his mother on the small side, Oswald? That would explain his lack of inches.' She had not waited for his reply. 'You're what – twenty? You don't look as if you shave. Not a sign of stubble. Do you – in fact – shave?'

'No, I don't. Yet. Miss Carstairs.'

'I'm Marge to my chums. There was no butter to be had in the war, but Reggie will vouchsafe he never went short of Marge.' She had continued, in a coquettish baritone, 'I'm that ruin's blushing bride-to-be. I'm only waiting for the day he's capable of walking a straight line to the altar.'

'Sometime never – eh, Reggie?'

'I'll be hung, drawn and quartered if I say yes, Oswald. Don't lay me open to risk. Have you a suitable libation for a man dying of thirst?'

'And woman, too, Oswald. Don't forget Marge. He's too pretty, your son. He should have been a girl.'

'Nonsense, Marge.'

And now my father was telling his Christmas guests that I had run away from the comforts of 'Blenheim' at the tender age of seventeen. Had he gone after the blithering young idiot? No, he had not. Had he left the ungrateful son and heir to stew in his own juice? Yes, he most definitely had.

'Still, you must admit – Reggie, Marge – the boy showed pluck. He didn't come back snivelling, as I half-expected he would. It wasn't long before I found out where he was hiding –

I do have connections, though I say so myself – but did I go and reason with the whippersnapper? No, I did not; leastways, not until he'd been cooped up there for a longish stretch. You should see the place. You should meet the odds and sods who live in it. You wouldn't believe your ears and eyes.'

'The darkie with the ploy?'

'He's one of them, Reggie. I met a batty old countess, too, who had the gall to scream at me when I asked her a perfectly polite question.'

'I'd have slapped her face, Oswald. Didn't you slap her face?'

'No, Marge. Me, a gentleman, strike a lady? Heaven forbid. Besides, she's Polish.'

'Ah, that accounts for it.'

It didn't account for anything. I chose not to remark. It accounted for nothing sane, nothing temperate. I did not correct my father, since I suspected that he had changed Countess Bolina's nationality deliberately, in order to goad the son who was even now remembering that he, the gentleman, had once struck a lady, heaven forbid – Oswald Harvey's wife, Mr Van Pelt; Gabriel Harvey's mother, Miss Carstairs.

Rubens let out a howl then, and I had cause to escape for a while.

'And what might you require, you cursèd beast?'

'Exercise, Father. I'll walk him for you. Give me his lead.'

'His lead? He'll lead him away and astray, Oswald. He'll drag him through a hedge backwards. Why, he's almost as big as your little Gabriel, if my sight can be trusted. Rubens'll whisk him off and you'll never see the pair of them again.'

'You take him, young man. Let him have a good long run. I think I can rely on you.'

On the common, in the growing dark, I ran and ran with Rubens. I found a branch to throw, which he always retrieved. I brought him home to 'Blenheim' in a state of happy exhaustion.

'Where's Miss Carstairs, Father?' Reginald Van Pelt was asleep on the larger of the two sitting-room sofas.

'What could you be wanting with her, for Christ's sake, young man?'

'Just to show her I've returned. In one piece. With the dog.'

'She's taking a well-earned rest. You've been gone for ages.'

(In the autumn of 1976, when he lay without legs on his deathbed, dependent upon his 'wet-nurse', Agnes Garrett, my father revealed that Margery Carstairs had been the last woman he had given a 'really thorough rogering'. I had looked at him with disgust, a look he was quick to misinterpret. 'She was no bloody oil painting, that bitch, I grant you. I'm not surprised you've curled your nose up, I took her, Gabriel lad, on the Because She Was There principle – she presented me with the challenge, and I was man enough to rise to it.' 'But Mummy –' I choked on the words; he did not hear them. 'I sent her blood racing. I had her grovelling for more. I found her truly detestable.')

'Why don't you stay overnight, young man? The buses stopped running at lunchtime. I've had the Quinlan air your bed for you.'

'No, thanks.'

'It wouldn't kill you to stay.'

'No, it wouldn't.'

'We'll get shot of Reggie and Marge and play a few games of dominoes. Eh? Or chess, even. I've an ivory set. Unused.'

'No, Father. Thank you for the scarf, and the tie, and the socks. I'm sorry I brought you the wrong brand of whisky.'

'Stop acting like a cursèd oaf, will you? You'll be reaching your majority in three months. Show a bit of grace and accept your old dad's offer.'

'I can't.'

'You mean you won't.'

George Fox looked down on me as I reflected on the day's absurdities, on the beginning of my Swedenborgian penance. I had endured every insult, ignored every attempt to goad and irritate me. My behaviour had been impeccable, I decided.

And then Aunt Kathleen's mysterious words came to me, as they were to come so often in Sorg, Minnesota: 'You must repair yourself.' They made me smile, as they were to do so often in the years before I broke into pieces, in America.

8

I arrived at the Jerusalem from several directions in the nine
years I worked there. I came from Clerkenwell, from Hackney,
from Fulham; I approached it by bus, by train, but mostly by
Shanks's pony – as I had heard my mother say once, to my
childish confusion. 'I shall be travelling to my secret place by
Shanks's pony today, Gabriel. Just look at the weather!' Who
was this Mr Shanks, and why had I never met him? And where
did he keep his pony? Wasn't it frightened of the London traffic?
And would she take me for a ride on it, please? 'Questions,
Gabriel, questions! It's an expression, you silly darling. It means
I shall be walking to work. As you will soon be doing, when
I've checked behind your ears.'

'Food to your liking, is it, young man?'

'Yes, thank you, Father.'

We were in a 'select' restaurant, the two of us, on the evening
of my twenty-first birthday.

'I should jolly well hope so, the price it is. It's high time you
bought yourself a new suit, if I may say so. I can see myself in
the shine on that one. I shall slip you a bundle of readies afore
we go.'

'I don't want your money, Father.'

'I shall have to dig deep into my pocket to pay for this lovely
grub, you realize. I can't for the life of me see the difference.'

'I can.'

'I suppose I ought to feel grateful you've allowed me to treat
you. It's more than I expected.'

(I'm with you tonight for Aunt Kathleen's sake, and in her
memory – I did not, could not, tell him.)

'I think we should have a serious talk. Man to man. It's the
appropriate occasion, isn't it?'

'Is it?'

'Don't be oafish. Your coming-of-age. At least, that's what I assume it is. A coming-of-age and a coming-to-your-senses. You don't propose to go on sorting letters, for Christ's sake, do you?'

'No, Father, I don't.'

'That's what your old dad wants to hear.'

(He would not have wanted to hear my reason for leaving the sorting office, and I did not bother to give it. Harold Mude was no longer around to make Mount Pleasant pleasanter. 'Poison Ivy's fangs have sunk themselves into him, and they're not likely to loosen their grip,' one of the older sorters revealed. 'The doctor has changed her drugs and she's seen through Mudey's scheme.' 'Why Poison Ivy? What scheme?' 'Because she's bloody poisonous, Gabriel. Tongue on her like a whip. The lashings it's meted out to him would have driven most of us, me included, to murder. "She's the victim of a depressive illness, Wally. She doesn't know what she's doing" – that's how the poor cheerful sod accounts for her rotten ways. And as for the scheme, Gabriel – well, he was on nights, wasn't he, in the main. You follow me? He slept while she was awake, and vice versa. Ideal arrangement for most of the week. That's all over now, no thanks to the quack. Mudey's postal paradise gone up the spout with a single prescription. Poison Ivy wants him there when she's *compos mentis* or the nearest she ever bloody gets to it. He soon won't have a soul to call his own. I guarantee.')

'I start a new job next Monday.'

'Where, might I inquire?'

'The Jerusalem.'

'And what, in all creation, is that? A pub?'

'It's a Home, Father. For elderly women.'

'The devil it is. You're joking, aren't you? Teasing me? Having me on?'

'No, I'm not, Father.'

'I'm at a loss to understand you, I honestly am. A Home for elderly women? You'd be better employed at the zoo. A son of mine emptying bedpans – God give me strength.'

'The nurses do that. I shall have other duties.'

'Why not a Home for old men, young man? They need looking after, too, in case you hadn't noticed.'

(Did he have Oswald Harvey in mind? I was tempted to ask.)

'Another whisky, *garçon, civil play.*'

'*Oui, monsieur.*'

The waiter, who had a distinct Welsh accent, filled my glass with the red wine he had recommended.

'Swedie had a taste for that stuff, I seem to recollect. Her ice-cream husband started her off on it.'

'This is the best I've drunk, Father. It's delicious.'

(I refrained from saying that the only wine I'd had before was from Algeria, mulled to a boiling-point by Diana Sparey: 'It's a bit too vinegary straight from the bottle. I've added sugar and cinnamon to sweeten it up.' And many pieces of cork, and quite a few hairs.)

'Gives me an acid gut. You're welcome to the foul concoction. Now, please explain for your old dad's benefit, and in words he'll understand, why you've chosen to work at this Jerusalem place. Sounds fishy to me. Sounds to me as though that Bethlehem or Nazareth has had a hand in it.'

'No, Father, he hasn't. It's pure coincidence – the names.'

'Why, then?'

'Oh – the history,' I said.

'The history, young man?'

Yes, the history, I tried to tell him. The commonplace, every-day history of lives that were lived. The history I hadn't read about in books like *Our Island Story*, in which Sir Walter flourished his cloak and Alfred burnt the cakes and Sir Francis looked up calmly from his game of bowls and, oh, and all those famous heroes (British, mostly) killed all those infamous villains (foreign, usually); the history, I gabbled on, that Mr Nichol at Lily's was only able to hint at: 'Do remember, boys, that history is also concerned with millions of men and women who did nothing more special than raising their families and causing little or no harm to their fellows.' At the Jerusalem – I said, courting ridicule – I expect to be among ordinary ghosts, for the place had been a workhouse once. It suited the mood I was in for me to go there.

'And a daft bloody mood it is, too, if you ask me. I can't fathom what goes on in that skull of yours, I really can't. It's gibberish you're spouting.'

'Perhaps.'

'Perhaps nothing. It's drivel. And don't shrug, young man, when sense is being spoken to you.'

He fumed loudly in the ensuing silence.

'Father?'

'Yes?'

'Your friend Mr Van Pelt wears suede shoes.'

'What if he does? It's a free world, isn't it. At least, it was the last time I looked.'

'When I was a boy, you' – I nearly said 'lectured' – 'you warned me that people who wore them weren't to be trusted. I would be wise to steer clear of suede – that was the gist of it. A true aristocrat, you taught me, sticks to leather.'

'So he does, so he does. Most definitely, he does. You don't for a minute imagine that I trust Reggie, do you?'

'Don't you?'

'Blimey O'Riley, no. Reggie's a cove, a bounder. Reggie is a crook. Not an actual criminal with a record, of course. Your old dad doesn't keep that kind of company in a hurry. No, it's just that Reggie does business with some fairly shady types – I shall say no more on the subject. Reggie amuses me, that's all. He tickles me pink when he's on form.'

'Amuses you?'

'You sound amazed. He's a wit, a wag, is Reggie.'

(Reginald Van Pelt had said nothing witty, nothing waggish, that endless Christmas Day. He had tickled none of us pink, though the hollow guffaw with which he had responded to one of my father's many humorous observations had startled Rubens into a frenzy of dervish-like activity. He had played the blazered Bardolph to Oswald Harvey's tweed-suited Falstaff with a sycophancy alarming to behold, for it was sustained against all the drunken odds. My father had revelled in his admirer's approval, had even encouraged it: 'Wouldn't you agree, Reggie?' 'I would indeed, Oswald. I hope your son is listening, and marking well your words of wisdom.')

'Wish he'd get shot of that corset cow. If ever a female stuck in my craw, it's her.'

'What's wrong with Miss Carstairs?' I inquired, with studied innocence.

'What's right with her, you mean, young man? Precious little, in my considered opinion. She's an ugly eater, and that's a terrible fault in a woman – especially in one who prides herself on being a lady. Lady, my arse! Think of the disgrace she'd bring on me if I'd brought her here.'

(I thought, instead, of Margery Carstairs addressing her sovereign. 'Bless your little cotton socks, Your Majesty,' she had said to the Queen, who was seated at her desk in Windsor

Castle. 'Bless your beautiful cotton socks!' When Elizabeth the Second reminded Her subjects that there were those in Her Commonwealth who would not be enjoying the traditional fare of roast turkey and plum pudding this Christmas, Margery Carstairs had nodded vigorous assent: 'The poor creatures! The poor blighters!' At the end of the monarch's speech, Margery Carstairs declared – through tears – that Lillibet had made a most impressive television debut, bless her cotton socks, and that she, a royalist to her fingertips, would be penning a letter to *The Times* to that effect.)

'I begrudge every mouthful she scoffed at "Blenheim". I only put up with her for Reggie's sake.'

For Reggie's sake? For the sake of that purple-faced fool?

'Cheese, *messieurs*? Or a sweet, perhaps?'

'We'll have both. My son could do with fattening up. He doesn't eat in this style very often.'

As I drank an after-dinner brandy, and smoked a small after-dinner cigar, which made me feel slightly queasy, I wondered if I was to be spared the threatened twenty-first birthday lecture. It seemed likely.

'Kindly inform the chef', my father was addressing the head waiter, 'that his *entrecôte* with *Bercy* butter was worthy of the great August S. Coffier himself.'

'Escoffier? *Monsieur* flatters him, and us.'

'I'm not free with my compliments. I give them when they're due. I am not, and never have been, a man for flannel.'

'I will convey your message, *monsieur*.'

'Do.'

I thanked my father for a wonderful meal, a pleasant evening.

'I've enjoyed myself, too, young man. Up to a point, that is. Your old dad would be a much happier parent if his son saw the folly of his ways and found himself a proper job. And by a proper job I don't mean whatever it is you've landed yourself in at this Jerusalem. It can't have a future. I'm talking about prospects.'

'Yes, Father.'

'Now where's that cursed Sparrow?' he demanded of nobody in particular when we were in the street. 'I told him to be waiting outside by eleven at the latest.'

'Sparrow? Waiting?'

'Harry Sparrow, young man. He drives my car for me.'

'Your car?'

'That's what I call a vehicle on four wheels that isn't a taxi, a van, a bus or a lorry.'

'I didn't know you had one.'

'You weren't to know, were you? It's a recent addition to the household. Walking any distance pains my pins these days, so a car seemed like a good idea for getting around. I'd have driven it myself a short while ago, but I'm too old to sit behind a wheel. Where are you, Sparrow?'

'He's your chauffeur, is he, Father?'

'Only in a manner of speaking. He's not available round the clock. I have to give him a day's notice if I require his services. He doesn't wear a uniform.'

I soon saw why not. A uniformed chauffeur would have looked incongruous in Oswald Harvey's tiny car, which was a black Morris Minor.

'I had my eyes on a bigger motor – I fancied a Humber, or even a Princess. The beauty of this little fellow is that Rubens, my so-called watchdog, considers it too small for his doggy person and won't climb into it. Claustrophobia, I presume. His refusal to join me in the back decided me to buy it. If a man can't find peace and quiet in his own jalopy, as those Yanks say, where *can* he find it, eh, young man?'

It was a question I felt unequipped to answer.

'Why so late, Sparrow?'

'I'm not late, Mr Harvey. Not late late. Ten minutes isn't really late. Hop in!'

'Sparrow, this is the son I was telling you about.'

'He's not wearing his wig and gown, is he?'

'Of course he isn't.'

'Pleased to meet you, Your Honour-to-be.' Sparrow put his hand out of the car. I shook it. 'I envy you, sir. I'm fascinated by crime in all its forms, but a nice juicy murder's the best of the lot. I'm expecting a ticket for your first murder trial, as I've told your old dad.'

'I'll make sure you receive one, Mr Sparrow. You may have to wait a considerable time for it, though. Wouldn't you agree, Father?'

'Patience is a virtue, they say. There's no virtue quite like patience, Sparrow.'

My father hopped in on that philosophical note.

'Would you mind signing my autograph book, sir? I take it everywhere with me. London's a city where you're always bumping into the famous. When you're Judge Harvey, I'll be able to show this to my kiddies and tell them I met you while you were still studying for the bar in Lincoln's Inn Fields.'

'Your kiddies' kiddies, I think. Have you a pen, Mr Sparrow?'

'Never without one.'

I placed Mr Sparrow's autograph book on the bonnet of my father's shining new Morris Minor and wrote in it: *To Harry Sparrow. With best wishes from Gabriel Harvey, 'Wretches hang that jurymen may dine.' March 20, 1958.*

'There you are, Mr Sparrow.'

'Much obliged.'

'I'll walk back to Clerkenwell, Father, in case you were wondering whether to offer me a lift. Good night, Mr Sparrow.'

'A very good night to you, sir.'

'Good night, Father. Thanks again for the meal.'

'My pleasure, young man. Take care of yourself, won't you. If you need anything, any help or anything, you know where "Blenheim" is. Home, Sparrow, and don't spare the horses.'

A present awaited me at Vineyard Walk: a gold watch from the Crown Jewellers with my initials inscribed on the back. There was a card in the box that contained it, on which was written: *To my son on his coming of age. Your old Dad wellcomes you to a Man's world.*

'I hope you won't object to my giving you a short history lesson.' The Matron smiled, shut the smile off quickly.

'No. Of course not.'

'Did you notice the bust in the entrance hall?'

'Yes, I did.'

'It represents our founder, Lord Endon. He lived from 1857 to 1888. Not a long life, by anybody's reckoning. A mere thirty-one years.'

'The same as Schubert.'

'Oh? The "Trout", isn't it? How interesting. On with the lesson, Mr Harvey.'

'Yes, Matron.'

' "Matron" does sound so institutional. Please call me Mrs Ricks. Shall we settle for that? Mrs Ricks. Back to Lord Endon, Mr Harvey. Well, he had a wretched childhood. Both his parents died before he was ten. He was a lord, in fact, at the distinctly tender age of nine and a half. It was then that an uncle took charge of him: a man of loose morals who drank and gambled.

By the time Lord Endon inherited his father's fortune, he himself was a drunkard. He had wasted his youth in low dens and such places.' Matron accompanied the words 'low dens' with her quickly shut-off smile. 'At the age of twenty-eight His Lordship, on an impulse, journeyed to the East. In 1885 he saw the Light. In Jerusalem. He returned to England to spread the Word. He lived among the London poor. He bought a property, a workhouse, and made it into a Home for the elderly and dying. He named it the Jerusalem. Which is how, Mr Harvey, we began.'

(I was intrigued by the details of Lord Endon's brief life, by his progress from those 'low dens' to the Light in the East and the spreading of the Word in London's slums. They suited my view of history: the view from the laystall; the view my father would soon dismiss as gibberish. Besides, I had the feeling that Oswald Harvey, who had been born three whole years before the Light had struck the lord, would not have approved of an aristocrat lowering himself in such an airy-fairy, nonsensical way: 'I can't fathom out what's going on in that skull of yours, Your Lordship, begging Your Lordship's pardon, I really can't.')

'You are a surprising applicant, Mr Harvey.'

'Am I, Matron? Mrs Ricks.'

'I'll say. A young man who listens to Schubert wanting to scrub the floors – you do realize that scrubbing floors will be one of the required duties?'

'Yes, I do.'

'You must see that it's unusual.' She smiled, shut the smile off quickly. 'You're not exactly robust, are you?'

'I suppose not. But I can manage, Mrs Ricks. Don't worry.'

'Would a trial period be acceptable? I can imagine you – and I intend no disrespect – getting easily bored with the menial tasks I shall have to ask you to undertake. You will be longing for your Schubert when you are cleaning out, I'm afraid, the toilets.'

(I mentioned other composers to Mrs Ricks while I worked at the Jerusalem – Mozart, Beethoven, Handel, Brahms – but they seemed not to exist for her. It was Schubert, and Schubert alone, to whom she always referred. 'I heard Klemperer at the Festival Hall last night, Mrs Ricks. The "Eroica". He took it slower than most conductors would dare to, but it was still wonderful.' 'No Schubert on the programme?' And months later: 'Bartók's my great passion now, Mrs R. You should hear Geza Anda play his piano concertos.' 'You're not leaving Schubert out in the cold, I hope.')

'Do you have any experience of old people, Mr Harvey?'

'My father's in his seventies.'

'That means your mother must be –'

'She's forty, Mrs Ricks. Just. It was her birthday yesterday.'

'Did you celebrate?'

(No I did not celebrate. I sat in my room – Mrs Ricks might have been horrified to learn – in perfect quiet, in a Moygashel frock – oh, yes – of the kind Amy Harvey was wearing, would for ever be wearing, on that day of recurring brightness. Its shade was sugar bag blue. I had bought it, on an impulse as inexplicable as the one that led Lord Endon Eastwards, from a second-hand clothes dealer in Petticoat Lane. 'This for your bit of fluff, eh, matey?' I'd nodded. 'Lucky girl. I'm giving it away at two quid.' I'd nodded again, and handed him the money. 'Foreigner – you?' The question had set me nodding in earnest. 'A *Parlez-vous* or a *Sprechen Sie*?' 'Swedish,' I'd answered. 'What's the Swedish for "blushing"?' I'd shrugged my shoulders, in the supposed manner of mystified aliens. 'Because that, matey, is what you're doing.')

'No, we didn't. My mother lives abroad. My parents split up in 1950.'

'I'm sorry, Mr Harvey.'

'She was in Malta, the last time she wrote to – to me.'

'That's somewhere I've never visited. I haven't, in all truth, had much opportunity for travel. I envy her.'

And as for grandparents, I went on to explain, I was in the unique position of not having any. My father's mother and father had died of natural causes, long ago; my mother's had been 'wiped-out' – the phrase had stayed with me – in a train crash.

'It sounds, Mr Harvey, as if you haven't had a very happy childhood.'

'I'm not complaining.'

'My ladies will have to grow accustomed to seeing a man about the Home.' She smiled, shut the smile off quickly. She picked up the telephone on her desk and spoke into it: 'Nurse Barrow, would you be a dear and ask Mrs Capes to come to my office? I'd like her to do one of her famous guided tours. Thank you so much.' She replaced the receiver. 'Mrs Capes is extremely energetic for her age. She's retained her lively mind. I think you will find her a "character".'

(Ah yes, a 'character'. I had cause, after my father's death, to ponder the notion of what constitutes a 'character'. There were times, listening to Oswald Harvey, when I felt that I had walked on to a stage and into a play. There he was, spotlit; there was I, in the shadows, waiting impatiently for the rare silence I would have to fill with my few miserable lines. How often I fed him the wrong cues; how often I longed for the performance to come to a lasting close. Vain longing – for the curtain has yet to descend, and while I live it will remain above 'Blenheim', the set in which he strutted and lectured and cursed the cursèd.)

'She will amuse you, I can promise. I'll leave it to her to introduce you to the other residents.'

'My first name's Louise,' said Mrs Capes. ' "Louise" is French.'

'I haven't met a Louïse before.'

'It isn't common. Not in England, anyhow. In France, I expect, you'd meet Louises wherever you went.'

'Yes, I expect you would.'

'And what's yours?'

'Mine's Gabriel.'

'That's lovely. Oh, that *is* lovely. Religious.'

'I don't think I live up to it.'

'I bet you do. I'm a student of people in my way, and I can tell that you do.' Mrs Capes winked at me. 'Pure as the driven snow. There won't be much temptation for you in this hole, will there? Amongst a lot of old crocks and leftovers. You'll have no problem keeping your hands to yourself.'

'That's true.'

'I was hoping you'd disagree with me. I've taken a fancy to you already. You've got the sort of features I like in a man. Refined.'

'Cradle snatching are you now, Louise Capes?' The sharp voice came from behind us. I turned and stopped. The speaker was a tall, upright woman. Mrs Capes came to a halt, but did not turn.

'This lady is Edith Trimmer. Miss Edith Trimmer. She never married.'

'In her wisdom. Who are you and what are you doing here?'

'He's Mr Harvey to you,' said Mrs Capes, with her back to Miss Trimmer. 'And what he'll be doing here is working.'

'Working? A man? I don't mean a man, do I, I mean a boy, a pretty little boy, by the looks of him.'

'Take no notice, Gabriel. It's Edith's nature to find fault. Let me show you the lounge.'

I was duly shown the lounge, where most of the Jerusalem's inhabitants were huddled into themselves that cold March afternoon. One of them started from her sleep as we entered. She sucked in a thin length of spit that was secured to her lower lip and announced: 'Dan and me was fighting like thieves again. It was horrible.'

'Mrs Affery – Maggy – meet Gabriel.'

'Gabriel? Am I dead then?' Mrs Affery looked about her wildly. 'No. I can't be. Not yet. There's Nell there, and Queenie, and Niagara Alice. And there's you, Louise.'

'Gabriel's our new dogsbody. And a very pleasantly spoken one he is, too. Not like that common Rowena we had up until last week, with her dyed red hair and her tarty habits.'

'Pleased to meet you,' said Mrs Affery, wiping her toothless mouth on the end of the mangy tippet that hung from her shoulders. 'Nice to know you. Glad to see you.'

Mrs Temple, Mrs Crane and Mrs Gross were also pleased to see me, they said. Miss Trimmer alone was circumspect: 'I'll keep you posted if I'm happy to have made your acquaintance when I've actually made it, and providing I'm happy – and not before, and that's that. How do you do, Mr Harvey?'

'I'm well, thank you. Miss Trimmer.'

'Come along, Gabriel,' ordered Mrs Capes. 'Ignore crabby old Edith. She'd try the patience of Job himself.'

I said goodbye to the women, and followed my leader into the corridor.

'I only sit in the lounge of an evening, when there's something worth watching on the TV, which isn't often. I enjoy a nice play, or a ballet. I'm very partial to a ballet. The others aren't, but then they haven't my first-hand knowledge of the subject. My son was a dancer, you see. We'll have a photo session one day when you're not too busy. I have lots of snaps of him.'

'I look forward to it, Mrs Capes.'

'So do I. Yes, dear, as soon as my hospital serial's over, I usually trudge up to the ward and settle down with a good book. I don't want my brain to addle, even if the rest of me's ready for the knacker's yard. This is where we eat, Gabriel, though I wouldn't honour the table manners of two

I could name with the word "eating". Slobbering's what *they* do.'

We went into a long hall.

'According to Matron, this is where the paupers used to have their meals. What was it they ate? Gruel, was it?'

'Yes.'

'And up there, on that balcony – '

'A balcony!'

' – was where, according to Matron, the workhouse master used to watch to see that they ate it. Their gruel. Scarcely a dinner goes by without me picturing poor Oliver Twist in my mind. Asking for more, of course.'

'To no avail.'

'As you say. We mustn't be gloomy, must we? Why be gloomy? That's what I ask myself when I'm in the dumps, Gabriel. "Why be gloomy, Louise, when you've no cause?" '

Mrs Capes drew my attention to a notice on the wall. It was in a gilt frame, and read: 'DO NOT SPIT. MATRON.'

'That's from when they had men in the Home. Before I arrived, worse luck. My joke, Gabriel. No one's ever bothered to take it down. The "Do not spit" bit wasn't our matron's doing. That was Miss Unwin's handiwork. A tartar, by all reports.'

('DO NOT SPIT. MATRON.' is in my kitchen here at Chiswick. Its gilt frame has been cleaned and restored. My other memento of the Jerusalem, the strange journal of Roger Kemp, lies under George Fox's gaze in this room in which I am trying to make sense of Gabriel Harvey's life.)

'At Christmas we hang up streamers; we put up bunting. Ever so festive, it looks. We have singsongs. A man comes in and builds a little stage and we each of us do a turn. I tend to oblige with a ballad or two. By public demand.' She laughed. 'But you're young. That old-fashioned stuff wouldn't appeal to you.'

'Don't be so sure, Mrs Capes.'

'Louise, please. My one and only poem, that is: "Louise, please." '

'Louise, I have a question for you.'

'Yes, Gabriel?'

'Why did Mrs Affery call Mrs Temple "Niagara Alice"?'

'Because of the trouble she has with her waterworks. She's perched on her chamber half the night as a rule. She has a rubber sheet on her bed – just in case of accidents.'

(I'd had a hundred accidents on my rubber sheet - 'It's a very popular piece of equipment, I hear tell, in lunatic asylums' – I did not see fit to inform Mrs Capes. I'd thrown the thing away with a confidence I was now startled to realize had not been misplaced.)

'She has my sympathy.'

'Does she? That's nice. Talking of rubber sheets, I've a couple of introductions to make, I don't think. Let's go upstairs to the sleeping quarters.'

Mrs Capes giggled into her hand as soon as were were in the ward.

'Oh, I mustn't. Control yourself, Louise Capes. Mrs Hibbs, I want you to meet Mr Harvey. Can you hear me? Obviously not. I shouldn't mock, should I? She can't help being gaga, helpless old soul. There – you're honoured. She's opened one eye.'

Miss Burns had both eyes open. They seemed to look beyond me.

'She was staring like that the first time I saw her. Dark or light's no different for Miss Burns. You could stand in the buff in front of her, Gabriel, and she wouldn't turn a hair.'

'I shan't test the truth of that remark.'

'Spoilsport!'

The little money my aunt left me amounted to nearly three hundred pounds. I was to spend it how I chose, said the solicitor's letter that accompanied the first cheque I ever received – a magical piece of paper I carried about with me for several days before reluctantly parting with it at a branch of the National Provincial Bank.

Mrs di Salvo's instructions are that you should be 'imaginatively profligate' with the sum enclosed. I assume that you are sufficiently familiar with her use of English to understand what she meant by this odd combination of words. I am, sir, Yours faithfully, Nigel M. Draper.

'I'm a man of means all of a sudden,' I told Mr Nazareth. 'Can I tempt you into excess and buy you a celebratory pint?'

'Means, Harvey? You? Impossible. Your curry-hating parent has not died?'

'No, no.' I heard myself add: 'Not yet.'

'That is welcome news. It would upset me to learn of his decease. I find him a most engaging fellow.'

'It's my aunt. His sister.'

'She has remembered you in her will?'

'Yes, she has.'

'How much, Harvey? How much?'

'That's a very direct question, Mr Nazareth.'

'You have categorically stated that you are a man of means. I am curious to ascertain the extent of those means. How much?'

'I have enough to open a bank account.'

'That is not a satisfactory answer, Harvey.'

'Isn't it? Anyway, that's what I've done. With my wealth, I mean.'

'An account can be opened with a pittance, with the risible contents of a begging bowl. How much? Thousands?'

'Perhaps.'

'You are playing an English game with me, I fear. The truly rich in this country are secretive about their money. They pretend to be paupers, and you are emulating them already – with your hundreds, yes?'

'Perhaps.'

'I shall not be teased. I shall assume that your means are inconsiderable until I learn to the contrary.'

'A safe assumption, Mr Nazareth. Now, must I celebrate alone?'

'No, you must not. I have developed a thirst, and it has to be quenched. I shall allow you to tempt me. A little modest indulgence is appropriate to the occasion and to the size of your inheritance. Proceed, Tempter, and I shall follow.'

In the Three Crowns that evening, Mr Nazareth permitted me to get him slightly drunk. He would neglect to burn the midnight oil, even if the relapse resulted in his attainment of a diploma in chartered accountancy being delayed by a few hours. He studied to a system, methodically, and here he was imbibing his third – or was it his fourth? – pint, good grief. His future partner, Sippaimalani, would be appalled by his dissipated behaviour: 'He is a devout Hindu, Harvey, but a financial wizard none the less.'

'Why are you laughing?'

'At the picture I am seeing in my head of his appalled features. It really is hugely diverting. I have never known Sippaimalani smile. He is a naturally frowning man, my accomplice in commerce. The idea of his disapproving face looking more appalled than it habitually does fills me with mirth, Harvey. Oh my, I am spluttering!'

Some days later, Aunt Kathleen's promised twenty books were delivered. Not one of them, I was relieved to find, was by Swedenborg, whose *Heaven and Hell* was beyond my inadequate powers of comprehension. I could not keep pace with his thinking, and marvelled at the translator's undoubted ability to do just that. How had he contrived to make those familiar English words appear so alien, so almost-Swedish in their inaccessibility? I had only to stare my way through a fogbound paragraph and a dull ache started up behind my eyes. It was impossible, then, to persevere – in that thickening fog, and with that ache such a hindrance.

All but two of the small selection had belonged to Mr Tiverley, the ancient eccentric who had proclaimed my aunt a young phoenix on his death-bed. *Ex Libris, Cedric Tiverley* – whenever I look at the shipmaster's plate, I try to imagine Kathleen Harvey and Nora Rosen pushing a barrow from the grand house in Wellclose Square to their humble lodgings in Southwark. What an odd sight they must have presented to the poor Londoners they passed on that day in 1899, with their copious pickings from a gentleman's library, and what jibes they must have endured – the cockney skinnyshanks and her chosen mother, the big-boned, ruddy-cheeked, unrespectable Rosie Rotbagga. What could a pair of slaveys – a 'blastpheming' foreigner and a snotty scrag from the worst stretch of Cable Street – be doing with a cartload of books, of all things? And where in hell were they going with them?

Oh, Mr Tiverley, how often I have envisaged you, in your brocade weskit, reading Shakespeare or Donne or Milton or Spenser by candlelight; how often I have looked up from those same editions you once held in your hands and wondered at the commonplace accident – an unlettered girl darting into the nearest church to shelter from the rain – that caused them to be in my eventual possession. How often have I thought of you at the end of your good, long life, sipping a medicinal, fortifying brandy and listening to the faithful Nora making dear Charlie's prose the more melodious; how often, and with what gratitude, have I considered your existence, Mr Tiverley – its charm, its grace, its kindliness.

'What do you suppose you're wearing, young man?'

'Clothes, Father.'

'On your legs, I'm talking about.'

'So am I.'

'I can't see trousers.'

'That's because they're jeans.'

'Not Mabel's or Muriel's?' He awarded himself a brief chuckle. 'Cursed Yanks and their notions. A couple of old sacks would look smarter.'

'I bought them for work. They didn't cost much.'

'I should hope they didn't.'

'Who let you in?'

'Not the batty old Pole, and not that Indian neither. The street door was open to the four winds, as a matter of fact. "Is anybody there?" I asked. "Is anyone at home?" What was the answer I got? Silence. So in I stepped and up I climbed.'

'Why?'

'There's a welcome for you! Why, he wants to know. I *am* your dad – or was, at least, when I last looked.'

'Yes, Father. But why?'

'I've been to the City on business is why. I ordered Sparrow to drop me off here for an hour is why. He has a rheumatic mother-in-law lives in Blackfriars, and he's gone to pay his respects with a box of Turkish Delight, courtesy of yours truly. Now is that enough "whys", young man, or shall I throw in a few "wherefores" for luck?'

'You're sitting on my bed, Father.'

'Of course I bloody am. There's no other place I can park my arse, is there? You surely don't expect me to try to get into that desk contraption.'

'When you came before, you spurned it, as I remember. You said something about a certain stench offending your nostrils.'

'Yes, well, I probably did. I wasn't to know, was I, then, that you'd been cured.'

'No, Father, you probably weren't.'

'Pissing the way you used to. Making the stink you used to.'

'That's right.'

'All in the past, eh?'

'Right again.'

'Swedie's left you a pile of her battered old books, I notice.'

'She has.'

'There's nothing in them, young man, you can't learn better

at what I call the University of Life. That's where I've done my schooling, I'm proud to say.'

'It so happens, Father – ' I faltered. What *was* happening? And what was I on the brink of declaring? 'It so happens that I'm writing one myself. A book, Father. In my free time.'

'The devil you are.'

'The devil I am,' I lied.

'You? A book-writer? Wearing – what are they – jeans? Has Swedie's money given you more mad ideas than you've got already in that skull of yours?'

'Who told you about the money?'

'She did, you oaf. She'd made plans to leave you some of her ice-cream pickings while you were still in the cradle.'

(And Tom? Had she made plans for him, too, from his cradle onwards? I was tempted, greatly tempted, to startle him suddenly with that question.)

'Sir Vincent counted a couple of book-writers among his pals, if my memory's not playing tricks on me. Real gentlemen of leisure they were, in their hound's-tooth and sea island cotton. Why you should want to be a book-writer when the best book-writers are all dead and buried is beyond my understanding, it really is, young man.'

'I shan't give up my job at the Jerusalem, Father. I shall go on being gainfully employed.'

'Employed? Gainfully? On your knees for a pittance gainfully employed? Your hands soon won't be a book-writer's hands if you stay there much longer.'

(Oh yes, they would be; seven years later, they would be a writer's hands in earnest. It was then that I informed my father that I had abandoned all hope of ever producing a book; it was then that I feigned hopelessness, when I was most hopeful of achieving my strange ambition.)

'How's Rubens?' I asked, to divert him from the subject of the Home.

'What a considerate son I have in you. Always anxious to find out how your old dad's faring.'

'Are you keeping well, Father?'

'Funny you should inquire. Actually, I'm not. Keeping well. My leg's giving me frightful gyp. The penalty for living too long, I suppose.'

'I really do think you should see a doctor,' I said, hearing the lack of urgency in my voice.

'And I think different. I think very different. As for the dog, he's in the lap of luxury, where he's blooming, thank you kindly. I can't exercise him any more, so I get the Quinlan woman to take him out on the common – when her cursed ulcer isn't making her as useful as a spare prick at a wedding, that is. If she's clutching at her gut, and Cole's not tending the garden, I have to slip that born bloody scrounger Sparrow an extra pound or two to stop the beast from wrecking "Blenheim" and everything in it. That's your beloved Rubens for you – a liability.'

'You'll have to excuse me. It's my turn for a bath, Father. We have a strict rota. The water only heats up twice a day.'

'Lend me a hand, will you, and help me off this torturer's rack you use for a bed.'

He rose with difficulty, clinging to both my hands.

'Jeans for Christ's sake, and he wants to be a book-writer! I need a stiff Scotch. You don't have one, locked away?'

'No, Father.'

'No, you wouldn't have. Put a razor to your face yet?'

'No, Father.'

'You won't be growing a beard, then, will you?'

'Of course not.'

'You'd be sprouting all over the shop if you could, I'd wager. Out of sheer cussedness. The sight of you with fungus on your chops isn't a prospect I look forward to, young man. You can see me down to the street – the least you can do for me – before you take your turn in the tub.'

'I'm sorry you're going, Gabriel. I'm genuinely sorry. You've been a sane, a calming, influence, I don't mind telling you. Hackney, did you say?'

'Yes, Diana. It's a bit nearer to the Jerusalem. By a few miles.'

'I shall miss you, and so will the blight on my life, though you'll never catch her admitting it. I've some wine left over from our New Year shindig, Gabriel. Let's drink a toast to your Hackney health.'

'Thank you.' I added, with forced cheeriness: 'That will be lovely.'

'No, it won't. It will most probably be foul. I thought I'd trained you not to be so damned English. You know I don't have a connoisseur's cellar. Open it, Gabriel, there's a dear, while I fetch the Woolworth Waterford.'

I filled the glasses.

'To Hackney,' said Diana Sparey. 'To Gabriel.'

We sat at the scullery table and drank.

'It's better mulled, isn't it?'

'Yes, it is.'

'A fraction. If I let you in on a little secret, will you promise me faithfully that you'll pass it on to no one else?'

'A secret?'

'It concerns the Countess.'

'I promise, Diana.'

'Oh, you must. And don't you dare break it. I've no wish to hurt the old duck.'

'Perhaps you shouldn't confide in me. For safety's sake.'

'I shouldn't be confiding in you at all if you weren't leaving us. The Countess has a nephew, Gabriel. In London.'

'She hasn't ever mentioned him.'

'She wouldn't. She's too ashamed.'

'She's talked about her brothers. I was under the impression that they stayed on in Russia and were both dead.'

'They did stay on, Gabriel, and they are. Dead. Michael is Nikolai's son. He came here when he was a boy. Now for the secret. Micky Petritsky and his wife, Doris, sell fish and chips – the best for miles around, people say – in Woolwich somewhere. It's thanks to Micky that Countess Bolina can afford to do nothing for a living. It's Micky's money that pays her rent and buys her posh chocolate and guarantees that she doesn't have to pawn her jewellery. It's Micky, my angel of a tenant, who's let the Countess go on being the Countess for more years than you've been born.'

'What is it she's ashamed of?'

'Fish and chips, Gabriel, fish and chips. It shames her that a Petritsky fries food for the peasants. She allows Micky to support her, but not to visit her. Visiting is strictly *verboten*. He turned up once unexpectedly and she screamed and raged at him – in Russian, naturally – and the poor, sweet man went off in a very tearful state indeed. And yet ... and yet, he still keeps sending her monthly cheque. She's twice complained to him, to my certain knowledge, that his loan – yes, dear, loan – is not large enough. "I shall pay back every penny when my ship comes in," she says. "The details are all recorded in this ledger." And twice he's increased it, the loan, the stupid saint of a man. Micky believes it's an honour – his privilege – to help her, and

164

she encourages him in his belief, fish and chips or no fish and chips.'

I took the secret with me to 13 Holly Villas, Clapton Square Passage, Hackney, along with my accusing desk, my books and clothes, my radio, the picture of George Fox, and several jars of Diana Sparey's marmalade and chutney.

'I hope you will remember your friend when you are tucking in.'

'Yes, of course I shall. Diana, I have a great favour to ask of you.'

'A reference, would it be? Something like that?'

'No, nothing like that at all. It's my father. I don't want him to know my new address.'

'I shan't tell him, Gabriel. I shall be at my most absent-minded if he tries to coax it out of me. I shall put on a scatter-brained show just for his benefit. Your Hackney privacy is ensured.'

'Thank you.'

'Sad though she is at losing her favourite serf, the Countess is already preparing for the arrival of the new lodger. The *hypothetical* new lodger, Gabriel, because I'm not quite certain that I can cope with someone else in the house. I shan't find another mediator as patient as you, to remind the Countess what she always chooses to forget when she's in one of her uppity moods, when she's crowing in that maddening way she has: that the Russian invasion of Hungary killed any remaining hopes I may have had in Kremlin communism. Now I shall have to remind her myself, and I don't honestly feel equipped for the task any more – oh, it's too much of an effort. I think I might well murder her.'

'I shall give evidence at your trial, Diana. You're bound to be acquitted.'

'And if Mr Pringle springs to my defence, too, Gabriel, I could have a peaceful old age, couldn't I?'

We both must have pictured a springing Mr Pringle in the same instant, for we both began to laugh – loudly, immoderately, in each other's arms.

I would tell my friend Mudey, whom I hadn't seen for many months, that I was moving to Holly Villas. I would tell him in person, I decided, impulsively, on my last Saturday at Mrs Sparey's. I would go to his house, knock on his door, and give him what I did not doubt would be a very pleasant surprise.

I knocked, and waited. I knocked again.

'Who is it?'

'It's me, Mudey. Gabriel. Open up.'

'Gabriel?'

'The same.'

'How dare you?'

'How dare I?' I laughed.

'You've no right,' said Mudey, in a furious whisper, from behind the closed door. 'You've no right and it's no joke. Be off with you. Go away.'

'I've come to – '

'Come to, come to, come to, come to,' he jabbered. 'I don't care what you've come to. I'll call the police, I have a phone just here, I'll call the police this instant.'

'But, Mudey – '

'It's a terrible thing when a person can't rest easy in his own home. I say you have no right. I say you have no right in the world.'

Then the letter-box's flap was pushed out, and I glimpsed Mudey's tongue.

'Go, youngster. Please go, youngster. You mustn't see me now.'

'I'm your friend, Mudey.'

'You are. Yes, that's true. You are.'

I bent down to talk to him.

'Goodbye, youngster.'

I remained crouched there until a sob broke the silence. It was like the shot from a starting pistol. It told me to run.

9

'The Campbells are coming,' said my father. 'That jumped-up grocer next door has sold "The Cloisters" to a family called Campbell. Scotch, I'd wager, to judge by the moniker. I've always got on well with them.'

'Why is that, Father?'

My question was 'typically oafish'. Wasn't it obvious – hadn't it sunk into my cast-iron skull; if it hadn't yet, it ought to have done, damn it – that of all the Celtic races, the only one with any rightful claim to civilization was the Scottish? 'It's a fact, young man, an undeniable fact.'

I knew that glare; I knew what it forebode. A 'Blenheim' lecture was under way.

'You just listen, and take heed. In your path through life, you'll meet twisters and crooks by the dozen, most likely by the hundreds, but I'm willing to stake the contents of this room that there won't be a man jack among them from north of the border. I'm not peering into a crystal ball, young man, I'm talking out of my own experience. No Scot I've met has ever fiddled me, has ever shown me more faces than the clock he was born with, and that's why my prediction must be treated with respect. I speak as I find, and I haven't found a single, solitary Jock who's been anything but fair in his dealings and open in his behaviour.'

'Haven't you?'

'No, I haven't. And I've never seen a Jock in those cursed Yanks' jeans things you're still wearing neither. A kilt's a daft bloody outfit for a burly bloke to walk about in, I grant you, but at least it has history on its side, and it gives you a good laugh wondering what you'd clap eyes on if the wind suddenly sneaked up under it. But those! You might have thought of putting on decent trousers before you came to honour me with your presence.'

I did not explain that I was dressed indecently because I was there to exercise Rubens on the muddy common, at his request, free of charge. I did not remind him of the favour I was doing him – a favour necessitated by the chronic condition of Mrs Quinlan's ulcer, by Cole's refusal to go anywhere but to church on the sabbath, by Harry Sparrow's housemaid's knee. A shrug seemed appropriate.

'You'd look smarter with an old piece of sackcloth tied round your legs. Your mother would be turning – ' He stopped, stared at me wildly. 'I mean, she would be turning red – blushing, young man, blushing – with embarrassment, young man, at the sight of you, if she could see you as I'm seeing you now.'

(How fair you were in your dealings, Father. How open in your behaviour.)

'The Scotsman, I was remarking, is a stalwart fellow. It's the average Scotsman I'm describing, of course. Scotland's had her share of rogues same as any other country, it stands to reason. Macbeth and that wandering half-witted wife of his, they were a prize pair of fiends, a disgrace to their tartan, baying for bloody blood, but they did live long ago, when stabbing and poisoning and similar was considered normal. It's recent times, since I was a lad, that I'm referring to.'

'Shall I make myself useful, Father?'

'The dog can wait.'

'I was thinking of your glass. It's empty. Do you want another whisky and soda?'

'I do believe I do.'

'Just a splash?'

'Why bother to ask? You've been mixing my drinks since you were thirteen.'

'I was still twelve, Father. On February 1, 1950, I was still twelve. That's when I started mixing them for you.'

'Twelve or thirteen – it's really no matter. I could die of thirst while you're nitpicking.'

'I'm at your service, Father.'

'Take a dram yourself.'

'A what?'

'A dram, you Sassenach oaf. That's what they say in Bonnie Scotland. A wee dram.'

'Do they? No, thanks.'

'You can't say I didn't offer. Yes, young man, the Scot is the only straightforward Celt there is. I don't know exactly why that should be, I couldn't give you a reason if pressed, but such is the case. Just compare him to a Welshman and you'll follow my line of argument. The average Taffy is sly and oily – he's pricing your shoes while you're trying to catch his darting eye. Devious, he is, devilish devious. Low cunning is in his nature. He's the master of the word that comes out dripping with honey, and I wouldn't trust him a tittle and a jot, specially while my back was turned, especially then, I can tell you. Your old dad isn't taken in by those melodious tones, all that "look you"-ing and gog-gog-gog-goging they go in for, nothing but singsong it is, no wonder they form so many choirs. Oswald Harvey isn't deceived by the tuneful Welsh, young man. No, sirree – as your friends, those Yanks, say.'

'Is the mixture to your taste?'

'Yes, yes, yes. You're a capable barman, if you're not good for much else. Let me offer another comparison – as regards the Scot, and with regard to what I'm saying. Just compare him to an Irishman and you're duty bound to agree that he's the better of the two. I haven't met a Paddy yet who isn't a walking pisstank. I drink, I make no bones about the fact that I drink. I enjoy a tipple, a wee dram, I'd be a hypocrite if I said otherwise, I'll even admit I've been the worse for wear once or twice – but has anyone ever had to pick me up off the floor, Paddy-fashion, in seventy-nine years? The answer, young man, is no.'

'Is it?'

'It is. It is, indeed. Most definitely. There was a priest used to knock on certain doors in Shylock's stables, you wouldn't remember him, he was Irish – well, his name, and this is the gospel truth, was Father Flood. And did that Floodie have a thirst! Inbloodysatiable, it was. Unbloodyslakable. No greater guzzler has drawn breath. And talking of breath, his was – what's the word? – hazardous. Only a born idiot would have struck a match when Father Flood was in the neighbourhood. I had to laugh the day I heard he'd snuffed it. He was giving some poor, pious Mrs Paddy the last rites, and would you believe, he keeled over himself and went to his eternal rest before the old biddy. Fell across her bed, he did, startling her out of the few wits she had left. It took two strong men to lift him off, with the Mrs Paddy screaming all the while that he hadn't fulfilled his mission, he hadn't, saints preserve her. And that, young man, is the average bogtrotter for you. In the Emerald

Isle, even the Holy Joes are pie-eyed and floor-prone, when they should be clear-headed and upright.'

'You've never said you've been to Ireland.'

'I've never said because I haven't. You must take a dim view of your dad's sanity if you think he'd waste a precious minute of his life on that moonstruck stretch of peat. I don't have to go there, young man, to learn what a hell of a place it is. I'm judging it by the odds and sods who get tearful for the home country every Saturday night in every public bar in every London pub. If they miss it so much, I ask you, why were they so quick to leave it?'

'Work, Father. They needed work.'

'Work, my flaming backside. Work, the oaf says! I've worked alongside of Paddies, and I'm here to testify that I did all the working and they did all the talking. From dawn to sunset, their mouths were cluttered with daftness.'

'Like Johnny Tuohy's?'

'Whose?'

'Johnny Tuohy's.'

'Who on earth are you talking about?'

'The man you rescued, Father. From the Thames.'

'Rescued? Thames? Oh yes, by God, him, him. Johnny Tuohy's part of my Stone Age, as it were, lost in the mists of time, as you might say. He was another typical gabbling pisstank – the first I ever met, back in Vicky's century it would have been. I couldn't fish him out, hard as I tried. I can't say that wretch I leaped in after was much of a loss to the human race, because he wasn't. Still, young man, still and all, a life's a life, and it's terrible when a person decides – if decides is what he does – to take it.'

(Yes, Father.)

'Even the likes of him. What did you have to go and dredge his memory up for? I was – I damned well am – in a cheerful mood. I was just thinking to myself that I'm looking forward to meeting the Campbells. I shall greet them as friends, seeing as how they're Scots. I shall enjoy a dram with them, I don't doubt, and perhaps they'll invite me to celebrate Burns Night – Burns *Nicht*, rather – in their new hoose. I shall go over with a lump of coal at Hogmanay, as if I was their neighbour in Perth or Bonnie Dundee or Edinburgh, or wherever. It'll be a real hame from hame for them, I'll see to it, you can bet on it.'

(Now that I have you on the tip of my pen, Oswald Harvey, almost – at last – at my command, now that I have you where you never expected to be, I could easily transform you into a dedicated despiser of all things Scottish – those skinflint Scots could join the drunken Irish, the smarmy Welsh, in your mind's eye's menagerie. In Chiswick, now, on this dull spring morning, I am tempted to compose the 'Blenheim' lecture you didn't choose to deliver: The Caledonian Menace, say. I could set down, if I chose to, your awful warnings on the haggis, for example: 'Don't touch it – that's my advice. It's sheep's offal, young man, stuffed into a piece of skin from the animal's gut. It sounds inbloodydigestible, and it is'; your thoughts on the sporran – 'Who but a Jock would gad about with a fur pouch dangling from his belt? A dafter, more useless, article has yet to be invented'; your opinion of the bagpipes – 'Was there ever such a cursèd caterwauling? It's worse than that symphony stuff you fill your skull with. Only a bunch of hairy-arsed heathens would call it music.'

I must live with you as you were, Father, and I cannot allow myself imaginative liberties, however harmless. I have to resist the urge to fabricate. My business is to tell the truth, as you so often, and so skilfully, failed to do. I shan't have you inveighing against the Scots, for such an outburst would be my conceit and mine alone. No, I shall try to preserve you, if I can, exactly as you were.

'Our esteemed parent's conversion to the Scottish cause happened on an evening in 1900, when he was an impressionable youth, believe it or not,' my half-brother, Tom, told me recently. 'He loved to boast that he'd been present at an historic event – Harry Lauder's London début, at Gatti's-Over-The-Water. It was love at first sight, Gabriel – on Daddykins's part, anyway.'

And then I remembered that my father had impersonated the comedian once, for my mother's benefit, just before the one and only New Year she celebrated in 'Blenheim': 'I love you best when you're being mad like this.')

During supper that Sunday, which I'd prepared in the kitchen 'Escoffier was welcome to', my father nearly begged me to give him my new address. That scruffy bitch with the stuck-together glasses had put him into a rage with her smiling prevarication, her 'I'm a respecter of confidences, Mr Harvey', her closing the door on him with some nonsense about his being careful not to buy fruit that came from South Africa, because it was tainted with innocent blood. He wasn't accustomed to that kind of treatment, most definitely he wasn't.

'I asked her to keep it a secret. She was respecting my confidence, as she said.'

'Secret? Secrets are for children, young man.'

(Are they, Father?)

'Are they, Father?'

'Of course they are. It's common knowledge. I don't understand the funny game you're playing with me, but I do know it's childish. What's the harm in a father wanting to find out where his son is living? Answer me.'

'I can't.'

'I'm not surprised.'

(I could not admit to him that I intended to fulfil my Swedenborgian penance on my own terms, in my own time, at a certain necessary remove. Better a secret than that admittance – what it involved, what it implied.)

'Then give me your address, if you please.'

'I would prefer not to.'

'I'd be easier in my mind, young man, if I had it. Accidents, emergencies, nasty tricks up Fate's sleeve – there's method in your old dad's madness.'

'I'll phone you regularly, Father. Never fear.'

'It'd please me very much to have it.'

'Shall I cut you off another slice of pork?'

'No. I'll have what's left for lunch tomorrow, with some piccalilli. Don't change the subject. I was saying, in case you hadn't heard, that I'd be easier in my mind.'

(You had a mind, Father – on that occasion, at least. I always had to make do with a skull.)

'I did hear you. I'm keeping my secret.'

'The devil you are, curse your stubborn hide. I take it I am right in assuming that your new hovel is an improvement on that Spare-eye woman's doss-house?'

'Yes, Father. You are.'

(An improvement? No, not in Oswald Harvey's 'Blenheim'-biased view. Scarcely that. Mr Pearce's little villa was the humblest of dwellings. I was his sole lodger, occupying the adjoining upstairs rooms, neither of which was large enough for a man of means to strut in. I did my ones and my still troublesome twos in his outside privy, and made breakfast and washed myself – usually in cold water – in his tiny kitchen, to the chirruping accompaniment of his budgerigars, Gypsy Rose Lee and Fatty Arbuckle, whom he thought were either celibate or impotent, for nothing – not even the merest vestige of an egg – had come from their lovey-doveying, if that's what their perpetual commotion signified.)

'I certainly don't have to wait an eternity to use the bathroom, as I had to when Countess Bolina was at her *toilette*.'

(The drawn-out *toilette*, of an hour or more's duration, was not encouraged at Hackney Public Baths, where I went each Friday evening for my weekly soak.)

'Eternity's too short for her to turn herself into a sight fit for decent people. You've probably lumbered yourself with worse raving bloody lunatics than her, if I know you as well as I think I do. In whichever run-down part of London it is you've chosen to hibernate – yes, that's the word, hibernate. Yet more Poles and Nazareths, I expect.'

'You haven't remarked on the meal, Father.'

'Should I have done? You're after a compliment, are you? Here it comes.' He belched loudly, laughed, and belched again. 'There you are, young man. Ready at your request. Finer than any words, the stomach voicing its gratitude.'

'Thanks.'

'I hope and trust that you aren't thinking of becoming a chef. I seem to remember warning you on that particular front after the omelette went to your head years ago.'

'I heeded the warning, Father. Have you forgotten already that I'm writing a book?'

'Forgotten? You and your cursèd nonsense.'

'You never warned me against being a writer – sorry, bookwriter. Perhaps you should have. I'll wash the dishes, and then I'll leave.'

'Quinlan will see to them in the morning, ulcer permitting. I don't like the thought of you doing woman's work.'

'You can't say', I said, 'that I didn't offer.'

I have to write that I was relieved when Mrs Gadny was taken away from the Jerusalem. My relief, though, was of a different order from that felt by the older women, who had come to detest her. Mine was altogether more subtle, I imagined, for it was not compounded of anything so strong, or so simple, as detestation. Her presence there had caused me to see a second presence – a presence I had no wish to see in Mrs Gadny's –

with hair like hers, hands like hers, legs like hers. Mine was a sweet relief. When Faith Gadny was removed from the Jerusalem that September morning, a not-to-be-envisaged Amy Harvey went with her. Heddle's lady's glory was restored.

'I fear the worst for her now, Gabriel,' sighed Mrs Capes. She continued, with increasing liveliness, 'I've heard it's a terrible place they're putting her in. It's set in its own grounds, off the beaten track, in the depths of the countryside. She'll have electric wires attached to her if she's not careful and starts having one of her tantrums – and doctors in white coats will rush in and give her the shocks treatment, the way they're prone to do. If only she'd accepted my friendship when I offered it, instead of behaving high and mighty and reaping the consequence.'

Faith Ethel Gadny's 'reaping' was six months in the sowing. Days after her arrival at the Home, Mrs Ricks was advising the staff to handle her with velvet paws. She had become hysterical when the doctor had attempted to examine her: 'I'm used to a man,' she had mumbled in bewildered fright. 'That's what I'm accustomed to. I've never had to suffer another woman looking at me naked.' And then Nurse Trembath and Mrs Capes had stood by amazed as she tore into shreds the photographs of her dead husband, Tom, and her dead daughter, Celia – snaps she had clearly treasured but now, in her hysteria, was driven to destroy. And then it was discovered that she had been writing letters to her dear friend Mrs Barber, to whose funeral she and Celia had sent a beautiful wreath of lilies two years earlier. And then Mrs Ricks decided that the widow she had considered gentle and remote was too disturbed to sleep in the same ward with Queenie Crane, Edith Trimmer, Peggy O'Blath, Maggy Affery, Alice Temple, Ellen Gross, Louise Capes, and her pair of 'vegetables', Winifred Hibbs and Myrtle Burns: 'Mrs Gadny will have a room of her own for a while.'

'Dotty Faith's got mad Annie Erskine's ghost for company now,' said Miss Trimmer. 'Old Annie was shoved up there by Unwin the Tartar soon as she entered her second childhood. Had a dummy stuck in her gob at the end – gurgling and dribbling, they say she was, and only wanting a cot to turn her cell into a nursery.'

(On Thursday May 25, 1967, when the last traces of the Jerusalem were finally razed to the ground, I learned that it was in that same room or cell that the dying Roger Kemp of

Liverpool invited Mrs Parchment to become his amanuensis: *You must to fetch pen and ink and paper and you must to listen and to mark my every words. And you must to put them down without adorning for I must to tell how the wonder came to me and how the wonder left me and no adorning must to be in the telling. And you must to be patient Dorothy and I must to be in truth for you have spelling out of words in your power and I have the words that must to be spelled.*)

Dotty Faith – as Miss Trimmer and Mrs Crane persisted in calling her – was brought down from her cell only once before her removal to the Home in the country. The occasion was Mrs Hibbs's ninetieth birthday party, which was held in the ward. I had spent the morning helping with the preparations: hanging streamers from the ceiling, laying the table under the critical eye of the Jerusalem's cook, Mrs Clements, who had baked a special cake decorated with nine candles ('That's one for every ten reckless years'), and arranging long-stemmed roses in a silver bowl it had taken me an hour to polish to my satisfaction.

Everyone was seated when Mrs Gadny was led in by Nurse Barrow and Nurse Perceval. Mrs Gadny did as she was told, returning the 'Hullo' of Mrs Gross and 'Good afternoon' of Mrs Capes at Nurse Barrow's discreet insistence.

Winnie stayed insensible throughout, even when a knife was put into her quivering hand for the cutting of the cake; even when a celebratory glass was placed at her lips; even when her friends sang 'Happy Birthday to You'; even when Matron read out a telegram from the mayor and mayoress in her brightest voice; even when Faith Gadny suddenly screamed, and went on screaming and spoiled everybody's fun.

'Get rid of her,' shouted Mrs Temple, while Mrs Gadny raged.

'Send her away,' shrieked Mrs Crane. 'Send her to a bin.'

'Bedlam'd do for her,' observed Mrs Affery.

I stared at Mrs Gadny, who was struggling to break free from Nurse Barrow's arms; stared, and saw my mother – an image of my mother – struggling too. It was Amy Harvey who was whimpering; Amy Harvey who was being restrained and consoled.

'Come now, Faith. We'll go to your room. The two of us. We'll go to your room. Together. We'll go. Come now.'

Come now, Amy. We'll go to your room: but she's in Malta, I assured myself. Or somewhere. She has rooms, rooms.

(Of course she had rooms. She lived in that vast, mysterious, unvisited Abroad – in a villa overlooking the sea, perhaps – and had all the light and air and space she wanted. At forty-six, she was surely in her prime, and as glowingly beautiful – I did not doubt – as she had been for me on that far-off morning of her departure. Wherever she was, she was still her own woman – of that I was convinced.

And when she grew old, there would be no restraints on Amy Harvey. She'd not be cast aside, ever. Impossible to think of her seeking consolation from some future Nurse Barrow, in some future Home that may or may not once have been a workhouse. Ridiculous idea. Her husband, her darling Ossie, wasn't Jerusalemed, and he was older than poor Faith Ethel Gadny. No, she'd not be degraded – she had her pride to sustain her, and my unfailing love.

Yet Mrs Gadny was proud, and fiercely so – and wasn't it her pride, nothing else, that was making her scream, that was ensuring her the dislike, the contempt of the other inmates? Ah, yes, that was the word: inmates. Mrs Gadny could not reconcile herself to becoming one, and that was why I saw my mother in her. Amy Harvey an inmate? Pigs would be flying first.)

'Tell it not in Gath, Gabriel' – Mrs Ricks looked about her to see if anyone was in listening distance – 'but hasn't life been happier for us since we've been Faith-less, so to speak?'

'Yes,' I had to agree. 'It has.'

'Close your eyes and put out your hands.'

'What for, Mummy?'

'Oh, you know what for, you imp. You know very well what for. Do as you're told.'

I was quick to obey her.

'I'm not expecting a present. It isn't my birthday.'

'I'm aware of that, for obvious reasons. And anyhow, Gabriel, the nicest presents are always unexpected.'

'But it's October – '

'There you are.'

'It feels like a book.'

'It feels like a book because it is a book, though it's not a brand new one.' She kissed my forehead, and then, as was her custom, wiped the kiss away. 'You have my permission to unscrew your eyelids now.'

The book in my outstretched hands was definitely not brand

new. Its pages had begun to yellow, and its binding was buckled and stained.

'*Moby-Dick*,' I said.

'I must come clean, Gabriel, and confess to you that it's not a proper present – not a present I went out and bought for you specially, in a proper shop. I found it on a seat on the top deck of the 39 bus which was bringing me home in state from my secret place this afternoon. There's no name and address inside, so I didn't feel terribly guilty about taking it.'

'It looks very long,' I said.

'And far too difficult for your simple mother to make any sense of, I'm afraid. I opened it at a couple of places and felt my poor brain reeling. It reminded me of those bits of the Bible I can't manage to read, however hard I try – all those family trees following each other, Gabriel, starting with Esau's and ending with I don't remember whose. The Jesus parts are much more my cup of tea. The truth is, I would have left *Moby-Dick, or, The Whale* right there where I found it, if I hadn't seen a certain person mentioned in Chapter LXXI – whatever number that is.'

'Seventy-one.'

'Trust my little scholar to have it at his fingertips. In Chapter 71, you'll meet a Gabriel, Gabriel, who's not the kind of Gabriel I should have cared to have brought into the world. You're not going to grow into a holy terror, a fanatic, are you?'

'No, Mummy.'

'That's good to hear.'

On a bench, in the gardens of St John-at-Hackney, for three successive balmy July days, I read every chapter of my mother's 'improper' present. I'd had the battered copy in our nameless house, in 'Blenheim', in my Clerkenwell attic: I had held it lovingly, as if it were a precious object; I had protected it from further assault by keeping it wrapped in thick brown paper; I had cherished it, but of Captain Ahab's doomed search for the great white whale he was compelled to destroy I was still stupidly ignorant. On the first of those July mornings, I had caught an echo of Heddle singing of his lady:

> Shaming the rose and lily
> For she is twice as fair

and this erstwhile Lily had taken *Moby-Dick* from beneath his pillow and had decided that he would start his summer holiday by reading it, if he could.

I reached the seventy-first chapter late on the afternoon of the second day. It was then that I made the acquaintance – what my mother might have called the 'proper' acquaintance – of my fearsome namesake, the self-appointed archangel on the whaler *Jeroboam of Nantucket*. Melville's 'deliverer of the isles of the sea and vicar-general of all Oceanica', encountered in a London churchyard that still contained the parish stocks and whipping post, made me think – in his wild ravings – of George Fox walking barefoot through the streets of Lichfield, crying woe unto that bloody city. Yet the prophet Gabriel – raised among the Neskyeuna Shakers, for whose edification he had often descended from heaven by means of a trap door; warning his terrified fellow-sailors on the *Jeroboam* that Moby-Dick was the Shaker God incarnate – was plainly crazy, a full-fledged lunatic, a ranting monster, and George Fox, my benevolent George Fox, quite as plainly wasn't. George's humanness, his essential sanity, was there in the lithograph I had bought in an Islington junk shop, was there in his *Journal*, given to me by a grinning Mr Nazareth ('You have his mug shot, Harvey – here is his criminal record') – it was wonderfully there, I believed, in the winter fields outside Lichfield, when he confounded the shepherds by taking off his shoes and walking away from them with his feet burning like fire. The fictional Gabriel, the actual George – Mr Nazareth, who considered the Archbishop of Canterbury to be certifiably insane, would say there was no difference between them. I would say there was.

I shook, literally shook, with excitement then, for the thought had come to me that I could write about that very difference. I had a subject. History must have seen hundreds of Gabriels, I reasoned, and there had been other Georges, shaking their fists at steeple house spires. I'd track them down, somehow; I'd seek them out; I'd make them live again, the cranks and the visionaries. I had a subject.

The Campbells had come to 'The Cloisters' from Coventry, via Trinidad. The Campbells had come, and they were black.

'As the ace of spades, God help us,' spluttered my father, his inventive powers of description for once failing him. They were dark brown, the Campbells, to be absolutely precise, I said. I had been greeted by two of them – a tall young man and an old woman – on my arrival.

'You just tell that Nazareth chum of yours that I'd rather have him as a neighbour, if I had the choice – which I haven't, obviously. I think I could grow used to seeing his sarcastic face over the garden wall. But people who move into a house at dead of night when decent citizens are in their beds, they're not to be trusted. It doesn't bode well, that sneaky sort of behaviour. I've signed a petition.'

'A petition? What kind of petition?'

'I can't remember the exact words. A fellow called Weekes wrote it, solicitor type, command of the language – he's our spokesman, you might say. The gist of it is that the residents hereabouts don't relish the prospect of them, those Campbells, living in the Avenue. Not at all, they don't. Most definitely not.'

'Why, Father?'

'Oaf, oaf, oaf – do I have to spell it out?'

'You do.'

'They lower the tone.'

'The tone, Father?'

'Yes, the tone, Father. They bring the neighbourhood down. What if I wanted to sell "Blenheim"? A fine price I'd get for it now with Sambo and his tribe practising their voodoo next door. I was going to buy a property on the right side of the river, and here I am ruing the day I didn't. They have ways of keeping Campbells and such at a safe distance in Belgrave Square and Kensington Gore.'

'They most probably have.'

'And by a safe distance I mean a long distance. Miles, I mean. I was cautious, young man, with the money Sir Vincent left me, which is why I bought "Blenheim", mainly to please your mother – '

(My mother's pleasure at occupying 'Blenheim' – its large, high-ceilinged rooms, its wide central staircase, its echoing bathroom, its kitchen that 'Escoffier was welcome to' – had not been made evident to me, her doting, watchful son.)

'Yes, you can look amazed, but it's the truth. Your mother argued my head off against our crossing the Thames, and I gave in to her, as I always did. She hated the idea – I still can't fathom why – of settling down in a snooty district. That was her word, that "snooty", not mine. And then there was the price to be paid.

I picked up "Blenheim" for a very reasonable figure, considering. What it's worth now I dread to think.'

'Who'll be receiving your petition, Father?'

'You're determined to be oafish today, to judge by these damned-fool questions. The Mayor, to begin with. My Member of Parliament, for another. Men with influence. You don't hand over a petition to somebody without any, do you?'

'No, Father.'

'It's that jumped-up grocer's doing, the two-faced Deptford-born bastard. He must have known, even while he and his mutton-garnished-as-lamb wife were drinking my best whisky out of my best glasses in *my* sitting-room, thank you kindly – he must have known, blast him, and she must have known, blast her, that those Campbells he'd sold "The Cloisters" to weren't Scottish, blast him, weren't Scottish one bit, were no more Scottish than I'm Scottish or they're Scottish. They must have known, while they were oiling their hypocrites' throats at my expense, that the Campbells weren't white-skinned, like most of the Campbells you meet. They knew, blast them, they knew; they knew the fine pickle they'd be leaving me in.'

'Pickle?'

'That's what I said. Imagine what having them in "The Cloisters" will do to my standing locally. I shall lose respect, because of them. Cole has already threatened to resign, and Quinlan's sure her ulcer'll burst, if not explode. A pretty pickle, indeed. Are you smiling, young man?'

'No, Father.'

'I could have sworn you were, after your fashion. You've a smirk, a curl of the lip, that's special just to you, in case you hadn't noticed.'

'I don't practise it in the mirror, if that's what you're implying.'

'Take the beast for his run, for Christ's sake, and spare me your cursèd nonsense. And give those Campbells a wide berth. They were a Scotsman's slaves not so long ago, remember. That's how they got hold of their name.'

The Gabriel Harvey that I was at twenty-seven: I stop and wonder at him now.

An odd little man, a stranger might have said, seeing Mr Harvey at work in the Jerusalem – sweeping the corridors, scrubbing down the refectory table, washing the plastic daffodils that Mrs Gadny had complained were dusty. A surprisingly boyish-looking man, that stranger might have observed, with no trace of stubble on his chin, and the sort of faint moustache you find on many pubescent girls. A happy man, clearly, in the way that the slightly retarded seem happy – so the stranger might have assumed, taking a casual glance. How humane of the Matron to employ him, the stranger might have thought. And how perceptive, for he was a cheerful drudge, performing his dull and unpleasant tasks without complaint.

A glance would have revealed that much about me to the casually curious stranger. I *was* a noticeably odd little man: I had heard people, women mostly, make remarks to that effect. 'There's Peter Pan come to life'; 'Is he a puppet, do you suppose, Daphne? Escaped from his ventriloquist?'; 'He looks peculiar, him with the pretty-pretty face.' I was flattered, rather than offended, by their comment. Ah, but you don't know the extent of my oddness, I told them silently; I am odder than you can possibly imagine, and I am far more peculiar than I look.

Yet was I? I don't think I really thought so. I didn't consider myself remotely peculiar, for all my silent boasting. If I appeared odd to strangers, then that was nature's fault, I reasoned. I was different from other young men that I had met, and that difference signified the true extent of my oddness – or did, at least, until I was twenty-eight, when Mr Pearce disturbed me one evening, and I had to leave Hackney, where I had indeed been happy.

The reasonably contented Gabriel Harvey, at twenty-seven, was only disheartened by his mother's absence. He still hoped for her return, and still summoned a shadow of her to him with the incantation HMV B9719:

> Surely you heard my lady
> Go down the garden singing,
> Silencing all the songbirds
> And setting the alleys ringing –

but there were times, and they were increasing in number, when he ached for her loving presence. It was then – the ache inside him not abating – that he needed to put on his Moygashel frock, to sit in perfect quiet, allowing himself to hope that the charm of Abroad would soon wear off. A natural need, ensuring a blissful peace of mind.

It had to be a secret need, of that I was aware. I had blushed while buying my reminder of a vanished day because of that very awareness. I could anticipate derisive laughter even as I handed the dealer the two pound notes that made it mine. I wasn't peculiar, though: I didn't want to change into a woman. Heaven forbid. I simply wanted a fraction of the past retrieved, that was all. Yes, my natural, secret need was perfectly ordinary.

That I had no cause to wonder at the man I was then is what causes me to stop and wonder now.

'Hop in, young man. Your carriage awaits.'

My father was calling to me from the back seat of his Morris Minor, which was parked outside the entrance of the Jerusalem.

'I'll take you home, if that's what it is, in style.'

'No, you won't. Thank you, Father.'

I was about to greet Mr Sparrow when I realized that someone else was acting as Oswald Harvey's chauffeur.

'This, young man, is Flint. Edward – or Teddy – Flint.'

'How do you do, Mr Flint.'

Mr Flint smiled at me and nodded.

'I'll answer on Flint's behalf. I have his permission to say that he's well. Except for his stutter, that is. He has his good days, when he can almost talk a stream, and his bad days, when his tongue goes haywire in his mouth. Today's a bad 'un, isn't it, Flint?'

A brisk nod from Flint indicated that it was.

'But does he moan about his affliction? No, he does not. Flint's like me in that one respect – he keeps his aches and pains to himself. Quinlan's cursèd ulcer I've learned to live with, but Sparrow's housemaid's knee I'm buggered if I'll suffer. I have sent him and it packing. The last straw was when he started referring to the damned thing by its medical name – patellar bursary, or some such quack's nonsense. "Blenheim" is a house, I told him, a family mansion, not a bloody hospital for clapped-out skivvies. Now just tell Flint your destination.'

'No, Father. I don't want to. Goodbye, Mr Flint.'

I heard my father instruct his new driver to 'follow that oaf' as I set off in the opposite direction to Hackney.

In my anxiety, my absurd anxiety, to ensure that 13 Holly Villas remained untainted by my father, I changed trains five times before ascending into safe London streets at King's Cross.

My accusing desk had yet to imprison me. I was still a doodler, a scribbler, for although I was in possession of a subject and even a title – *Lords of Light* – I lacked the stuff, the matter, with which to make a book. I should have to start searching for it.

I did not ask myself how; I did not ask myself where. It sounds ridiculous now, like so much else in my life, but I sought my lords – the genuine and the crooked; the wildly crazed and the cynically intelligent – in London's junk and second-hand book shops. Jesse Page's admiring biography of C.H. Spurgeon was my first find, Lady Jasmine Rowell's *Life of Eustace Barnes*, the reformed thief who preached under the name Barabbas, my second. Soon I had lords galore from which to choose.

It was only when the Jerusalem was razed, when Mrs Ricks handed me the two fat ledgers that contained the story of Roger Kemp of Liverpool told in his own words to an enthralled Mrs Parchment, that I gained the courage to begin my long incarceration.

Queen Elizabeth the Second's little cotton socks were blessed, as usual, on that grisliest of all grisly Christmas Days.

'Her Majesty doesn't have natives living next door to her.'

'She doesn't have anyone living next door to her, Van P.,' snorted Margery Carstairs. 'Buckingham Palace is entirely separate from the rest of the world, which is quite right and proper. Fancy my having to remind you, a supposed royalist, that a monarch never knows the bother of neighbours.'

'*If* Her Majesty had people living next door to her, *if*, they would not be natives, is what I am attempting to say, Marge.'

'If, if, if! Since Her Majesty, bless her, is never likely to move out of her palace – her palace without a next door, let me tell you – your "if", Van P., is totally, if not completely, ludicrous.'

'No, it's not. Use your imagination, Marge, instead of criticizing a chap when he's trying – '

'That's exactly what you are – trying.'

' – trying to make a perfectly valid point. If Oswald here, just imagine, had been born into royalty, do you think he'd have tribesmen living next door to him?'

'Impossible "if". Out-of-the-question "if". Man-in-the-moon "if". King Oswald, Van P.? Prince Oswald? Our Oswald bearing the orb and sceptre? You are talking twaddle, my dear Van P., which is unlike you, very unlike you. If you're going to be iffy, you have to offer "ifs" that look as if they might happen.

Oswald's coronation will not be taking place while I live and breathe, and there's no "if" about that.'

'Who said there was? I didn't. I wish you'd listen to a chap, instead of jumping down his throat. My hypothesis, Marge, is that if, and I do mean if, Oswald was a higher Oswald, then he wouldn't be where he is. Would he?'

'And if I'd been Joan of Arc, I'd have gone up in smoke. Really, Van P., I think you've left your brains with your brolly in the hall. Either that or you are teasing your Marge deliberately. Bad Reggie, to tease me so.'

The teaser glowered at the teased and drained his glass.

'I've said it before and I'll say it again, but you are far too pretty to be a man,' Miss Carstairs suddenly boomed at me. 'Far too pretty!'

'Leave the boy be,' snapped my father.

'No offence, Oswald.'

'None taken, Miss Carstairs.' I hadn't spoken for at least an hour. 'I'm not offended.'

(I was, though, and bitterly, but not by her familiar taunt. That afternoon, for some deep reason in me, I was more than ever offended by the hospitality my father lavished on Reginald Van Pelt and the woman who was still waiting to be led to the altar. Couldn't he see what I saw, clearly – that they were bona fide oafs, the genuine oafish articles? Perhaps he could, and was secretly revelling in their oafishness. Perhaps he regarded them as his licensed jesters, their payment for humouring him the food that Margery Carstairs gobbled up with such untidy eagerness, the drink her promised bridegroom swallowed until achieving his desired stupor. But perhaps not – he had told me of his admiration for the waggish Reggie and his loathing of Clapham's corsetière. My father suffered Margery Carstairs for the sake of his friend – the friend who had supplied him with the goose my mother had roasted thirty-seven days before she left "Blenheim"; the friend I was certain she must have despised, she who was so quickly, so easily embarrassed by inconsiderate behaviour.)

'Is everyone present of the opinion that an Englishman's home is his castle?'

He's off, I thought, in panic; he's away; he doesn't require an answer, but he's bound to get one.

'Of course we are, Oswald. Reggie and I are, anyway. I, or rather we, can't vouch for your offspring.'

My father sent me his special glare and then embarked on the most confused of all his 'Blenheim' lectures: The Mental Moat.

'I have a mental moat.'

'You have a what, Oswald?'

'Be patient, Reggie, and I'll explain.'

'I could have sworn you said moat.'

'I did, Reggie. I did, indeed. Most definitely. A moat I said and a moat I meant. A stretch of dividing water surrounding a castle – that's my idea of a moat. Well, the castle I am referring to is "Blenheim", my "Blenheim", this Englishman's home. It lacks a moat, but that is not to say that it doesn't have one.'

My father looked delighted with his conundrum, and paused that we might ponder it.

'Because it does. Up here it does.' He tapped his forehead. 'That's where the "Blenheim" moat does its work, and does it better than the real garden wall. Mine's a mental moat, and I'm finding it a godsend.'

'Are you, Oswald?'

'I am, Marge, I am. The jumped-up tradesman, by the name of Williams, who had this house built for him in 1867, I think it was, had no need of one. It was peaceful in these parts then, almost a rustic retreat. Ironmonger Williams was living in a London paradise and he knew it. I thought I was, too, until those foreign bodies appeared on the horizon. That's why I've invented, so to speak, my mental moat. It keeps the nigger Campbells at bay.'

'What about a drawbridge, Oswald? Every moat has a drawbridge. Otherwise your castle's completely cut off.'

'Quick thinking, Reggie. Yes, there's a drawbridge. Entirely mental, mind you. It's up most of the time, you won't be surprised to learn. I let it down when the coast's clear, after Quinlan has given me a signal from the garden. Oh yes, I've a drawbridge. I amuse myself raising and lowering it over my moat. Keeps the old grey matter healthily occupied, I do assure you.'

'Does it, Oswald?'

'It does, Marge. I've become a bit of a philosopher, though I say it as shouldn't. It was their hollyhocks that first made me picture a moat. I hate the hollyhock, it's such a common bloody flower. It has no place, a hollyhock hasn't, in a gentleman's garden, and neither, come to that, has the dahlia, which they grow, too, those so-called Campbells. I nearly had a fit when I saw them, and was ready to explode, but then, I tell you no lie, the moat came to me in a flash of inspiration. I took stock, I did, of my plight – I had coloured neighbours who grew holly-hocks, and a respectable person can't have worse, I reckoned, to contend with, short of living in a mud hut in some infected swamp up the Limpopo. Bugger them, I thought, they won't get Oswald Harvey in a tizzy. He has a moat, he has. He has his own private mental moat.'

'Mental or not, Oswald, a moat's a strange thing for an Englishman to have round his property in 1964.'

'You're right, as per always, Reggie. But needs must, old pal. It's positively medieval, I grant you, a moat, and the same applies to a drawbridge, but it serves its purpose. Yes, indeed. Most definitely.'

(Years later, on the day the proud inventor of the mental moat was buried, a tearful Mrs Campbell told me that my dear old father had given her family no harm. The neighbours to their left, the Robinsons, in 'Tintagel', had sorely tried their Christian patience – turds, human turds, Robinson turds, had been dropped through their letter-box or dumped on their door-step, and Mr Robinson, who was a church warden, had phoned them for several weeks at three in the morning to let them know they were monkeys. 'Your daddy was a true gentleman, Mr Harvey. A little eccentric, if you'll pardon me saying so. I remember how he used to stand under his magnolia tree, smiling to himself, staring into space, as happy as a sandpiper. That was when we were new here. I couldn't count the number of times I said hullo to him and he didn't hear me. He was lost in his own joyous thoughts, I expect, God rest his soul.')

The mental moat, the lecturer continued, could be recom-mended as a means of restoring general sanity in an England going, if not already gone, raving mad. If every decent white citizen, present company included, owned a mental moat, civi-lization as we once knew it might well be preserved. It was as simple as Isaac Newton's apple, the notion that a man – or woman, Marge, mustn't leave out the fair sex – could keep his distance from the black, brown and yellow enemy in his midst, courtesy of Oswald Harvey's moat.

'Your moat may be fine for you, Oswald, but it wouldn't do for me. I can feel it in my bones. If a black man approached me I'd see red. I'd hit him with my handbag where it would damage him most, or slap his face, providing I had my gloves on. A

186

helpless woman in a dark alley would not have much use for a moat, Oswald.'

'A helpless woman who goes down a dark alley deserves anything she gets, the stupid bitch,' said Reginald Van Pelt. 'You're not helpless, Marge, and you wouldn't be seen dead in a dark alley, so your argument doesn't hold water.'

'Oswald's moat doesn't either.' Margery Carstairs guffawed. 'Being mental.'

I took Rubens for his run then – our last together, as it transpired. Away from mental moats and unrespectable holly-hocks, away from the endless drivel that passed for normal discourse in 'Blenheim', I seriously considered breaking the unspoken promise I had made to my aunt. I'd done penance enough, in view of the fact that I had nothing to be penitent about: I'd put up with his insults and remained open-eyed during his lectures; I had been a most attentive son, given that I held no affection for him, not a residue, not a drop. I actually hated him.

I stopped at the thought, to the dog's annoyance. Yes, it was hatred I felt for Oswald Harvey, the hatred his third wife, my mother, must have felt when she deserted him. This was a renewed, a refreshed hatred, stronger by far than the mere loathing that had caused me to escape from 'Blenheim' a decade earlier. By honouring a vow my aunt hadn't even heard, I was behaving like a hypocrite, I was practising a constant deceit. *He is a poor creature, and he should be pitied* – that was a 'should be' beyond my emotional powers, for I could not pity him, and saw no reason to. I was finished with hypocrisy.

So I told myself on the bleak common, in the ailing light. So, I think, I told Rubens too. Reckoning without life, the way life has of nurturing our deceits, I could imagine the newly refreshed-in-hatred Gabriel Harvey as a very paragon of honesty: 'You're a madman, Father, and I am sick and tired of you.'

But my aunt had loved me, and my aunt had values. She had entrusted me with a duty I was, and for ever would be, unequipped to fulfil. Kathleen di Salvo had been totally aware of the mockery her brother had heaped upon the doting sister he had nicknamed Swedie, and she had seen fit to forgive his every gibe. Were I to be honest now, I would be committing an act of betrayal against my aunt's loving values. They mattered to me, since I had once been their grateful recipient. They persuaded me not to tell the truth.

'Your father says you are writing a book.'

'My father's wrong, Miss Carstairs.'

'The devil he isn't. Speak up for yourself, young man. Don't be modest all the time. I happen to know you're burning the midnight oil.'

'I've abandoned the idea.'

'You've done what?'

'I've abandoned the whole idea of writing a book. You ought to be pleased.'

'Pleased, I'll only be pleased when you make something of yourself. If I live to see the day dawn, that is.'

'He's a shilly-shallier, your son, Oswald. I've said it before and I'll say it again. I recognize the type – there's not much in human nature that slips through my net, as some have noticed to their cost. You've been too gentle, too easy-going, with him. You've encouraged him to think the world owes him a living.'

'When I want your opinion, Marge, I shall ask for it. I understand that young man better than anyone, himself included.'

'Of course you do, Oswald.'

'Just you remember,'

'I will, Oswald. I will.'

I let myself out of 'Blenheim', quietly, while my father and Margery Carstairs were enjoying Reginald Van Pelt's recitation of 'Eskimo Nell' – an exceedingly filthy monologue, running to some fifty verses, that seemed to be little concerned with the occupant of an igloo. The manic reciter's fiancée honked with laughter at the numerous indignities visited upon the body of a tireless Chinese maiden by a flotilla-full of drunken sailors: 'Oh, I shall burst, Van P., I warn you, burst!' My father, however, was more amused by the many faecal mishaps that beset the insanitary crew: 'You're the Laurence Olivier of smut, that's who you are, you dirty-minded old bugger.'

10

'You'll have to buy me a parrot now, young man.'

'A parrot? What do you mean?'

'A book-reader like you ought to be quicker on the uptake. Hazard a guess.'

'A parrot, Father?'

'That was the word I used. Put on your thinking cap. Why would your old dad be wanting a parrot?'

'I can't imagine.'

'Yes, you can.'

'To keep you company, I suppose.'

'By Christ but you're dimwitted today. Does "Pieces of eight! Pieces of eight!" strike a chord, ring a bell?'

'Yes, it does.'

'There's your answer.'

'I'm mystified.'

'If I had a parrot to perch on my shoulder, I could pretend I was Long John Silver, couldn't I?'

I stared at my grinning father. Only days before he had railed against whatever it was in cursèd nature that had brought him to this pretty pass. To be stuck in a hospital, among a lot of rheumy old wheezers, coughers and spewers, was the worst bloody humiliation of his life – and that meant eighty-three, coming on eighty-four, years. And then to be told by some medical pup calling himself a surgeon that he had a thrombo-angi-something-or-other, which in plain English turned out to be a clot, and that he would have to undergo an operation, which might result in his left leg being amputated – which it did, which it bloody did; well, it was a terrible shock, and a terrible loss, and he was in a terrible state, he didn't mind admitting.

'I'll have to have a wooden leg fitted first. No point in owning a parrot if I can't stand up.'

'No, Father,' I agreed, to my astonishment.

'I think I'd like an oak one.'

'Do you?'

'Yes, I fancy oak. Oak's dependable. I shall cut quite a dash with an oak leg. I intend to take myself off to the best leg-makers in London and have it specially carved – that's the next plan on the agenda, when these ghouls in here have finished with me.'

'You should have seen a doctor ages ago, when the pain started troubling you.'

'I don't require a lecture,' snapped the lecturer. 'Particularly from you. I've had my gutful of tongue-lashings from the pup with the scalpel, thanks very much. What I should have done in the past can't be done or undone now, and there's an end of it. Subject closed. I'm glad you've decided to show me some respect in your person at least.'

'Respect?'

'That's what I said. By not wearing those Yankee-bloody-jeans things is how you're showing it, young man. Corduroys are a real improvement, even if they are a bit on the arty-farty side.'

'Oswald's himself again, by the sound of it,' said a voice behind me. I turned and saw a plump, grey-haired man, carrying a bouquet of spring flowers.

'I wasn't expecting you until this evening.'

'I knew you'd be pining for my company, so I've come earlier.'

'It's not convenient.'

'Stop talking piffle. It's perfectly convenient.'

'I'd rather you went away. This minute.'

'Are you', I dared to ask the stranger, 'my half-brother Thomas, by any chance?'

'Yes, Gabriel. I am.'

(Oh, it was wonderfully inconvenient, that chance encounter in St James's Hospital. I relished my father's confusion as I shook hands at last with Thomas Harvey, the flesh of his flesh I had known about for fifteen years. Secretive Oswald Harvey stared in amazement at his secretive younger son, the son who was even now exulting in the fact that his daring had paid off so satisfactorily. I had rendered the man of words speechless, and I felt triumphant.)

'We've communicated with each other before, Gabriel,

though you probably don't realize it. I seem to remember I phoned our father one evening and you answered. I think you said he was doing business in Paddington – up to something shady, I've no doubt. It was a long time ago, anyway, when you were still a boy and I still had some youthful blood in me.'

'Tuesday, March 7, 1950. That was the day you rang. At a little after half-past six in the evening. I picked up the phone because I was expecting a call and Mrs Gould had her hands in flour in the kitchen. She was making an apple pie.'

'The devil she was,' said Thomas Harvey, smiling at his father. 'You've produced a phenomenon in Gabriel, Daddykins. The lad has a truly remarkable memory.'

'Watch how you address me, will you. March 7 happens to be his mother's birthday. There's nothing remarkable in a son remembering that. And he's far too long in the tooth to be a lad.'

'I stand corrected. Or perhaps I don't. This tasteful floral arrangement is for you.'

'Is it?'

'Yes, it is. Most definitely.'

'Stick it in a vase then.'

'I would if I had a vase to stick it in.'

'Stop your daft fussing, will you, Tommy Rotter. And do sit yourself down, if you're planning to stay, which I hope you aren't. I never could abide my children hovering.'

'You'll be relieved to hear that I have to dash off. I've a taxi merrily ticking over outside.'

'It wouldn't be ticking over inside, would it?'

'No, you sharp old sod, it wouldn't.'

'Get going.'

'It's been a fruitful lightning visit, Daddykins. You're obviously on the road to recovery and I have met the legendary Gabriel.'

'Bring me a bottle of decent Scotch when you fly in again.'

'Only if it's with the doctor's permission. I don't want to be accused of spoiling all the good work.'

'Good work? A perfectly useful leg thrown out with the scraps and slops good work? Be a pal to me, Tommy. Just bring it as a present and forget the doctor. He thinks every bloody thing in creation's bad for me, except pap, pap, and more pap.'

Thomas Harvey bent down and kissed his father on the forehead.

'I shall do as I'm told. I'll be back tomorrow.'

'You needn't bother.'

'I know I needn't, but I must. *Au revoir*. Take these cursèd flowers from me, please, Gabriel, and see that someone sticks them in a vase for our grumpy daddy – would you?'

I took the bouquet from him.

'And here's my card. Give me a tinkle on Sunday. We must meet and talk, And talk. And talk.'

'Well,' said my father when Thomas Harvey had gone. 'That was your half-brother.'

'Yes.'

'Always in a rush.'

'Is he?'

'Daft fusspot. Not your type of person, young man.'

'Isn't he?'

'Definitely not. Most definitely not. Who told you you had a half-brother? It wasn't me, was it?'

'It wasn't you.'

'I didn't think it was. Then who was it?'

'Aunt Kathleen.'

'Who else? I might have guessed it was Swedie.'

'She told me about Thomas that Easter I stayed with her.'

'Why have you never asked me about him?'

'Why have you never mentioned him?'

'If I were you, I'd tear up that card he gave you. Tommy's a prattler, a gossip. He'll have your ears humming with his tittle-tattle.'

'Will he, Father?'

'And most of it's his own daft invention. That's why I call him Tommy Rotter.'

'Is that why?'

'Yes, young man, it is. He's sarcastic, too, in case you hadn't noticed.'

'I hadn't,' I lied.

'You should have. He isn't serious like you. He treats life as a joke.'

'Does he?'

'Yes, yes, yes, he does. Heed my advice. Steer clear of Tommy.'

I was prevented from asking him to explain why I should steer clear of my half-brother by the arrival of the 'pup with the scalpel', who was middle-aged and stooped. I got up to leave, promising to return soon.

'Not tomorrow. I don't want the pair of you bothering me.'

I handed the bouquet to the ward Sister, who pronounced it exquisite: 'This will brighten your dear grandad's bedside.'

In the corridor, I passed an old coloured woman, who waved to me. I waved back, delighted by her spontaneous show of friendliness.

It wasn't until I had left the hospital that I realized she was one of the Campbells who lived in 'The Cloisters', beyond the mental moat that now surrounded 'Blenheim'.

My father lowered his mental drawbridge with reluctance when I visited him on Sunday, January 31, 1965. I had insulted his closest chum by staging my cursed vanishing trick during Reggie's brilliant party-piece at Christmas. Sneaking off without a by-your-leave was the behaviour of a bad-mannered lout, not the son of decent and respectable parents.

'I was bored, Father.'

'You were what?'

'I was bored. I was bored by that witless filth Mr Van Pelt was spouting.'

'Then there's something wrong with you.'

I reminded him, gently, that he had rarely sworn in my mother's presence; that it was he who had threatened to strap me till my skin was raw if I ever said certain words in her hearing.

'A word like "shit", for instance. A word much favoured by the poet – is that the word? – of "Eskimo Nell".'

'And a bloody fine word it is, too. By Christ, you can be pompous. Butter stands no chance of melting inside your refrigerated mouth. You're a grown man now, you oaf, small as you are, with blood running in your veins. Live in the present, can't you. You were still only a boy when I threatened you with the strap.'

'Mummy wouldn't have been amused either. Mummy wouldn't have endured it. If there's something wrong with me, there's something wrong with her as well.'

'Men and women laugh at different things. Hasn't that simple truth of human nature dawned on you yet? You're not a bloody monk.'

'Miss Carstairs laughed.'

'She's not a woman in my book, young man. She's what I call a female.'

I said that I didn't understand, although in fact I did. I had become a connoisseur of Oswald Harvey's distinctions.

'Use that skull of yours for a minute while I explain. A woman is someone you look up to. A woman is someone you treat with respect. A woman is someone you buy pretty clothes and luxuries for. Could you look up to, could you respect, that corset cow?'

'No, Father. But Mr Van Pelt could. And does.'

'She's Reggie's blind spot. She's the fly in his ointment. Reggie's a splendid fellow, one of the very best, but even he isn't perfect. Everybody has a blemish in their character, and in his case it's the devotion he shows his precious Marge.'

'What's yours, Father?'

'What's my what?'

'Everybody has a blemish. What's yours?'

'That's for other people to say. Make yourself useful. My leg's giving me gyp and it's a long journey to the drinks cabinet.'

(Three weeks later, that leg would give him gyp no more.)

'Am I preparing lunch today?'

'Quinlan's seeing to it. She hasn't clutched her gut since breakfast. No escape to the kitchen for you, young man. You're lumbered with your old dad.'

(As I am still, Father. As I still am.)

'If Reggie pops in on the off-chance, you'll have the opportunity to apologize to him.'

'I thought I left discreetly. I didn't disturb the audience's pleasure.'

'Reggie was offended, whatever you thought.'

'I wasn't aware that Mr Van Pelt has such sensitive feelings.'

'There's a great deal, Horatio, that's not been dreamt of in your philosophy, young man.'

(Oswald Harvey a Shakespearian? He had called Mr Middleton, the owner of our nameless house, 'Shylock', but that was a common term for Jews in the London of my childhood – except that Mr Middleton wasn't Jewish. I tried to remember if I had ever heard him say 'Lead on, Macduff' or 'All that glitters is not gold' and similar misquotations, and was sure that I hadn't. Would I, who had not been his Gabriel for fifteen years, be his Horatio from now on?)

'You're wearing your smirk.'

'Am I?'

'That's what it looks like to me. I hope you removed it when you went to Westminster Hall.'

'I've been nowhere near Westminster Hall, Father.'

'You should be ashamed, you should, to admit it. What's your excuse?'

'I was working. At the Jerusalem.'

'So were most of those who stirred themselves to go and pay their respects to Winnie – they were working, too. They found the time, they did, to file past the old warrior.'

'Did you find the time?' I asked, in the certainty of receiving no for an answer.

'Yes, as a matter of fact I did.'

(Yes, as a matter of fact he did. Oswald Harvey's brief homage to Winston Churchill was reported in an American newspaper. 'A friend sent me the cutting. Amazing, isn't it? Dale found it quite by chance in the New York Public Library. He was flicking over the pages in search of the item he wanted – a homicide, that was his word, in Connecticut – when his beady eye alighted on the name of our dear dead Daddykins. Read it, Gabriel. It's priceless.'

Among the thousands of ordinary British citizens who thronged London's famed Westminster Hall to honor the memory of Sir Winston Churchill was one Oswald Harvey, a survivor of the Somme. 'I am nobody special,' said Mr Harvey, a dapper old English gentleman in a snazzy Savile Row suit. 'I was just a humble private doing his duty in the trenches.' Humble Private Harvey's stiff upper lip quivered for a split second as he spoke of his hero. 'I had to come to Winnie's lying-in-state. It was the least I could do for the man who saved my country.'

'How inconsiderate of Churchill to have died in the January. If he'd lingered on for another couple of months, our father could have – no, would have – hopped along to Westminster Hall on his remaining leg. "I lost it doing my duty in the trenches. A Gerry sniper got me in his sights" – et cetera, et cetera. What a tale the sharp old sod might have told! What a wasted opportunity!')

'It was the least I could do for the man who saved my country.'

'I watched the funeral on television.'

'Do you have a set, then? In wherever it is that you live?'

195

'No, Father. There's a set in the Jerusalem.'

(The ceremony moved all but one of the women to tears. 'Sniff, sniff, sniff,' said Miss Trimmer. 'Sob, sob, sob. I blame him for the last war and I don't care who contradicts me. You won't catch me crying for him. I remember a terrible air raid over Peckham and a doodlebug missing the Trimmer house by a whisker. I blamed him for that at the time, and I still blame him, and no amount of boo-hooing and blubbering will make me alter my mind. I went out the next morning with my ration book and I surrendered my precious coupons for a tin of pineapple chunks, to which my sister and myself was extremely partial, being born with the identical sweet tooth. I brought home that tin as if it was the Crown Jewels and I set it on the kitchen table and I said to Enid, "This is to celebrate our narrow escape." I got the best spoons out of the family cutlery chest and Enid fetched the evaporated milk and I put the chunks – ten for Edith, ten for Enid, share and share alike – into our breakfast bowls and the pair of us sat down to a special treat. Or so we thought. We weren't to know, honest and open in our dealings as we'd been since children, that some of those chunks wasn't pineapple by a long chalk. Oh, no. They was swedes or parsnips and they was mixed in with the real fruit and swimming in the syrup, just as if they'd come off the tree instead of dug up for cattle fodder. I was that angry I was incensed, and I wrote a stiff letter to that man you're weeping for, telling him in no uncertain terms that when I parted with coupons for pineapple, it was pineapple I expected to find, not nasty little bits of vegetable. Him the conquering hero? He couldn't even be bothered to write a reply. Wail away, wail away, but I'll not be joining in the wailing.'

'Pineapples', said a distressed Mrs Capes, 'do not grow on trees, you jaded, ignorant old woman.')

'That was history you were looking at, young man. The passing of an age.'

'Yes.' I answered my father's glare.

'We were saying goodbye to Winnie's England.'

'Were we?'

'We were indeed. Most definitely.' He cut a cigar and lit it. He took a deep puff. 'That's exactly what we were doing.'

'You usually smoke cigars at night, after a meal.'

'There's no law against me having one now, is there? If there is such a law, I haven't noticed it. What was my drift before your oafish interruption?'

'The passing of an age, Father. Winnie's England.'

'Ah, yes. Well, it's gone, hasn't it? It was in the coffin with him.'

'Was it really?'

Oswald Harvey, cigar in hand, explained that it was. The England he conjured up that Sunday – the England of Sir Vincent as well as that of the man he was now calling Winnie – was a feudal paradise occupied by trusting masters and cheerfully obliging servants. Only foreign invaders, soon vanquished, ever disturbed its peace. It lacked a laystall history, this fanciful England – the history with which the storyteller had once beguiled me under the faintly hissing gaslight while his wife was at her 'secret place'; the history he had long ago eradicated from his memory when he transformed himself into the 'Blenheim' lecturer.

'Mummy said you both voted Labour in 1945.'

'What Mummy said and what Daddy did are two different things, young man.'

'I don't believe you, Father.'

'As you please.'

'It isn't as I please at all. It's a fact that you voted for Mr Attlee.'

'Is it?'

'Yes, Father. You had no money then.'

'Enough of your nonsense.'

Mrs Quinlan entered without knocking and announced that dinner was ready to be served.

'It's luncheon,' my father corrected her. 'It's luncheon we eat at lunch time in Liberty Hall.'

Then, on my mother's forty-seventh birthday, my charmed Hackney life – for so I considered it – came to an end.

'You, you, you – why, you little powder puff, you – '

'Mr Pearce?'

'That's me. Mis-ter Pearce. Mis-ter Pearce. That's who I am, little Miss Harvey.'

I smiled at my startled landlord.

'This, this frock I'm wearing, Mr Pearce, it's – '

'It's to play the little minx in, isn't it?'

I actually laughed at the absurd suggestion.

'No, of course it isn't. It helps me, this frock, to remember someone.'

'The man of your dreams, perhaps, Miss Harvey?'

'Please stop calling me that, Mr Pearce.'

'I'll call you anything I want to. I might even call the police, come to think of it.'

'Don't be silly.'

'Me silly? Mis-ter Pearce silly? You've got a nerve, Miss Harvey. You've got an almighty nerve, you dirty little pansy.'

'I'm not what you say I am. I'm not at all like that.'

'I have eyes, Miss Harvey. I can see. The evidence is in front of me, in a blue dress. Not a blue suit, a blue dress.'

'And that's the extent of it, if you look closely. I'm not wearing earrings, am I? I'm not wearing make-up, am I? I'm not wearing bracelets or a necklace, am I? I'm not wearing women's shoes, am I? Have I a wig on my head? No, Mr Pearce, I haven't.'

'But you *are* wearing a dress. A woman's dress, Miss Harvey.'

'I know I am. And I tried to tell you the reason. I can still tell you, if you'll let me, if you promise you won't scoff.'

'I won't promise you anything. You're one of nature's mistakes, Miss Harvey. It strikes me your mother would have been better off if she'd thrown you away and kept the afterbirth.'

I could not, would not, try to tell him my reason, I decided in that instant. Why risk further ridicule? HMV B9719, the day of recurring brightness, the need to sit in perfect quiet – he'd say I was mad; he'd laugh me to scorn.

'I'm waiting for your reason.'

'I'm afraid it's too private. I can't tell you. I can't expect anyone else to understand it.'

'Is that so, Miss Harvey?'

'Yes, Mr Pearce, it is so.'

'Your private reason looks very simple to me. You wish to be a woman.'

'That's never, never been my wish.'

'Hasn't it, darling?'

'No, Mr Pearce,' I shouted. 'It hasn't, it hasn't. Never for a single minute.'

'Temper, temper, darling. You'd be tossing your curls at me if you had them. You just listen to me, you freak, you freak in a frock, and listen carefully. You can sleep your unnatural sleep under some other roof tonight. Do you hear me, Miss Harvey?'

'I hear you, Mr Pearce.'

'Pack your bags and vamoose. And take all your junk with you. I want you out of my house in double-quick time.'

'It's after eleven, Mr Pearce.'

'I know.'

'I could leave in the morning. Very early.'

'Early in the morning's too late for me. Get going now. I'd be obliged if you went out of my front door in men's clothes, Miss Harvey. The neighbours might see you and jump to conclusions about their old friend Jack Pearce.'

'I can't take the desk with me.'

'I'm a reasonable man. A fragile young lady struggling along the streets with a heavy desk? Perish the thought. You must arrange to have it removed. Within the week, Miss Harvey. It'll be firewood afterwards.'

Mr Pearce stood there, watching me get out of my Moygashel frock, which I folded neatly. He can see for himself that I'm not really peculiar, I thought. I'm not wearing knickers, am I, Mr Pearce? But I refrained from asking him.

'You haven't any hairs on your chest.'

'That's true.'

'You're a pretty pathetic specimen.' He waited for a response. In the silence, I took down my suitcase from the top of his walnut wardrobe. 'An apology, that's you, Miss Harvey.'

He continued to watch me as I packed. He can see for himself, I thought, that the frock is the only item of women's clothing I possess. Shirts, pullovers, underpants, socks, trousers, those 'cursèd jeans things' – surely he can see, if he has eyes.

'A word of warning, Miss Harvey. Keep out of Hackney. This borough's forbidden territory where you're concerned. *Comprendy?*'

'I understand, Mr Pearce.'

'There's a sensible girl,' he said, slamming behind him the door I should have locked.

I shall never know why Mr Pearce came upstairs that night. In the few happy months I stayed in his 'villa', I rarely saw him, let alone spoke to him. A retired signalman, he spent most evenings at a railwaymen's club. He was usually asleep when I breakfasted. In the course of the longest conversation I had with him – on the day he accepted me as his tenant – I learned that his wife had run off with a dance band crooner named Pepe, and that his daughter and her engineer husband lived in Toronto. He had yet to meet his six grandchildren. I learned, too, that he enjoyed the thrillers of Hank Janson, his favourite being *Dead Dames Don't Talk*. Had I read it? No? I should. It was strong stuff, he assured me in his dull voice.

And it's that same dull voice I hear as I set down his insulting 'Miss Harvey'. The surprise of chancing upon me in my Moygashel frock was registered on his face, in the form of a suddenly twitching right cheek, but his taunts were expressed without emphasis, without colour. Even his 'Mis-ter Pearce' was leaden, his vocal cords refusing to give the sarcasm its sarcastic due. His word of warning ought to have sounded melodramatic – as melodramatic as it looks on the page. In 13 Holly Villas, on Sunday March 7, 1965, it came out on a monotone.

I heeded it, nevertheless. I kept out of Hackney for over a decade. I suppose I dreaded the public ridicule Mr Pearce had it in his power to inflict upon me – a power he would never have attained if I'd locked myself in that evening. What a truly stupid oaf I'd been, and how I regretted that stupidity in the years that followed. In dream after dream I was taunted by Hank Janson's admirer, who sometimes led a braying mob in pursuit of the freak in a frock. The imagined Mr Pearce would screech for Miss Harvey's blood, and I would race across a Clapton Square that went on into infinity.

Walking away from Mr Pearce's that Sunday night – weighed down by a suitcase that contained my clothes, my radio, the portrait of George Fox, and those of my books from which I could not bear to be parted, even for a few days – I was suddenly possessed of a treacherous thought. 'If you were here, Mummy, in England, I should have no need of the blue frock. It's because of you that this has happened. It's really you, Mummy, who's to blame.'

I stopped then, in the actual Clapton Square, and begged her forgiveness. 'I didn't mean it, Mummy,' I said aloud. 'I honestly didn't mean it.'

In my frustration to convince her she was blameless, I started to weep.

Remembering those tears in Sorg, Minnesota, I had to laugh.

I awoke the next morning in the Jerusalem – in the room to which Mrs Gadny, alias 'Dotty Faith', had been exiled.

'My landlord's had a brainstorm,' I told Mrs Ricks. 'He's decided that he doesn't like me. He didn't give me a reason.'

'People are most peculiar, Gabriel. That's the one certainty in life.' She smiled, shut the smile off quickly. 'Did he insult you, this peculiar man?'

'He said he hated the sight of me.'

'I don't think he was flattering you. Oh, you poor boy.'

'I'll survive, Mrs Ricks.'

'Of course you will.'

'I must find somewhere else. I feel guilty about sleeping upstairs.'

'What on earth for?'

'I shouldn't be there, Mrs Ricks.'

'You're not depriving anybody of the pleasure of staying in that room, I do assure you, Gabriel. The ladies look on it with horror. You know you're welcome to it until you're comfortably settled. It isn't your fault that a madman in Hackney takes against you.'

'No.'

'You can move up in the world now.' She smiled her quick smile. 'Hackney's not my idea of paradise.'

(Paradise? Mrs Ricks lived in paradisiacal Kensington, in a service flat that denied her even so much as a glimpse of the sky and stars. All she could see from her three windows was a section of the massive red-bricked back of a department store. 'The woman in the flat above me swears that her bricks are pale and interesting compared to mine. "It's the pigeons," I tell her. "You're nearer the roof." It's our standing joke, Gabriel. Since we can't invite friends to admire the view, we ask them to chuckle over it instead.'

How could I explain to Mrs Ricks, or indeed to anyone, that Hackney, in the here-and-now, appealed to me more than any paradise? Until yesterday, I had been its happiest inhabitant. In Navarino Road – I did not remark – was a pretty house called 'Muse Cottage'; it pleased me to imagine a poet inside, in thrall to his Cockney Calliope, writing the London epic she demanded of him. No, that was a Hackney diversion it was impossible to describe – it was too private, by far. Gabriel Harvey, whom the Muse had yet to visit, felt tongue-tied at the prospect of relating how the subject for the book he had yet to write had come to him on a bench in the gardens of St John, near the tomb of the Loddiges family. What if *Lords of Light* never materialized? What if he failed to make his cranks and visionaries live? It was best to stay silent.

And those Loddigeses, those dead Hackney Loddigeses – who

were they, and where had their descendants gone? Enchanted by the unusual name, I had looked for it in the telephone directory, but no surviving Loddigeses – not a single, solitary Loddiges – adorned its columns. One day, perhaps, I would trace their history, which must have been imposing, to judge by their tomb. Another diversion, to keep to myself.

I kept the *fauteuils* to myself as well – and the fact that a man in the Elephant's Head, where I drank a pint of beer every Friday night after my soaking in the borough's baths, had talked glowingly of the Empire's foothills. 'Comfiest seats in the house, them foothills. The wife and me would never sit nowhere else.' The Empire he was referring to was the local variety theatre, and its foothills were – I discovered later that same Friday – *fauteuils*. I stood on the steps of the Hackney Empire and smiled at my discovery, for there was the magic word on one of its doors. 'I courted Mabel in them foothills. Nearly made a criminal of me, it did, finding the lucre to pay for the privilege. But once you've sat in a foothill, no other seat ain't good enough.')

'I'm not sure that I want to move up in the world.'

'I was teasing you, Gabriel.'

'Yes. Of course.'

'My predecessor, Miss Unwin, dubbed your temporary abode the "difficults' room". So just remember, Gabriel, that while you're our guest upstairs, I shall have to consider you a "difficult". And I am still teasing.'

'Yes, Mrs Ricks. Thank you.'

I was a 'difficult' for a week and five days.

'He ought to be foaming at the mouth,' Miss Trimmer observed to Mrs Gross, as the two women passed me in the corridor. 'I wonder if he's been visited by Annie Erskine's ghost yet.'

'No, I haven't, Miss Trimmer,' I said, looking up from the floor, which I was busy scrubbing. 'I didn't think that you, of all people, would believe in ghosts.'

'I don't, Mr Harvey. But then, I'm sane. Edith Trimmer's in no danger of ending up up there.'

'What's it like inside, dear?' Mrs Gross asked me. 'It sounds silly, but I've always been too frightened to take a peep.'

'It's very like a prison cell.'

'How would you know? Aren't you a bit young to be an old lag already?'

'Rest your tongue, Edie, and let Gabriel answer.'

There was only one tiny window, I said, offering a little light, and the walls had not been plastered. The ceiling was less than a yard above my head, and I was an unusually small man. It was really very like a prison cell.

(When I was writing *Lords of Light*, I remembered the claustrophobia I felt in that room, and tried to picture Roger Kemp, who stood six-foot-three without his shoes, in his long workhouse confinement. What misery he must have endured, where I knew irritation.)

'I shall be moving out of there tomorrow, Mrs Gross.'

'I'm relieved, Gabriel, I must say. I'm not superstitious by nature –'

'Yes, you are,' interrupted her constant companion. 'You're as superstitious as they come. You told me once you lived next door to a man who'd got a message from the Beyond – or the Other Side, or wherever – from his dead wife, who warned him not to marry a girl half his age. He didn't heed her warning, and dropped down dead himself for not heeding her – so you told me, Nell, as evidence that those spiritualists have a point, you said. I remarked at the time that Mr Gamfield didn't hear no voice from the Beyond – it was his human brain advising him not to act like a bloody fool. It was his own brain he should have heeded, Nell, but he couldn't, him being the kind of man he was. Lust was his undoing, not his poor faithful wife still warm in her grave sending his messages from daft Beyonds and Other Sides. He heeded what he kept in his trousers and he paid the price for it with his tired ticker conking out on him. A lot of men die that way, in my experience.'

'What a rigmarole! Have you quite finished, Edie? I am not superstitious by nature. You only see things that are stuck in front of you, that's your trouble. I'm glad you're leaving that room, Gabriel, because it's my opinion there's forces in there I'd rather not reckon with, and I'm relieved you won't have to – reckon with them, that is. Do you follow me?'

'Yes, Mrs Gross. I think I do.'

'Follow her? Forces? Forces, my fanny! The eye-wash a sensible person has to listen to in this place! Come along now, Nell, and leave this boy here to his women's work. You watch out for yourself tonight, Mr Harvey, in case those forces decide to drop in on you. You're not safe yet, according to Nellie Gross.'

'You can scoff, Edie. Gabriel understands what I mean.'

'Then he must be a mind-reader.'

'Perhaps I am,' I said.

'I'm sure he is,' said Mrs Gross, and patted me on the shoulder.

I had Diana Sparey to thank for my swift delivery from Mrs Gross's disquieting 'forces'. I had visited her soon after my expulsion from Hackney, and had repeated the story about Mr Pearce's sudden change of character. She had clucked in sympathy.

'Why don't you return to the Sparey fold? You can't have Walter's eyrie, I'm afraid, because there's a budding ballerina occupying it. Esther's a skeleton, Gabriel, though the Countess thinks differently: "For a dancer, my dear blind Diana, she is *obese*." But the basement's yours, if you want it.'

'Mr Pringle's basement?'

'Mr Pringle's no longer. A lady rambler bewitched him on the Yorkshire moors last summer, and he has gone to live with her. In delicious sin.'

'How ever did you find out?'

'He announced it, Gabriel – in thunderous tones. He threw a farewell party, on the spur of the moment: a slap-up champagne do, with teeny fishy corpses on slivers of toast, right here in the scullery. The Countess deigned to honour us with her presence, mostly out of curiosity, as she hadn't seen him at close quarters in all the years they'd lived under the same roof. "I have never rambled," she informed Brenda, Mr Pringle's girlfriend, who seems to be permanently in shorts. "The great outdoors holds no allure for me." Mr Pringle got riotously drunk, and kissed everyone goodbye, including Mr Nazareth, who would have turned pale if it were possible. It was an enchanting occasion.'

'I'm sorry I missed it.'

'So am I. Anyway, my trusted mediator, the basement is going a-begging.'

'It isn't that I'm not grateful, Diana,' I began, 'but I don't think I could live in a basement. In fact, I know I couldn't.'

(I knew I couldn't because I had a particular basement in mind – a Bloomsbury basement, in a Georgian wilderness.)

'I understand how you feel. There's not much light down there.'

'It's very kind of you to offer – '

'You annoy me, Gabriel, when you're being polite in that awful English way. I'm not kind in the least. You'd have to pay me rent, wouldn't you? It's you who'd be doing me the kindness by taking Mr Pringle's place.'

'Hardly, Diana.'

'Oh, yes. My before-Brenda Mr Pringle enjoyed the gloom and ignored the damp and didn't once complain in twenty years. I shan't find his curious like again unless I'm very lucky. Actually, Gabriel, it was pretty rotten of me to suggest the basement. Go up and pay your respects to the bane of my existence while I make a few telephone calls. Let me try and earn your genuine gratitude.'

'Vanish,' said the Countess when I knocked at her door.

'It's me, Countess, Gabriel Harvey.'

'Who? I receive no visitors except by appointment. My diary is blank for today.'

'Gabriel Harvey,' I shouted. 'Don't you remember me? I used to run errands for you.'

'Ah, *le petit Anglais*. Enter.'

I was commanded to kiss her right hand, and to sit in my customary chair.

'How pleasant to look upon someone who is neither robust nor fat,' said the Countess, peering down at me. 'You have met the ballerina *manquée*?'

'No, I haven't.'

'She is grotesque, believe me, my young friend. I tried to disillusion her, in her own best interests, from pursuing a career in the ballet, and was insulted for my expert advice. I, who have sat at the incomparable feet of Karsavina, to be put in my place by a suet pudding from a London suburb! She has been raised on fish and chips, this Esther Boddington.'

(I did not ask if Micky Petritsky had fried them.)

'The last ballet I saw', the Countess continued, 'was at Covent Garden. I cackled – that is the word, isn't it? – cackled at the *spectacle* of Serge Lifar in *L'Après-midi d'un faune*. It was *L'Après-midi d'un éléphant*, even though he wisely wore a girdle. He should have retired with grace, the vain old thing, instead of clumping so late in life on to a foreign stage – thud, thud, thud – and making an *idiot* of himself. This insolent Esther Boddington, she is already a jumbo, and she is still but a chit.'

'Diana was just telling me about Mr Pringle's surprise party, Countess. It sounds as if it was fun.'

'The *champagne* was inferior, and the food provided was excessively salty. Mr Pringle I was pleased to meet to say goodbye to, and as for his rambleress – she was attired, my dear, like a Boy Scout. Her bosom was emblazoned with badges. She was wearing, Mr Harvey, socks. Thick, thick, ugly socks. And sandals. And her knees, her silly knees, were exposed beneath her – oh, ludicrous creature! – shorts. Shorts. At fifty! Fifty years of age – probably more – and shorts!' The Countess was cackling now. 'And this rambling Brenda has captured Mr Pringle's heart. I presume she is passionate. Her panting lover certainly has next to nothing to remove – her blouse, her shorts, and her thick ugly socks! I doubt that she delights in beautiful *lingerie*. By the way, what would a robust woman wear under her *culottes courtes*? Do you happen to know, Mr Harvey?'

'I don't, Countess, I'm afraid.'

'Afraid? You should be afraid – afraid of rambleresses. You must keep yourself off the moors of Yorkshire, for fear of being captured by one.'

I had never seen Countess Bolina so happy.

'This Brenda, this *excursionniste*, she has awakened in me a dreadful – what is it when you are intrigued by the bedroom behaviour of other people?'

'Prurience, I think you mean. *Lasciveté*, perhaps.'

'You speak a little French? The English only ever speak a little. Well, Mr Harvey my dear, I have this prurience in my thoughts since meeting this Brenda, and I cannot control it! I giggle to myself when I picture him peeling off those thick ugly socks in a state of ecstasy, and I have badly aching ribs from imagining the blouse with all its badges being torn off by the lusty Pringle. Am I not wicked to enjoy this prurience?'

'Yes, you are,' I answered, to the Countess's great amusement.

'You've obviously put Bolina in a merry mood, you clever Gabriel, you,' said Diana Sparey as I walked into the scullery. 'What magic did you work?'

'None. I barely spoke. It's Mr Pringle's Brenda you have to thank for her wild laughter.'

'The vindictive bitch. The awful snob. As a matter of fact, I find Brenda slightly comic, too – but I like to think that I'm not malicious about her. Let's drink some plonk to celebrate your good news.'

'What's plonk, Diana? And what's my good news?'

'Which world are you living in? "Plonk" is what everybody's calling the kind of wine I drink – have always drunk. "Plonk" is the name the Tommies in the trenches gave to *vin blanc*. I haven't heard it for twenty years, but now – as I say – everybody's using it. Draw the cork for me, there's my angel. And the good news is that I've found you somewhere to live. Telephone call number four did the trick. It's a small flat, above an antique shop, in Fulham, owned by a friend of a friend. Here's the address. I hope it turns up trumps.'

The friend of Diana Sparey's friend's friend was a former mannequin. Sadie Jennings had modelled the New Look in London in 1948 – that same New Look my mother had coveted in Paris in that terrible February two years later. 'It's the smartest outfit on the market for Amy Harvey to return to England in. It's what her Ossie is giving her as a homecoming present.'

Sadie Jennings lived in a boat on the Thames at Chelsea Reach. 'Welcome aboard, darling. It's been this choppy the entire week. You must be utterly perished. Don't you possess an overcoat?'

'This keeps me warm enough.'

'A mackintosh? Either you have an enviable constitution, darling, or you're telling me a fib. Come in and huddle by the oil stove.'

'Thank you, Mrs Jennings.'

'*Miss* Jennings, darling, if you please. Watch your step on the gangplank.'

I did so, and slid into the boat.

'You seem nervous, darling? Are you?'

'No, of course not.'

'There's really no need for nervousness. A nice drinky will help you relax. I'm a gin-and-it girl, darling. Mother's ruin's all I have to offer.'

'That's fine,' I lied. 'Thank you.'

'Do you think I'm batty, darling? Be honest. My closest chums say I'm a belfry case. First impressions, now – they're usually right. What's your first impression of me?'

(That you are another performer, Miss Jennings, into whose play I find myself suddenly propelled.)

'I haven't formed one yet.'

'That's the whole point about a first impression, darling – it comes naturally; you don't have to form it. It's instinct, pure and unadulterated.'

'I've only just met you.' I faltered. 'I can hardly be your darling.'

'No, I suppose you can't. Especially since I've forgotten your name.'

'It's Gabriel Harvey.'

'So it is. It's lovely, darling – there I go! The Gabriel half, anyway, is lovely. What's your job, Gabriel Harvey? Oh, do do sit down. I simply know it has to be artistic.'

'I work in a Home, Miss Jennings. For old women.'

'You're far too young to be a doctor. Are you a nurse? A male nurse?'

'I'm not a doctor or a nurse. I'm a skivvy.'

'You, darling?' She handed me my gin-and-it. 'Skivvying?'

'Yes, I sweep and scrub and polish. Things like that.'

'But your face, darling – it's soulful. It's sort of Giotto. You can't possibly be a skivvy with such sensitive features.'

'That's what I am, though, Miss Jennings, at the moment.'

'But not for long? Are you an actor, perhaps, darling, resting between engagements?'

'No, no. Most definitely no. An actor's the last thing in the world I'd ever want to be.'

'Very sensible of you, darling. It's an artificial life.'

She had once been, she confessed, a bit of an actress herself, smiling for the photographers when she felt like utter death, and looking radiant, radiant, radiant, darling, until her jaw was paralysed from the effort. A dab hand at the dogged radiance was the Sadie Jennings that was. Rheumatism had put an end to her modelling career. It was such an elderly-sounding complaint for a woman barely touching thirty, rheumatism – rheumatic fever, to be absolutely precise – but that was the diagnosis.

'I can't expect you to have heard of the New Look.'

(I was Piss-a-Bed again for a moment, waiting to rush to greet her. Those two words had set my young heart thumping.)

'Yes, I have, Miss Jennings. I believe my mother wore it.'

'Inspired by Sadie Jennings no doubt. I was in several magazines, darling, at the time. I was splashed, as they say, everywhere. Christian Dior – he designed it – wrote me the most heavenly letter of thanks.'

Which she proceeded to show me.

'Charming, isn't it?'

'Yes, it is, Miss Jennings. Very.'

'Shall we talk business now? Shall we get the agony over?'

'Yes.'

'Money's such a grubby subject.'

Sadie Jennings talked business while I listened. She could tell I was a suitable tenant because I had made the desired first impression, which was completely favourable. Always supposing, of course, that I wanted the flat: 'It's quite desperately *bijou*, darling. But then, you're not a beanpole. You won't feel restricted there. I felt restricted there, boxed-in. Life on the ocean wave – *almost* on the ocean wave – suits me much better.'

The rent – dared she mention it? – was rather steep. No fault of hers, she hastened to add. I was to blame those nasty little interfering bureaucrats who assessed the rateable value of other people's property. Her rates were colossal.

'How much would you charge me?'

'Ten pounds a week,' she whispered. 'Shocking, isn't it, darling?'

'Can I see the flat?'

'I'll transport you to Fulham in the Jennings chariot. I shall give you a guided tour.'

'Thank you.'

'After we've had a second drinky.'

We had a second drinky, and a third, and a fourth, I think, but my memory is hazy. Waking the next morning in the Jerusalem, I vowed that I would never risk spirits again.

(I broke that vow in 1977, in Sorg, Minnesota, when and where I befriended Jack Daniel and Jim Beam, my temporary comforters.)

The charioteer ignored three red traffic signals on our hectic, and mercifully short, progress towards Fulham. A crash was only narrowly averted as we crossed the King's Road with the light against us. Impervious to the shrieks and curses of drivers and suddenly alarmed pedestrians, Sadie Jennings chattered to her terrified passenger about the married men with whom she had been romantically involved. 'I enjoy the sadness of parting, darling. A last tearful goodbye at the end of a brief but passionate affair gives me such exquisite anguish, darling, that I actually look forward to it – the inevitable parting – whenever I take a new lover. Batty, aren't I? Bitter experience has taught me a lesson, and it's this: if it's batty to revel in sweet sorrow, then battiness is preferable to wretchedness, and God knows I've known that, darling. Would you believe that I came close to V. Woolf-ing myself over a man once?'

'You did?' I yelled.

'I did, I did. Yes, darling, I walked into the sea, I shudder to remember it, at Cromer, with the full intention of – well, succumbing to the Great Wave.'

'Drowning?'

'What else, darling? I didn't succeed. Obviously. I no sooner had my head under water than I realized that Dorian – that was his name, Dorian – wasn't worth dying for. No man is. I dashed back up the beach, soaked to the skin, and flew into the nearest hotel, dripping all the while, and ordered a bottle of the bestest bubbly they had. I paid for that delicious – never more delicious! – champagne with soggy fivers, darling. Oh, we seem to have reached our destination.'

We had – with a jolt that shot me forwards and an excruciating screech of brakes.

'I'm sending up a prayer, darling, that you'll take the flat. You'd be the perfect tenant. You're so quiet and reserved, I can't imagine you offending the neighbours.'

I freed myself from the chariot and stood in the street and drew in a very deep breath, by way of reminding myself that I was still alive.

'This is my little shop, darling. Do you see what's painted above the window?'

'Yes. It says "Fido Chambers", Miss Jennings.'

'Isn't it too absurd? One of my married Romeos thought of it. The "Fido", darling, is because I specialize in those hideous Victorian china doggies, and the "Chambers" is because I also specialize in pos. Just doggies and pos, darling, nothing else. Batty, really, aren't I?'

The flat, to my delighted surprise, was considerably more spacious than I had been led to expect by its owner, who apologized for what she called its 'bijouness' as she led through its three, high-ceilinged rooms. 'It's your boat that's *bijou*,' I did not remark. 'You have to duck your mauve head, you batty creature. You almost concussed yourself when you were mixing the drinkies.'

'I like the flat very much, Miss Jennings.'

'Are you sure? Are you utterly certain, darling? The kitchen and the bathroom are such – well, disgraceful apologies. But, of course, you *are* small, aren't you, darling?'

'I am, Miss Jennings. It's true.'

'You have furniture, I suppose?'

'Some bits and pieces.'

'That's good. Dare I ask you, darling, to pay me a month's rent in advance?'

I wrote her a cheque that instant, and dared to ask her, in turn, if I could rid the walls of their Regency stripes and paint them white instead.

'Must you, darling? It sounds frightfully stark to me.'

'That's how I like to live.'

'I'd say no to anyone else, darling, but since it's you, I'll give you my reluctant consent. And it *is* reluctant.'

'Thank you.'

'Now I simply have to whizz. I have an assignation, darling, with the latest of my marrieds. Candelit Greek dinner, then beddybyes on the boat. Can I drop you somewhere?'

'From the chariot? It's very kind of you to offer, but I think I'd prefer to walk. It's a pleasant evening – '

'It isn't pleasant at all. It's quite horribly cold. The weather's beastly, surely, darling.'

'I've known it to be worse,' I said in desperation. 'Very much worse.'

'At the North Pole, probably. Not here in London. You're determined to be hardy, are you?'

'Yes, Miss Jennings.'

'The next time we meet, darling, do please remove your raincoat. You're the nervousest person I've ever come across. Dare I ask if there will be trouble with the cheque?'

'Trouble? What trouble?'

'How rotten of me. Your bank account, darling – it *is* healthy? Don't answer – I can tell, I can tell by your look of utter outrage that it is. No more embarrassing questions, I promise.'

She handed me the keys to the flat, blew me a kiss, and said she really had to whizz or there'd be a lovers' tiff and she couldn't face one of those, darling, they did drain you of so much energy, didn't I find? Or perhaps I didn't? Was I, or had I been, in love? No, I was not to tell her, it was utter impertinence on her part, we had only just become acquainted, and would I please forgive her?

'Terribly sorry, darling. *Ciao.*'

'Goodbye.'

I hugged myself with pleasure as soon as Sadie Jennings had gone, had really gone, had swung her chariot out of Parsons Green and was aiming it in the direction of her impatient lover. If I was her darling – and oh, how I had been darlinged these last two incredible hours! – then what was he? Her precious? Her beloved? The terms seemed inadequate to express her feelings.

'Whatever you are', I told him loudly, 'she won't V. Woolf herself when you break her heart.'

I was laughing before I had finished cautioning the married Romeo. I gave him further advice, which induced further laughter, while I walked happily from room to room.

The following evening, my bits and pieces were delivered by Mr Nazareth, in his friend Sippaimalani's brand new van.

'Mr Pearce has a fascinating twitch, Harvey. A neurological masterpiece. I was hypnotized by the frenzied activity of his right cheek – hypnotized to the point of rudeness, I fear. He appeared to be disconcerted by my *swarthy* complexion.'

'Did he say anything?'

'He said a number of things, Harvey, most of them strange. He mentioned a person I assume to be your sister.'

'I don't have a sister, Mr Nazareth.'

(I had not met Ethel then.)

'The poor twitching fellow is clearly deluded. "So Miss Harvey fancies the tar brush" – what could he have meant by that inexplicable observation?'

'I've no idea.'

'He repeated it several times.'

'He's a peculiar man, Mr Nazareth.'

'He must be, Harvey.'

I made certain that Mr Pearce's peculiarities were not dwelt on again, despite – and because of – my friend's bewildered interest in them. Over dinner at the Bengal Lancer, I chattered incessantly about Oswald Harvey and his neighbours, the not-Scottish Campbells. Mr Nazareth found the notion of a mental moat delightfully whimsical. Then I mentioned, casually, that my father's left leg had been amputated, and he was horrified. He was also very much annoyed that I had not bothered to apprise him of the upsetting news sooner.

'Your manner dismays me, Harvey. I admire the old boy; I genuinely admire him. You have been frivolous, you realize. You have not behaved responsibly.'

I was too startled to speak.

'You have been flippant where you should have been serious. You are surely aware that I am unable to visit the poor man in hospital. My presence – my *swarthy* presence – at his bedside would cause him embarrassment and distress. You must hurriedly, and with apologies, convey my sympathy to him.'

'I will,' I muttered.

'I sincerely hope you do, Harvey.'

'If you insist. He'll only – '

'Laugh? Sneer? Curse? Very likely. It is nevertheless important that my sympathy is conveyed.'

'All right.'

'I am in earnest, you know.'

Mr Nazareth's display of feeling for the Oswald Harvey who had treated him with open contempt was not the only surprise I received that night. Alone in my flat, I was drawn to sit down at my accusing desk, to rest my hand on the lid that FK, PA, RW and JB had scarred, and to wonder if it would be here, in Parsons Green, high above the doggies and the pos, that I would feel the acutely desired compulsion to write. 'Please let it be here,' I begged. 'For Mummy's sake, let it happen here.'

I got up, and opened the desk. The corpse of Fatty Arbuckle confronted me. Mr Pearce had wrung his neck. A note addressed to Miss Harvey explained why he had killed the little bird: *Hes one like you Hes useless Pity I cant do for you what I have done for him but the Law is the Law and I am abiding you Filth I shall get myself a Budgie whose Natural and Normal for Company Perhaps you will die from Shock Heres Hoping No Yours Truly for you you Filth I sign my Name Jack Pearce (Mister!)*

'There you are, young man, alive and well, I see. I was beginning to think you'd gone and kicked an early bucket.'

'I've been busy, Father.'

'I should hope you have. Too busy to visit your old dad, that's certain. And how, exactly, have you been busy?'

'I had to move. I was thrown out of my lodgings.'

'The devil you were. Caught rogering, were you? In flagrant deliquency, eh, with your bare thrusting bottom, eh, in some biddy of a landlady's line of fire? When I was younger than you, I was discovered in the lovely act, I remember, over Wapping way, by a gorgon who went for me with an aspidistra, which was the nearest thing she could get her hands on. Painful, isn't it, having to make a hasty exit? Tough on the party underneath, too, especially if she's doing it for fun and not for England. Oh, you're a dark horse, you're a sly villain.'

'Am I, Father?'

'Aren't you? You *were* caught rogering, weren't you?'

I sensed that my answer would disappoint him. 'No, I wasn't. My landlord turned against me for no reason. He threw me out in a fit of temper.'

'So where are you now?'

'In Fulham. At Parsons Green, to be precise. I have a flat with a kitchen and bathroom.'

'That's all very nice, young man, and fine and dandy, as those Yanks say, for you, but I've needed you here these last few days – ' He paused, and added, in a ferocious whisper, 'for protection.'

'From what?'

'From a pest is what. From a daft old black mammy with the Almighty in her noddle is what. From the mother of that upstart who moved into "The Cloisters" when decent citizens were fast asleep is what. She's trying to save me, she says. She says that He has His eye on me. I can't understand the half of what she says.'

'Are you talking about the elder Mrs Campbell?'

'Yes, I bloody am. She's worse than Swedie ever was. Far, far worse. Swedie was intelligent. Correction: Swedie was very intelligent, as women go, before she fell for that Swedish balderdash after her ice-cream husband croaked and she turned her back on good red meat. This Campbell creature with her perpetual hallelujahing never had a brain in the first instant. A white woman who's got God is bad enough, but a coloured one is the cursèd limit.'

The Dowager Mrs Campbell had been his regular, unwanted visitor for more than a week now, he complained. She merely smiled her lunatic smile at the other patients, the lucky bastards, and breezed past them waving vaguely, like royalty, but at Oswald Harvey's bed she stopped in her tracks with a vengeance, and stayed. He had asked her, politely, to sling her celestial hook, in so many words. She had smiled at him, and stayed. He had begged the nurses to get rid of her. She had smiled at them, and stayed. He had feigned sleep – but would she take the hint? No, curse her. She had been sent to comfort him – comfort him! – by a Higher Power, she said, thumping her cheap-looking Bible and shouting 'Hallelujah!' What had he done to deserve such a fate? Why him, whose sins were on the pinkish side compared to those of certain wicked perishers in the universe?

'I don't understand, Father, how I can protect you.'

'Then you're a bigger oaf than I thought you were.'

'Thanks.'

'Because you have tact, young man. You have charm – I believe it's called – when you're not curling your lip up at your old dad. You've the knack of speaking to the odds and sods as if they had their wits together instead of being raving barmy. And besides, you're used to darkies.'

'I assume you're referring to Mr Nazareth.'

'The man with the ploy, yes.'

'He sends you his sympathy, Father. His sincere sympathy.'

'Him?'

'Him.'

'For the leg?'

'Yes.'

'Are you sure.'

'Quite sure.'

'That's decent. Extremely decent. You're not kidding me?'

'No, Father.'

'Well, that is decent.'

'I still don't understand how I'm supposed to protect you from Mrs Campbell.'

'I want you, young man, to tell her to bugger off, in your most educated voice. You shouldn't find it difficult.'

What unsuspected virtues I suddenly seemed to possess! 'You're more confident of my powers than I am, Father.'

'I've watched you at work,' he said, 'over the years. I've studied you, young man. I know your capabilities.'

Wasn't his other son, I wondered aloud, similarly capable?

'Tommy Rotter? Don't be oafish. He'd have her hallelujahing at twice the volume, Tommy would. He'd set her off just by looking at her, always providing he spared her the time. Tommy burst too fast from his mother and he's been in a hurry ever since. Anyway, if I wanted his help, which I most definitely don't, young man, I'd need to hop across to Egypt for it. That's where the mad sod's taken himself, without a moment's thought for his father's plight.'

(I had given my brother the requested tinkle – a succession of tinkles, in fact – but had received no answer. Now I understood why.)

'He blew in here and announced he was going to Cairo. "Take care" – those were his parting words – "Take care." I'll bloody take care of him when I'm on my feet again.'

('On your foot, surely, Father,' I managed not to say.)

I stayed at the hospital until the bell was sounded for visitors to depart. Mrs Campbell did not appear, to my father's intense irritation, for he was being denied a 'scene' that he had anticipated with relish. 'Where is the cursèd pest? What's keeping her? She has no right to be late on the one day she'd be welcome, so to speak. Where on earth could she have got to? Tact and charm, remember, young man, when she arrives – they'll do the trick. I'd bet my life on it. Come on, Mammy, come on.'

I most definitely didn't employ tact and charm in the letter I wrote to Mr Campbell at my desk that evening. I recall that the lies I set down in order to rescue my father from Mr Campbell's mother's attentions gave me a sneaking satisfaction, and that I laughed as they came to me. Daddy, I wrote – of the man I could not, would not, address as Daddy – had led a long and devout earthly life, which was now drawing to its inevitable close. Oswald Harvey's consideration for others was legendary in South London, I added, in my mischief; his name had become synonymous with self-sacrifice. It was very kind of Mrs Campbell to worry about Daddy's chances in the Hereafter, but she really should stop fretting herself. Speaking as his proud and dutiful son, I had every hope that he would enjoy a serene eternity, if simple goodness was to receive its just reward. Mrs Campbell ought to seek out a genuine sinner and not waste her energy attempting to save my already saintly daddy. I begged Mr Campbell to intervene on my daddy's behalf. He must understand that Oswald Harvey was too sweet-natured, and altogether too humble, to ask Mrs Campbell to leave him in peace, for that was what he craved. I signed myself, Yours sincerely.

Dear Mr Harvey, I thank you for your courteous letter. You have my personal guarantee that Mother has given me her solemn word that she will respect your wishes with regard to your father. We had no idea we were living next door to a legend. God be with you, Royston Campbell.

'The cold shoulder, young man, that's what she's giving me, the pious old bitch. I'm even begrudged her royal wave, let alone her cursèd "Hallelujah". And I never once raised my voice to her – do you realise? Sheer bloody spite it is.'

'You said she was a pest when I saw you on Sunday.'

'And I was speaking the exact truth, as per always. Of course she's a pest. Show me a Bible-basher who isn't. What riles me is that I kept my temper with her, which is more than I did with Swedie when she went God-barmy. I do not like being snubbed by a female two weeks out of the jungle, young man. No, I don't like it one bit.'

The Dowager, he continued, was now celestially pestering a Wandsworth tobacconist who'd had a stroke. He was so gaga that her sodding hallelujah prattle just washed over him: she could as well be telling the poor bastard about Lady Connie and that gamekeeper chap for all he took in. There was still a little justice in the world.

'Reggie was here earlier. His breath reeked of Dutch courage. Hospitals scare him shitless. He kept looking round as if he thought the quacks were going to pounce on him. I used to feel the same. It was bloody decent of him to come, considering. Bloody decent. You might care to know that the pup with the scalpel's arranged for me to be moved to the country. Convalescence, he said. Rehabilitation. I told him I'd rather be back in "Blenheim", I'd rather croak in the comfort of my own home, I'd no need for convalescence and rehabilitation. Then what do you think he did? He smiled. He smiled and walked away, on both his legs, young man, on both his good legs, as though my feelings weren't worth a fig.'

II

Had I been alive in 1789, and a resident of Strand-under-the-Green, I would have had as my immediate neighbour in that pleasant Chiswick village the portrait painter John, or Johann, Zoffany, who was newly returned from India, where he had enjoyed the lavish patronage of the Nabob of Oudh.

Zoffany kept a shallop moored on the Thames opposite the miniature mansion he had bought as his country home. Perhaps he would have invited me on to his green, pink and drab sailing vessel – 'elegantly and conveniently fitted up', as a contemporary, Mrs Papendieck, described it in her diary – to mingle with the distinguished guests at one of his costly musical parties. On fine summer nights, the greatest singers of the age sang Handel arias from the shore, and the sounds carried over the calm water. I might have heard those sounds, had I been among the privileged few who were waited on by Zoffany's servants, in their livery of scarlet and gold with blue facings.

> Did you not hear my lady
> Go down the garden singing?
> Blackbird and thrush were silent
> To hear the alleys ringing

I might have heard, had I become then what I have become now – accidentally wealthy.

But I wouldn't have joined the few; I'd have remained with the many, I feel certain, in that laystallish London some miles down-river. Hollywood, Gabriel Harvey's Nabob, did not exist, and Roger Kemp of Liverpool had not been born – and it's because of the former's fascination with the latter that I live here in Strand-on-the-Green, in a miniature mansion very like Zoffany's.

And Roger Kemp himself would have stayed obscure in his pauper's grave had Mrs Ricks not said to me, 'Throw these dusty old ledgers out, Gabriel', early in the morning of Thursday, 25 May, 1967, before the men arrived to raze the Jerusalem. 'They can't be of interest to anybody any more. They're ancient, unimportant history. The sheer junk that accumulates.'

'Ancient, unimportant history' – it was that phrase, I think, that made me stop and look inside the ledgers. I was suddenly curious to discover how unimportant it actually was. Expecting columns of figures, neatly audited to the ultimate farthing, I found instead the *must tos* of Roger Kemp: *I must to say that there fell upon my tongue in Liverpool such a wonder of speech that I stopped amazed; I must to remember that my mother cast me out in her white woman's fear; I must to tell how I was sore distressed when my illness flowered.*

Sore distressed he was, indeed, for Roger Kemp died from the flowering ravages of syphilis, contracted while the 'wonder' was still with him. In the film *Mersey Messiah* a vague plague – not smallpox, not scarlatina – dispatches Roger heavenwards, with an absence of spots on his glowing black skin. 'I'm reaching out, I'm climbing, Lord,' he warbles from his pristine death-bed, while an invisible chorus urges him to place his (manicured) hands on the ladder Saint Peter has thoughtfully lowered on his behalf. Or so the dying Roger hears and sees in the last of his radiant cinematic delusions, set – like the others – to a music of sorts.

I did not throw the ledgers away. I carried them back with me to Parsons Green, where I studied their strange contents throughout the night. On Friday morning I went to bed secure in the knowledge that I was ready to begin writing the book I had been working on circuitously since the day of its inception in the gardens of St John-at-Hackney. Roger Kemp of Liverpool, befriended and nursed by the disgraced Mrs Parchment, was the saddest of all my preachers, and the one I was most anxious to restore to life, if I could. Of course I could. I had been the accidental recipient of an extraordinary gift, and I must to – I said aloud – express my gratitude.

('I'll be a great deal happier, young man, when I know for a fact that a certain Gabriel Harvey has started rogering the girls. I can't abide the idea that a son of mine's a eunuch' – how often, and with what sly insistence, my father wondered if I had yet become a rogerer. Once, after he had exhorted me, in my own best interests, to roger like the red-blooded male he hoped I was, I asked him why he always used that particular verb: I had never heard anyone else use it, and I hadn't seen it written down either. Was it, perhaps, Oswald Harvey's invention?

'No, it bloody isn't, you oaf. It's a gentleman's word, "roger" is. I'm not the least surprised you've never heard it, the funny company you keep. You won't catch an upstart or a foreigner saying it. You should count yourself honoured that your old dad has passed it on to you. The aristocracy rogers, remember, young man – the rest of the population fucks.'

'Yes, Father.'

The only time he'd had a blazing row with his dear chum Reggie, a thunder-and-lightning job, was over the origins of 'roger'. The dirty-minded buffer maintained that it had to do with Roger the lodger, him in the jokes. Oswald Harvey knew otherwise. Reggie had cited as evidence the poem that went:

> A fervent young Baptist, Miss Pod,
> Believed that her babe came from God –
> But it wasn't the Almighty
> Who lifted her nightie,
> It was Roger the lodger, the sod.

which had made him chuckle, naturally. ' "You're wrong, though, Reggie, wrong," I said. "Sir Vincent's father, Sir Randolph, boasted in his cups one night how he'd rogered every female servant on the estate – Nanny and Cook excepted – in what he called his flaming youth. That was in 1913, by my memory, and he was talking about forty years earlier, because he was sixty-odd then. So don't give me your Roger-the-lodger nonsense." You'd have thought I'd insulted him personally, the rage he flew into. He jumped in the air, Reggie did, and bellowed that he was the "roger" expert, not me. He carried on jumping and bellowing until I lost my temper, too, and reminded him that I had mingled with the *cream de la cream*, so to speak, whereas his acquaintances were suede shoe types and worse. I could have bitten my tongue off for speaking to the old rogue like that, but for him to lay claim to "roger" knowledge he hadn't bloody got was more than flesh and blood was able to bear, it really was, young man. You have rogered, haven't you?'

'That's my business.'

'Cursed oaf.'

Writing Roger Kemp's story, in the last weeks of 1969, I did not thank my father for the honour he had passed on to me. Roger, Roger – it was impossible to dissociate the boy's name from that ludicrous verb with its aristocratic connotations. 'Now I'm scuppered on the larboard side, my rogering days are over.' The Master of 'Blenheim' smiled appreciatively at his nautical turn of phrase. 'Well and truly over. Yours, you lucky young man, have only just begun. Eh? Yes?' Roger, Roger – I went on writing. 'Still, I've plenty of rogering memories to keep me cheerful.')

I finished *Lords of Light* in 1970, on my mother's fifty-second birthday. The front door of my flat was bolted and barred, as usual, when I got into the Moygashel frock to think of her. *For Mummy, with undying love* – there was the dedication, written on Friday, May 26, 1967, on the first page of my bulky, much-corrected manuscript. She would read my book, I knew, and the reading of it – in Italy or France, wherever she was – would bring about our reunion. She would send a letter care of my publisher expressing her pride in me, and I would fly in a plane – 'higher up than birds can get to' – and speed through foreign streets and be gathered into her outstretched arms. I cried for joy at the prospect.

Care of my publisher! Six months later, it was obvious that no London publisher cared to publish me. Twenty houses had been offered *Lords of Light* and twenty houses had rejected it, most of them with humiliating speed. I was encouraged slightly by the managing director of a firm that had its offices in a Georgian square in Bloomsbury, who advised me to transfer my attention to India: Buddhism was the 'in' religion, it had mystery, it spoke to the liberated young; he could sell a book on Indian mysticism, because it was a subject that appealed to people who were sick of material things. Christianity, by contrast, was too earth-bound, too bourgeois, too obvious. The good news from the East was what the public wanted.

'Eastern or Western, Harvey, bunk is bunk' – that opinion of Mr Nazareth's came to me as I listened to the managing director, who wore his shirt open to the navel. When he had finished speaking, with the compliment 'I like your style', I tried to explain that *Lords of Light* was a work of social history. Its title was intended to be ironic. Hadn't he noticed that many of those lords were scoundrels, and that others were mad? Didn't he realize that my book was concerned with the effect those preachers made upon the poor, whose pennies they extracted with assurances of a better life in the next world? Surely he had understood that I had no faith at all in the existence of that much promised Canaan? I had not produced a Christian tract. To each of these questions I received a nod. There was a silence. He looked at his watch. I waited. 'India,' he said. I picked up the typescript, thanked him for his encouragement, and left.

Three years' hard labour at my imprisoning desk had ended in disaster, it seemed. I had failed. I had slaved in vain. 'How you'd gloat if you knew,' I said to the father I had wisely kept ignorant of the book's long, and sometimes difficult, composition. 'Oh, how you'd laugh!' And I was tempted to laugh, too, in the manner of Oswald Harvey, at my wasted effort.

In a side street near the British Museum, I passed a publisher's that hadn't been encumbered with *Lords of Light*. I walked to the corner and stopped. Was there any point in offering them the cursèd thing? The typescript, so neatly prepared for me by a Mrs Shand, was battered now and torn in places. Its cover was stained with coffee or tea. It had obviously been read, and as obviously rejected. Its appearance signalled failure. What was the point in soliciting yet another rejection?

'Shove it on the pile,' said the receptionist at Leopold Stern. 'Will you be calling back for it, or do you want it posted?'

'I'm not sure.'

'Postage will cost you at least a pound, judging by the size of it. You don't look rich to me. We'll phone you, shall we, when it's ready for collection?'

I gave the girl the number of the ironmonger's shop I had been working in since the destruction of the Jerusalem.

When the phone call came from someone at Leopold Stern, I would say to him or her, 'I shan't bother to collect it, thank you very much. I'd be obliged if you disposed of it for me.' That's what I would say, and the whole sorry episode would be over.

I had turned into Montague Street and was only yards away from Matthew's 'wilderness'. It was a wilderness no longer, that house in which I had feared for my life on an August evening seventeen years ago. The near-ruin of my memory had been restored to its original splendour. I could not see its present occupants, but they had to be bright and confident and wealthy. The glow that the house gave off suggested as much.

'My wilderness,' Matthew had said. 'My place of desolation. Does it scare you, Gabriel?'

'Of course it doesn't.'

'Ah, but it isn't dark yet. The rats and mice haven't come out to play. You must partake of my hospitality long enough to hear them. I think I can rustle up a sardine or twain, or a smoked sprat perhaps. Shall we descend to my living quarters for a spot of low, as opposed to high, tea?'

'Yes, thank you.'

'Bleak up here, isn't it? This was our bedroom, hers and mine. We slept in state, in a four-poster. She has neglected to inform me if she shares it with anyone now. She has custody, you understand, Gabriel, complete with the three children who were conceived in it.'

I had known Matthew — I was never to learn his surname — for five days. 'I am an awful warning to them,' he had announced mysteriously when I sat down beside him on a public bench in Lincoln's Inn Fields. I had been wandering about the centre of London since eight that Monday morning, and had stopped to eat the tomato sandwiches I had prepared in the kitchen Escoffier was welcome to. I hadn't noticed there was a man at the other end of the bench until he spoke. 'I cause them embarrassment.'

'Who?' I asked, turning to look at the speaker.

'My fellow-barristers. My *erstwhile* fellow-barristers.' He seemed to be addressing everyone and no one, for he stared straight ahead of him. 'Pleaders for justice in the higher courts.'

'You are a barrister?'

'I was. I still dress for the part. The togs are a trifle frayed in places, and there's a shine on the seat of my pin-stripes. From a discreet distance, it's impossible to make out the algae that's establishing itself on my jacket. I dress for the part, but I'm not allowed to play it. Not that I want to — oh dear, no. Not any more.'

'Why not?'

'You are most inquisitive. I'm touched by your curiosity. The time, however, is not right. Our acquaintanceship has barely commenced. It is too soon for revelations. Suffice it to say that I am barred from donning wig and gown for a number of embarrassing reasons.'

'Are you?' I persisted.

'Suffice it to say, I said to you, I am.'

He showed me his face with this reprimand. I thought for an absurd instant that it was a circus clown who was glaring at me. He had whitened his cheeks, surely, and reddened his nose.

'My name, I can reveal, is Matthew.'

'Is it?'

'You are put off by my familiarity. You wish to keep yours secret.'

'Mine's Gabriel. Harvey. Gabriel Harvey.'

'Delighted to meet you.'

I shook the shaking hand he offered me. The bulbous nose, I saw, was nearer purple than red.

'You have the distinction of being the first Gabriel, Gabriel, I have met. I am not making idle conversation. That is the plain truth.'

'I was the only Gabriel at school.'

'I believe you. Which school is that?'

'Lily's. I mean, Sir William Lilliburn's.'

'And did you shine in your solitary splendour there?'

'Not really.'

No, not really: I told the stranger, in a gabble, that I had been a good, probably better than good, pupil once. Then something had happened, and a change had come over me, and I lost all my will to learn. Music, music alone, excited me. I'd shone for a little while, perhaps, before the spark went out, but as for solitary splendour, oh no, not really.

· 'You are a musician?'

'No. I go to lots of concerts. And I read scores.'

'I have a daughter somewhere who, I think, plays the clarinet. She began with the recorder and progressed.'

'You *think* she plays the clarinet?'

'Precisely. I don't know for certain that she does now. She may have abandoned her studies. She played the instrument when I last clapped eyes on her.'

'When was that?' I surprised myself by asking.

'You would make a formidable prosecuting counsel. When? Oh, five years ago, at least. Shortly after my – my demise.' He snorted. 'Yes, that was when.'

He rummaged in a shopping basket and brought out a bottle, which he held above his head.

'I've just caught sight of my esteemed colleague – former colleague – Henry Allam shuffling across the green sward yonder. "The green sward" is the kind of antiquated English that legal tortoise speaks. "Two", for him, is "twain". A master, Henry Allam, of obfuscation. It is essential to his work.'

I had no idea what 'obfuscation' meant, and said so.

'The obfuscation for which Henry Allam is noted drapes a pall over light and reason and common sense. He has only to open his mouth and the world is stupefied. He is the sworn enemy of clarity.'

'I wouldn't understand him?'

'He doesn't understand himself. That, you might say, is his genius – he obfuscates with such inspired assurance that his brain gives up on him and retires from the battle, wounded. His greatest achievement, his *tour de force*, was to end the case for the Crown in mid-sentence, with an indefinite article hanging in the air, deprived of a noun. And there it stayed, never to be supported. Logic suffered its severest defeat that day, thanks to Henry Allam. Masterly.'

He lowered the bottle and unscrewed its cap.

'I always toast him as he trudges by. He deserves my respects. He will pretend not to see me.' Matthew drank. 'Salutations, dear Henry! Greetings from your old opponent! Have you mislaid the Crown's noun in the grass? Is that why you're scanning the green sward?'

My strange new acquaintance laughed loudly at these insults. I hoped that Henry Allam, who really did resemble a tortoise, would acknowledge them, would stop in front of the bench and shoot his head up out of his chest and obfuscate. But the barrister was not to be goaded. He shuffled past, oblivious.

'He disapproves of the wine I toast him in. It's British, it's foul, and he's quite right. The label does not reveal the whereabouts of the vineyard, but my taste buds tell me it has to be in the far north. I call this gut-rot Château Cawdor. Drinking it – allowing it entrance to my oesophagus, to be precise – I can conjure up the blighted grapes on that windblown estate, picked by gnarled arthritic hands and trod by chilblained feet. It has a distinctly salty flavour, redolent of the nearby Moray Firth, which causes one to splutter, should one be unwise enough to gulp it down. Which I don't. I sip the filthy stuff. I linger over it. That is the extent of my remaining wisdom, Gabriel.'

'Mister – ' I began.

'Matthew. Nothing else. Sufficient.'

'If that wine is as foul, Matthew, as you say it is, then why do you drink it?'

'Look at me. Take me in. Isn't it obvious why? I'm almost a tramp. I don't belong in polite company any more, begging your young pardon. You'll notice that I said "almost". I have yet to achieve the full status of gentleman of the road, since I am still a man of property. It's a wilderness now, my town house. My wife – my former wife – and I have denuded it between us. What she neglected to appropriate, I sold. Chairs, tables, carpets, china – I sold them all for ready cash. In order, Gabriel, to drink. Or imbibe, as Henry Allam would say. I had a connoisseur's palate when I practised at the bar.' He snorted. 'Oh, yes. I maintained a particular affection for those delicate, delicate beauties from Alsace: the Sylvaner and the Riesling. These days necessity demands that I take my pleasure gloomily, courtesy of Château Cawdor, a vintage with so many reasons to be secretive about its origins that it hides its shame behind the vagueness of "British". Cheers!'

He raised his bottle to me, and drank.

'I like to think of myself as a restricted vagabond. The broad highway does not lure me. I keep to my old haunts – but on the periphery, of course. I go where I'm recognized. Life wouldn't be such fun if I didn't. It'd be hell. There's Marcus Strang ignoring me, the odious prig. Cut me dead, Strang, cut me dead! Here's your health in British wine! You see, Gabriel, the rare fun I have?'

'Yes.'

'You really really do? Then you're perceptive beyond your years. What age are you?'

'Sixteen.'

'You look younger. My vision, I have to confess, is far from perfect.'

'Sixteen and a half, very nearly.'

'A pedant. Well, Master Gabriel, I have enjoyed our conversation. Goodbye to you. I intend to sleep for an hour or twain.' He grinned at me, revealing cracked yellow teeth. 'Please feel free to leave, and please don't worry yourself about my wife's – my former wife's – shopping basket and its brinish contents. They should be perfectly safe. No one is likely to steal them. No one of sound mind. I shall be here tomorrow.'

Within seconds, he was snoring lightly.

In 'Blenheim' that evening, while I was making myself useful at the Jacobean-style cocktail cabinet, I asked my father if he had ever drunk British wine.

'What kind of oaf's question is that, Piss-a-Bed? Wine's

foreign and always has been. And as for me drinking the muck, I'll have you know I'm not the type. Swedie is – or was when her ice-cream husband was around. And as for there being such a thing as British wine, it only proves to me that you're more uneducated than I reckoned. It's back to school with you. Yes, it's back to school.'

'There is such a thing, Father.'

'Such a thing as what?'

'As British wine.'

'Are you contradicting me, Piss-a-Bed?'

'I saw a bottle today. Of British wine.'

'The devil you did. What on earth have you been up to?'

'A man showed me the label. He was sitting on a bench, drinking British wine, in broad daylight. He said it has a horrible taste.'

'Where was this bench, and who is this man? And bring me my whisky and soda before you answer.'

'In Hyde Park, Father,' I lied. 'By the Round Pond.'

'The Round Pond is in Kensington Gardens. It was, anyhow, when I last looked. But perhaps you've heard different. Perhaps somebody's come along and shifted it.'

'It's an easy mistake to make. The Gardens lead into the Park, Father.'

'Who's this man?'

'Just a stranger.'

'If he's a stranger, why were you talking to him?'

'I didn't say much. I listened.'

'To some bloody ragbag boozing straight out of a bottle in a royal park?'

'Gardens.'

'Watch your tongue. Why, Piss-a-Bed, why?'

'Actually, Father, he was quite well-dressed. He wore a black jacket, pin-striped trousers, and a bowler hat.'

(I did not describe the state they were in, those respectable clothes. I said nothing more of their unrespectable owner, boasting of his accumulating algae. The real Matthew belonged on his chosen bench in a different part of London among my store of secrets.)

'Worse and worse. People should be what they seem. A man togged up like a City gent ought to behave like one. Which means that he oughtn't to be tosspotting by the Round Pond, where children and their nannies can see him. This is a soda and whisky you've brought me, Piss-a-Bed. It's all arse-uppards. The proper mixture, if you please.'

'Yes, Father.'

'Your mother won't be overjoyed when I let her know you've been keeping the company of a public tippler.'

'He only spoke to me for a little while.'

'Long enough. Definitely long enough for him to discover he'd met a dunce in Gabriel Harvey. He fooled you well and truly, most definitely he did, with his poppycock about British wine. If us British had been wine-makers and wine-drinkers, do you honestly imagine we'd have won the wars we've won down through the ages? Of course we wouldn't've. You and your oafish nonsense!'

'I had a feeling you would come back for more,' Matthew said to me the next day. 'I can't say I'm surprised to see you here.'

'You're not?'

'No. You are intrigued, aren't you?'

'Am I?'

'Yes, yes. Spellbound. Shall we get the cross-examination under way? I am ready to stand trial.' He snorted. 'You can safely assume that I have taken the oath and am in the box.'

I couldn't safely assume any such thing. I was embarrassed by his invitation, even though I wanted to accept it.

'Do begin.'

'I can't.'

'Can't, Gabriel? After the steady bombardment of yesterday? You surely haven't changed character so soon.'

'Is your wine really British?'

'Oh, that's no question. That won't intimidate the accused. It's British, yes, beyond a doubt. The sharp bouquet of herring offers sufficient proof of its nationality. You are welcome to sample a drop.'

'No, thank you. I believe you. It's my father who doesn't.'

'Fortunate man, not to have had recourse to Cawdor. Those who live in, or near, Carey Street are all too painfully aware of its existence. Your health, Gabriel.'

He drank, cautiously, from the bottle.

'What age is he? Your father?'

'Seventy.'

'Ah, then it's unlikely that he'll find himself in Carey Street, quaffing – as Henry Allam would say – British wine. Most unlikely. Let him enjoy his ignorance. Now we've cleared that little matter up, we can proceed with the important business. I don't have to remind you that I'm still in the dock.'

In the silence that followed I wondered why Matthew apparently assumed there was nothing extraordinary about a seventy-year-old man having a sixteen-year-old son. Most people, especially my fellow-Lilies, found it very odd indeed.

'My mother', I said, 'is much younger. By exactly half.'

'No concern of mine.' He shook a finger at me. 'In the dock.'

A word came to me in my confusion: 'demise'. Matthew had used it, I remembered.

'What did you mean by your "demise"?'

'Excellent, Gabriel, excellent. That's the ticket. My demise is central to your purpose.' He snorted. 'What led to it is. The events that led to it. And one event, one terrible event, in particular.'

'Why was it terrible?'

'Because it was,' he shouted. 'Because it was,' he muttered.

'What happened?'

'I defended an innocent man and the jury found him guilty. They were guided towards that decision by the judge, who insinuated that my wretched, gullible client possessed reserves of cunning behind his timid exterior. Theirs was a unanimous verdict, Gabriel. And mine was a total defeat.'

'He wasn't hanged, was he?'

'No, my eager inquisitor, he wasn't. He was given a long prison sentence. He's free now, now that the true criminal has come forward and confessed. But the harm, the injustice, has been done. A mere pardon can't alter that.'

'You must have felt pleased when he was freed.'

'Pleased? Was I? At being proved right! I was past feeling pleasure. Oh, I certainly smirked. I walked into one of those shabby so-called studios where you can have your passport photograph taken and had the so-called photographer capture my smirking likeness. I sent the most telling snap to the judge, in the hope that it would cause him at least a moment's discomfort. Who knows if the old swine squirmed? Perhaps he did.'

I listened, enthralled, as the accused proceeded to chastise himself in the dock. I was grateful to Matthew for asking his own embarrassing questions.

'How could a single failure in the courtroom bring about

my – my demise? Ah, but this, Gabriel, was the failure of failures. I had nothing to lose, and I lost it.' He snorted. 'What an achievement! I had an open-and-shut case – the open so open and the shut so shut – and somehow I shut the open and opened the shut, and everyone was astounded. I was baffled. I had sustained a thorough and reasonable defence. I had pointed out the obvious in plain language. How obvious is obvious? I didn't stop to consider there might be degrees of obviousness. I'd no reason to. It was the judge who did that, at length, by subtle insinuation. Oh, Gabriel, the hours I've spent studying His Honour's summing-up! I read it again just this morning, in search of the hidden fact that continues to elude me, and was again appalled. Inference, inference: the jury were not to assume that the feeble-minded lack guile – quite the contrary, some of the darkest crimes had been committed by supposed simpletons; he had sat in judgment on many such, and could be said to speak with authority – the man before them had witnessed (had he not?) brutality of a most repugnant kind, in the dismal slum in which his natural mother and her paramour had raised him, and it was therefore not entirely improbable that this same young man might choose, in his simple heart, to emulate his nearest and dearest. Et cetera, et cetera. A short pause for Cawdor, methinks.'

He gave me his yellow grin, and drank.

'Ah, Gabriel, the way he coloured the word "darkest". You would have appreciated those two notes on the double bass, with your love of music.' He snorted. 'And the disdain in his voice when he said "paramour". And the infinite condescension behind that "simple heart". They guaranteed my demise, those artful little touches. They dug my grave. Congratulations, Your Honour!'

He drained the bottle, then placed it in his shopping basket.

'First of the day's empties. Where had I got to in my sorry tale? Ah, yes, demise, commencement of. I'd shown signs of demising before, but my dear wife – the former one – had always brought me to heel. Under her firm guidance, I had done what millions of worried people are doing this very minute: I had pulled myself together. My annoyance at the law's delays, my impatience with obfuscation, my gathering doubts about justice, or rather, punishment – these I kept in check. I had my reputation as a barrister to think of, and the status in society that went with it. I exercised quite incredible control – give or take the odd binge or twain – until I failed to achieve a just and proper and necessary acquittal for my ignorant and guileless lad from Tottenham. Why control myself any longer? Why keep my wildness in check?' He snorted. 'I lost control, Gabriel, and I went wild. That is exactly what I did. I had no reason not to, was how I reasoned, afterwards. You have taxed my remaining brain cells to their limits, you merciless boy. I've meandered enough for your amusement.'

'Not amusement, Matthew.'

'No? Exceptional creature, to be unamused. At sixteen, I'd have laughed, I'm sure. If, that is, I had stopped to listen to the prattle of a wreck on a bench. But I would not have stopped, Gabriel. I would have been frightened stiff of someone like me. I'd have hurried past, as Marcus Strang is now doing. I'd have run at the very sight of a Matthew – whoosh, at a sprinter's pace. "A stranger spells danger" – that motto of my Mama's would have been ringing in my ears. And yet you, you have actually sought out my company a second time. I salute your courage.'

He opened another bottle, and drank from it.

'Cork appears to be scarce around Inverness. Hence these horrid metal caps. You can imagine my irritation when the damned things don't unscrew properly. Sometimes they catch, with a mocking little click. It's then that they threaten to go round and round for ever. I broke a canine once, trying to snap one of the buggers off. To be locked out of Cawdor was more than I could bear.' He yawned. 'The audience is over for today, Gabriel. I must snooze. I shall see you on the morrow – to quote Henry Allam – perhaps?'

He was asleep before I could answer.

Carey Street: The Spendthrift's Purgatory was the 'Blenheim' lecture I brought down upon my head that evening.

'Carey Street? Who's been telling you about Carey Street? The City sot by the Round Pond, is that who?'

'No, Father.'

'Your half-Abdul chum, then?'

'He's on holiday in Dorset. It was a woman, actually. On a bus.'

'And what was this woman, actually, on a bus, doing, I should like to know, picking a conversation with you, Piss-a-Bed, on the topic of Carey Street? It smells fishy to me. It's not in your nature, anyhow, to travel on a bus, judging by the shoe leather you wear out. And why should she – this woman on this bus – pick on you to discuss a matter like Carey Street with? Fishy, I'd say – most definitely.'

'She didn't actually speak to me, Father.'

'Didn't she, actually? I'm not surprised. What *did* she do to you, in that case, to make you pester me about Carey Street?'

'I overheard her say to another woman, "He'll end up in Carey Street," ' I lied. And I had her continue: ' "If he's not very careful." '

'Now you're talking sense, Piss-a-Bed. This woman on this bus obviously has a husband with holes in his pockets. His head's got champagne ideas while his hand's clutching only enough cash for a small glass of stout. Yet it's the champagne he orders, despite the shortage of funds, the reckless bloody fool. He and his like are never careful. Did she look upset to you, this woman?'

'Oh, yes, Father.'

'Not without reason. It's a shame I wasn't with you – not that you seem to want my company – to give the poor cow the benefit of my advice. How was she dressed, young man? I don't suppose you bothered to notice.'

'She was rather smart. She wore a fur coat.'

'In August? She must be desperate, and that's a fact. She's wearing her fur, it strikes me, because she's afraid he'll sell it, the sod, or pawn it, or trade it in for more of whatever it is that's made him skint. She probably keeps her fur on day and night, I'd be willing to wager. He's fixed his hawk's eye on it, and that's a load on her mind. I'm willing to wager, young man, she wears it in bed, even, and has it wrapped round her when she's perched where legend has it that Dictionary Sam did all his best thinking. Her one last little luxury, that fur is.'

'Is it, Father?'

'Use your skull and work it out for yourself. It has to be. Why else would she be dolled up in it, in August, on a bus, gabbing her mouth off about Carey Street? Yes, she's a spendthrift's better half, or my name's not Oswald Harvey.'

'I still don't understand why she mentioned Carey Street.'

'You'll understand, I hope and trust, by the time I've finished talking to you. Now just you listen and take heed. Carey Street, young man, is the spendthrift's Purgatory – it's where he goes, in a manner of speaking, when he's got nothing left in the kitty; when he's finally down and finally out; when his creditors are baying for his blood, let alone his missing money; when the law, in other words, declares him bankrupt. That's exactly when he goes to Carey Street.'

'But why Carey Street?'

'If you wish to learn, don't interrupt. He goes to Carey Street, this spendthrift does – in a manner of speaking, mark you – because he would have had to go there in the olden days, in history, when Carey Street boasted the biggest bankruptcy court in the land. He doesn't go to the real Carey Street any more, only – as I say – in a manner of speaking. It's a turn of phrase, is "Carey Street". It means a man's on his uppers.'

'Or a woman.'

'Seldom, Piss-a-Bed. Seldom, if ever, a woman. It's a rare woman who's a bread-winner – '

('Then my mother was rare,' I did not interrupt to remind him. 'While she worked at her "secret place" she was rare, Father.' 'She's the toiler now,' he'd told me in our nameless house, under the hissing gaslight. 'We'll have to depend on her, the two of us.')

'There's the occasional widow, I grant you, who squanders her late lamented's spondulicks and has to put her pearls in hock to pay the milkman, but she's the exception that proves the rule. No, it's men, by and large, you'll find in Carey Street – men who've been breadwinners but have turned into what I would call breadlosers. And if you don't pull your socks up, Piss-a-Bed, and stop mooning about, Carey Street'll be your address, too.'

'No, it won't, Father,' I said forcefully. 'No, it won't.'

'That remains to be seen. You're hardly in a position to know, the tender age you are. A lot can happen, and not for the best. Purgatory, remember. Purgatory.'

'Yes, Father.'

'This woman on this bus you heard – it's my opinion she's a lady more than a woman, and if you listen I'll explain what I mean. When a man from low down the social ladder falls on hard times, he doesn't fall into Carey Street, not by a long chalk he doesn't. It's any old alley for him, and a bed and a bite from the Sallies, providing he joins in the hymn singing, poor bugger. No, Carey Street's where the wheelers, dealers, swindlers and gamblers, Mayfair types with thousands to throw about, take their shoes off at night, in a manner of speaking. This lady on this bus is probably accustomed to a chauffeur driving her everywhere in a Rolls-Royce, I'd wager, except that him and the car have gone where her husband's money's gone – into thin bloody air. And that's why you saw her on a bus, in her fur coat in August, and heard her mention Carey Street. It's purgatory for her, having to travel like that, wearing what's left of her best. Come to think of it, Piss-a-Bed, you'll never earn enough to lose enough to warrant entry to Carey Street, the way you're going. You won't have a wife stranded on a bus. It'll be the Salvation Army, dosshouse Purgatory for you, that's what it'll be.'

'Will it, Father?'

'Of course it will, you cursed oaf, unless you change your spots, like the leopard can't. You've had a warning of Purgatory today, so heed it. You're being very slow about making yourself useful.'

'I'm sorry, Father.'

'So you should be, young man. Jump to it.'

I jumped to it, as demanded.

'I wonder, I just wonder, who the hell you'll be meeting or overhearing tomorrow.'

I met Matthew, of course, on his bench.

'You find me in a convivial mood, Gabriel. You have read *The Times* today?'

'No, I haven't. My father doesn't part with it until the evening.'

('The old strutter upstairs, His Toffiness, Gabriel, would like us to believe he reads that posh paper he once had the nerve to ask me to iron for him.' Ellen Gould shook her head and chuckled. 'The truth is that it's my Charlie's rag he really enjoys, bless him. There it was, open at the cartoons page, on his little table, next to his cigarette box. He must have forgotten to hide it, or sneak it out to the dustbin, or whatever he does with it afterwards. I think your father buys *The Times* for show, bless him.')

'It contains a hugely diverting obituary.'

'Does it?'

'Yes, yes. Listen. "The House of Lords has lost one of its most flamboyant characters with the death of Simon Evelyn, fourth Lord Spiller, at the age of eighty-nine. He succeeded to the title in 1900, but did not take his seat in the Upper Chamber until the following year, when he gave a maiden speech of unusual, but characteristic, brevity. He was not to speak in the

House again, although he never missed a debate in over half a century. He was an unmistakable presence at Westminster, due to his penchant for colourful neckwear. The identity of 'Stocky' Spiller's tie-maker was the subject of much happy speculation among his fellow-peers." Isn't that heart-warming, Gabriel? Isn't that wonderful? Fifty-three years, and not a word out of him! To be remembered for one's ties! I must drink to silent "Stocky" Spiller.'

And he did.

'Oh, that all our lords were so quiet and so harmless.'

On the Friday, the fifth and last day of our friendship, I understood what he meant by that then bewildering statement.

'Aim for the bastard's eyes, Gabriel. Injure him. Do him grievous bodily harm.'

I slung the dart he handed me. It missed the board and landed sideways on the floor.

'Butterfingers, Gabriel. I'm swimming in Cawdor but I didn't miss him. Have another go.'

My second dart struck the tip of the judge's nose.

'Excellent work. Keep it up.'

My third quivered for a second on his chin, then fell.

'It was the great Beccaria who said, Gabriel, that the fate of a delinquent changed many times in passing through the different courts of judicature, and that his life and liberty were victims to the false ideas or ill humour of the judge – well, that so-and-so on the dartboard is in a permanent ill humour. That's the expression he wears when he's passing sentence. His Lordship is enamoured of neckwear, too, Gabriel, but not the colourful kind that dear, departed "Stocky" Spiller favoured. Ah, no. It's the noose this old lord fancies – round other necks than his own, naturally. He's arranged for two innocent men to wear it lately. I am speaking the truth. Two innocent men, at the very least.'

(They were innocents, in truth, those two – the simpleton Timothy; the simpleton Derek. I was to learn of their short, wretched lives from Harold Mude, my teacher at Mount Pleasant. In Matthew's wilderness that Friday, I was ignorant even of their names.)

'Since I cajoled you into coming here for a spot of low tea, I really ought to provide it. Let me see what's in the larder. Yes, as I thought, sardines. I wouldn't be offended if you ate them straight out of the tin, but I shall treat you like an honoured guest and empty the dainty tiddlers on to a serviceable plate. I say "serviceable" because You Know Who appropriated the decorative china. And you may sit, what's more, in my one remaining chair, Gabriel. Please make yourself quasi-comfortable.'

The chair had lost its back and all its legs were loose. I sat in complete discomfort while Matthew gave me his 'potted history of tinned food'.

'My post-demise preoccupation.'

He talked of syruping and brining, of cooling and processing, of the Balling Scale and of Norwegian Plate.

'You look mystified, Gabriel. Are you familiar with the phrase "sweet Fanny Adams"?'

'Yes, I am. My father uses it.'

'She owes her immortality to a canning factory.'

'Does she?'

Her sweetness, Matthew said, was not of the kind a man usually associates with an attractive young lady. He snorted at this remark. In 1867, he went on, a canning factory was established in the Victualling Yard at Deptford. In that same year, a Mr Frederick Baker, now forgotten, murdered a Miss Fanny Adams at Alton in Hampshire. Baker proved himself to be something of a butcher, for he hacked the unfortunate Miss Adams into dozens, if not hundreds, of little pieces. He was hanged at Winchester Gaol on Christmas Eve, on or about which day Her Majesty's Navy at Portsmouth received its first consignment of tinned meat from Deptford. The sailors, seeing the chunks of bully beef that plopped out of the tins, inquired of the cook if – by any coincidence – they would be sitting down to dine that night on 'sweet Fanny Adams'. The cook's reply had gone unrecorded.

'I don't feel like eating, thank you very much.'

There was rust on the sardine tin, and an insect was walking across the serviceable plate.

'It's fish, Gabriel. You're in no danger of tucking into Fanny Adams.'

'I'm not hungry.'

'Are you scorning my hospitality?'

'No, Matthew.'

'Then accept it. With grace.'

'I'm sorry, but I can't.'

'What is wrong?'

'Nothing. Nothing at all.'

'Fibber.'

'I swear to you, Matthew – '

'Swear, swear. You swear to me lies, lies.'

I stood up. 'It's getting late,' I said. 'I live on the other side of London. My father will be worried if I'm not home by seven.'

'You won't be home by seven. You certainly won't be home by seven.'

'Yes, I will.'

'It is my intention that you won't. You will stay here, in my living quarters, until I decide to release you.'

'Don't be ridiculous.'

'I shall be as ridiculous as I choose. You're going to be my guest for the evening.'

'I shouldn't have come,' I heard myself blurt out. 'I'll visit you on your bench again, I promise.'

'Will you, indeed? You may not be welcome.'

He dropped the bottle from which he had been drinking on to the stone floor, where it smashed.

'You'll do as you're told, you impudent boy. I cannot brook insolence in the young.' He snorted. 'I thrashed my eldest son whenever he answered me back.'

'No, you didn't, Matthew.'

'Contradict me, would you, Gabriel Harvey? If I said I did, I probably did. Pick up the pieces.'

'What?'

'The pieces of broken glass. Pick them up. I have the vermin's continuing good health in mind. They could cut themselves, couldn't they? Graze their teeny backsides. That is your present duty, my boy – to pick up the pieces.'

'You're drunk, Matthew.'

'Am I really? Really, really? Ah, but I've passed beyond mere drunkenness. I am preserved – yes, preserved – in Cawdor. Down on your knees, boy.'

'Have you a dustpan and brush?'

'I shouldn't think so for a minute. I've no cause to keep such housewifely objects. Use your hands.'

And use my hands I did: I would placate him, I reasoned; I'd win his favour and make a quick escape. I was suddenly scared of him, and wanted to be away.

'Every last bit, remember.'

'Yes, Matthew.'

'We English are seldom cruel to animals.' He snorted. 'Other forms of life, maybe, but not our furry and feathered friends. What a lot of "f"s I put into that observation. It will soon be time to light the candles.'

'Candles?'

'I've survived without electricity for two years now. Priorities, Gabriel Harvey, priorities. The vineyard at Cawdor has to be maintained. It is dependent upon my unwavering support.'

'What shall I do with the pieces of glass?'

'They're yours to do with as you so desire. Oh, shove them wherever you wish. Try the fireplace, boy. Yes, the fireplace would seem to be best.'

'The vermin are out of danger,' I remarked, with a smile, once I was certain that I had picked up 'every last bit'.

'Your humour holds no charm for me. I dislike facetiousness, particularly in the young.'

I said goodbye then, and repeated my promise to visit him on his bench.

'You sound and look terrified. Why is that, Gabriel Harvey?'

'I'm not, Matthew. Honestly, I'm not.'

'Yes, you are.'

Yes, I was, and not for any reason he could suppose. He had a carving knife in his right hand, but that did not frighten me. 'I shall not hesitate to kill you if you attempt to leave,' he threatened, brandishing it with a patent lack of conviction. 'You have been duly warned.'

I feared for my life, all the same – for the life ahead of me, the life I had yet to live. I sensed deception the more Matthew talked, the drunker he grew. 'I went to Eton, boy, not to some twopenny-halfpenny grammar school' – it wasn't the would-be rescuer of a feeble-minded innocent speaking, it was an English gentleman gone to the dogs through his own inherent weakness. I began to doubt that he had ever tried to save the man whose unjust prison sentence had caused his 'demise'. Perhaps the confidence he had displayed in the courtroom was merely the self-assurance that comes with class: the flaunting of the silver spoon. Perhaps the darts he hurled at the Lord Chief Justice were only the darts of envy.

Outside the wilderness-that-was, I remembered the fear that had seized me in its mouldy-smelling basement. A hero had disintegrated before me inside those once fungi-coated walls. On that October afternoon seventeen years later, I recalled the heroism I had attributed to Matthew in Lincoln's Inn Fields; the grand nature of his 'demise'. He had failed nobly, and had been brought down by intractable foes – experts in legal obfuscation and judges bent on vengeance. His determination to remind his former colleagues of that failure had struck me as more heroic than ridiculous. Then, in the house in Montague Street, after I had refused his tinned sardines, he had glowered at me, and I'd grown afraid, not so much *of* him as *for* him, for what he intended to reveal of himself. 'You will stay and listen, you common little boy.'

I needn't have stayed, needn't have listened – I could have fled, easily. I allowed him to go on playing his taunting game with me until it ended in tears. I tried to summon Heddle out of the enveloping dampness, and jabbered, 'HMV B9719, HMV B9719, HMV B9719', like a madman, while Matthew bawled: 'Matty's lonely, Sheila, Matty's awful lonely, Sheila, Matty's lost without his Sheila, Sheila, Matty hates this common boy, Sheila, this grammar-school guttersnipe, Sheila, he really really does, he does really, I swear to you, Sheila, my darling darling Sheila, I swear to you, I swear, I swear, I swear, Sheila, oh, I swear.'

I stepped over my idol of five days and left him where he lay, still crying out for Sheila.

(In Sorg, Minnesota, when I was forty, I was as abject, often.)

'I'm sorry I deserted you, Matthew,' I mumbled, from the safe distance of seventeen years. 'I was a stupid coward.'

And with that apology came a strange feeling of elation. I had exorcised the worst of his ghost and restored the best of him to its proper place in my memory. He was my absurd idol again, never again to be toppled. So I felt as I turned out of Montague Street, and so I feel now in Chiswick.

The call from someone at Leopold Stern came quicker than I had anticipated, and it was not the expected call of rejection and regret. I took it in the perpetually untidy office in which Bertie Faunce, the ironmonger, played patience, brewed tea, wrote up his diary and sometimes did his accounts.

'It's a Miss Bacon to speak to you. Keep your conversation brief. You know how I hate minding shop.'

'Yes, Bertie.'

'You're paid to meet the public.'

'Yes, Bertie.'

Miss Bacon announced herself as Leopold Stern's personal assistant. Mr Stern, she was pleased to tell me, had read *Lords of Light* with great interest and – he had used the phrase in her hearing – 'diabolical pleasure'. It would be a difficult book to publish – very difficult, in fact – but Mr Stern enjoyed a challenge. He was prepared to offer me £40: half on signature of the contract, half on publication. She did not doubt but that I would accept Mr Stern's offer, gratefully.

'Yes, I will. I will. Thank you.'

'Thank Mr Stern, Mr Harvey.'

'Yes, thank Mr Stern for me, thank you.'

'Where shall we send our letter of acceptance and your contract?'

'Where, Miss Bacon?'

'Where, Mr Harvey. I assume you have an address.'

'Of course. In Fulham.'

'Where in Fulham?'

I told her where.

'I've had wonderful news, Bertie.'

'You were a long time on that telephone. I pay you to look after the shop.'

'Forgive me, Bertie. I'm going to be published. I mean, my book is. Isn't that wonderful?'

'How did your Miss Bacon get a hold of my number?'

'I left it at Leopold Stern's, Bertie. In case they decided to reject the book. They would have rung here and said no. But they didn't, Bertie, they didn't.'

'It isn't prudent, parting with another person's telephone number. It could end up in the wrong hands altogether.'

'I shan't give it to anyone else.'

'That's a comfort. Back to your post. You're employed to stand behind the counter.'

'Yes, Bertie. Thank you. For the phone call. I'll let you have a copy of the book.'

'Writing's more my line than reading is. I shall want it inscribed, I shall, and properly. "To Albert Faunce", in your neatest lettering. None of your "Bertie", if you don't mind. I shouldn't care to see "Bertie" on your title page. It wouldn't look good, "Bertie". It's a vulgarization. Yes, "To Albert Faunce", followed by a polite message – I think I'd find that agreeable.'

Dear Mr Harvey,

Mr Leopold Stern is in Finland at the present time on urgent business. Before his hasty departure, he requested me to convey to you his sincerest congratulations on the book he will be publishing. Of your many and various Lords, Mr Stern was most taken with Frederick Charrington, heir to the brewery fortune, who devoted himself to the cause of teetotalism. Mr Stern was 'tickled pink' by his story.

Kindly read the enclosed contract with care. Initial the clauses in the boxes provided, and sign and return it to me at your earliest convenience.

Yours faithfully

Leonie Bacon

PS I have glanced at *Lords of Light*. My verdict is Curious.

12

'It's bespoke.'

'What is, Father?'

'This boot, you oaf, on my remaining foot. The boot I'm wearing. I've had it made to order and made to measure.'

'A single boot?'

'No point in having two, is there? Yes, young man, a single boot. A marvel of a boot, if I may say so. The best that J. C. Cording could provide.'

'You've never worn a boot like that before.'

'For obvious reasons. Open your lugs and I'll explain. I had a brainwave while I was convalescing in that cursèd nursing home. A picture came to me of a famous boot, a waterproof boot, that was stood in water in the window of a shop in Piccadilly for as many years as you've been with us. It was stood in water, young man, to show passers-by that water couldn't harm it. It was like inflammable is to fire, to put it in a nutshell.'

'Do you need a waterproof boot, Father?'

'Yes, I bloody do. It's exactly what I need. I can't be expected to rest content with odd shoes.'

I was mystified. 'Can't you?' I asked. 'Can't you?'

'No, I can't. An odd shoe, missing its partner, won't catch the eye, but a boot will. Especially my boot, young man, my beauty of a boot from J. C. Cording. People, passing strangers, will remark on it, you wait and see. "There goes Oswald Harvey in his famous boot," they'll say.'

'But why waterproof?'

'England, in case you hadn't noticed, has a rainy climate. The Sahara's a long way off.'

'Even when you had – ' I stopped short, embarrassed.

'Even when I had – what?'

'Both your legs, Father. Even then, you seldom walked anywhere. Not any distance. Not so that you'd need galoshes. Or a waterproof boot.'

'Walk or no, I'd be daft to buy a boot that couldn't withstand the elements. Get it into your skull that there's more to this splendid creation than the fact that it's waterproof. The man at Cording's made a note of all my requirements, and all my requirements have been accommodated, I'm happy to report. He's a splendid fellow – gracious, courteous, a real gentleman's gentleman. He's come up with the perfect boot.'

'The perfect boot,' I repeated, flatly.

'Yes sirree, as the Yanks say. Yes, sirree. You'll understand why when I decide to tell you. I haven't mentioned, have I, that Quinlan's done a bunk?'

'No, you haven't. Has she?'

'If you'd bothered to stay at "Blenheim", as I'd requested, while I was being rehabloodybilitated, you'd know she has. You might – you just might – have caught her in the act. As it was, Flint dropped in one night at two in the morning – he'd heard sounds of merry-making from the road – and found Quinlan and some bog-Irish tyke arseholed with drink in the sitting-room. *My* drink, it was, young man – only my finest whisky.'

'Mrs Quinlan drunk? It's hard to believe, Father.'

'Nevertheless, it's true. What riles me, what sticks in my craw, is that cursèd ulcer she bamboozled me into sympathizing with. God, the sympathy she drew out of me, thanks to that thing in her gut. Correction: that thing she didn't have in her gut, but which she convinced me – me, Oswald Harvey – she *did* have. "It's paining me bad today, sir" – that was always her ploy. "Go and lie down, then, Quinlan. You go and rest." "Are you sure, sir? I don't like to, when there's so many tasks undone." "They can wait, Quinlan" – by Christ, the times I told her they could wait. The work she didn't get round to, the corners the swindling bitch cut, the money she accepted but never earned – it's me who deserves the ulcer, most definitely it is, for being made a fool of by a conniving female. It isn't as if I rogered her, either. She had no excuse. She took me for a ride through sheer bloody spite.'

'Aren't you exaggerating, Father? It doesn't sound credible.'

'No, I am not exaggerating. I should have realized ages ago that you can't nurse an ulcer for as long as Quinlan nursed hers. Years, she's had it. Except that she hasn't, which is why she's still alive. She'd have croaked else. I could curse Gould for moving up north. I had a good and loyal servant in her.'

'Yes, you had,' I agreed, remembering Ellen's gentle mockery of the Toff and his foibles.

'She didn't treat "Blenheim" like Liberty Hall, like that Quinlan cow did. I tell you, the next woman who enters this house will have to pass a very severe test indeed. I shan't be playing into the hands of another Jezebel in a hurry, young man, not now that the pup with the scalpel has deprived me of a limb. Yes, a very severe test.'

I waited for him to specify the nature of his severe test, but he chose not to be specific. He said, 'Of course there is a solution to my housekeeping problem, and he's sitting here in front of me, looking at his father holding an empty glass and doing sod all about filling it. In other words, you. You could come and run "Blenheim" for me until a suitable person turns up. I'd pay you a decent wage. More, considerably more, than you're getting for Jerusalem donkey-work.'

'No, thank you.'

I took his empty glass.

'Why ever not? You'd be doing your Christian duty and earning an honest penny at the same time. I don't see what's so dreadful about giving your old dad – your incapacitated old dad – a helping hand.'

'You once remarked, Father, that you didn't want a son of yours doing woman's work.'

'Yes, I did remark, and I meant it, too. That was before you took it into your skull to turn your back on the opportunities ahead of you. If what you're doing in that there Jerusalem dump isn't woman's work, I don't rightly know what is. Come to think of it, playing housekeeper at "Blenheim" will be near enough the classiest job you've had.'

'No, thank you.'

'Much the classiest, by far. A real leap up the ladder after the letter-sorting and skivvying you've been used to. I wouldn't treat you like a servant, young man. Not for a minute I wouldn't. I give you my solemn word.'

'No, thank you.'

'You'd have plenty of free hours in the day. I'm not the man to make unnecessary demands. You could get on with that book-writing you started and then oafishly abandoned.'

(I did not say that I ached to get on with it, that I longed to be happily imprisoned.)

'No, thank you, Father.'

'Curse your obstinate hide. You can't say I didn't offer you the chance to better yourself. Stop being oafish.'

'Your whisky and soda.'

'Even the cursed dog's deserted me.'

'No, he hasn't. I saw him when I arrived.'

'Yes, he has. Where did you see him?'

'In the Campbells' garden.'

'Exactly.'

'I assumed he'd jumped over the fence.'

'Jumped? He was lured over it, enticed he was, while I was in the convalescent home. You assumed wrong, which is your way with assumptions. Those not-Scots tempted Rubens, Flint told me, with green tripe. Lashings and lashings of green tripe.'

'What's green tripe?'

'Tripe, young man, is the stomach lining of oxes, cows, and sheep and such. The green variety is due to grass – the grass the animals were chewing prior to being slaughtered. The grass that hasn't become manure. The butchers who don't sling it out sell it to the owners of pet shops. I never bought the muck for the beast because I can't abide the diabolical stink of it. Those Campbells can, obviously. Especially that tall streak of black piss who walks him on the common. It was he did the luring.'

'I'll fetch Rubens back for you, Father.'

'No, you won't. You'll leave him where he is. Let the ungrateful great thing stay with the company he prefers. I wouldn't give him house room now.'

'But he belongs to *you,* Father. He's your property. The Campbells were only looking after him out of kindness.'

'How in hell would you know that? Kindness my arse. They haven't returned him, have they? No, if he wishes to feather his nest in the jungle, let him. Besides, I should imagine his breath is so foul it infects as far as Land's End, or upwards to John O'Groats. He's not wanted, he isn't, in "Blenheim".'

To amuse my enraged father, I dared to ask if the captain of HMS *Canis* had ever mentioned green tripe on one of his twice-yearly visits to the Prodigal's Return.

'What are you gabbing on about? Which captain is this, you oaf?'

'Don't you remember? When I was a little boy, you explained

to me how the Isle of Dogs got its name. You told me how the captain of HMS *Canis* had told you that the wild dogs on the Isle of Dogs were fed by Royal Charter. I just wondered', I ended feebly, 'if the sailors had ever thrown them green tripe?'

'Well, wonder on. I never talked such twaddle. I never met a captain neither.'

'Oh, it doesn't matter.'

'Then why bring the daft subject up? It's typical of you, it is, to wander off down some bloody side-track of your own creating when I'm talking sense. I blame your airy-fairyness on music.'

'Music?'

'Yes, music. Your mother encouraged you in your musical mooniness, with disastrous consequences.'

'Hardly disastrous.'

'Yes, young man, disastrous. You'll soon be thirty, and you're scrubbing floors for crones to tread on. There's no spirit in you, no adventure. I suppose you consider yourself a success?'

'Not particularly.'

'Your room's as you left it. Nothing's been moved. Stay here for a couple of days – or longer, or longer – and see how you make out. Eh? Flint'll do the heavy work, I promise.'

'I'm sorry, Father, but no.'

'I'll keep the offer open, in case you decide to change your mind.'

'You must be Gabriel.'

'Yes, I am.'

'Miss Garrett. Miss Agnes Garrett.'

'Pleased to meet you.'

'Likewise. Your father is in my care, as you have probably been notified.'

'Yes, I have.'

'Do come in. Oswald is expecting you. He is in the sitting-room. Would you be offended if I addressed you by your Christian name?'

'Not in the least.'

'To business, then, Gabriel. You may mix Oswald a single drink. I recommend an overdose of soda. Should he attempt to wangle a second whisky out of you, kindly threaten him with my displeasure.'

'Yes, Miss Garrett, I will.'

'Agnes, please. You find my displeasure amusing?'

'No, no,' I faltered. 'I'm simply surprised that my father – '

'That your father – ?'

'Can be threatened.'

'Certainly he can.' She smiled at me. 'That was almost the first thing I ascertained.' She opened the sitting-room door. 'Here's Gabriel, Oswald – a little earlier than you expected.'

'Hullo, young man.'

'Hullo, Father.'

'Luncheon will be ready in twenty minutes. Plain fare, Gabriel, but satisfying.'

'Remarkable woman, Agnes,' said my father, when Agnes Garrett was out of earshot. 'Quite remarkable.'

'You called her Agnes.'

'Is there a law that says I shouldn't? I called her Agnes because Agnes happens to be her name.'

'I never heard you call Mrs Gould Ellen, or Mrs Quinlan Mavis.'

'I had to show them who was boss. Not that the Quinlan female took much notice. They were servants. It isn't wise to get too familiar with servants.'

'And Miss Garrett's not a servant?'

'Not a servant servant, young man. She *is* a servant, of course she is, I mean, I pay her a wage, but she's more than someone who cleans and cooks. She is, in a word, remarkable.'

I mixed my father's drink to the remarkable woman's instructions.

'I've allowed Agnes to live in. She's chosen to sleep in the room where a certain person pissed his bed night after night a few years back. She likes the view over the common.'

'She keeps you company, then.'

'Yes, young man, she does.'

(She was to keep him company until his death a decade later. She was to be his 'companion', his 'source of strength', his 'guiding light at the end of life's dark tunnel' and, finally, his 'wet-nurse'. She was to inherit 'Blenheim' as a 'small return for her faithful service'. She was to sell it immediately, and to travel round the world on the proceeds.)

'How did you find her?'

'I stuck an advertisement in *The Times* personal column. Flint did the wording of it for me. I thought to myself "Christ, what a frowzy-looking frump!" when she turned up on the doorstep. Even you, who're no judge of women, as far as I can tell; even you can see she's no oil painting with those pop-eyes of hers. She's titless into the bargain. And then, there's the rest of her – all over the shop, it is, what with that enormous great arse and those silly tiny legs, and her head much too big for her body. She's completely out of proportion is Agnes Garrett. Nature went haywire bringing her about, and that's a truth.'

My father listed Agnes Garrett's deformities as though he were extolling her beauty.

'Not a lass to roger, by any stretch of the imagination. In my rogering days, I wouldn't have given her a glance. No, it's her mind's her strength. Agnes is the only woman I've met in my eighty and some years who's got a mind.'

'Mummy has a mind, Mummy's intelligent.'

'Agreed, agreed. Your mother's was more of a feminine mind – no disrespect intended – whereas hers, Agnes's, is nearer the masculine. What I'm saying is that Agnes could argue the toss with a clever man, I'm willing to wager, and not miss a single pro or a single con in the arguing.'

'Were there any other applicants?'

'Applicants?'

'For the job. Did anyone else answer your advertisement?'

'Oafish question. Bloody sure they did. Several women wrote to me at the box number. Different types, different ages, but none of them with her qualifications. She's looked after an admiral before me, and a professor of Greek, and yet she's still on the right side of fifty.'

'Remarkable,' I said, with no sarcasm, I thought, in my tone. My father detected it, none the less.

'Yes, she is, you sneering oaf. You might have put a suit on today for once in your life.'

'At least I'm not wearing jeans.'

'That's true enough. I suppose I ought to be thankful.'

The door opened, and the remarkable woman with the masculine mind and the severely disproportionate physique came in to announce that luncheon was ready. 'Leave Oswald, to me, Gabriel. I'll support him. I have the knack.'

We ate Agnes Garrett's plain fare in the kitchen: 'The most agreeable room in any household, I always think.' The meal began with potted shrimps ('The admiral's favourite'), continued with *ragoût* of lamb ('I hope I haven't been too free and easy with the cayenne. My hand tends to slip') and closed with an exquisite sweet made, to my amazement, with fresh beef suet and a large lemon ('A Sussex Pond pudding, Gabriel. Do gobble the rest of it up. I'd love to, and so would Oswald, but we mustn't').

'You may smoke a small cigar, Oswald, and then I insist that you lie down for a good two hours. Gabriel will dry the dishes for me.'

'Yes, Miss Garrett.'

'Agnes. A task shared is a task halved.'

The task was shared and halved while my father took his afternoon nap in the former dining-room. 'I asked Mr Flint to move Oswald's bed in there. It's much more convenient for all concerned.'

'My father seems most impressed with you.'

'Only "seems"? Yes, Oswald does seem to approve of me. If he didn't, I would pack my bags and go, Gabriel. I cannot function where there is animosity.'

('Then you'll soon be packing your bags,' I refrained from saying.)

'I foresaw certain difficulties. They were overcome almost at once. I nipped them smartly in the bud.'

'What difficulties?' I was curious to learn.

'I shall have to be frank with you.'

'Be frank.'

'I think I should like a glass of Tokay. Will you join me?'

'I've never drunk it.'

'It is rather sweet.'

'A little, thank you.'

'It is not to be consumed in large quantities.'

'Of course.'

'Tiptoe into the sitting-room, Gabriel, and quietly remove a couple of liqueur glasses from that – that – '

'Jacobean-style cocktail cabinet?'

'Yes. If that's what it is. Yes.'

('These thimbles, Amy, are for you.' / 'Why me, Ossie?' / 'Because they are, that's why. You've had to drink your fancy drinks out of the wrong glasses for far too long.' / 'Oh, Ossie, don't be ridiculous. I'm fond of my old medicine glass.' / 'These are for after dinner, to show off to our friends.' / 'Friends? What friends?')

'I'm sure these haven't been used since my father bought them.'

'Chin-chin, Gabriel.'

'Chin-chin.'

'Frankness, yes? Well. I was not surprised by Oswald's – shall I say – overtures. Indeed, no. Men of his type are loath to admit that their sexual day is done. "Game to the last" might be said to be their motto. I rebuffed his advances with firmness and levity. Outrage acts as a spur to the Oswald kind, in my experience, but a smile and a joke will usually cool their ardour. What an appalling cross for an old man to bear. Passion, I'm referring to.'

'Is it?'

'So I have found. But back to Oswald. I had not been in his presence half an hour before he let out a stream, a positive stream, of coarse language. I was not shocked. I was, rather, prepared for such an exhibition. It is a sad fact that people newly deprived of a limb or limbs indulge in compulsive swearing as a means of venting their anger and frustration. I encouraged him to continue. "Swear away," I said. "Let's hear every dirty word you can think of. The dirtier the better." When the spring finally dried up, I thanked him, Gabriel. I thanked him warmly. "That's it, Oswald. I've heard my fill. You have been so thorough, you have covered so much mucky ground, that a repeat performance will not be necessary." Nor, I added, would it be welcome. Are you enjoying your first taste of Tokay?'

'It's pleasant.'

'Unlike the matter I'm telling you about. However, I anticipate no further trouble. I feel confident that I have nipped, as I said, poor Oswald's brutishness in the bud. If I haven't succeeded – which I doubt – then some other woman will be put to the test of coping with his priapism.'

I left 'Blenheim' that Sunday afternoon with an enriched vocabulary.

Winnie Hibbs was still alive when the Jerusalem was razed, and so was Myrtle Burns. Both insensible women were taken by ambulance to a Home in Broadstairs – just a stone's throw, Mrs Ricks assured them, from the sea.

'The sea, did you say, Matron?' asked Edith Trimmer, the third surviving inmate.

'Yes, Miss Trimmer, I did.'

'Think they'll go bathing, do you? Dip a toe each in the briny? Play in the sand with their buckets and spades?'

'No, Miss Trimmer. Of course I don't. Try and calm yourself.'

'They've no notion where they are, and haven't had for years. They're living nothings, those two. Whether they're near the sea or whether they're near a cesspit – it makes no odds to Hibbs and Burns. Honestly, Matron, you're talking eye-wash. If you was to string that pair up in the Hanging Gardens of – of Oojamaflick – '

'Babylon.'

'That's the place. If you was to string them up, arsy-versy, in flower baskets in the Hanging Gardens of Babylon, they'd be none the wiser – would they now? You can't answer me nay because you know I'm bloody well right. It strikes me there ought to be a tablet and it ought to be lawful.'

'What do you mean, my dear?'

'A tablet, Matron, is like a pill you swallow. The tablet or pill I'm speaking of is designed to send a person off to sleep for good and all. Hibbs and Burns, the staring awful daft things, should have been given a tablet long ago, in my humble opinion. That tablet would have saved you a lot of wasted effort, Matron my dear.'

'I'm not sure that I wholly approve of euthanasia.'

'Approve of euthawhat or not, that's your lookout, but it's my belief there ought to be a lawful tablet. You could give it to me this minute and I'd be grateful to you. Oh, yes.'

'Miss Trimmer, Edith, you mustn't be so morbid. You won't be leaving your beloved London, as I keep on telling you. The Home in Shoreditch is really terribly nice – very modern, very comfortable, very up-to-date. The complete opposite of the Jerusalem. You're bound to make lots of new friends – '

'No, I'm not. I'm not bound to at all. If you were any judge of character, Matron, you'd know I'm not, and never have been, the friendly type. I pick and I choose who I'm pals with, and now my days for picking and choosing are over. I stomached the likes of Queenie and Alice and Maggy and even that snob of a Louise Capes, but Nell was the one true friend I had in here. I shan't find another and I don't want to neither.'

'You could be pleasantly surprised in Shoreditch.'

'And then again I couldn't. I wish there was a way of getting in touch with Nell, just to show her she was wrong about the Beyond. I'd have heard from her by this time – it's six months and two days since she went – if there was anything in that message from the Other Side eye-wash she was always pestering me with. There isn't, I was positive in my bones there wasn't, and her silence is the proof. I was the closest to Nell, and it's the closest who are supposed to hear. I'd have certainly heard, if there *was* anything in it, me being the closest, after six whole months and two days.'

'Yes, Miss Trimmer.'

'It stands to reason.'

'Of course it does, Edith dear. Mrs Taylor from Shoreditch is waiting down in the hall. She's a busy woman. Gabriel will carry your suitcase for you.'

'At least portering's a man's job. I hope you'll be saying goodbye to women's work, Gabriel Harvey, once this old Jerusalem's gone.'

'I shall be selling nails and hammers and screws and hinges, Miss Trimmer. In an ironmonger's. I start next week.'

'That's better. That's more natural.'

'Gabriel's kept the Jerusalem spick and span for us, Edith. I think you should thank him.'

'You do, do you? Thank you, Mr Harvey. There, I've said it, Matron, and to his face. I still maintain that it's against nature — a man scrubbing floors.'

'Let's go down, Edith, shall we?'

'I'd prefer to go for ever, that's what I'd prefer. A lawful tablet would soon put me out of this misery.'

'You're not miserable, Edith. Not while there's cause for complaint. Not you.'

'If you say so.'

As I helped her into Mrs Taylor's car, Miss Trimmer confided, 'My skin hasn't been the same without Nell's caring for it. Soap and water aren't enough with the type of open pores my ma and my pa wished on me. Clogged up, it's been, my skin has, these last six months, and it'll get worse, I'm convinced it will, in Shoreditch.'

'Goodbye, Edie.'

'Nell was a wonder with my blackheads. She could see them sprouting on my moosh before they was there. She hurt me sometimes with her pinching and squeezing, but she always had my clear complexion at heart. Oh, but she was special, was my Nell.'

'This is for you, Father.'

'A book? What would I want with a cursed book? I haven't gone through a book since before you were born.'

'Take it, Father. Look at it.'

'Why should I? I'm past the age for books and book-reading. Why the hell should I?'

'Take a look at it,' I shouted, slinging the book into his lap. 'Take a look at it at least, you hateful swine.'

'Watch your language, young man,' he said quietly. 'There's no need for that kind of talk.'

I heard myself apologize to him.

'I should think so, too. Now, what is this? *Lords of Light*? Good bloody grief! Electricians, are they?'

'No, Father. Keep looking.'

'*Lords of Light*. Gabriel Harvey. That's your name. There's a book-writer around, is there, called Gabriel Harvey?'

'It's me.'

'You? Stop pulling my leg.' He chortled at this remark. 'Correction: stop pulling my right leg. It's the only one left, in a manner of speaking. You didn't do this, young man.'

'I did.'

'It's so bloody long.'

'Two hundred and fifty pages. I've read far longer books.'

'You couldn't have written this. You haven't had the time. You've been working in that cursèd ironmonger's, like the oaf you are.'

'I burned the midnight oil, Father. In a manner of speaking.'

'The devil you did. You let me believe different, you artful villain. You'd "abandoned all hope" of becoming a book-writer – that's the fancy way you put it. Abandoned, my arsehole. You went ahead with it behind my back just to spite me.'

'Spite you? Stop being absurd.'

I watched him read the dedication.

'I see. "With undying love." Well, that's very nice. Very nice, indeed. "For Mummy." I see. "For Mummy, with undying love" – yes, that's very thoughtful of her darling son. I had a hand in your conception, you know.'

'Yes, Father.'

'"Yes, Father", he says. There's no "For Daddy", though, is there?'

'No, there isn't.'

'I see. Who are these lords of light, anyhow?'

'Preachers, Father. Itinerant preachers, mostly.'

'Preachers? Do you mean to say you've been filling your skull up with stuff about men of the cloth?'

'Very few of them were actually ordained. They weren't strictly men of the cloth at all.'

'That's as maybe, but they still had God in their noddles, didn't they? This is Swedie's influence, I'll wager.'

'Perhaps.'

'She changed you. She said something to you that Whitsun –'

'Easter.'

'Easter, then. She said something that changed you from being a normal, healthy lad into – into –'

'Into?'

'Oh, into a lad I hardly recognized. You went off straightforward and you came back moody. Swedie's to blame for this bit of book-writing.'

He hit *Lords of Light* with his fist.

'I must say I'm relieved – relieved, do you hear? – that you decided not to stick a "For Daddy" in your preacher-book.'

'Why is that, Father?'

'Because people would think I was responsible. They'd put two and two together and come up with Oswald Harvey as the culprit. And that wouldn't be fair on your old dad, who tried to bring you up honest and decent, which means giving clergymen and such a wide berth. "For Daddy" indeed!'

'Try and read some of it. You might be surprised.'

'Might I? You could make yourself useful, young man. My throat always goes dry when I'm niggled and upset. And a Christmas measure, if you please. Agnes is bending the rules today.'

'Only a fraction,' said that lady, entering the room to announce the arrival of Mr and Mrs Van Pelt.

'Close the door, Agnes. Quickly. I haven't told him here about Reggie's – well, accident.'

Agnes Garrett closed the door and stood against it.

'Tell Gabriel, then, Oswald.'

'Reggie, poor Reggie, he's had a stroke. His face has gone funny down one side and his voice sounds daft, like he's speaking through a ventriloquist.'

'Elegantly and tactfully phrased,' murmured Agnes Garrett, as if to herself.

'Has he married Miss Carstairs?' I asked.

'She's married him. He was too ill to resist her. He'd have crawled to his grave a bachelor else.'

'I'll show them in, Oswald.'

Reginald Van Pelt, seeing me, let out a high, throttled laugh. I recognized the awful sound as laughter, since that was how he had always greeted me – with derision.

'Congratulations, Mr Van Pelt,' I said, in as neutral a tone as I could manage. 'Are you allowed to drink?'

Mr Van Pelt nodded vigorously.

'I ration him,' his wife boomed. 'Don't I, Van P.? Ration you? That means half his usual. You can fill my glass to the jolly old brim, though.'

'Certainly, Mrs Van Pelt. Congratulations.'

'I think I deserve a long-service medal. Ours must have been the longest engagement in history. When are you getting spliced?'

'Me?'

'Yes, of course you. You're the only unattached male in present company. You, yes.'

'He's still playing the field, Marge. Sowing his wild oats.'

'Roger. Ing,' came from Reginald Van Pelt.

'That's it, Reggie my boy. That's the word. Keep your voice down, remember, when you talk about rogering, there's a good chap. Agnes doesn't approve of swearing and such.'

'This *is* your house, Oswald.'

'I know damned well it is, Marge. What's your drift?'

'My drift is that an Englishman can swear to his heart's content within his own four walls if he so desires, Oswald. He's not at the whim of a mere housekeeper.'

'I'm at nobody's whim and never have been. And Agnes isn't mere neither. I swear as much as I want to in "Blenheim", but I don't do it in front of a lady, out of respect for her wishes.'

'I'm not offended that you don't consider me a lady, Oswald. Reggie, when he's feeling lovey-dovey, always calls me his pal. I'd rather be a pal to a man any day of the week than a lady, thank you very much.' She snatched the drink I offered her. 'You don't grow any bigger, do you?'

'No, Mrs Van Pelt, I don't. And it's not likely that I shall. I'll be thirty-four soon.'

'If you doubt who exactly owns "Blenheim", Marge, you have only to shove your hand in my boot.'

'Whatever is it you're saying, Oswald? It sounds like complete and utter nonsense to me.'

'Deeds. Of house. Oswald's. In boot.'

'Reggie's right. I keep the deeds of "Blenheim" in this wonderful boot. All my money, too.'

'Your money, Oswald?'

'Drew the lot out of that cursèd bank last June. I said to the cashier, "I want the lot, this minute." Pandemonium followed. "Are you absolutely certain, sir?" asked the manager, appearing out of nowhere. "Yes, I absolutely am," I said. "I'm fed up to the gills with you and your fellow-sharpies" – those were my words, and I have to tell you he winced – "you and your fellow-sharpies charging me for the pleasure of looking after my friend Sir Vincent's bequest to me. From now on, I'm looking after it myself." "Yourself, sir? You can't possibly" – this with a sniff and a sneer. "I possibly can," I said, "and I probably will." "How, sir, may I inquire?" "With the assistance of J. C. Cording," I told Sniff-and-Sneer, and that knocked him sideways. "Is he a banker, sir?" "Yes," I said, "the best." Speechless, he was, then. And speechless he stayed while Flint filled a bag with hundred-pound notes. Which, Marge, have been transferred down here.'

'You're not serious, Oswald.'

'Never more so, Marge. It's the safest place, when you stop to think about it. Even banks get raided, and some of the City ones go bust.'

'But burglars, Oswald. Burglars.'

'I'm a step ahead of you there, Marge. What self-respecting burglar would dream of looking in an old man's boot? He'd tear "Blenheim" apart first, and still leave swagless. I stick a smelly sock inside it overnight, as an added precaution.'

'Cun. Ning. Cun. Ning.'

'Is that what I am, Reggie? You should know, you devil. Talking of cunning, you'll never guess what this young man's been and gone and done.'

'Something unpleasant, I shouldn't wonder,' snapped Mrs Van Pelt.

'Stop jumping to wrong conclusions, Marge. He's written a book, he has.'

'Him?'

'None other. And what's more, he's been and gone and got it printed.'

'Him?'

'Show it to the disbelieving female, young man. Let her see it with her own eyes.'

I handed Mrs Van Pelt the copy of *Lords of Light*.

'I'll need to put on my reading specs for this.' She delved into her large black handbag and eventually produced them. '"*Lords of Light* by Gabriel Harvey." Well, well. Oswald isn't having a game with us, Van P. He's speaking the truth.'

'Of course I'm speaking the cursèd truth. Lying's not my style.'

'No, Oswald. Of course it isn't.'

(No, Father. Of course it wasn't.)

'Open it, Marge. Take a peep at what the book-writer's written.'

'He's dedicated it to his mother, I notice. Aren't you a little long in the tooth to be calling her Mummy?'

'No, Mrs Van Pelt. She's Mummy to me. It's the word I prefer.'

'And who are these lords of light? Peculiar title. George Fox, John Wesley – clergymen, I seem to remember. This Roger Kemp of Liverpool – who's he?'

'Some people thought he was the Messiah, Mrs Van Pelt. He died in obscurity in a London workhouse.'

'Like your grandfather, you mean? He wasn't a Messiah, but he died in the workhouse. Didn't he, Oswald?'

I looked at my father. He avoided my glance.

'The book's all about preachers, Marge. Not your cup of tea, really.'

'No, not really, though I do tend to favour the historical when I'm in the reading mood. It's the pageantry I enjoy. Intrigues at court – that kind of spicy stuff. Colourful characters, too – you know, Oswald, swashbucklers. Any buckling of the swash in *Lords of Light*?'

'No, Mrs Van Pelt.'

'A pity. I'll have a borrow of it some time, Oswald, if I may. Unless, that is, your son's brought a spare one with him for his father's friends – '

'He hasn't, Mrs Van Pelt.'

'I think we'll survive without it – won't we, Van P.? This Leopold Stern, I assume, is the publisher. Would he be foreign?'

'German, Mrs Van Pelt.'

'And a Jew-boy by the sound of him.'

'He's Jewish, yes, Mrs Van Pelt.'

'What's a German Jew-boy doing publishing a book about English Christian clergymen?'

'He admires it, I believe. I haven't had a chance to discuss it with him, I'm afraid. As yet.'

(I have still to meet Leopold Stern; still to talk to him on the phone; still to receive a letter from him. Even when I wrote to thank him for negotiating a Hollywood contract on my behalf, his thanks for my thanks were expressed by Leonie Bacon: *Mr Leopold Stern has instructed me to convey his gratitude for your appreciation of his services. The deal was 'clinched' in a matter of minutes. He hopes you realize that had you not written the book, he would not have earned his ten per cent.*)

'Have you ever considered wearing a corset?' Mrs Van Pelt asked Agnes Garrett during Christmas lunch.

'I haven't, actually.'

'I wish more women would, and not just for the sake of business either. The modern corset is a light and fragile thing compared to those fearful Victorian monstrosities our poor dear ancestors were forced to suffer. You must have come across the latest design – complete with Direct Buttock Control – in your women's magazines.'

'I do not read women's magazines, Mrs Van Pelt. Complete with direct-what-did-you-say?'

'Buttock Control. We refer to it as DBC in the trade. Shall I elaborate?'

'Please do.'

'The latest corset – and it's a revolutionary undergarment, in my humble opinion – rests snugly on the wearer's bum. Oh, what have I said? You must forgive me, Miss Garrett, for swearing in your presence.'

' "Bum" is perfectly acceptable, Mrs Van Pelt.'

'Bum. Bum. Titty. Bum.'

'That's enough, Van P. Behave yourself. Yes, it rests snugly on the wearer's bottom, thanks to a wonderful elastic named Lycra. The corset is therefore controlled directly from below. It's caused a revolution among us corsetières.'

'A revolution?'

'Nothing less. The nipped-in waist is a thing of the past. DBC is here to stay.'

'How fascinating.'

'I find it so. I am directly controlled even as I speak to you,

Miss Garrett. Yes, yes. That lovely Lycra is keeping all my secrets hidden.'

Agnes Garrett smiled at this revelation. 'I've grown accustomed to my unbridled state, Mrs Van Pelt. Far too accustomed. I rather think I should loathe being controlled from below. Mine's a bum that won't be restricted, I fear.'

I heard Elizabeth the Second's little cotton socks blessed for the last time that Christmas. Reginald Van Pelt dropped dead in the saloon bar of the Windmill the following spring, and his wife – 'an honest woman of eight months' duration', as she styled herself at his funeral – was strongly discouraged from visiting 'Blenheim'. 'She has only to open her mouth and Oswald's blood pressure goes rocketing up. It's dangerous for him to lose his temper. Mrs Van Pelt and her elasticated buttocks have been shown the door in no uncertain manner. A welcome riddance, I am sure you will agree, Gabriel.'

'Reggie couldn't have had a better death. On his pins with a large Scotch in his paw one minute, and then – whoosh, out for the final count the next. He deserved it if anyone did, the dear old wag. I shall miss him, I can tell you. I won't have his bloody luck when it's my turn.'

'Perhaps you will,' said the outwardly dutiful son who almost believed that his father's turn would never, never come. 'You might be as lucky.'

'Fat chance. We had some good laughs, Reggie and me, especially when that corset cow wasn't around putting her female's spoke in. I feel a stitch coming on just remembering the way he used to do *The Times* crossword. He had a system, he said. The Van Pelt system. He showed me how it worked once, but I couldn't get the hang of it, not having his command of words. I bust a gut laughing at his cleverness.'

'Tell me about his system.'

'You were always so high-handed with him, so bloody rude, I'm surprised you want to know. Reggie's system, young man, was to look for the clue that had the most blank squares in it. He was in his seventh heaven if it was a twenty-letter job, because that was a test of his intelligence. Once he'd filled that first one in, he was well and truly away, the old cove.'

'But that's how most people do crosswords.'

'Of course it is, you oaf, of course it is. Most people put the right answers in, don't they? Reggie made it more of a challenge for himself by putting in answers that made absolutely no bloody sense at all. The beauty of it was, though, that everything fitted. The answers were wrong, but they linked up a treat. Most people wouldn't have the diabolical wherewithal to do that to a crossword, but my chum Reggie had. Genius, I call it, the Van Pelt system. Pure, cockeyed genius. And now it's gone up in smoke along with its inventor.'

'I suspect it has.'

'When it's my turn, I'm not to be incinerated, like Reggie was. I want what's left of me left down here.'

'So you're the clever Gabriel. I'm the not-very-clever Ethel.'

'I'm sorry. Ought I to know you?'

'I'm only your half-sister.'

'I didn't realize I had one.'

'Well, you have, and here she stands. Pleased to meet you.'

'Yes,' I said. 'Yes, indeed.'

'How old are you now, clever Gabriel?'

'Thirty-eight.'

'My, my. I suppose you must be. I shall be sixty-one next birthday. That's four years younger than Tom. I wonder if Tom's really his first and you're really his last.'

'I'm sorry, I –'

'Not quick on the uptake, it seems, for all your cleverness. I am wondering, Gabriel, how many bastards our bastard of a father spawned. I can't believe he confined himself to three legitimate children.'

'It's something I've never thought about.'

'Haven't you? Since you didn't know of my existence, that's hardly surprising. He's told you who Tom is, has he?'

'I've met Tom, yes.'

'It's something I've thought about a lot, Gabriel, and for a damned good reason. He walked out on my mum and me when I was nearly thirteen, and I can't forgive him. To this day, I can't forgive him. He'd found another woman, and she wasn't your mother, because by my reckoning – and you can correct me if I'm wrong – little Amy Prentice would have been ten years old in 1927. He liked his lady-loves young, but even he drew the line at ten.'

'I don't understand, Mrs – Miss –'

'Ethel will do. I'm Mrs Knight, actually. Mr Knight – Alec, my husband – suffers from asthma, but there's nothing wrong with our son, Martin, except perhaps his wife. Now what is it you don't understand? I was given to understand by the old bastard that you understood everything.'

'No, Ethel. I don't understand why you're here in the hospital if you can't forgive him.'

'I want to make thoroughly sure he's going this time. I've had my hopes raised before. The doctor says it's only a matter of weeks, hip hip hooray. I've got the bunting ready, Gabriel. There'll be singing and dancing in the Knight household when Oswald Harvey drops off his perch, by God there will.'

I found myself shocked by her honesty.

'You'll weep buckets, I suppose, Gabriel.'

'No, I won't.'

'Tom'll miss him. Tom's always seen the funny side of him. But then, Tom's pretty funny, too.'

I made no response.

'When we meet again, Gabriel, it'll be at the grand send-off. Goodbye for the present. I must get home to my casserole. Alec's helpless at a stove.'

'Goodbye, Ethel. It was nice meeting you.'

'No, it wasn't,' she said, without looking back at me.

'Gabriel's come, Oswald.' Agnes Garrett opened the door for me. 'I'll leave you alone together.'

'Why?'

'You have urgent business to discuss with him.'

'Ah, yes. You're not going far, are you, Agnes?'

'No, no, Oswald. Push the button and I shall be right along.'

'How are you, Father?' I asked when I was alone with him.

'Oafish bloody question, as per usual. I've got no legs – that's how I am.'

'They've given you a pleasant room.'

'So they should have, for the price. Still, it's quiet, and I'm away from the riff-raff.'

'I met Ethel in the corridor.'

'She's her mother's double.'

'She told me she's my half-sister.'

'I bet she did. Change the subject. What's your news?'

'Nothing much. I've moved to Chiswick.'

(To a beautiful eighteenth-century house, I did not reveal. 'I paid two hundred thousand pounds for it,' I refrained from saying. 'Roger Kemp of Liverpool has made me rich.')

'Peter Fisher's come back into my life. He invited me to his wedding.'

'Was that the half-Abdul who took the piss out of me?'

'Yes.'

'Is his wife touched with the tar-brush?'

'No, she's not.'

'You ought to marry. There must be a woman somewhere in the bloody universe who'd have you.'

'Agnes Garrett mentioned urgent business.'

'I've altered my last will and t. I'm leaving you something.'

'I don't want or need your money.'

'That's gone where my legs went. I'd be surprised if there's much more than a brass farthing and an old collar stud in the kitty. No, my son, I wouldn't insult you with filthy lucre. Others, yes, but not you.'

'Thanks,' I said, 'for having my interests at heart.'

'I know you'll thank me – in my absence, of course – for my parting gift. Oh, I'm sure you will. You're the only person in the entire world, Gabriel, who would appreciate it.'

I did not ask him why. I had stopped asking him questions ages past – the questions, that is, I knew he wanted to answer.

His hands were suddenly restless, pummelling the eiderdown. 'Signs of life, signs of life,' he hissed. 'Yes, there is definite activity below. I feel a turd worming its way out. Be a good lad and ring for my wet-nurse.'

I was happy to press the button.

'My son' and 'Gabriel' and 'Be a good lad' – it was far too late for such endearments.

In the autumn of 1976, Oswald Harvey delivered his last 'Blenheim' lecture. The subject was Cunt.

'A slave to cunt I've been, and that's a truth. In my rogering days, I couldn't have enough of it. There never was a man so cunt-struck. Heed my warning, and ration your cunt. By Christ, what a fool, what an oaf, it's made of me.'

I was silent.

'I even got trapped in that corset cow's. I haven't been near one since. I gave her a really thorough rogering.'

I looked at him with disgust. It was a look he was quick to misinterpret.

'She was no bloody oil painting, that bitch, I grant you. I'm not surprised you've curled your nose up. I took her, Gabriel lad, on the Because She Was There principle – she presented me with the challenge, and I was man enough to rise to it.'

'But Mummy – '

'I sent her blood racing. I had her grovelling for more. I found her truly detestable. It was cunt, cunt. She lifted her skirt on the staircase while Reggie was in the sitting-room knocked out for six, and there was her rotten cunt sending me a clear signal – '

'But Mummy – '

'And in I went, and she was screaming, and when she wasn't screaming she was treating my neck like Dracula, and the more I pushed the more she pulled, and this was on the staircase, mind you, not behind the bedroom door – '

'Shut up.'

'I'm telling you for your benefit. You look and behave like a monk, but you've my blood in your veins, so you can't be. Have your cunt, by all means, Gabriel lad, but show a bit of thrift in regards to it.'

'Don't call me Gabriel. Don't you call me lad.'

'Your mother had her cunty tricks. She knew what power she kept between her legs.'

'You're vile.'

'Listen to me. This is for your benefit. Agnes washes my dirty arse for me. That's love in my book, you book-writer. She's never worked her cunty tricks on me.'

'Mummy would have washed your arse. Mummy loved you. It was your fault she walked out on us.'

'Cunt, cunt, cunt. Give it a wide berth. Find yourself an Agnes if you can and you might die happy.'

' "Ashes to ashes, dust to dust" ' – a hated clergyman spoke over my father's grave.

'You said you wouldn't weep,' said Ethel.

'I shall see her now, now he's gone, now he's dead. We'll be reunited, I know we will. She'll come back when she hears. I shall see her now.'

'Yes, Gabriel, the bastard's gone.'

'We'll be reunited, won't we, Mummy and me. Mummy and I. Mummy and me's terrible grammar for a book-writer. I think I'm crying for joy, Ethel.'

The Summer in Sorg

Gabriel Harvey was met at Minneapolis-St Paul airport by the widest man in the world.

'Hi. Is it Dr Gabriel Harvey I'm speaking with?'

'Yes, it is. I'm Gabriel Harvey.'

'Dale Armsted.'

'Hullo.'

'I figured you had to be British.'

'How?'

'You got that pasty look. This your first time in the States, Gabe?'

'No. I've been to New York.'

'Then this is your first time in the States. New York ain't in America. New York's someplace else. New York's separate.'

'Really?' asked Gabriel Harvey, lost for other words.

'You betcha. Bomb it sky high, no ordinary decent folks'd miss it. New York's where the kooks hang out. Ain't no kooks in Sorg, Gabe. Leastwise, none I've heard tell of.'

This man's a colossus, thought Gabriel Harvey, as Dale Armsted relieved him of his suitcases with two vast pink hands. A check-trousered, check-shirted Stetsoned colossus.

'You sure don't believe in travelling light, Gabe. These are mighty heavy. What you brought with you? Bricks?'

'Just clothes, Dale. And a few books and papers.'

('And my father's bequest to me,' Gabriel Harvey could have added. His still unopened bequest, sealed in the box that had once contained Oswald Harvey's beauty of a boot.)

'Mighty heavy, Gabe. And you such a little guy.'

'Yes, I'm not very big,' said Gabriel Harvey, who had never felt as little as he did now.

'You couldn't start growing, and I couldn't stop. Right, Gabe?'

'Right, Dale.'

> Wastin' away again in Margaritaville,
> Searchin' for my lost shaker of salt

sang the voice on Dale Armsted's daddy's car radio.

> Some people claim
> That there's a woman to blame
> But I know it's nobody's fault . . .

Gabriel Harvey, stretched out on the back seat of the air-conditioned Lincoln Continental, asked the driver to please explain the meaning of the song. This was the second time it had been played since they'd left Minneapolis, and he was at a loss to understand what it was about.

'Well, Gabe, Jimmy Buffett's singing about this guy that's getting shnockered in this bar. You know what a Margarita is?'

'No, Dale, I'm afraid I don't.'

'Well, it's a Mexican drink, Gabe, made of tequila and lemon juice. Barman rubs salt around the rim of the glass. I ain't never drank one. I'm a beer boy by nature.'

'And he's in Mexico, the man in the song?'

'You betcha. Drowning his sorrows, Gabe. Woman trouble. Ain't never had none of that, myself.'

'You haven't?'

'Nope. Debbie's a wife in a million. Majored in Home Ec. over at NDSU. You'll visit with her, Gabe. She's a real neat lady.'

'I look forward to meeting her.'

'She sure can't wait to see you. Debbie just loves those British accents on TV. Creases me up when she copies them.'

'I hope she'll find mine worth impersonating.'

'She will, Gabe. She will. You're married?'

'No.'

'Divorced?'

'No.'

'Ain't been bereaved, have you?'

'No, Dale. Most definitely not.'

'How old are you, then?'

'Forty.'

'Forty, Gabe? And you ain't, nor never been, married? What's wrong with you?'

'Oh, many things, I should imagine, Dale.'

'Reckon there must be. Don't take me serious. Matter of fact, we've only one bachelor guy in Sorg, and he's a cripple. Like from birth onwards.' Dale Armsted let out a surprisingly high-pitched, almost girlish laugh. 'I ain't broke wind, if that's what you're thinking. That's an animal's smell.'

'Which animal?'

'Why, the Minnesota skunk. Ain't no other smell gets through the air-conditioning, 'cepting for the skunk's. Enjoy, Gabe.'

'It isn't unpleasant, Dale.'

'Ain't exactly appreciated in the boudoir neither. You're sniffing the filtered kind. Tell you something, Gabe – there's a stink over in Moorhead worse'n any skunk's. Comes out of the American Crystal sugar beet plant. It's like as if somebody's left a big potty up there in the sky and ain't nobody emptied it. Don't happen too frequent, Gabe, but when it happens, my, you sure know it's happening.'

'Thanks for alerting me.'

'You're welcome. How's about us stopping for a bite to eat, Gabe? My belly's sending me lonesome messages.'

'Whatever you wish, Dale.'

'Steak's real good at Pete's Platter.'

The restaurant was a few miles off the highway near a town called Alexandria.

'Hi, gentlemen. I'm Cheryl, your cocktail waitress.' The speaker was a tall blonde in a very short red skirt. She seemed to be introducing herself to unseen persons in the ceiling, for her gaze was directed upwards.

'A Michelob for me, honey. And can you fix a Margarita for my buddy here? He's from London, England, where folks drink different.'

'Sure thing,' said Cheryl, aiming a tired smile at the gentlemen above her head.

'You're in lake country, Gabe. There's two hundred and some around Alexandria.'

'That leaves nine thousand, eight hundred in the rest of Minnesota. According to your number plate.'

'To what, Gabe? I guess you mean license plate. It's my daddy's, anyhow. I drive a beat-up Chevy. Ten thousand lakes,

Gabe – you better believe it. More'n you have in Britain, I reckon.'

'Yes, Dale. You're right.'

'My daddy's got a home on Eighth Crow Wing Lake, over by Park Rapids. Me and Debbie and the kids visit with him almost every weekend in the summer.'

'There you go.' Cheryl, her eyes still concentrating on the ceiling, set down the drinks. 'Enjoy,' she added, mournfully.

'That's some dippy broad,' said Dale Armsted. 'Cute little toosh, though.'

'Yes,' Gabriel Harvey responded, not daring to ask what a toosh might be.

'You should of gotten married, Gabe. All the toosh you can grab hold of in your own bedroom.'

'Yes. Indeed.'

'How's your Margarita?'

'It's unusual,' he answered. He actually found the drink rather disgusting.

'You British, Gabe. Unusual. You sure pick your words.'

Dale Armsted mumbled a prayer over the large T-bone steak, French fries and pickles brought to him by another tall blonde ('Hi, I'm Karen') in a short red skirt. Gabriel Harvey heard a 'Thee', a 'Thy', a 'Thou', a 'Lord' and – finally – an 'Amen'.

'This is an enormous sandwich, Dale. One, two, three – yes, there are three layers of it. I really wasn't expecting anything quite so big.'

'Eat as much as you can,' Dale Armsted advised, champing on a thick piece of meat. 'Gal'll give you a doggy-bag.'

'Have you ever seen such dreadful manners?' Gabriel Harvey, starting at the voice, turned and saw his mother. She was wearing her blue summer dress. 'You won't show me up in public will you, my angel child, by speaking with your mouth full?'

'No, Mummy.'

'What's that, Gabe? What d'you say?'

'Oh, nothing, Dale. I thought I recognized someone from England. It was an optical illusion. The result of tiredness, I suppose. I couldn't sleep on either of the planes.'

'We owe you an apology, Mr Harvey,' said Betty Pedersen.

'What for?'

'Betty's alluding to Dale Armsted, our resident redneck. We feel we kind of foisted him on to you.'

270

'Foisted? I'm sorry, but I don't understand.'

'We should've told you to book your flight through to Fargo. We could've met you easy. Go ahead and explain why we didn't, Carl.'

'We figured, Betty and I, that if you saw the worst Sorg has to offer the moment you landed on American soil, then everything that followed just had to be an improvement. After four hours of Dale's company, you'd find a grizzly bear civilized.'

'Carl's kidding, Mr Harvey. We thought you would want to see something of Minnesota, and Dale meeting you in the Cities sounded like a neat idea. He wasn't too gross, was he?'

'Please call me Gabriel. No, he wasn't too gross – if gross means what I assume it does.'

'Coarse, I guess, Gabriel. I'm glad we've gotten around to first names so soon. And that it was you broke the ice. You English can be real reserved – you know that? We had a guy at the college from – where was Jeremy Collins from, Carl?'

'England.'

'Where in England, smart ass?'

'Manchester – for what it matters.'

'It could just matter. Could be that people from Manchester are more uptight than people from London. *Uffda*, Gabriel, Jeremy Collins sure was mad when Dr Olson – no less a person than Dr Olson – went up to him at Fargo airport and said, "Hi, Jeremy. Good to meet you." '

'Which gave your fellow-countryman apoplexy, Gabriel. "I am not aware that we have been properly introduced. I am Mr – *Mis-ter* – Collins. Are you, by any chance, Dr Frederick Olson?" Jeez, poor Fred had never been spoken to like that in all his born days. He sort of reeled, as though the Limey had left-hooked him. "Delighted to make your acquaintance, Mr Collins" – those were Fred's words soon as he'd picked himself up off the floor. Old Allow-as-how's the sweetest guy going, but he took his revenge on Mr Jeremy Collins. Only time he called him Jeremy was when he shook his hand to say goodbye. It'd been "Mr Collins", "Mr Collins" for a whole goddam year.'

' "Allow-as-how"? Is that a nickname?'

'Sure is, Gabriel. Betty and I, we don't use it to Fred's face. It's our little joke.'

'Fred has his own way of talking. "I allow as how you may be correct on this particular issue" – that's for when he agrees with you. Reluctantly. "I allow as how Harry Truman, all things taken into proper consideration, is – on balance – the most effectual of recent White House incumbents" – can you work that one out, Gabriel?'

'I think so, Betty.'

'Oh, but he's dear to us. Isn't he, Carl?'

'Yeah. He is that. Allow me to freshen your drink, Gabriel.'

'Thanks, Carl. I rather think I like the taste of bourbon.'

'Try not to like it too much. Otherwise Betty'll be counselling you. She works with the quote chemically dependent unquote.'

'Don't knock it, treasure. Yes, Gabriel, I help folks that get hooked on booze. There's quite a lot of them around here.'

'Old Allow-as-how's just about the only friend we have who's never, but never, surrendered to the sauce. He's a real got-together person. Jeez, poor Fred's had more reason than most to hit the bottle.'

'Oh, Carl, it's Gabriel's very first evening with us!'

'Okay, babe. I'll cool it.'

'Be sure you do. We're eating fried chicken, Gabriel. If I would have known your favourite recipe, I'd have been happy to prepare it for you.'

'Fried chicken sounds very nice.'

When they had finished eating, Carl Pedersen remarked to his wife that the time had come for some straight talking. Gabriel had better be put in the picture.

'We're atheists, you see.'

'So am I, probably. I suppose I'd describe myself as an agnostic.'

'But your book, Gabriel – '

'Have you read it?'

'No, we haven't. We figured you'd be religious. We took a look at the movie.'

'The kids at the college think it's just beautiful,' Betty Pedersen intervened.

'We thought it was crap.'

'That would be my assessment of it, too.'

The real Roger Kemp of Liverpool, Gabriel Harvey told the Pedersens, was not remotely like the saintly automaton they had seen in *Mersey Messiah*. No, no, no. *His* Roger – and he had to admit that he did feel curiously proprietorial towards him – his Roger was one of the world's unfortunates. He was 'born to endless night', to use Blake's phrase, and didn't, couldn't, die radiantly, as the elegant young black had done in the film.

According to Mrs Parchment, who was present on the grim occasion, no celestial choir sang for him on his death-bed in the London workhouse. She wrote that he howled with pain.

'He had tertiary syphilis.'

'*Uffda*!' said Betty Pedersen.

'D'you happen to know how he got it, Gabriel?'

'Yes, I do. He caught it from a girl who had come to hear him preach in Southwark. It seems that she had contracted the disease from a wealthy gentleman – a "toff" – who paid Mrs Parchment a considerable sum for the pleasure, if that's the word, of taking the child's virginity. He did so, and immediately infected her. I should explain that Mrs Parchment ran a discreet and exclusive brothel a stone's throw from Southwark Cathedral. She supplied very young girls from very poor homes to very rich pillars of London society. That was her thriving trade before the news spread through the gentlemen's clubs that Mrs P.'s pretty little Minnie had the clap. If Minnie Higgins hadn't sneaked out of the brothel that September evening and tempted the Messiah from Liverpool, and if the Messiah hadn't disappeared as abruptly as he'd arrived – well, his story might have been a happier one. Because you see, there was a scandal. A newspaper reporter named Herbert Oakes pretended that Roger Kemp had converted him, cleansed him of sin, made him see the folly of his evil ways – Herbert Oakes was an insistent convert. He was also a snooper. He wheedled his way into Roger's entourage and travelled with the faithful from town to town. He was with them after the meeting at the temperance hall in Southwark, and went back with them to the lodgings they had hired for the night. Herbert Oakes heard Roger and Minnie – '

Gabriel Harvey found himself unable to complete the sentence.

'Screwing?' suggested Carl Pedersen.

'Ignore my tacky husband. Making love, Gabriel?'

'Yes. And, two or three weeks later, when the chancre appeared – '

'On Roger's dong?'

'Yes, Carl. That's another new word for me. I must have learnt about twenty already and the day isn't over. Yes, it was there, on his penis. I'm sorry, Betty, this talk must be embarrassing for you.'

'Oh, you sweet old-fashioned thing. Don't worry. This gal's

been married to Carl Pedersen for thirty years, Gabriel. He's seen to it that I'm no lady.'

'They sure didn't show the lump on Roger's dong in the movie. I read someplace that the guy who played him had his nose altered. He said he wanted Roger to look real beautiful.'

'Quit interrupting, Carl. Carry on, Gabriel. This reporter – what did he do?'

'He realized what had happened to Roger. He denounced him in his paper as a fiend from hell, who had posed as a son of God. He mentioned Mrs Parchment and the type of house she maintained. He revealed that Roger Kemp of Liverpool had known one of her pathetic charges carnally, and was now paying the penalty for his wicked knowledge. Roger and Mrs Parchment both vanished, without trace. Minnie Higgins died of cholera a few months after the scandal broke, and with her death the whole affair came to an end. The Messiah and the brothel-keeper were soon forgotten. And that's how they stayed until I opened three dusty old ledgers in the Jerusalem.'

'You opened *what*?'

'In the *where*?'

Gabriel Harvey answered the Pedersens' questions.

'It seems I gave birth to an angel who's in love with the sound of his own voice.'

His mother was standing at the foot of Dr Olson's bed.

'Mummy?'

'Yes, it's your mummy. Really, Gabriel, I'm surprised at you. What a dreadful gasbag you've become.'

'Carl and Betty wanted to hear about Roger Kemp and the Jerusalem and – '

'Oh, it's "Carl" and "Betty", is it? I thought I brought you up to be wary of strangers. You've hardly met them, and here you are on Christian-name terms.'

'They're very friendly.'

'On the surface, perhaps. You know what your daddy thinks of Americans. Do please be cautious, Gabriel.'

'Yes, Mummy. I'll try.'

'And do please stop talking so much. It isn't in your character. Not the one I helped to mould, anyway.'

'No, it isn't,' he agreed.

She was gone, then. Between blinks, she was gone.

> Don't know the reason
> I stayed here all season
> With nothing to show but this brand new tattoo

sang Jimmy Buffett on the radio in Dr Olson's green-tiled bathroom.

> But it's a real beauty,
> A Mexican cutie –
> How it got here I haven't a clue.

Gabriel Harvey stepped out of the shower and wrapped himself in the oriental dressing-gown his mother had been wearing on February 1, 1950.

'She took it with her, you cursèd oaf.'

The dressing-gown was his own, and made of towelling material, not Chinese silk. It ended at his knees, whereas hers – 'My slant-eyed maiden's hostess gown' – had touched the floor.

There was light everywhere in Dr Olson's house this glorious May morning. Gabriel Harvey felt himself glow as he ambled through each sunlit room.

He made a pot of tea – Dr Olson had provided him with a choice of Assam, Darjeeling or Lapsang Souchong – and carried it out to the back porch. He surprised a grey squirrel, which darted down the steps and across the lawn.

'Hi there!' Betty Pedersen called from the adjoining yard. 'Could I visit with you, or are you thinking deep thoughts?'

'It's too early for those.'

'I'll go get my coffee.'

The deepest thought he'd had in the hour or so he'd been awake concerned the precise location of Jimmy Buffett's drunkard. Dale Armsted was wrong: the man was definitely not in a bar. Most definitely not. He was searching for his lost shaker of salt in a sleazy hotel. Or then again, a *mo*tel – yes, it was probably in a *mo*tel that he was wasting away.

> I blew out my flip-flop,
> Stepped on a pop top;
> Cut my heel, had to cruise on back home.

A motel would be home to a man on the move, a man without a home to go to.

> But there's booze in the blender,
> And soon it will render
> That frozen concoction that helps me hang on

suggested that Jimmy Buffett's drunkard was an expert at mixing Margaritas. An expert wouldn't be patronizing a bar. Since he was intent on getting – what was the colossus's word? – *schnockered*, he would save himself a great deal of time and money by staying put in his motel and ...

'Did you sleep okay?'

'In fits and starts, thank you.'

'You're jet-lagged. You'll be fine in a couple of days. How are you enjoying Fred's house?'

'Very much. It's absolutely luxurious. I've never known such comfort. Those sofas of Dr Olson's are the length of ocean liners.'

'They were Ingrid's idea. The curtains, the carpets, the art work – they were all Ingrid's idea. Ingrid was Fred's wife, Gabriel. She died a year ago. She had cancer. Both breasts off. The whole goddam works. Fred took her to Rochester for chemo treatment. Hell, it just broke him up, her death. And us.'

'I'm sorry.'

'Ingrid's the reason he's on sabbatical. Fred swears he's gonna finish the Elizabethan book he started writing when God was a boy, but we don't rate his chances. He'd have nothing left if he finished it.'

'An Elizabethan book?'

'Sure. Carl'll fill you in on the details. It's way way above my dumb Norwegian head. English poets, I gather, nobody's ever heard of. Except, of course, for our clever old Allow-as-how. Didn't he mention it in his letters to you?'

'No.'

'*Uffda*, but that's typical. We figure, Carl and I, that Fred's shifted his butt out of Sorg because the pain of losing Ingrid's finally gotten to him, and he'd hate for folks to see him upset. I mean, real upset. Weeping around the place upset.'

'The poor man.'

'He'll do his research at Yale, and then he'll come back to us in sleepy little Sorg, allowing as how like everything's hunky-dory. I'd sure appreciate it, Gabriel, if I could talk with you for a minute about something else.'

'Please do.'

'Carl and I, we had a kid. His name's Eric. He went and got himself killed in Vietnam. If he would've listened to his dad, you'd be visiting with him today. But he didn't listen, and Carl's still hurting. I'm still hurting. Why I'm telling you like this, Gabriel, is just because Carl's bitter. He talks bitter. He calls Eric real horrible names when the bitter mood hits him. You better believe that Carl Pedersen loves his son, though you may find it difficult. That's enough of that. You know what I propose to do? I propose to fix my new friend from England a huge American breakfast.'

'Only if you're certain – '

'I'm certain.'

'I was a dreadful gasbag last night, Betty. I monopolized the conversation. Do please forgive me.'

'You were fascinating. We were fascinated. You're welcome to be a gasbag just whenever it suits you. Let's go.'

'A drunken angel is a contradiction in terms.'

'Is that you, Mummy?'

'It certainly is. Can't you see me through the haze of drink?'

'Yes. I can see you.'

'Then what am I wearing?'

'Your dressing-gown, Mummy. The February 1 one.'

'The assistant in Galeries Lafayette in Regent Street said I looked *sédui*-something-or-other in it.'

'*Séduisante*, Mummy. It means seductive.'

'That's a very naughty French word for my drunken angel child to know. Would you say I look seductive?'

'Yes, Mummy.'

'Then I mustn't keep your daddy waiting. I *shall* keep him waiting, though, while I give you a ticking-off.'

'Why, Mummy?'

'Because you deserve it. You had no right, no right at all, to talk about me in that sickening way.'

'I only said – '

'I am well aware of what you said. I caught every sickening word. I won't have you telling perfect strangers that you love me. Do you hear?'

'Yes, Mummy.'

'And in that maudlin tone of voice. You ought to understand, if anyone ought, that you don't have to announce to the world that you love someone if you love them deeply. There's no need.'

'Yes, Mummy.'

'It's a private matter. Or should be. Yours and mine, Gabriel.'

'I know. I know.'

'So do stop trumpeting your feelings.'

'I will, Mummy. I promise.'

'Be sure you do. It embarrasses me.'

Gabriel Harvey switched on Dr Olson's bedside lamp to confirm that he was now alone.

On Gabriel Harvey's first Sunday in Sorg, the Pedersens invited him to a Bloody Mary brunch.

'You're in for one hell of a surprise, Gabriel. Take your drink and go join Carl in the den. He's glaring at a faith healer – ha ha – on TV.'

The faith healer was small and dumpy and given to sudden fits of screaming. Whenever he screamed, his blond wig shifted perceptibly – to the left, to the right; backwards and forwards. An ear was momentarily concealed, and then an eye.

'Ker-rist!' screamed the faith healer.

'Jesus,' mumbled Carl Pedersen. 'Take a look at this jerk, Gabriel. His method of healing'll be a revelation to you.'

The Reverend Billy Tarbox's method was to thump each invalid granted admission to his therapeutic presence. 'I'm gonna knock the sin out of you,' he promised an old woman in a wheelchair. 'Them doctors that's been mistreating you, Dorothy, they calls it a illness, but I calls it a sin. Them doctors lie. Them doctors sweet-talked you, Dorothy, so's they could steal your dollars. You tell the folks gathered here in God's name how many dollars them doctors have stole from you.'

'Fifteen thou', Reverend Father,' replied the outraged Dorothy. 'Fifteen grand they've took off of me, Reverend Father.'

'And you still can't walk?'

'I still can't walk. That's the truth.'

'That ain't the truth! I says unto you them doctors have lied, lied, lied! I well recall, folks, a wise man telling me when I was no more than a itty-bitty boy that them doctors has to take a hypocritic oath before they's fit to cut us up and sell us the poisons they persuades us is medicines. "That's as why they's hypocrites," that wise man said. Forget them hypocrites, Dorothy, and forgive them they trespasses against you. I'm gonna

278

hit you, Dorothy, and then I'm gonna command you to confess your sin.'

The Reverend Billy Tarbox thumped the woman on the crown of her head. She winced.

'I confess, Reverend Father, that I have sinned.'

'How did you sin, Dorothy? I can't heal you if you don't confess how.'

'I committed the sin of adultery, Reverend Father.'

'That's what I wanna hear. That's what the congregation wants to hear. That's what the Lord God wants to hear.'

'It was with my best friend's husband, Reverend Father. She was in Des Moines, Iowa, tending her sick mother.' Dorothy began to cry. 'I snuck out to hers and Leroy's home whiles Duane, my late hubby, was watching Superbowl. I felt dirty afterwards, Reverend Father, and I've felt dirty ever' day since.'

'Listen up, folks. Listen to what Dorothy's confessing in behalf of everyone of you. God saw Dorothy sinning with Leroy and He, in His mighty wisdom, paralysed her. That's the honest truth them doctors ain't privy to. I calls upon You, Christ Jesus, to unparalyse this poor repenting woman. I calls upon You with all the love in my heart!'

The Reverend Billy Tarbox thumped Dorothy hard. She winced again. He screamed, and his wig shifted.

'Billy Tarbox was Ingrid's favourite,' said Carl Pedersen. 'He was at his most grotesque the Sunday before she died. He quote uncancerized unquote some guy that looked like a skeleton. When the Rev. hit him, there was a rattling noise, I swear. Betty and Fred and I, we all felt sick, but Ingrid laughed. "At least I've been spared Billy Tarbox's faith healing," she said. "Weak as I am, I'd have been tempted to hit him back." '

'This has been the Reverend Billy Tarbox's Hour of Healing,' a sepulchral voice announced. 'If you wish to aid the Reverend Billy in his inspirational work, then mail your donation to the address on your screen. If you would prefer to make your donation by charge card, then call the toll-free number below the address. And, remember, folks, if there is someone in your home that is illiterate or blind, don't deprive them of the joy of making their donation. Do your Christian duty and write our address on the donation envelope for them. They will be in your debt eternally.'

'That Dorothy intrigues me, Gabriel. There's something funny peculiar about her confession. She told the Rev. she got in the sack with Leroy while her old man was watching Super-bowl – on TV, presumably. I figure she was into her sixties when God paralysed her, judging by the way she looks now. She has to be eighty plus – and boy, do I mean plus. I reckon she was a sexual athlete who should have retired from the field of combat in her prime. She couldn't admit she was past her peak. Instead of telling her pussy to call it a day, she snuck off to Leroy's for some advanced gymnastics and did herself one heck of an injury. The Rev. might live to regret unparalysing her. Dorothy could take a shine to him, and God would have to reparalyse her, I imagine. It's a tricky business, faith healing.'

'Has Kirk started up yet?' Betty Pedersen asked her husband as she pushed a trolley into the room.

'Just about to, honey. You timed your entrance to perfection. Get a load of these titles, Gabriel. Seeing is believing, after all.'

Gabriel Harvey looked at the television set and saw:

KIRK'S KRISTIAN KITCHEN
OPEN FOR SERVICE

on the screen.

'Hi, I'm Kirk, and I'm mighty pleased you've chosen to drop by to see what's cookin' in the Kristian Kitchen at this time,' said a madly smiling man in a chef's hat. 'I don't have to remind you folks that in a true Kristian kitchen there's always somethin' beautiful cookin'. So let's inquire of my darlin' Darlene what she's preparin' for us. It sure smells mouth-waterin' from here.'

A madly smiling woman, holding an enormous ladle, was revealed.

'How about givin' me a Kristian kiss, Darlene?'

'Have I ever denied you your conjugal rights, Kirk?'

'Never, Darlene. But that's because you're a Kristian wife.'

'Face-lift meets face-lift,' muttered Betty Pedersen when Darlene gave Kirk his required Kristian kiss. 'Have some heathen ham and eggs, Gabriel.'

'Thank you, Betty.'

'That was yummy, Darlene. I'm goin' to help myself to more of that later, if I may.'

'Of course you may, Kirk.'

'I've got a feelin' our guests are gettin' a little bit hungry out there. Why don't you read them the Kristian menu at this time, Darlene?'

'Surely, Kirk. Well, folks, first for dinner today's a delicious cold soup.'

'What are the ingredients, Darlene?'

'Morning-gathered mushrooms, Kirk, and whipped cream, and fresh herbs, and a cube of chicken stock – and last but not least, Kristian love.'

'I'd say that's an essential ingredient in everythin', Darlene. What's to follow?'

'A good old reliable pot roast, Kirk.'

'Nothin' finer – in Carolina, nor any place else. Specially when it's cooked with Kristian love. What's for dessert?'

'Can't you guess, Kirk?'

'Jello, Darlene?'

'Wrong, Kirk. Try again.'

'Not your apple pie?'

'You got it, Kirk! You guessed right.'

'Aren't they terminally cute, Gabriel?'

'Yes, Carl. They are.'

'An apple pie baked with Kristian love, as Darlene's is, brings to my mind that fruit – that fatal fruit, folks – on the Tree of Life the serpent beguiled Eve into pluckin' off thereof. She did eat, the Holy Bible tells us, and gave unto her husband, and he did eat. It was an apple that opened the eyes of Adam and Eve to their sinful nakedness. Isn't that so, Darlene?'

'It is, Kirk. It surely is.'

'But what Darlene is givin' unto her husband at this time is an apple pie baked with Kristian love. And that, my friends and guests, is the difference.'

'I can't say I grab his meaning.'

'Oh, Carl, quit being picky. Since when did Kirk make any sense?'

'I'd welcome a joyful song of praise from the Kristian Kitchen Choir at this time. Wouldn't you, Darlene?'

'Need you ask, Kirk? Which one is it to be?'

'You heard me talkin' about the serpent in the midst of the Garden of Eden. That wicked critter brings to my mind the insects that pester folks with their nasty bites and stings. I'm proud to tell you that the Kristian Kitchen is fully protected against mosquitoes and beetles and cockroaches and all kinds of bugs – hey, I'm nearly forgettin' the flies! Jesus was fully protected, too, and that's why I'm goin' to invite our Kristian Kitchen Choir to give us their rendition of "There ain't no flies on Jesus". Take it away!'

It was a large choir: 200-strong, Betty Pedersen informed Gabriel Harvey. Then a small orchestra came into view. The men were dressed as chefs; the women wore decorative aprons.

'Why is Kirk Kristian with a "K"?'

'His ancestors hail from Kristianopel in Sweden,' Carl Pedersen explained. 'The "K" is his tribute to the old country. I don't think the dumb-bell realized when he dreamed up Kirk's Kristian Kitchen that three "k"'s stand for something else down South. Somebody was quick to give him a history lesson. That's why he now has a half-dozen blacks in his choir.'

'It occurs to me that when Kirk dies Darlene'll have to go into hospital to get her face dropped. She can't attend his funeral smiling like that.'

'Kirk would have to have the op as well. If his darlin' Darlene precedes him upstairs.'

'*Uffda!*'

'You can write your friends in England that you've crossed the mighty Mississippi.'

The Pedersens had brought Gabriel Harvey to the source of the river at Lake Itasca.

'I shan't reveal that it's only a trickle.'

He stood on one of the stepping-stones traversing the infant Mississippi while Betty Pedersen photographed him.

'Pretend you're happy, Gabriel.'

'I don't have to pretend,' he heard himself lie.

('I have come to America to open a box,' he wanted to confide to these kind Pedersens. That was the ridiculous long and short of it. Yes, he knew he had agreed to deliver the 1977 Thomas J. Swenson Memorial Lecture at Wilkin County College – but that was his wonderfully opportune excuse. The box, bequeathed to him by a much more practised lecturer – The Suede Shoe, Men Who Cook, and The Fool Looks Backward, The Wise Chap Plans Ahead had been among Oswald Harvey's 'Blenheim' subjects – that box had been in his possession now for almost six months. He'd sensed on receiving it from the solicitors in Rose and Crown Court that its contents were probably malign – and that the chance of their being in any way beneficial to him was just as probably remote. *I bequeath to my youngest son, Gabriel Harvey, some papers of a very private nature, for his instruction* – the ridiculous long and short of it was that he feared to read them in London. 'I'd burn the bloody things if I were you,' his half-brother had advised; his half-sister had concurred: 'Take a match to them, Gabriel. He's up to his tricks from the grave, I'll be bound.' To confide in the Pedersens would be to act like a coward. No amount of drink would loosen his tongue to that extent. He was in America to deliver a lecture on how and why he wrote a book called *Lords of Light*, for a generous fee of $2,000, plus expenses.)

His fear seemed doubly ridiculous to him as he wandered with the Pedersens in Itasca State Park that hot afternoon. Nothing the box contained could approach the horror these generous people had endured, and were still enduring.

> Immortal, Invisible
> God only wise,
> Through light inaccessible
> Hid from our eyes

sang a wispy voice at the foot of Dr Olson's bed.

'Mummy?'

'Yes, it *is* Mummy, and she's wondering at her angel child's behaviour again. She's wondering why he sat and watched those blastphemers pretending to be clergymen.'

'You never said "blastphemer", Mummy. That wasn't you. It was the thief's wife who insulted Nora Rosen – she said "blastphemer".'

'All right, all right, blasphemer, you prig, since you insist on correcting me.'

'I laughed at them, Mummy. I did laugh at them.'

'I heard your cackles. You didn't laugh at the vicar of St Mary's when I took you to be confirmed. You were my solemn little angel that day. You knew then what you seem to have forgotten now – that religion's no laughing matter.'

'I haven't forgotten, Mummy. I truly haven't.'

'What a way to spend a Sunday morning. You're drunk, aren't you?'

'No, Mummy – '

'Please don't lie to me, Gabriel. Please don't. Remember what happened to the wretched Matthew.'

'I will. I will, Mummy.'

'And wash and comb your stubborn hair. It's looking a positive disgrace.'

'Yes, Mummy.'

'Sloven's the word for you, my darling. Won't you ever improve?'

'I'll try.'

'Trying's not good enough. Succeeding's better.'

She was gone before his hand had even reached the switch.

9 Elm Street
Sorg, Minnesota
June 3, 1977

Dear Peter and Hannah,

I am due to deliver the Thomas J. Swenson Memorial Lecture at six this evening and I have just begun to quake in my boots. I fear that I am going to make a perfect fool of myself, as I am not – most definitely not – a lecturer by nature. I spoke to my reflection in the bathroom mirror a few moments ago and found that I had a frog in my throat. Stage fright, I suppose.

I have been in Sorg a week now, and have taken note of all its landmarks. There is a Lutheran church. There is a gas station (gas being petrol, of course). There is a water tower. There is a grain elevator belonging to a Mr Dahl, who farms on the immediate outskirts. There used to be a general store, but the business folded when its owner, Mr Rentheim, died at the same great age as a certain Oswald Harvey. The good people of Sorg buy their groceries in nearby Moorhead at the felicitously named Piggly Wiggly – though my friends and next-door neighbours, the Pedersens, favour Hornbacher's in Fargo, North Dakota. I trust you are riveted by this exotic information.

The Pedersens, Betty and Carl, are an unusual couple. They claim they are Sorg's only atheists. He teaches maths (Correction: he teaches MATH) at Wilkin County College, and she works in a rehabilitation centre for alcoholics, alias the chemically dependent. (The winter here has been known to last from late in October until the middle of April. Despite the fact that they have lived on the prairie all their lives, many people find themselves doubting – in February and March – that the spring will ever return. It is then that they fall victim to 'cabin fever' and start drinking heavily to overcome their depression. They hibernate, a bottle always within easy reach.)

Gabriel Harvey sipped his whiskey and continued:

Carl Pedersen's great-great-grandfather and his young family were the first pioneers to settle in Sorg. The year was 1861. It wasn't Sorg then, naturally – just a flat stretch of earth in the Minnesotan wilderness that the exhausted Casper Pedersen was thankful to stake out as his own. The Pedersens had survived a gruelling voyage across the choppy Atlantic from their native Heradsbygd, only to endure the long, long trek by covered waggon – you can imagine how they felt when they reached their journey's end. Five Pedersens sat around the fire that September evening, eating the meagre broth Casper's wife, Beret, had prepared. Five Pedersens prayed to the God who had delivered them safely, and five Pedersens craved His merciful blessing on their new life in a new land. Five Pedersens lay down to sleep, vowing to rise with the dawn. They had work, important work, to do.

Four Pedersens rose early the next morning. Casper, Beret and the two boys, Henrik and Olaf, agreed to leave little Maja to her dreams. She would awaken soon enough, in the heat of the day. Their Lazybones, always.

But Maja wasn't dreaming. She was dead. Olaf made the terrible discovery: 'Maja cold! Maja cold! Maja cold!'

They buried her that afternoon, in a grave dug by the weeping Casper. And that night, so Beret wrote in the journal that is now in Carl's possession, Casper gave the stretch of Minnesotan earth the name it still bears. 'Sorg' is 'sorrow' in Norwegian, and sorrow is what the Pedersens first experienced in America.

I find this rather a beautiful story, and I have tried to set it down much as Carl related it. Sorg's present inhabitants – all 350 of them – pronounce the name of their home town with a hard 'g'. In Norwegian, however, that particular 'g', coming at the end of a word, has a soft sound, very like – but not quite like – the English 'y'. Correctly pronounced, 'sorg' sounds almost like 'sorry'.

Maja Pedersen has a marble memorial in Sorg's small

cemetery. This was put up in 1893, when her family had become prosperous. Before that, there had been a simple wooden cross to mark where the seven-year-old lay. Now a marble angel, sculpted in Minneapolis by a Mr Hyltoft, watches over the child.

I am staying in the house of Dr Frederick Olson, and very comfortable it is – deep armchairs, sofas long as ocean liners, carpets my feet sink into. It was Dr Olson who sent me the original invitation, but he won't be around today to savour the Harvey wit and wisdom. He was widowed last year, at about this time, and grief has made him 'shift his butt' (Betty's phrase) out of Minnesota. He is at Yale, working in the university library on a study of six Elizabethan poets. ('My field is English Elizabethan,' he once observed to Carl, who was amused by the agricultural ring.) Their identity – the poets – is his secret, though I have a hunch one of them might be Giles Fletcher, who is – strictly speaking – more Jacobean than Elizabethan. I lifted the blotter on the doc's desk the other day and came across a scrap of paper on which had been typed some lines from Fletcher's 'Wooing Song':

> Love is the blossom where there blows
> Everything that lives or grows:
> Love doth make the Heav'ns to move,
> And the sun doth burn in love

and so on. Peter, I learnt this poem by heart when I was a Lily.

'Harvey is a 3-A's romantic,' Gabriel Harvey remembered th English master, Mr Penfold, joking to the class. 'All the poem he chooses from the *Oxford Book* are to do with love – mostl unrequited. Let's have Drayton's "Agincourt" next Tuesda} boy. Fine stirring stuff. Plenty of blood and guts.'

'You learnt it for me, didn't you, darling.'

'Yes, Mummy.'

'So that you could recite it to me when I came back from m holiday.'

'That's right.'

'Recite it for me now. There's my angel child.'

'I couldn't. I can't.'

'Try.'

'I can't.'

'There is no such word as "can't" in a man's vocabulary.'

' "Love the strong and weak doth yoke" ...'

'Go on.'

' "And makes the ivy climb the oak" ...'

'Go on.'

'I can't. I really can't.'

'Drink destroys the brain cells, Gabriel. Drink clouds the memory.'

'I know it does.'

'Take care of your brain, angel child. Preserve your memory.'

'I will, Mummy. I will.'

'Go on with your poem, then.'

'I can't. I can't any more.'

'Who's the crybaby? I'm not staying in the same room as a crybaby.'

And she didn't.

Gabriel Harvey took another sip of whiskey and continued:

The Pedersens gave a party in my honour yesterday. It was held in their yard. ('Yard' has poky connotations for me – cramped, dingy, walled-in, like the yard behind the house where I was born. The Pedersens' yard is a garden, with a vast lawn that rolls down to a small stream. No fence divides it from Dr Olson's. As Carl says, 'Fred and I allow as how Robert Frost got it all wrong when he wrote "Good fences make good neighbours". We're here to prove it.') There were nearly a hundred guests, including most of the faculty of Wilkin County. I played several drunken (yes) games of croquet with various partners before falling asleep on the grass. I can't recall ever being so reckless, so irresponsible.

And I was actually rude to someone, though I don't think she noticed. It isn't in my nature to be blunt and direct, but – spurred on by Jack Daniel's, a delicious-tasting whiskey – I was blunt and I was direct. The woman I insulted fancies herself as a mimic and is labouring under the delusion that she can impersonate Gabriel Harvey. To that end, she trailed behind me for two hours or more, repeating my every remark. This ghastly echo kept coming back at me: if I, answering a polite inquiry, said I was enjoying my stay in Sorg very much, then Debbie Doppelgänger at my rear would repeat, a second later, 'I am enjoying my stay in Sorg veddy much.' It was her tin-eared 'veddy' that finally drove me to tell her she was a pain in the arse. 'You are a pain in the arse,' she repeated in 'my' voice. Debbie's 'arse' is closer to 'horse': 'You are a pain in the horse' is certain to haunt me all my life, I fear.

It was Debbie's husband, Dale, who met me at the airport and drove me to Sorg. Dale must be the widest, if not the tallest, man in the world. He is gigantic. Debbie, by startling contrast, is only slightly taller than the victim of her inaccurate and unrelenting mimicry. She is also extremely skinny. 'A real neat lady' is how the adoring Dale describes her. The Pedersens affect to loathe Dale, but I have a feeling that they are secretly fond of him. His eyes indicate depths of kindness and concern even as his lips give expression to opinions of a – to me – depressingly familiar unloveliness. (He might have found Oswald Harvey a kindred spirit – but then, my father would never have lowered the drawbridge over his mental moat for a cursèd Yank. Which reminds me: I can't remember the 'Blenheim' lecturer ever using 'jew' as a verb. Dale does. 'Folks don't jew you in Minnesota,' he informed me.) Perhaps I am being fanciful, but Dale strikes me as a 'nice guy' at heart. He is taking me to the Badlands of North Dakota next week: they are, he assures me, 'something else'.

I have much, much more to tell you, but it will have to wait. I shall be home in a fortnight (I'm having a restful little holiday care of Dr Olson) and propose to bore you both rigid at the earliest opportunity. It is now after four, and I must shave and shower, and pour myself a single drink to steady my nerves, and put on the suit – Gabriel Harvey in a suit! – I bought especially for the Thomas J. Swenson Memorial Lecture.

Gabriel Harvey drained his glass and concluded:

I am a creature of reserve, Peter, as you know. Let me say here what I am unable to say to your face – that the renewal of our friendship, after so many intervening years, is a source of considerable joy to me. As is my friendship with you, dear, lovely Hannah. Please give Sophie a great big godfatherly kiss. I have bought her an unusual toy from the shop at the university (the Varsity Mart) in Fargo.

North Dakota State has a football team, and its mascot is a bison. There in the shop were rows and rows of bison, in varying sizes. I shall be staggering under the weight of a biggish cuddly brown bison when I see you all again. So much smarter than the common-or-garden teddy bear!

This jumble of impressions comes with my love.

Starch-angel

Gabriel Harvey heard the dean, Glenn Holmqvist, tell the audience what most of its number probably knew already: Thomas J. Swenson, farmer–philosopher and founder of Wilkin County College, was one of the most remarkable Minnesotans. His place alongside Charles A. Lindbergh, Scott Fitzgerald, Dr Charles Mayo and Senator Hubert Humphrey in the state's Hall of Fame was assured.

'It was through Tom Swenson's inspiration – and bankroll, ladies and gentlemen – that Wilkin got to be built. It stands today as a monument to his questing spirit. Our famed course in Comparative Religion was his idea. One of Tom's heroes (and Tom had a great capacity for hero-worship) was Bishop Henry Whipple, who befriended the Indians. Those of you who have visited the Cathedral of Our Merciful Saviour in Faribault will have seen the stained-glass window commemorating Whipple's friendship with the Sioux. It features a symbolic peace pipe and was a gift from the tribe that – in Whipple's words to President Lincoln – had been "shamelessly cheated and victimized". Tom was brought up to regard the Indians as savages, and it wasn't until he read about Bishop Whipple that he altered his viewpoint.

'Tom was in his forties when he enrolled at the University of Minnesota, leaving his sons to look after the farm. It was while he was a student that he hit upon the simple but profound notion that every religion contains its core of truth, and that a proper knowledge of the differences between one religion and another is the only chance Man has of achieving tolerance and understanding on planet Earth. It dismayed Tom that there are Christians so entrenched and even imprisoned in their own kinds of Christianity that they deny the members of different Christian sects the right to call themselves Christians. It's because of Tom Swenson's dismay that we have our course in Comparative Religion here at Wilkin.

'Last year's Thomas J. Swenson Memorial Lecture was given by Dr Edwin Riley, a convert to Buddhism. Dr Riley left us with a lot of controversial and thought-provoking material for our discussion groups, and I feel confident that Mr Gabriel Harvey is going to do the same. Mr Harvey is an agnostic who has written an important book, not yet published in America, about the preachers who broke away from the Established Church in his native England. Dr Frederick Olson, who is regrettably unable to be with us this evening, has read Mr Harvey's *Lords of Light* and finds it of tremendous interest. "It's better than the movie," he said. Fred was referring, of course, to *Mersey Messiah*, the rock musical that Mr Harvey tells me is very loosely based on the life of Roger Kemp, the preacher he discovered by accident. I visited with Gabriel last evening and I am still smarting from the defeat he inflicted on me. He plays a mean game of croquet. Ladies and gentlemen, would you welcome our Thomas J. Swenson Memorial lecturer for 1977 – Mr Gabriel Harvey.'

When the applause had subsided, Gabriel Harvey, looking down on a sea of blond heads, cleared his throat and began:

'My mother had a beautiful old Bible, printed in London in 1787, with a gold clasp which she secured whenever she finished reading from it. As a child, I thought her Bible a magical book, a book like no other, simply because of that bright gold clasp. I used to imagine, in my childish fancy, that Adam and Eve, and Moses, and Abraham and Isaac, and Samson and Delilah, and Joseph, and "gentle Jesus, meek and mild" were all being let out for my benefit whenever the clasp was released again. One day in 1950, not long after my thirteenth birthday, I undid the clasp myself. There, on the title page, was an astonishing piece of information. It told me what I could scarcely believe, even at that still impressionable age – that the world had been created at nine a.m. on October 23 in the year 4004 BC. All its living creatures, I read on in astonishment, had been produced in the following six days. God's mighty work of creation, I therefore deduced, was completed by midnight on the twenty-ninth.

'It struck me as extremely perverse of God to bring the world into being in the tenth month of the year. Reason, my schoolboy's reason, demanded that Life should have begun in springtime. It made sense that way round, with the trees coming into blossom. In misty October, they would be shedding their leaves and that made no sense at all. Why start things off in a state of decay? And why at *nine* a.m., when the most glorious part of the day – the dawn – was already over? The more I thought about it, the less plausible the information looked.

'I was twenty-nine when I discovered that the implausible information was the work of two highly respected men – James Ussher and John Lightfoot. In the latter years of the seventeenth century, Ussher was Archbishop of Armagh, while Lightfoot was regarded as the most learned Hebraist alive. Their findings had to be taken seriously – Ussher and Lightfoot were considerable scholars as well as devout Christians. They had consulted medieval texts, and if the date and time they agreed upon was an inspired guess, they had enough facts at their fingertips to disprove any alternative date and time. Thus, in 1701, the information appeared at the front of the Authorized Version. It reappeared in subsequent editions until the 1850s, when it was suddenly removed. In other words, it was still being disseminated after Charles Darwin had published *The Voyage of HMS 'Beagle'*, with all that book implied about the origins of life on earth.

'Ussher and Lightfoot were men possessed, in their scholarly fashion. They wanted to know exactly when God created the heaven and the earth. "In the beginning" was too vague for them. You could say they had scientific minds. Misapplied science, perhaps – but weren't they fired by curiosity? I care to think so. They refused to rest content with vagueness. They craved the specific. They finally settled on nine a.m., on October 23, on 4004 BC. They were obviously, literally wrong – wrong according to the scribes who penned the Book of Genesis; and wrong, most definitely wrong, in the light of Darwin's momentous theory. I doubt that they were charlatans, however. I am coming to the charlatans.'

'Who forgot to comb his stubborn hair?'

Gabriel Harvey ignored the question and resumed:

'But before I do, I must mention George Fox. He was born in 1624 in Leicestershire. In 1647 he founded the Society of Friends, otherwise known as the Quakers. He was a big man, a peasant, a shepherd by profession. I encountered him in an Islington – that's a borough in north London, by the way – in an Islington junk shop. In a lithograph, I should add. He stared at me, and I stared back at him. The anonymous portraitist has caught wonderfully his fervent, yet calm, expression. I paid two shillings and sixpence for my portrait of George. "It's the maple frame you're wanting," said the Irishman who sold it to me. It wasn't, but I didn't bother to contradict him.

'I was acquainted with George's likeness for several months. Just his likeness. I hung it above my desk in the attic I was living in. Then a friend and neighbour, Mr Nazareth – I see you are smiling; well, I smiled too when he introduced himself – gave me George Fox's *Journal* as a present. It was a surprising present to come from him, for Mr Nazareth was – is – the most determined (I would even say exultant) atheist I have ever met. Yes, he is exultant in his belief in non-belief. Thanks to Mr Nazareth, I became acquainted with George's heart and mind – with the whole man, in fact. He is a man for whom I feel affection and respect.'

'And what do you feel for your daddy?'

Gabriel Harvey willed himself not to answer the question. He went on:

'I respect George Fox for not removing his hat. Let me explain. It was his passionate conviction that human beings are equal in the sight of God. This is a commonly held conviction, and one to which the majority of Christians pay lip-service at least. But George, rare creature that he was, actually lived by that conviction. He practised what he preached. "Moreover when the Lord sent me forth into the world, he forbade me to put off my hat to any, high or low; and I was required to 'thee' and 'thou' all men and women, without any respect to rich or poor, great or small." A couple of lines later, he adds: " ... neither might I bow or scrape with my leg to any one; and this made the sects and professions to rage. But the Lord's power carried me all over to his glory ... " For George, there was only one higher authority, the God who had told him to keep his hat on.

'He refused to take it off when he and other Friends were dragged into the court at Launceston. Judge Glynne, the Chief Justice of England, was presiding. George writes: " 'Why do you not put off your hats?' said the judge to us; we said nothing. 'Put off your hats,' said the judge again. Still we said nothing. Then said the judge, 'The Court commands you to put off your hats.' Then I spoke and said, 'Where did ever any magistrate, king or judge from Moses to Daniel, command any to put off their hats, when they came before them in the courts ... ? And if the law of England doth command any such thing, shew me that law either written or printed.' " Judge Glynne flew into a rage and ordered the prisoners to be taken to the cells.

'A short while later, the Chief Justice called them back into his presence. " 'Come,' said he, 'where had they hats from Moses to Daniel? Come, answer me. I have you fast now.' " But Judge Glynne was reckoning without George Fox's thorough knowledge of the scriptures, for George instantly replied: " 'Thou mayest read in the 3rd of Daniel that the three children were cast into the fiery furnace by Nebuchadnezzar's command, with their coats, their hose and their hats on.' This plain instance stopped him so that not having anything else to say to the point, he cried again, 'Take them away, jailer.' "

'Many of you will be familiar with those great lines of John Donne:

> Churches are best for prayer, that have least light:
> To see God only, I go out of sight:
>   And to 'scape stormy days, I choose
>   An everlasting night.

George Fox thought otherwise. He prayed everywhere but in church. He worshipped his Maker in the streets, in the fields, and in the market place. He prayed most often, though, in the houses of the Friends, in company he found congenial. And there was no day so stormy that he wished to escape from it. On the contrary: he sought out storms; he revelled in trouble and argument. He did not have to skulk to see his God. The Almighty, for George Fox, was there among the clenched fists, the raised voices.

' "The Lord walks among the pots and pans," said St Teresa of Ávila, and George Fox would have concurred. There can be no doubting the sincerity, the almost embarrassing sincerity, of the saint and the Quaker. The totally embarrassing insincerity – no, inauthenticity is more exact – of Kirk and Darlene in their improbable and profitable Kristian Kitchen is a spectacle that invites only derision, if not disgust. The Lord would surely think twice before He walked among Kirk and Darlene's pots and pans. I hope they have no admirers in the audience. I am going to assert, unequivocally, that they are charlatans.

'They are not the first, however, and they will not be the last. Let me tell you tonight about some of their English predecessors. Eustace Barnes, for instance. Now Eustace was a robber in his youth – so Eustace said. No evidence exists for Eustace's claim. But then, the people who flocked to his meetings needed no evidence. The breast-beating of the self-named Barabbas was sufficient to convince them that he had been a criminal once and was now properly ashamed and repentant. On Good Friday, especially and appropriately, he attracted huge congregations. "I am he who should have died on the Cross," Eustace/Barabbas screamed. "I am the thief who was set free." You will observe that this false Barabbas did not confess to the crimes of sedition and murder for which the real Barabbas was imprisoned and sentenced to die on the Cross. Heavens, no. The wily Eustace was well aware that such a confession might lead to complications. Theft would do nicely. And it did. It did him very nicely.'

'It did him veddy nicely,' came back at Gabriel Harvey from somewhere in the centre of the hall.

Then Dale Armsted was heard ordering his wife to quit fooling.

'How this reformed thief prospered, with his cautionary tales of the darkness that had enveloped his young days! If he was to be believed – and thousands did believe him – he was the artfullest dodger of them all. Those vast Easter congregations thrilled to his exploits, laughed at his brazen cheek, for "Barabbas" Barnes was a lovable rogue. So roguish was he that people wondered if they were really attending a service, since you didn't go to church to laugh, and here they were laughing. "Why do you laugh?" he suddenly asked them. "I am he who should have died on the Cross. Your laughter mocks the Son of God." And with that he rounded on the mockers and castigated them, and said they were the very rabble who had called for Barabbas to be freed. They would have Christ crucified again, were it in their power.

'So this Barabbas thrived – a more insidious robber than any he conjured up in his usual sermons. The contrite poor gave him their pennies, and those pennies accumulated. So he would have continued, had not Lady Jasmine Rowell attended one of his Good Friday meetings. Her Ladyship was overawed by the magnetism of the preacher, and had a servant deliver her card to him. "You have inspired me with your words of penitence," she wrote. "Please to break bread with me in my town house." He would be greatly pleased, deeply honoured. It was a sign of the noble Lady's true Christian forgiveness that she was ready to open her doors to an erstwhile thief.

'The pastor met with the wealthy young widow, and after

only a little persuasion agreed to act as her spiritual guide. In return for a handsome endowment, and a suite of rooms – complete with chapel – in her Northumberland manor house, "Barabbas" Barnes would endeavour to teach Her Ladyship those values he had painfully acquired on the rough road of Life. And that is what he did for his remaining twenty years, according to Lady Jasmine's biography – hagiography, rather – which I bought for sixpence in a junk shop. This is a book which continually attracts the sceptical reader to read between the lines, for its hyperbolic prose is seldom informative. Very few facts emerge from its three hundred pages. One of them is a curious reference to the healing properties of Madeira, which the "ruddy-faced" mentor of the chastened Lady Jasmine drank in ever larger quantities. He called for a last glass as he "set fair to embark on that sublime journey the humble mortal must undergo before attaining celestial bliss", and Lady Jasmine brought it to him. As he departed, she avowed she heard welcoming trumpets sound. I suspect it was the local brass band tuning up for a rehearsal.'

'Who's my cynical little angel child?'

Gabriel Harvey was aware that it would not be sensible to acknowledge this gibe. He talked instead of other charlatans, allowing no pauses for similar insults from that woman who looked and sounded like his young mother. The audience were most diverted by the story of the barn-storming Dr B. Wilson Kell, who prophesied the Second Coming with the aid of inexplicable diagrams which were projected on to a screen. Kell fancied himself as a composer, and was in the habit of breaking into tuneless song in the course of his lectures. At these moments his wife Lavinia, whose features were set in a permanent glare, struggled to accompany him on an upright piano. Gabriel Harvey's audience laughed at the picture he drew of that other audience in faraway, Edwardian Manchester, unable to sing the hymns sent to Dr Kell's pen by divine inspiration. "Join in! Join in!" yelled the pounding, glaring Lavinia. "Open your throats for Jesus, you sluggards!" Those sluggards who did manage to open their throats did so with the music of Isaac Watts or Charles Wesley hesitantly, faintly emerging. And Dr B. Wilson Kell, deaf to their treachery, boomed on.

Gabriel Harvey paused. The laughter subsided and there was silence. He listened. Yes, silence.

'But Roger Kemp of Liverpool was not a charlatan. How do

I know? I sense that he wasn't. My deepest instinct tells me his fervour was genuine. After all, it first manifested itself when he was only ten years old, in the Myrtle Street Orphanage where he had been raised from a baby. Words, strange words, words an uneducated child of ten could not possibly have learnt, suddenly dropped from his tongue in a torrent. Words like "amaze" and "wonder" and "seraphic" and "oracle" were in that deluge. What was its source? That remains a mystery. Here was a boy who hadn't even mastered his alphabet speaking a high-flown and syntactically eccentric English: *I must to say that the Lord God Almighty has commanded that the Wonder be mine in this city of Liverpool. I must to say that He has sent me to cause the shining of that Wonder in all that are darkened and fearful. I must to say that I am in His merciful and bountiful power and that I will strike those in amaze that do walk in their darkness content.* And I must to say to you that I felt elation when I came upon the *must tos* of Roger Kemp on a May evening in 1967. They were contained in a pair of ledgers I had been requested to throw out with the rubbish. I didn't comply with the request. I took the ledgers home and read what was written inside them. I like to think that no one else has read what Mrs Parchment set down to Roger Kemp's dictation in an upper room in a London workhouse almost a century ago, and that the gangly, half-caste Messiah and his unusual amanuensis have found in me a worthy rescuer.'

'Who's a conceited little angel, then? Who fancies himself as the bee's knees?'

Gabriel Harvey paused.

'You've swallowed the dictionary, and now you're spewing it up.'

Gabriel Harvey cleared his throat. He scanned the audience for the woman who was pretending to be his young mother. She was not to be seen. Of course she was not to be seen.

The lecture had to go on, in spite of her.

The real Roger Kemp, Gabriel Harvey went on, had been left on the steps of the Myrtle Street Orphanage when he was just a few hours old. He was given his name by one of the institution's benefactors, Lionel Kemp, a former ship's doctor who had campaigned for the abolition of slavery. Kemp, a bachelor, planned to raise the foundling in his own home, but died before Roger could walk. It was supposed that the curiously coloured boy was the son of a newly released slave and a woman of the streets, but the supposition was never authenticated. Roger Kemp grew to an alarming height, and by the time he was possessed of the Wonder was already more than six feet tall. Within a matter of days of the Wonder's seizing him, the news spread across Liverpool that a Myrtle Street waif was claiming that he had divine powers. The news reached Randolph and Ena Cussell, who offered to adopt the 'gabbler', as he was now known in the orphanage. Their offer was immediately accepted, papers were signed, and the evangelical career of Roger Kemp of Liverpool had begun.

'It lasted until he was seventeen. The Cussells dressed him in a flowing white robe and transported him from town to town, where his appearance attracted large gatherings. It was a little like a circus act or a fairground show, for the same people who flocked to see the Bearded Lady or Tom Thumb or the Musical Mastiff turned out to catch a glimpse of the nigger orphan with the gift of tongues. They were not disappointed. Many, indeed, were chastened and moved by the spectacle.'

'And you're a spectacle yourself, and not my angel, if ever you were my angel.'

'I was,' Gabriel Harvey assured her. 'I am.'

'I was,' he resumed, in a quieter voice, 'moved myself, just reading about him. I am still moved at the thought of this innocent contracting syphilis, and the horrible agonies of body and mind the disease wrought upon him.'

'There's a crafty Gabriel. Devilishly crafty, I'd say. You slipped out of my net, didn't you?'

Yes, he had, and that was where he was determined to remain, at least until this ordeal was over. Gabriel Harvey warned his audience that he now intended to elaborate on those syphilitic agonies the makers of *Mersey Messiah* had omitted from their exercise in dogged uplift. The real Roger Kemp's real nose rotted away, he said, and there was no beautician from Los Angeles to build him a new one. Even healthy noses weren't replaceable in the 1860s.

Gabriel Harvey paused when he had finished recounting the unpleasant details. A voice, not hers, uttered the single word 'gross'. He turned, then, to happier and more familiar preachers – to John and Charles Wesley, and their friendship with a founder of the colony of Georgia, General Oglethorpe, who brought the Creek Indian chief, Tomo-Chi-Chi, to England in 1734; to Edward Irving, whose sermons at the Caledonian

Church in Hatton Garden were admired by Bentham, Coleridge, Lamb, Blake and De Quincey, and who secured his quick fall from grace by haranguing and denouncing those very admirers; to C. H. Spurgeon, the chain-smoking Baptist who advised the poor to pull their spiritual socks up and consider the life to come. 'Presented with a choice between Pastor Spurgeon and an evening at the music hall, I should have opted for the latter. No threats of hell-fire at the Alhambra, no promise of harps, no leering Satan or welcoming St Peter – only a lightening of the pain of the here-and-now, administered by comics and singers who were themselves veterans in distress. Had I been poor in Spurgeon's time, I'd have needed their immediate comfort.'

Gabriel Harvey looked at his watch. He had been speaking for nearly an hour, and had yet to reach the crux of his lecture.

'Let me mention two other lords of light before I make my concluding observations.'

The chosen two were 'Orator' Henley, an eighteenth-century atheist so wild in his reasoning that he was pronounced harmlessly mad and allowed to rant in the streets of London, and Frederick Charrington, heir to a brewery fortune, who began his long mission against the demon alcohol and its attendant crimes outside his own family's public houses in the East End. Charrington was an ineffectual speaker: his voice was pitched too low to be heard above the drunken rabble, and he was frequently kicked and beaten by the brutes to whom he was quietly recommending the advantages of teetotalism. A picture of Charrington hung in every East London brothel because the keepers wished to have a ready means of identifying the man who was breaking up their trade – and break up their trade he slowly and steadfastly did, this Sir Galahad armed with the Gospel. 'I find him an endearing obsessive. He, too, had an eye on the life to come, but he was also aware that the life that is, the life of penury and deprivation, could do with improving in practical ways. He saw how this world goes. In 1912, for example, during the famous Dock Strike, Charrington organized the feeding of the hungry strikers' families at his Assembly Hall. He championed the rights of women, especially those women who were most exploited, at the bottom of the social heap. His was a genuine, and generous, charity. He deserves not to be forgotten.'

'He won't be, thanks to you!'

'I wrote *Lords of Light*, I realize now, as the result of a series of – divine perhaps – accidents. The first accident was the name my parents chose for me – '

'I gave you Gabriel, Gabriel. And it wasn't an accident. I wanted an angel, and look what I got!'

'As I say, the first accident was that I was christened Gabriel. Then I bought a picture of George Fox. I knew nothing about him; I simply liked his face. Then I met a man, an amiable man, called Mr Nazareth. Then I worked for nine years in a Home for old women, the Jerusalem – '

'And then you?'

'And then I opened a book which my beloved mother – '

'Oh, yes?'

'My beloved mother had given me years before. Actually, someone had left it on a bus – '

'Aren't you going to tell us the number, you bloody little pedant? It was a 49 – '

'A 39 bus, to be boringly exact. The book was *Moby-Dick*. My mother – '

'Your *beloved* mother, please!'

' – had picked it up and noticed it contained a Gabriel – a Gabriel, she joked to me, who was not the kind of Gabriel she would have cared to bring into the world. He appears in Chapter 71, proclaiming himself as the "deliverer of the isles of the sea and vicar-general of all Oceanica", and warning his terrified fellow-sailors that Moby-Dick was really the Shaker God incarnate. Melville's Gabriel is a holy terror, a fanatic. When I made his acquaintance – on a bench, in the gardens of a London church – I shook with excitement, I remember. I felt I had a subject at last. I thought of the fictional Gabriel and the actual George Fox, of the crank and the visionary. My lords of light would be cranks and visionaries – and charlatans, too, as I was to discover. I had only to seek them out and track them down.'

'What a rigmarole!'

'I didn't seek Roger Kemp out, though, nor did I have to track him down. He came to me by accident, on Thursday, May 25 1967, to be precise. That was the day on which the Jerusalem was razed to the ground. My boss, Mrs Ricks, the matron of the Home, handed me a couple of dusty ledgers and asked me to throw them away, with the words: "They can't be of interest to anybody any more. They're ancient, unimportant history." If Matron hadn't used that phrase, I might well have slung the ledgers into the dustbin, as requested. It acted as a spur to me. Curious to learn how unimportant they were, I glanced inside and saw the *must tos*, the important *must tos*, of Roger Kemp.'

'Not them again!'

'And now I shall attempt to sum up. You may feel that I have offered you nothing more than a succession of anecdotes this evening. I hope, however, that some of you will find at least one or two of those anecdotes instructive. For all his claims of humility, a preacher is an individual who sets himself above his fellow-men. Lesser mortals flock to hear him because they consider themselves his inferiors. It has been my serious intention to put these superior beings into human perspective, to show them with their warts intact. Avarice, humbug, madness and charlatanism have all been referred to in this ragbag (I fear) of a lecture. Yet these, alas, were the prevailing characteristics of several of my lords of light. I mentioned the Wesleys earlier: even those good men were not free from class-consciousness. They dearly loved an aristocrat. I have to say that their friend General Oglethorpe strikes me as altogether more attractive. Like the temperate Frederick Charrington, he displayed a practical concern for the dispossessed. He liberated ten thousand debtors from English prisons, and supervised their transportation to America, where they could pursue a new life.'

'And did they all say, "Thank you kindly, General"? One after the other?'

'It will surely now be clear to you that I am no philosopher, certainly no theologian. I chose my lords of light because they intrigued me as people and their stories were worth telling. I should like to end with a passage from George Fox's *Journal*, which may serve as an explanation of my own agnosticism: "I lifted my head," he writes, "and I espied three steeplehouse spires. They struck at my life and I asked Friends what they were, and they said, Lichfield. The word of the Lord came to me thither I might go ... I went over hedge and ditch till I came within a mile of Lichfield. When I came into a great field where there were shepherds keeping their sheep, I was commanded of the Lord to pull off my shoes of a sudden; and I stood still, and the word of the Lord was like a fire in me; and being winter, I untied my shoes and put them off ..." The poor shepherds, Fox continues, trembled and were astonished at this strange behaviour. "As soon as I came within the town the word of the Lord came unto me again to cry 'Woe unto the bloody city of

Lichfield!' ... I went into the market place and went up and down in several places of it and made stands, crying 'Woe unto the bloody city of Lichfield!', and no one touched me nor laid hands on me. As I went down the town there ran like a channel of blood down the steeets, and the market place was like a pool of blood ... And so at last some friends and friendly people came to me and said, 'Alack George! where are thy shoes?' and I told them it was no matter ..."

'Ladies and gentlemen, I like to think that I might have been one of those friendly people, worried about the condition of George Fox's feet. They represent the best of which we are capable, thoughout history. And it says something for George's essential humanity that he should record what the friendly people said to him in the midst of his frantic "Woe"-ing. He noticed, and noted, their concern. George, in fact, can be counted our friend – with a small, as well as a capital, "f". I can't believe in his God, but I can admire his qualities as a believer. He took off his shoes at the Lord's bidding, but refused to remove his hat for a mere Chief Justice. His superiority as a human being is based for ever on that firmest of all his firm convictions – that he had only equals on earth. Such, anyway, is the ironic belief of the deliverer of this year's Thomas J. Swenson Memorial Lecture.'

Gabriel Harvey gathered up his notes and sat down. The audience applauded.

'I'll wager, as your daddy always says, you're relieved that's over. Yes, angel child?'

'Yes. Yes.'

'That goes for me, too.'

Gabriel Harvey stared at a point above the blond sea while Glenn Holmqvist congratulated him on a most stimulating lecture.

'Mr Harvey tells me he will be happy to answer **any** questions you may have.'

'Happy, is he? He knows I know he isn't. He's miserable as hell.'

'Very happy,' said Gabriel Harvey.

'Why don't you open Daddy's present?'

'How come your Roger Kemp story got turned into a movie?' asked a girl in the front row.

'It came to pass in this wise – '

'There's wit for you!'

'The film's producer, Michael Gazzard, bought a copy of *Lords of Light* on one of his trips to England. He read my Roger Kemp story and saw what he called its "inspirational potential". A contract was drawn up, and I was invited to write a "treatment". I did so, and was paid accordingly –'

'You were paid excessively!'

'The "treatment" was duly posted to Hollywood, where it was obviously relegated to the out-tray. Then, a few months ago, I was flown, courtesy of the film company, to New York, to attend the première. I have to confess that I got thoroughly schnockered afterwards, such was its inspirational effect upon me.'

'Dreadful American word,' she said distinctly through the laughter. 'Sucking up to a bunch of cursèd Yanks!'

And there she was, in the centre aisle, dressed all in silver. Yes, there she was, walking towards him, in her 'strapless wedding-cake'.

There could be no more questions, no more answers – not while her dark red velvet rose flared and flared and flared from that silver shimmer.

Late that night, the night of the brainstorm, Gabriel Harvey ripped off the sticky tape from his father's bequest.

In the morning, in the clear light of day, he would look inside, he assured himself. He had made a start, small though it was. He had only to pull back the lid.

'Then abracadabra!'

He had only to pull back the lid. It was as simple as that.

'Tomorrow it is.'

Gabriel Harvey realized when he awoke that he had slept undisturbed in Dr Olson's bed.

'You must have exhausted yourself, Mother.'

He waited and listened for her response. It did not come. The momentous day was beginning well. He listened. He heard a woman's voice. It was Betty, summoning him to breakfast.

'Don't you dare apologize,' she said, as he entered the Pedersens' kitchen. 'You apologized a hundred times too many last evening. You fainted, honey. It happens.'

'Not in such embarrassing circumstances.'

'You're getting to be a pain in the horse, as our dear friend Debbie Armsted would say. Eat.'

He ate. He ate heartily.

The Oswald Harvey bequest was not where he had left it, on the desk in Dr Olson's den. He had returned to the house with the intention of opening it immediately, and now it had vanished. His first, absurd thought was that she, his pretend young mother, had taken it.

'Hi there, Dr Harvey.'

He turned and saw the girl who had asked the question after his lecture.

'I'm Linda. Linda Engstrom.'

'What are you doing here?'

'Cleaning. Dr Olson pays me to clean for him once a week.'

'Ah.'

Within minutes, Gabriel Harvey learned that Linda had divorced her husband, who was weird, and was presently going steady with an older guy, who wasn't. Weird, she repeated. She had a baby son by Weirdo, which was why she needed the extra dollars from Dr Olson, and if things worked out with the older guy, she hoped to marry again, like for keeps. Oh, and she also hoped to graduate from Wilkin. With honours.

'I have to vacuum, Dr Harvey. I'll be through in a half-hour.'

'I'll sit in the garden. The yard. By the way, did you move a box, a largish box, from this desk?'

'Kinda battered? Sure. It's by your feet.'

'So it is. I'll take it with me.'

'Are you better today?'

'Better?'

'You had like a fit.'

'Yes, thank you. I really am much better. I feel ashamed that I couldn't answer more questions. I can't imagine what brought it on.'

'I can.' It wasn't Linda speaking. 'I can.'

'Tiredness, I suppose. I've been under a certain amount of strain.'

'I enjoyed your talk, Dr Harvey.'

'You're very kind. I'm plain Mister, not Doctor. And now I'll leave you to work in peace.'

'Don't forget your box.'

'Oh, no. Thank you.'

Gabriel Harvey picked it up and went out to the yard. The heat was already intense. He placed the box on the grass and sat down beside it.

He flicked back the lid.

'Who's my brave angel?'

'I am.'

(Then, suddenly, he remembered a different lawn and an entirely different day. He had arrived at 'Blenheim' during a hailstorm, and there in the front garden was the newly acquired Boot, unattached to its proud owner.

'Your boot, Father. It's out in the rain.'

'I know it is, you cursed oaf. If you'd had a grandmother, you'd have taught her to suck eggs. Have you any idea why my boot is out in the rain?'

'No, I haven't.'

'Because it's supposed to be waterproof is why. I'm putting it to the test, young man. I'm collecting proof, so to speak, that it's as waterproof as the chap at J. C. Cording says it is. Are you with me?'

'Yes, Father.'

'I've been waiting for a downpour like this one.'

'You could have tested it in the bath. The boot. Wouldn't that have been simpler?'

'Typical oafishness. Think, think. Use that skull of yours. Bath water's not the same as rain water, most definitely it isn't. The water you run into the bath is purified, which means it can't harm the skin. And boot leather's skin, young man, animal's skin, and all the tougher for having been treated. It follows, by my reckoning, that bath water's not going to cause a boot – particularly a special J. C. Cording boot – much trouble. And that's where rain water comes in. It stands to reason that water dropping straight from the sky on to London will be more harmful to a boot than the purified stuff. Would it have been simpler, young man? No, bloody perverse, that's what. Think, think.')

'I'm thinking, Father.'

Gabriel Harvey plunged his right hand into the boot box and pulled out a sheet of 'Blenheim' notepaper, on which was written:

Well Gabriel heres the whole truth and nothing but the truth for your perusal. You will find her letters in the order she sent them to me.

I am sorry you decided you did not wish to be my heir. You cannot do anything about being my son even if you

*change your name which would be daft of you due to the
fact that I shall be a goner when you read this and free
from hurts.*

*Well Gabriel I could have destroyed these and you would
never have been the wiser. I kept them for you alone.*

*Well Gabriel I want to tell you you were my favourite
my son allthough you did not have much competition from
the others allthough Tommy Rotter is good in his funny
way. Ethel is a thorn in every bodys flesh and was from a
girl.*

*Keep on rogering my son and don't make any of your
old Dad's mistakes. I have thrown in some photos for good
measure.*

'Love letters, angel child,' she whispered. 'They'll make you
jealous!'

Gabriel Harvey lowered his hand slowly into the box. When
he lifted it up, it was holding a postcard. On one side there was
a photograph of Sir Harry Lauder wearing a kilt and standing
on the steps of his mansion, 'Lauder Ha' ', and on the other the
message:

Just to say I LOVE YOU, OSSIE. I will be waiting outside our
usual place on Thursday. Try not to be late, you old
slowcoach. I don't want strange young men pestering
me.

Your darling Amy

He peered closely at the postmark: Sept 22, 1935.

'You won't listen, will you. You could easily destroy them.
You don't have to upset yourself.'

'Yes, I do.' Gabriel Harvey was alarmed at his reply. 'Yes, I
do have to.'

'Well, Father. Perhaps I shall be wiser now. Thanks to your
thoughtfulness.'

Gabriel Harvey locked himself in Dr Olson's bedroom.

'I'm ready. I'm prepared.'

'Are you?' she asked. 'Are you really?'

'Yes, I am.'

'I wonder.'

To show his readiness, he took a letter from the box.

His mother had written it in 'Blenheim' on Wednesday, February 1, 1950.

'On – '

'That's right!'

Dearest, darling Ossie,

   Guess what I am going to do with the money you gave me this morning? I am going to treat myself to a little holiday. I think I deserve it. You must be mad, expecting me to spend all that on clothes. I have made a fish pie for the pair of you. Haddock, shrimps and mashed potatoes. Good for the brains, Ossie. Heat it up and grate some cheese over it. You can just about manage that, can't you?

   I will drop you a line tonight. See you soon.

                                        Your Amy

Well Gabriel (his father had added) *that was the start of it. Next in the pile is the line she dropped me.*

She had dropped the line in the Monmouth Hotel, Paddington, London, West Two, on the evening of Wednesday, February 1, 1950.

Dearest, darling Ossie,

   I am having a lovely holiday.

   I have no idea, as yet, when I shall be coming home, if you can call that awful place a home. I need a rest from you. See that Gabriel eats properly and washes behind his ears and combs his hair. You can manage that, can't you?

   I shall be staying at another hotel tomorrow.

                                        Your Amy

On Thursday, February 2, she wrote from the Hôtel Mont Blanc, Pont Street, London, SW1:

Ossie mon cher,

   Who's come up in the world then? Moi. I'm helpless at French, which is just as well, as there isn't a single Froggy to be found on these small but ever so posh premises. Not a soul, Ossie, to tell me I look sedouit something.

306

There goes the gong for dindins. I shall have what my mother calls A Light Repast. I think I shall be very daring and wash it down with a teeny weeny gin or two.

How was the fish pie, Ossie? Has it improved your brains? I can only hope it has. There is room for improvement up there. I shall be leaving this Lap of Luxury at the crack of dawn and moving on to ... I haven't decided yet! I might even come – back to you. I nearly wrote home.

I am still Your Amy

She was back in Paddington the following evening – at Steeden's Guest House:

Dearest darling Ossie,

No headed notepaper in this dump! There's a chronic stench of cat's widdle coming up from the cracked dark brown lino. The only other guests I've seen look like gangsters and tarts. That's where Mrs Oswald Harvey is spending the night. Not to fear, Ossie. I have made it plain to the riff-raff that I am a Lady. A woman of means – that's what I am, isn't it?

And as you are a man of means, Ossie, I suggest you hire yourself a housekeeper until I come – back to you. Silly Amy. She nearly wrote home again. Gabriel's stomach must be in a dreadful state with your cooking.

I shall go out and post this. Then I shall return and try to sleep. If I can stop itching!

Needless to say, I shall be somewhere else tomorrow.

Your Amy

From Vaughan's Hotel, Maida Vale, London W9, she wrote on the evening of Monday, February 6:

Dearest darling Ossie,

Have you been biting your nails wondering what's happened to your Amy? I am safe and sound, so not to panic. I have been here since Saturday but I shall be leaving early in the morning.

If you ever find yourself in Steeden's Guest House, Ossie, make sure you bring your own toilet roll with you. Otherwise you will have to ask the frump on duty for some paper with which to wipe your dirty botty. That's what I had to do last Friday night. I was given three squares and told that was the allowance for ladies. What about gentlemen, I asked? It seems they get six. Mrs Steeden, who made the rule, clearly believes it's a man's world!

Have you hired a housekeeper yet? Silly Amy to ask, because you can't answer me, not having a clue where I am. London is a big city, thank God.

Always Your Amy

On Tuesday 7, she had moved to the Raven Hotel, Shepherd's Bush, London, W12:

Dearest darling Ossie,

For ever on the move! This is a funny way to live. And talking of funny, Ossie, you do come across some funny people in hotels. This one has the funniest I have met so far. A woman I passed on the stairs told me she was responsible for the death of Cleopatra. She had been a snake in her previous existence, she said.

I had fish for dindins at Vaughan's. A grilled fillet of plaice. Delicious. I hope you or your hired housekeeper is cooking plenty of fish in the kitchen that Froggy is welcome to. You know the reason why. I want to be with the Ossie I love. The old Ossie.

You can afford to pay a housekeeper a decent wage, with all that lolly your friend Sir Vincent left you.

My bags are packed for tomorrow's move.

Your Amy

The move took her to Paddington again – to the Presteigne Manor Hotel:

Dearest darling Ossie,

Why do I keep on writing that, when you haven't been my dearest darling for at least six months? It must be habit.

Give Gabriel my love.

Your Amy

308

The next letter, dated Wednesday, February 15, was from the Hotel Chrysanthemum, Hampstead, London NW3:

My dear Ossie

No more dearests and darlings for you. I hope you have been on tenterhooks this past week.

Ossie, I stayed at the Presteigne Manor for three days! You could have come and collected me. I had the curse rather badly and didn't feel like moving. You remember how I suffer every month, I trust. Would you have acted the outraged husband, Ossie, and given your wandering wife a thorough hiding? In full view of the staff and guests? What a scene that would have been!

Or would you have held me in your arms and kissed me gently and begged my forgiveness for behaving the way you have behaved since you came into that hateful bloody money?

The Presteigne Manor is run by a very nice Welsh couple. You always maintain that the Welsh are devious and not to be trusted, but Mr and Mrs Pugh are open and friendly and kind and I think I would trust them with my life. So there!

I went for a long and bracing walk on Hampstead Heath this afternoon. O God, it was cold – cold enough to freeze the balls off a brass monkey, to borrow one of your expressions. I was having a warming whisky in a pub called Jack Straw's Castle when who should waltz in but that queer son of yours by your first marriage. He had a really rough-looking gypsy type with him. He didn't get a look at me, I made sure of that. I put my head down and shot out of the pub while his eyes were still full of his lover-boy.

I shall be leaving here tomorrow. Most definitely.
Mrs Harvey The Third.
That was mean.

I am Your Amy

Two days later, she was in the Parkview Hotel, Kensington, London, SW7:

My Dear Ossie,

It's la-dee-da time again for the wife of the Man Of Means. This is just the right kind of place for the likes of Mrs Oswald Harvey. Even the porter speaks Cut Glass.

The Parkview Hotel is in a side street and you can't see the park for toffee! I often wonder what you have told Gabriel about his mummy's toings and froings. Give him my fondest love.

The Parkview Hotel may suit the wife of the Man Of Means but Amy Harvey, Ossie's girl, doesn't care for it one little bit. She will be staying at Pauper's Rest for the weekend.

Your Amy, I hope

The 'pauper's rest' was M. V. Dante's Hotel, in Paddington, from where she wrote on February 24:

My dear, dear husband,

I spied with my little eye someone beginning with O! Yes, I saw you, Ossie, in Praed Street at half-past twelve. I detest that tweed suit. You look ridiculous in it.

You were trying to find your Amy, weren't you? You had your furious face on, my old darling. I would have come out of the shop and kissed you but I was afraid that you might hit me. I know it hurts you terribly when you feel you have to hit me.

You walked straight past M. V. Dante's without giving it a glance. Silly old Ossie. Did you consider it too common for Mrs Man Of Means? O., read my letters, you fool, read my letters.

Read this one.

Your missing Amy

His father had written, on 'Blenheim' notepaper:

Well Gabriel lad I heard nothing more from her untill March 7 when blow me down she rang me up out of the blue in the middle of the morning. She asked me to meet her for a birthday drink. March 7 was her birthday in case you have forgotten. She said to meet her in the Cressida

Hotel at six o'clock and I was not to be late. I got there at 5 and waited in the reception for her. Come 6 and there was no sign of her. I went on waiting Gabriel untill past 8 like a right bloody lovesick idiot. Then I had a few whiskys in the bar but still no sign. It was gone 11 when I finally left. I was not best pleased I can tell you.

On the evening of March 8 she wrote from the hotel in Paddington where Oswald Harvey had waited in vain to see his missing wife:

Poor poor rich Ossie,

Did you inquire at the desk last night if a Mrs Oswald Harvey was in her room? And were you told there was no one of that name in the hotel? That's because I had booked in as Miss Amy Prentice. It took me ages to remove my wedding ring, Ossie. I had to use ever such a lot of soap.

You were waiting downstairs, you poor old Ossie, and I was upstairs, on the floor above, celebrating my thirty-third birthday. In Room 53, in case you want to know. I had company. You can't really celebrate alone, can you?

I have no desire to see him again. He is married anyhow and lives with his wife and daughter in Sheffield. He was in London on cutlery business. I caught him eyeing me at dindins on Monday and we struck up a conversation afterwards. He asked me my age, the cheeky devil, and I said I was on the brink of thirty-three and he said we must have a quiet celebration, if that would be agreeable.

He wined and dined me at an awful restaurant in Notting Hill, Ossie, then we returned to the Cressida in a taxi. I was scared coming into the reception. I saw you sitting over at the bar looking sorry for yourself. You didn't notice your Amy with her dyed red hair.

I went to his room. I let him do me. His big thing filled me up. I am sore today. I let him do me five times. Five changes of cock covers – that was his expression. He never travels without a supply, he said. He prides himself on his staying power.

With good reason.

On Sunday March 19 she wrote from the Blenheim Hotel, Marylebone, London, WI:

I have ended up here. You might have guessed I would.

I stood outside the other Blenheim late this afternoon. Did Gabriel's friends enjoy the party? Did that plain Jane you have hired put on a lavish spread?

Have you told her I used to be a vegetable cook at Buckingham Palace? Have you revealed my secret to our clever son?

I am mad to ask you these questions.

Wish Gabriel many happy returns of the day.

You could have sent the police after me, or a private detective.

You soon gave up the chase.

You didn't miss me very long.

Well Gabriel thats allmost it. There is one more letter from your darling Mummy. I never could open it. I often thought of doing so when I was half cut but even then I could not find the courage. Besides my son I allready knew she was dead. You were at school when the phone call came.

You open it. Always supposing you have got this far.

The envelope had turned a brownish-yellow. The stamp, which cost twopence-halfpenny, bore the head of King George the Sixth.

Gabriel Harvey opened the letter. She had written it in the Blenheim Hotel, on Monday, March 20, 1950, at 9 a.m.:

I am going to do it with bleach. I shall pretend it's gin.

We were so happy the two of us, then the three of us, once.

You and your Sir Vincent have put an end to happiness.

I shall pour myself a Brobat and tonic and toast you for the pompous old monster you have become.

I cannot love a man who is acting from daybreak to sunset. You used to act just for fun, when you were tiddly at Christmas.

The fun has gone.

I wonder if Mother and Father and Wendy will attend my funeral. I wonder what they will say to you. I wish I could come back as a fly on the wall.

There is a map of Ireland on the sheet on my bed. A

map of Ireland is what chambermaids call men's spunk when it's been spilt and leaves a stain.

He didn't have a supply, the man I let do me last night. He had to make a hasty exit.

Thirteen years ago today I gave birth to your child after hours and hours of terrible pain.

Perhaps you should have made a map of Ireland instead.

I am in Room Number 37. That's where they will find me. The wallpaper is hideous! It has a pattern of foaming champagne bottles.

No champagne for Miss Prentice. Brobat's her poison. Cheers!

I did love you.

I can't write any more.

His father had the last word, on the inevitable 'Blenheim' notepaper:

Well Gabriel I hope you showed more courage than your old Dad. Keep your chin up and try to see the sunny side of life. In the bottom are the photos and a bit from the local rag that I cut out with the coroner saying she was of unsound mind. I had your Mummy buried on the Monday March 27. A week to the day from when she did what she did. I had to hide the truth from you. I never meant you harm. You were my favourite.

You just keep your chin up my lad. This must have been a shock and a surprise for you.

What shocked and surprised Gabriel Harvey, what caused him to cry out in pain, was that he wasn't really shocked and surprised at all.

Grief woke Gabriel Harvey the next morning by gnawing at his gut. It told him that his mummy was dead; that he would never see her anywhere on earth.

It went on giving him the information while he showered and shaved, while he drank his tea and ate his buttered toast.

'Oh, my mummy, my mummy.'

It then commanded him to weep, with the authority it had gained over twenty-seven years.

'You sure were the life and soul of the party last evening, honey.'

313

Accepting Betty Pedersen's compliment with a bow, Gabriel Harvey smiled at the appropriateness of the cliché. 'I was in a frivolous mood.'

He had taken the Pedersens to a restaurant outside Moorhead. A waitress at the Viking's Shield had been astonished by the fact that he preferred to eat his salad *after* the main course. She had pronounced him weird.

'I suppose I am weird. I've often had reason to think so. But I know people who are weirder.'

Such as the Countess Bolina, whose rabbit's features his mobile mimic's face immediately assumed: 'Clutter! Is Sèvres clutter? Is Dresden? I have a few pieces of both'; such as Sadie Jennings, who adored the agony of parting, darling: 'Would you believe that I came close to V. Woolf-ing myself over a man once?'; such as Matthew, taunting his former colleagues from the bench in Lincoln's Inn Fields: 'Have you mislaid the Crown's noun in the grass, Henry? Is that why you're scanning the green sward?'; such as Oswald Harvey, the 'Blenheim' lecturer who believed that an Englishman's home was his castle: 'Oh yes, I've a drawbridge. I amuse myself raising it and lowering it over my moat. Keeps the old grey matter healthily occupied, I do assure you.'

It occurred to Gabriel Harvey, as he lay in Dr Olson's hammock, that his mummy, his dead mummy, had succeeded in V. Woolf-ing herself. She, too, had drowned her senses.

'Mummy,' he moaned. 'Mummy.'

In Room 37, in the Blenheim Hotel.

The life and soul of the party had added a new item to his repertoire. He had mimicked Debbie Armsted mimicking him, to the Pedersens' near-hysterical delight.

It was a Sunday morning, and God's television messengers were at their business.

A grey-haired smiling man, dressed in academic robes, was standing behind a lectern in a church that seemed to be built almost entirely of glass. His enraptured congregation were surrounded by hundreds of flowers, by exotic tropical plants, and by fountains.

He was talking about possibility thinking, which brought health, wealth and happiness. Jesus Christ had possibility thinking. Jesus was the greatest possibility thinker of them all.

'Nobody has a money problem, only an idea problem.'

'I don't recognize his Jesus,' said Gabriel Harvey. 'He makes the Son of God sound like a young American executive. Without a beard.'

'That's his appeal. For him, the meek and the poor are only meek and poor because they've an idea problem. If that's theology, it's shit.'

'We're a couple of negativity thinkers, aren't we, Carl.'

'That's us.'

A picture of Jesus came into Gabriel Harvey's mind: He had a beard, yes, and long flowing hair. He had children at his feet. Another child, a child called Gabriel, a boy with troublesome twos, was looking at the picture from a hospital bed.

'*Uffda*, Carl, he gives me the creeps. Switch to the Kristian Kitchen. Let's see what delicacy Darlene's preparin' for Kirk at this time.'

Gabriel's mummy bent down and kissed him. Then she brushed the kiss away with her fingertips.

'Put it back, Mummy. Please put it back.'

At Minneapolis-St Paul airport, two weeks later, Betty Pedersen cupped Gabriel Harvey's face in her hands and said to him, 'You were in hell when you made us laugh so much that evening in the restaurant. I call that honest-to-goodness goodness, the way you made us laugh. I call that real considerate. I know what hell's like, honey. Eric took us there. Let me tell you this, though – it's a better place to be than Kirk and Darlene's heaven.'

Part Two

Towards the end of my stay in Sorg, after I had come to grief, the Pedersens took me to visit Carl's cousin Sonia at her summer home by Lake Wilhelmine.

The old lady spoke carefully considered English with a slight Norwegian accent. She had been born and raised on a remote farm near Gilby, North Dakota, she said. Her hard-working parents ('From dawn to dusk, Gabriel, for almost fifty years') talked only in their native tongue. 'I grew up a Norsky. I did not meet an American – an American American – until I was ten years old.'

There wasn't even a Lutheran church, they were that isolated. On Sundays they read from the Bible – she, her mother and father, and her two brothers – and sang hymns at the harmonium. 'That same harmonium you see in the corner.'

'Do you play it, Mrs Loftsgard?'

'No, no more. My fingers, they are too arthritic. You must be a clever man, to have written a book, as Carl tells me.'

'I shan't write another,' I said. 'I am not a writer by profession.'

(*For Mummy, with undying love*. A gift for a corpse.)

'I am very backward, Gabriel. I am not educated, as I would have wished to have been. I blame my stupidity on the prairie winters. I and my brothers, we were too often absent from Miss Berglund's little school because of the snow drifts and, worse, the blizzards. You remind me now. A writer came to our farm once. On a hot afternoon, like today. A famous writer, Gabriel. Fourteen years before I was born. When my grandfather Olaf was the farmer. You know of Knut Hamsun?'

'Yes, I do. But I haven't read his novels.'

'*Hunger* I have read. It sickened me. It is on the shelf over there. He, Hamsun, sent it to my Grandpa Olaf from Norway.

319

Hamsun was in real life a Pedersen, but we are not related, unless very distantly.'

'Is Olaf', I asked, 'the Olaf who tried to awaken Maja?'

'Carl and Betty have told you the story? Yes, the same Olaf. The same sweet haunted Olaf. I have a memory of him. I was very small. I was lying asleep in the barn, in the hay. Then Grandpa was shaking me. He was shouting, over and over, the words "Not cold! Not cold! Not cold!" And, of course, I was not cold. I was warm, and alive. His were the first man's tears I ever saw. Oh, Gabriel, how my haunted grandpa wept! Yes, he gave Knut Hamsun a drink of water and the two men chattered in Norwegian and five years later the mailman brought the copy of *Hunger* to the farm. And now I myself will bring some food and beverage to the table. Fetch my stick, if you please, Carl.'

I went out to the porch and stared at the lake. A bronzed blond youth dived into it from a pier and I recalled the envy I had felt for those sleek and lithe guttersnipes swimming in the contaminated Thames. The reverie was broken by a swarm of mosquitoes making for my bare arms. I closed the screen door behind them and returned to find Betty pouring coffee and Sonia Loftsgard filling cones with cream and a fruit I recognized as bilberry, although I had never eaten it.

'You do not have in England *krumkake*, I believe, Gabriel.'

'*Krumkake*? No, we don't.'

'What is the matter? You look as if you have seen a ghost.'

'I have.'

(I had, and not the one I had been seeing since the previous Friday. This was a happier ghost, the ghost of a woman who had died of natural causes.)

'I talk of *krumkake* and you see a ghost?'

'It's my aunt. My Aunt Kathleen. She ate *krumkake* when she was a girl.'

In the basement kitchen of old Mr Tiverley's house, I added. And then, for a quarter of an hour or so, I had no mother and no hotel room. I had Nora Rosen and her benign employer, and my Swedenborgian aunt in her aromatic cottage, and the remembered joy of that best of all possible Easters.

That night, lying in bed with a bottle of Jack Daniel's – or was it Jim Beam? – I heard again what my aunt had shouted in her sleep. 'Push, Sandro. Push, push, Alessandro. Push.'

She had been begging her long-dead husband to fill her up, I realized.

Our father's marvel of a boot stood in its own glass case in the centre of my half-brother's sitting-room.

'Quite the museum piece, isn't it? You can walk around and admire it from every angle. Why the daft old bastard left it to me I can't imagine. Perhaps he expected me to lose a leg. Or perhaps he thought I would love it so much I'd rush out and order its partner. Anyway, Gabriel, make yourself comfy. A drink?'

'You don't have bourbon by any chance, do you?'

'There's exotic. Yes, as a matter of fact, I do. Wild Turkey. An unopened bottle. I maintain a cosmopolitan cocktail cabinet.'

I had given him a 'tinkle' that morning, and he had invited me over for a 'chinwag' and dinner.

'Have you been a sensible boy? Did you take the heartfelt advice that Ethel and I gave you?'

'No, I didn't.'

'That's a pity.'

'Why is it?'

'I may be wrong, I certainly hope I am wrong, but I think I have an idea what Daddykins put in the box.'

'Tell me your idea.'

'Letters and such, Gabriel. Stuff to do with her. His last wife. Your mother.'

'Yes.'

'You poor sod.'

'I'll survive,' I said, with the forced confidence of one who does not believe that he will.

'It must have knocked you sideways. Discovering the truth, I mean.'

'Yes, it did.'

(I could not say to Tommy that September evening what I have subsequently revealed to him: that my body expressed the grief my mind was unaware of, long ago. Indeed, it had even been premature in its expression, since I had become the despised Piss-a-Bed before she had consumed her fatal Brobat and tonic. When she was only three months dead, I had smeared myself with shit in a grieving ecstasy. And the chill that always followed the warmth of wearing the Moygashel frock – that was grief, surely; grief up to its icy tricks.)

'At the risk of upsetting you further and losing your company tonight, I have to admit, Gabriel, my dear, that I found the third Mrs Oswald Harvey a thoroughgoing bitch.'

'Tell me.'

'It's just my opinion, you understand. I could live with the fact that she hated me. It was her way of showing her hatred that rankled. She made it vividly plain that she considered me an undesirable presence. "You've brought queer weather with you," she once said as she opened the front door to me at the rented house. "But then you usually do." Ever the philosopher, I ignored the observation and inquired if my beloved father was in residence. She managed a nod. I flashed her my charm school smile and entered. "Queer", "queer" – she must have used the bloody word a dozen or more times that day. Did I respond to her sarcasm? No, I most definitely – copyright, Daddykins – did not. She actually remarked, Gabriel, apropos of nothing, that she – who was so fond of flowers – could not bring herself to like the common pansy. "What a coincidence!" I chirped back. "Neither can I." I think it dawned on her eventually that in Thomas Harvey she had chosen quite the wrong person to goad. My method of dealing with people who intend to abuse me is to breeze past them. I was always in a breezy mood when I met your mother.'

'What about our father? You most definitely breezed in and out of St James's when he'd had his leg removed.'

'Ah, but that was a different kind of breeziness, Gabriel. What you witnessed in the hospital was the performance I had to put on to counteract the performance he had to put on. We both rather enjoyed our little show as we both got older and – in my case – wiser. But as for your mother, well, I can't demonstrate how I breezed past her. I should need to see her in the flesh, and that – as you know – is impossible.'

'Have you read her letters? The ones she wrote in the hotels?'

'Yes, I'm afraid I have, my dear. You don't object to "my dear", do you?'

'No.'

'Please call me Tommy. I read them on the day of her funeral. What a grisly occasion that was! Her father spat in our father's face – a sizeable dollop it was, too. Mr Prentice had obviously been saving it up. And her mother went haywire. I am not exaggerating. She screamed, she stamped her feet, she said our father should be charged with her Amy's murder. She even ran

322

after a passing policeman and brought him back and insisted that he arrest Oswald Harvey. When the constable replied that he had no power to do her bidding, she hit him with her large black handbag. He then had to be dissuaded from arresting her for assault. I wish you had been there, Gabriel. I argued with him, I pleaded with him, to tell you the truth. He wanted to protect you, he said. You were too young to cope with such a dreadful state of affairs. Of course you weren't too young. You were exactly the right age because it was exactly the right time, the time it happened.'

'If he really meant to protect me, Tommy, he would have destroyed her letters.'

'Perhaps he felt that you're man enough now to cope. Perhaps you are.'

'Perhaps.'

'Have another bourbon.'

'Thank you.'

'I am going to ask you a very personal question. Are you Arthur or Martha?'

'I'm sorry, I – ?'

'Arthur means you fancy girls, and Martha means you fancy boys – as I used to do, in those not always happy days before I retired from active service.'

'I'm not Arthur or Martha,' I answered. 'I'm nothing.'

'Are you quite sure?'

(Yes, for I have loved a phantom.)

'Yes, I am. I'm a freak, I suppose. I'm weird.'

'Daddykins – oh, how he loathed that nickname, and how I adored teasing him with it! – Daddykins was so proud of you when you started to masturbate. I'm not making this up, Gabriel. It was Christmas 1949, and I'd met him by arrangement in a pub in Nightingale Lane. I was *persona non grata* at Blenheim Palace, you see. Your mother was worried that I might exert a queer influence on you. "Look at this, Tommy Rotter," he said, and flourished a handkerchief in front of me. It had the monogram "G" on it, I remember – a small sign of his new affluence. "What do you want me to look at? It's a hanky, Daddykins." "Don't use that cursed word in here, where I'm known," he growled. "Take hold of it. Feel it." I took hold of it and I felt it. "It's stiff, isn't it?" I agreed that it was stiff. "It was in the lad's bed. Between the sheets, not under the pillow. I'll wager it's stiff with the lad's first drops of spunk. Snot would have a bit of colour in it. There's no colour, is there?" I agreed there wasn't. "Proof positive, Tommy Rotter. He'll soon be rogering. Let's drink a toast to the lad's spunk." And we did, Gabriel, we did.'

'Well, I've never rogered.'

'He assumed otherwise. He was convinced you were secretive about your torrid sex life. "My Gabriel, he's sly, he's deep." You were a real chap, unlike me.'

'I *was* secretive, Tommy. About its non-existence.'

'An old queen and a middle-aged virgin – we're not cast in the Oswald Harvey mould, are we? Our father's sons?'

I put on the dress I had been frightened to take to America – a customs official, seeing it, could turn suspicious, and arrive in an instant at the correct conclusion – and spoke my magical HMV B9719, and there she was on that day of recurring brightness, and there was Heddle singing, faintly.

'Mummy.'

And then there she wasn't, and the day was gone, and the faint singing was now a scream, coming from my throat, and there I was, pulling and tearing at the dress, desperate to be free from the warmth it had given me – the terrible warmth of deception, that is no warmth at all.

'They were snobs, my dear. Unhappily for them, they were headed in opposite directions. Daddykins wanted to climb up the social ladder, and your mother wanted to descend it. He craved to be one of Them, she to be one of Us. Neither succeeded. His vowels gave him away, and although she went to work at Buckingham Palace as a skivvy, it was still Buckingham Palace. When she ran off with Oswald Harvey, she said ta-ta to her inheritance. He was poor, and married, and twelve years older than her father. Mr and Mrs Prentice weren't pleased with their eldest daughter's choice of husband. It isn't hard to see why.'

'Mummy – Mother – told me they were dead, her parents. Killed in a car crash.'

'You've been told a lot of lies, Gabriel.'

'Yes, I have.'

'Did Daddykins ever spill the beans about Sir Vincent?'

'I didn't realize there were beans to spill. He did say once that Sir Vincent's father, Sir Randolph, had rogered every woman, the nanny and cook excepted, on the estate.'

'Sir Vincent was caught *in flagrante delicto* – oh, to hear Daddykins struggle with that phrase again! – with not one, but two, grooms in his stables. He had a younger brother who hated him, and it was he who made the discovery and created what is called a "stink". Sir Vincent was never brought to trial because he had the sense to flee the country, but the scandal ruined him. For a very short period he joined Oscar Wilde as the outraged public's token pederast. Newspaper reporters trailed Sir Vincent and his wife across Europe, until more important events – the outbreak of a world war, for instance – captured their attention. By the twenties, Sir Vincent's misdemeanour near the horses was forgotten, except by our father.'

'He wasn't one of the grooms, was he?'

'He was. Having, he emphasized, a spot of innocent fun. What he and Alfred and Sir Vincent had been doing was nothing complicated and nasty – they were just "working their willies up into a froth". Sir Vincent was a proper chap, and he and Alfred were proper chaps as well, and that cursèd younger brother only created the stink because he wanted the estate for himself.'

'How absurd.'

'Isn't it.'

'I am thinking, Tommy, if our father –'

'Which most definitely art not in heaven. If our father – yes?'

'If our father hadn't worked his willy – or Sir Vincent's, or Alfred's – into a froth, in the stables, he wouldn't have been left the money. He wouldn't have become the master of "Blenheim".'

'Let us respect the facts, Gabriel. You are a historian and should be apprised of them. The frothing never happened. The younger brother's arrival preceded it. Nipped it, you might say, in the bud.'

'I cannot imagine what you hope to gain by this visit, Mr Harvey. Please make it brief.'

'I worshipped my mother, Mrs Gill. You're the remaining link with her.'

'Link, Mr Harvey? We were not attached in any way. Might I inquire how you traced me?'

'There was a photograph. Mummy – Mother – had scribbled on the back "Me with my big sister, Wendy, now Mrs Gill". I telephoned all the Gills in Salisbury.'

'To no good end, I fear. I have no revelations for you.'

'I lived in ignorance of her death for twenty-seven years. I don't expect any more revelations.'

'She was touched in the head, Mr Harvey. She had to be, to pursue that frightful old man. You don't seem to have his voice, which is a blessing.'

'She pursued him?'

'Yes, she did. I believe they met in rather squalid circumstances, in some cheap tea rooms. The parents tried to knock a sense of responsibility into her, but they failed. She broke their hearts twice, Mr Harvey, your dreadful mother. She killed them when she killed herself. They were ghosts long before they died.'

'I'm sorry.'

'Spare me your sympathy. Your father, I presume, is not alive?'

'No, he isn't.'

'Did you have any trouble coming to terms with being a bastard?'

'I'm not aware that I am a bastard. You mean illegitimate?'

'Of course, illegitimate. You, Mr Harvey, are what is termed a "love child". He did keep you in the dark, didn't he? I cannot say I am in the least surprised. He looked as if he had a great deal to be dark about.'

'You have my mother's beautiful green eyes, Mrs Gill.'

'No, I do not, Mr Harvey. They are entirely my own. I think I hear Mr Gill in the drive. He is always peckish after his golf. You will catch the three o'clock back to London if you leave this minute.'

'Thank you for seeing me.'

'It has not been a pleasure. You are very short, aren't you?'

'Yes, I am.'

'Something to do with that illness you had as a boy, I have no doubt?'

'Nothing to do with it, Mrs Gill. I had diphtheria.'

'I don't care what you had, Mr Harvey. Good day to you.'

'You even took away your kisses,' the love child screeched at his hated mother. 'As soon as you gave them, you took them away. Shitting H! Pissing M! Shitting V! Pissing B! Bloody shitting 9! Bloody pissing 7! Bloody shitting 1! Bloody pissing 9!'

The alleys rang with the love child's howling.

Five years have passed since I came to grief and the coldness of the whole truth struck at my life.

For three of those years I have laboured at this memoir, which I began writing at Tommy's instigation. 'It has to be much more interesting than that stodgy one about the preachers, my dear. You can dredge it up from your very heart.'

As I have. As I most definitely have.

The grief-stricken Gabriel Harvey that I was at forty: I stop and wonder at him now.

A fat woman, sitting opposite him on an underground train, tries to catch what he is saying to himself. She strains forward, and he lowers his voice to a whisper. He realizes that she considers him slightly dotty, if not wholly round the bend. He smiles at her. She blushes. She is suddenly fascinated by the advertisements above his head. She reads each one attentively, from left to right.

> Love no med'cine can appease,
> He burns the fishes in the seas:
> Not all the skill his wounds can stench,
> Not all the sea his fire can quench

is what he is muttering, this peculiar little man, who is making his way to Marylebone, where he is going to die.

'I learned it at Lily's,' he informs the student of advertising when he gets off the train at Edgware Road Station. 'For her.'

He is heading for the Hotel Malaga, formerly the Rankin Hotel, formerly the Garston, formerly the Blenheim.

He has booked into Room Number 37, by telephone, three weeks in advance.

'That is a double room, sir. There will be two of you?'

'No. I shall be alone.'

'We can offer you a choice of singles.'

'It must be number thirty-seven. No other will do.'

'We will have to charge you for a double.'

'I'll pay.'

He is at the reception desk. There is a sombrero hanging on the wall, next to a cuckoo clock. He signs his name, is handed his key, is told to take the lift to the third floor.

He locks himself into Room Number 37.

He opens his suitcase and takes out his father's bequest. He tears each letter into tiny pieces. He tears up the newspaper cutting and the photographs that were thrown in for good measure. The last of these shows Amy Harvey in front of 'Blenheim', in her Moygashel dress, looking glum.

He takes out a steak knife, which he has sharpened. A bleached farewell to the world does not appeal to him. He will slash his wrists, or go for his jugular.

He sits on the edge of the bed.

He sits on the edge of the bed, and hears Carl Pedersen speaking. Carl is drunk and is mourning the loss of his son, Eric. Carl has nothing kind to say about him, but what he says is bitterly affectionate. Eric was a dumb jock, an average among averages, a kid with no interests apart from cars and girls and football. Carl had worked his butt off fixing for Eric to dodge the draft. 'I bought him a one-way airplane ticket to Stockholm, but the asshole went to Vietnam and didn't come back.'

He puts the flat side of the knife to his throat. He rubs it gently against his skin.

He is with Dale Armsted in Dale's daddy's air-conditioned Lincoln Continental. They are driving through the Badlands in North Dakota, and Dale is impressing the Englishman who has recently come to grief with his knowledge, his genuine knowledge of the wilderness. Sorg's resident redneck talks of siltstone and bentonite, and how the Little Missouri River nourishes thick growths of cottonwoods and willows. He shows the Englishman a prairie dog town, and explains in great detail how those rodents live, with their intricate system of burrows. They watch the creatures dart in and out of the earth. They watch them kiss – for they are much given to kissing – and they see them spring up on their hind legs, anticipating danger.

He sits on the edge of the bed, and hears Dale tell him that that there sequoia stump was buried by volcanic ash sixty million years ago, and petrified.

'Sixty million years?'

'You betcha, Gabe.'

He rises from the edge of the bed and finds himself scraping at the green-and-white striped wallpaper with the steak knife. Minutes later, a different pattern is revealed: shepherds, shepherdesses, sheep. He scrapes the rural scene away and hits plaster. The foaming champagne bottles have gone.

He puts the knife into his suitcase, which he snaps shut.

He feels comforted by the notion of sixty million years, and thanks Dale for comforting him.

He hears Jimmy Buffett singing, and remembers that he had taken the score of Beethoven's Opus 131 to Sorg, Minnesota. He had been incapable of studying it. His pretend young mother had seen to that.

'And my chemical dependency.'

He is paying his bill.

'Is the room not to your satisfaction, sir?' asks the astonished receptionist.

'It was unexpectedly satisfying,' he replies.

On leaving the hotel, he decides to do his Christmas shopping. He has presents to get – for Peter, for Hannah, for Sophie, for Tommy. It is late October, it is raining, and the streets of central London are not too crowded.

In Liberty's, in Regent Street, he buys a red dress for his twin sister, whose measurements are roughly the same as her brother's. It is in raw silk, it has a slit on either side, and it will make a new woman of her.

I have not succeeded, Father, in what I set out to do. When I began this lament for my numb life three years ago, I meant to polish you off for ever, and I think I have failed. You are still here, curse you, in these pages.

You live on outside them, whenever I impersonate you. Oswald Harvey is my star turn. 'Be your father,' people say. 'He's your best.' So I oblige, and their laughter pleases and flatters me. What an unnatural son I am.

You have had your revenge on me, Father, if revenge it was. There are times, even now, I consider it my rightful inheritance. I should have gone in search of her. I should have made my way to Malta, or wherever it was that you said her last postcard came from. I should have travelled to – what was your phrase? – 'sunny climes'. If I had seriously attempted to go after her, would you have told me the truth my unhappy body was already hinting at? The truth my mind feared to acknowledge?

'You must repair yourself' – that was Aunt Kathleen's mysterious advice. She was your fellow-conspirator, it seems. Yet that unorthodox Swedenborgian also took pains to tell me that you were a poor creature, who must be pitied.

Often, during these past three years, I have set off from my grand house in Chiswick – purchased, like yours, with money unexpectedly, even absurdly, gained – and walked for miles in the city of our birth. Father, your Isle of Dogs is occupied nowadays by the kind of people you called 'upstarts'. They are rich, but hardly the *cream de la cream*. They are ambitious, unlike that dear ghost, Cedric Tiverley, who once lived so close to you, and whose treasured books are among my own treasures.

Father, the Jerusalem has been replaced by a shopping centre, and the hospital in Tite Street, in which I nearly died of diphtheria, by a convent; our nameless house and its neighbouring 'Shylock's stables' have been razed, and a computer factory stands where they stood, and 'Blenheim', Father, has become the Islamic Centre of South-West London. Muslims study and pray where once you strutted and lectured.

Do you remember, Father, the 'half-Abdul' I befriended at Lily's? Of course you do. You never forgave him for his 'cursèd insolence'. He and I are friends again, and I am the godfather of his and Hannah's daughter, Sophie. Not long ago, he confessed that he'd had a crush on me at school, a complete infatuation. I know that I envied him his beautiful black hair. Mine was 'stubborn' – her word – and dull by comparison. Perhaps we might have 'worked our willies up into a froth'.

Father, I have taken to rogering. It began with a map of Ireland that on close inspection more exactly resembled one of the tinier Orkneys. A small thing, but mine own. My lover is a 'quack', who works in the same hospital as Peter Fisher. She is researching into a dreadful new disease, which mostly claims as its victims 'chaps who aren't proper chaps'.

I see Tommy Rotter regularly. We give ourselves a brotherly kiss, Father, whenever we meet and part. He is frail, but resilient. After all, he is thirty years older than his sibling. We talk about you constantly – about your military career, your opinions, your reaction when he told you he was a Martha, not an Arthur: 'For Christ's sake, Tommy Rotter, don't start wearing suede shoes. Promise me that much, there's a good son.'

And only yesterday, Father, I remembered the present

you gave me at Christmas, 1950. You had overheard me saying to Mrs Gould that I adored the music of Mendelssohn. 'This doesn't sound like your usual moony stuff, young man,' you remarked as you handed me a record of 'The Moon of Manakoora' and 'Aloha, oe!', played by Felix Mendelssohn and His Hawaiian Serenaders.

We do not mention the woman you married in August, 1943, six years after your youngest son was born. Tommy is aware that I loved her, and that her going numbed me. I find I love her still, now that my numbness has gone.

Tommy Rotter has revealed most of your secrets, and uncovered more of your lies. My lecturer, my dissembler, my old dad. Whatever else is false, I care to think that your rescue of Johnny Tuohy actually happened. He was dead when you fished him out, and that has the ring of truth.

Discover more about our forthcoming books through Penguin's FREE newspaper...

Penguin
Quarterly

It's packed with:

- exciting features
- author interviews
- previews & reviews
- books from your favourite films & TV series
- exclusive competitions & much, much more...

Write off for your free copy today to:
Dept JC
Penguin Books Ltd
FREEPOST
West Drayton
Middlesex
UB7 0BR
NO STAMP REQUIRED

READ MORE IN PENGUIN

In every corner of the world, on every subject under the sun, Penguin represents quality and variety – the very best in publishing today.

For complete information about books available from Penguin – including Puffins, Penguin Classics and Arkana – and how to order them, write to us at the appropriate address below. Please note that for copyright reasons the selection of books varies from country to country.

In the United Kingdom: Please write to *Dept. JC, Penguin Books Ltd, FREEPOST, West Drayton, Middlesex UB7 OBR*

If you have any difficulty in obtaining a title, please send your order with the correct money, plus ten per cent for postage and packaging, to *PO Box No. 11, West Drayton, Middlesex UB7 OBR*

In the United States: Please write to *Penguin USA Inc., 375 Hudson Street, New York, NY 10014*

In Canada: Please write to *Penguin Books Canada Ltd, 10 Alcorn Avenue, Suite 300, Toronto, Ontario M4V 3B2*

In Australia: Please write to *Penguin Books Australia Ltd, 487 Maroondah Highway, Ringwood, Victoria 3134*

In New Zealand: Please write to *Penguin Books (NZ) Ltd,182–190 Wairau Road, Private Bag, Takapuna, Auckland 9*

In India: Please write to *Penguin Books India Pvt Ltd, 706 Eros Apartments, 56 Nehru Place, New Delhi 110 019*

In the Netherlands: Please write to *Penguin Books Netherlands B.V., Keizersgracht 231 NL–1016 DV Amsterdam*

In Germany: Please write to *Penguin Books Deutschland GmbH, Friedrichstrasse 10–12, W–6000 Frankfurt/Main 1*

In Spain: Please write to *Penguin Books S. A., C. San Bernardo 117–6° E–28015 Madrid*

In Italy: Please write to *Penguin Italia s.r.l., Via Felice Casati 20, I–20124 Milano*

In France: Please write to *Penguin France S. A., 17 rue Lejeune, F–31000 Toulouse*

In Japan: Please write to *Penguin Books Japan, Ishikiribashi Building, 2–5–4, Suido, Bunkyo-ku, Tokyo 112*

In Greece: Please write to *Penguin Hellas Ltd, Dimocritou 3, GR–106 71 Athens*

In South Africa: Please write to *Longman Penguin Southern Africa (Pty) Ltd, Private Bag X08, Bertsham 2013*

BY THE SAME AUTHOR

Sugar Cane

Esther Potocki is a venereologist in a London hospital. One day a young man named Stephen wanders into her clinic in search of his dying friend Tonio. Then, as suddenly as he appeared, Stephen vanishes, leaving behind a taped autobiography which describes the shocking circumstances of his life . . .

'Bailey has captured two remarkable voices, of a woman who comes to love a young man with maternal solicitude, and of the boy himself, an outcast within his own family . . . A powerful, painful and evocative novel . . . written with such feeling it makes the reader laugh and weep . . . Bailey is a master of emotion' – *Spectator*

'Bailey spins a beguiling romance which is perceptive, wise and tragi-comic' – Nicholas Lezard in *GQ*

and a volume of autobiography:

An Immaculate Mistake
Scenes from Childhood and Beyond

'An oddly wistful and affectionate account of a childhood spent in the shadow of a domineering but caring parent . . . *An Immaculate Mistake* weaves an account of its author's past from isolated scenes, memories of childhood and beyond, Joycean epiphanies and sundry fragments. Mr Bailey may have been a mistake, but he seems to have made up for it' – *Observer*

'A portrait that is without rancour, and full of affection and humour' – *Irish Times*

'Carries an emotional sting as powerful as that in any of Bailey's novels' – *Daily Telegraph*